We hope you enjoy this book. Please return or renew it by the due date.

You can renew it at www.norfolk.gov.uk/libraries or by using our free library app.

Otherwise you can phone 0344 800 8020 - please have your library card and PIN ready.

You can sign up for email reminders too.

About the author

Helen Wallen is a blogger, funny lady, mother, and all round gin, wine and cake enthusiast. Formerly a copywriter/PR-type person, she is now dedicated to growing human beings in her uterus and blogging about life with babies, toddlers and beyond.

The Mummy Lessons is her second novel.

Also by Helen Wallen

Baby Boom!

HELEN WALLEN

The Mummy Lessons

HODDER

First published in Great Britain in 2019 by Hodder & Stoughton
An Hachette UK company

1

A CIP catalogue record for this title is available from the British Library

Paperback ISBN 9781473691360
eBook ISBN 9781473691377

Typeset in Sabon MT Std
by Palimpsest Book Production Ltd, Falkirk, Stirlingshire

Printed and bound by CPI Group (UK) Ltd, Croydon, CR0 4YY

Hodder & Stoughton policy is to use papers that are natural, renewable
and recyclable products and made from wood grown in sustainable forests.
The logging and manufacturing processes are expected to conform to the
environmental regulations of the country of origin.

Hodder & Stoughton Ltd
Carmelite House
50 Victoria Embankment
London EC4Y 0DZ

www.hodder.co.uk

For my small people.
Thanks for being my babies.
(Otherwise I'd have no material for this book
and stuff.)
(PS You can't actually read it though, as it's
full of all the swears.)

CHAPTER LIST

THE RULES

1) Try to sleep when the baby sleeps. (SO NEVER. EVER. UNTIL YOU ARE AN EMPTY WINE-SOAKED HUSK AND FALL DOWN DEAD IN THE BABY AISLE AT TESCO)

2) Try to eat when the baby sleeps. (SEE POINT ABOVE)

3) Try to get basic household chores done when the baby sleeps. (ABOVE!!)

4) Batch cook food and freeze in individual portions for easy re-heating. (OR DELIVEROO . . . WITH WINE. AND CRYING)

5) Try hiring a cleaner to take the pressure off. (OR JUST USE BABY WIPES)

6) Take time to shower or bathe in the evenings when you can leave the baby with your partner. (OR JUST USE BABY WIPES)

7) Make tea or coffee in the Thermos so it stays hot. (WHAT IS THIS 'HOT' OF WHICH YOU SPEAK?!)

8) Don't be afraid to ask for help, or ask people to leave. (COMMUNICATION VIA WHATSAPP ONLY)

9) Remember to look after and take time for yourself.(AHAHAHAHAHAHAHAHAHAHAHA)

PROLOGUE

The Twelve Months of the First Year of Baby

I've done it. I've survived my entire first year without completely losing my shit or my sanity, and managing to keep the majority of my areolas intact.

I can't actually believe an entire twelve months have passed . . . It feels like a blur – an amazing, beautiful, wonderful, guilt-ridden, shitty, tearful, and occasionally all-a-bit-too-much-but-completely-incomparable blur.

So here, for every other amazing Mummy (and Daddy) out there who's made it through the first year, is a breakdown of THE FIRST YEAR OF BABY:

Month One

So small, so perfect, so fragile . . . Yes. Take a moment to remember your vagina the way it was.

Then re-grow all your pubic hair to form a secret forest around it, destroy every handheld mirror in the land, and NEVER THINK ABOUT IT AGAIN.

Once that's done, your first few weeks are spent trying to drown out the four thousand comments you get every day about how fast it goes, pretending breastfeeding doesn't hurt, and rediscovering wine . . .

Month Two

Okay you're EXHAUSTED but you can do this. You've totally got this parenting shit down. You've joined every baby class in the county and your main plan is to baby-sign the sensory-baby-massaging f@*k out of your newborn . . . (If you could only stop them shitting all over themselves, the pram and your only remaining clean pair of leggings every time you try to leave the house, that is.) But still. YOU GOT THIS. Who needs eight hours' sleep and a Perfect Prep machine anyway, right?

Month Three

You buy a Perfect Prep machine.

And Ewan the Dream Sheep, a Gro-clock, a Gro-blind and anything else that the Internet tells you to. At 3 a.m. Whilst crying.

THEN. Suddenly. One night. Your baby actually sleeps for five hours straight. This is amazing.

You're a new woman. You're so excited, you don't call your husband a penis-wielding voodoo-bastard that night. Instead, you plaster your new magic-sleeping-baby news all over Facebook. With a smug emoticon. And begin planning a city break. Which . . . means you JINX YOURSELF FOR LIFE . . . As every day from this point, they mainly survive on forty-five minutes' sleep a night. And the sound of you gently sobbing into a crusty muslin that's been on your shoulder since Tuesday.

Month Four

You used the Bumbo on the coffee table (you fucking rebel). But now, as well as not sleeping because you've been propped up in a nursing chair freezing one breast off at 4 a.m., you're also not sleeping due to the BPG (Bumbo Placement Guilt) so it probably wasn't worth it . . .

You try to sell the Bumbo on a Facebook selling site, but the experience is so horrendously tedious and time-wasting that you nearly murder someone who continuously calls you 'hun', and decide to just punch yourself in the fucking face next time instead.

Month Five

Jumperoo. That is all.

Month Six

Please remove any nice things from your life, as weaning means the end of those now. In fact – why not cut out the middleman, and begin hurling regurgitated broccoli and sweet potato at your own face and sofa. Perhaps some will trickle down your forehead into your mouth whilst still warm and you can count it as your first hot meal since you had a baby. Excellent.

Month Seven

You've made it. You've survived the first six months. This calls for celebration. An epic night out with breast pads, Spanx, and a new-found disrespect for your bladder . . . It is entirely amazing. Until forty seconds after you get in; when you know you'll be spending your impending hangover trying not to gag tequila into the face of your baby whilst desperately Googling 'breastfeeding after drinking A FUCK TON of alcohol' and punching Ewan the Dream Sheep in his stupid twatty face.

Month Eight

It's dawning on you that you're still in your maternity jeggings. And that breastfeeding somehow hasn't sucked you into a size 8 . . . but it's okay, because to make you feel better about that, you eat an entire cake without breathing and/or chewing. This then makes you feel sad and you start poking your stretch marks. So you manage that with a Toblerone and some gin. The end. #ginwin

Month Nine

Shit. It's started moving. Cafes aren't for you any more. You should know that. #beginningoftheend

Month Ten

You've discovered the power of CBeebies . . . But your shame crush on Mr Bloom may be getting out of hand . . . Heading to the toilet to watch CBeebies on the iPad 'one-handed' is just not motherly behaviour *coughs*

(But seriously; if you make it into the loo alone – down a Toffee Crisp and tweet about it so the rest of us have hope . . . please . . . *PLEASE*.)

Month Eleven

The Jumperoo doesn't work any more. And Facebook is NOTHING BUT LIES. And, if you're going back to work you're going to have to face the fact that you'll need to brush your hair and wear a real bra again soon . . . Shit.

5

Month Twelve

So your 'tiny baby' is suddenly capable of head-butting you in the area-formerly-known-as-your-vagina, capturing the footage on your iPhone and uploading it to their own YouTube channel . . . but the main thing is that you tell everyone four thousand times a day how fast it's gone, and that you've forgotten that breastfeeding ever hurt, and wine . . . Mainly wine. And wine.

#12monthsofbabydone
#ginwinetheend

Chapter 1

SHIT

'Where the fuckety-fuck is it?' Liz said out loud to herself as she rummaged clumsily in her over-sized designer handbag for the pregnancy test she'd just bought.

She'd scurried home quickly via the pharmacy after meeting her two best friends – Emily and Molly – and their newborn sons in a cafe in High Wycombe. Luckily they were both too distracted by breastfeeding and bone-shattering exhaustion to notice Liz's slightly rushed exit. The last thing she needed right now was awkward questions. Ones she didn't know the answers to herself yet . . .

It was a stuffy, hot, mid-August Saturday and the bathroom in Liz's neat, modern apartment suddenly seemed very small. And very sticky. And very impractical. Going for the minimal look was all well and good, except when you needed to find places to perch things. Even small things – such as plastic sticks you wee on that can potentially mess up your entire life quite massively, in a not *small* way at all.

She was aware she was huffing. A lot. She was keen to get on with this, just to know one way or the other. She couldn't think further than that right now – she wouldn't

allow herself to. She was ignoring the overwhelming feelings of anger, disappointment and stupidity as she located the test, scanned the instructions and quickly ripped the foil-lined wrapping away.

Thank fuck her boyfriend, Gerald, wasn't staying at hers this weekend, she thought, releasing a long sigh as she squatted down awkwardly on to the toilet, trying her best to wee in a straight line. Which, she now realised, was not quite as easy as the smug diagram on the box, and all the films and TV shows she'd ever watched where women did pregnancy tests, had suggested . . .

She was done.

She replaced the cap, pulled her knickers and shorts back up. And placed the test in front of her on the sink as she washed her hands, looking directly ahead at her reflection in the spotlit mirror above the basin.

She huffed at herself again.

Fuck.

Why the fuck was this happening?

This was not supposed to happen. Not to *her* . . .

She was the sensible one, the one with the soaring career, the one with her shit finally together. The one with the excellent fringe.

This sort of thing was supposed to happen to other people. This was the sort of thing that happened to Molly. In fact it HAD happened to Molly; one of her best friends, one of the most haphazard human beings she'd ever known, and the girl that believed contraception was a 'bit of a faff really'. And had quite frankly deserved to fall pregnant with that attitude . . . Which of course she had. But that wasn't Liz. She was careful, and considered, and in control. HOW COULD THIS HAVE HAPPENED TO HER?

Besides, she still wasn't a hundred per cent sure if she even wanted children . . . and if she did, now was possibly the worst timing in the history of all timings in the world ever. How was it that she could end up in this situation? Surely, she and Gerald had been careful – hadn't they? Clearly not careful enough.

Liz blew her fringe up out of her eyeline with a huff of hot breath, as she racked her brain. She began to come to the unsettling realisation that during the weekend she and Gerald had spent at her sister's house a few weeks ago, there might have been an unsanctioned moment of passion . . . thanks to an unsanctioned amount of red wine . . .

Liz frowned and rubbed her face in anguish, annoyed at herself for being so uncharacteristically reckless. She and Gerald had only been seeing each other for a few months, and it was clear that Gerald was a little more into the relationship than Liz was. Liz felt that familiar lump of guilt in her throat that appeared regularly when she questioned whether their relationship was still 'too much, too soon' for her. She couldn't help it. A past laden with shitty men and even shittier times had done that to her. People who didn't know might well view her as being cold, closed and a little career-obsessed, but she simply saw those things as necessary for self-preservation.

This was not a happy magical moment. This was one filled with utter dread and sickly anticipation, as she became aware that two minutes had more than passed and the result would be ready.

So she should look at the test.

It would be ready.

God, she didn't want to do this.

But she had to.

She filled her lungs with air and swiped the test up quickly from the sink, letting her eyes fall down on to the results window . . .

SHIT.

Chapter 2

THE NEWBORN BABY MYTH . . .

William was almost two weeks old. Emily had thought that by now, after a fortnight of being a real-life parent, she'd have motherhood 'down'. But the truth was, she didn't. She wasn't even close.

She'd barely moved out of the house. Other than meeting her friends Liz and Molly yesterday, one short-lived venture to the park, and a hospital appointment – to which she'd been forty-five minutes late because her baby had created a little bath of runny yellow poo in the car seat – she'd barely moved from her sofa, if she was honest with herself.

Everything still hurt a lot, and she just felt more comfortable being at home. Where she wouldn't be judged for not having washed her hair, or for wearing the same slightly funky-smelling T-shirt for the third day in a row. Or for awkwardly attempting to breastfeed a screaming newborn baby on a grotty park bench frequented by tramps while wayward sections of wobbly-boob got exposed and thrown around everywhere. Yes. Being at home just felt . . . easier. Even if it was a million miles from the formerly well-groomed, immaculately styled and always high-heeled girl known as Emily. Emily the PR

whizz, queen of being organised, life of every party and owner of more shoes than most of the known world – she was sure that girl was still lurking there under the surface. At least she certainly hoped so.

Right now, William was asleep in the bouncer at her feet, and as she curled up in the corner of the sofa, she began to feel quite suddenly and irrationally emotional. Disappointed in herself perhaps. She just wasn't quite the 'supermum' she'd thought she was going to be.

She had somehow thought that she'd simply bounce into action after a couple of weeks, that everything would feel so easy and natural, and the sleep would be returning by now. But it didn't. It wasn't. And to make matters worse she was still enormous – in fact, she still looked six months pregnant. Underneath her post-natal girdle, her midriff resembled a giant wobbly scrotum. With a belly button. And stretch marks.

She so wanted to be 'that mum' – the one she'd seen in magazines and on adverts . . . fresh-faced, with full make-up, brushed hair, looking slim and smiling as she breastfed her tiny tot in cafes whilst reading *Grazia* in normal-sized pants and debating which recipe to cook from scratch tonight . . . but she was beginning to realise that was complete bollocks, as she unpeeled another processed-cheese slice and stuffed it into her mouth.

Emily felt angry with herself for being sucked in. That perfect image of motherhood simply didn't exist. How could it? How could anyone find the energy to be 'perfect' when they'd been in the same underwear for at least forty-eight hours straight, and their nursing bra smelt like cheese. Cheese she'd made in her own armpits from her own son's infant-regurgitated breast milk.

That wasn't to say she wasn't utterly in love with her baby boy, or that she regretted becoming a parent in any way. She loved William more than she ever thought she could love another living thing. She just wished she'd prepared herself a little better – paid less attention to the bullshit media version of being a mummy. And been slightly more realistic about how often she'd actually wear mascara now, and have actual infant faeces on her face, her hair and/or in her mouth.

It now seemed utterly ridiculous that she'd imagined she'd be out of her maternity clothes by now, floating around in summer tops and short-shorts like the celebrities do . . . that was not something that existed in the real world; it mostly just happened on Instagram. Instead it seemed that just as she'd spent her entire third trimester eating Toblerones (whole, whilst crying), she was now spending the majority of new motherhood eating Toblerones whole, whilst crying and trying very hard to resist the urge to look at the area-formerly-known-as-her-vagina.

Emily had listened really hard in her NCT classes, she really had. It was her way. She'd made notes. She had a special folder. She'd colour-coded the sections and used special dividers. She'd even organised the end-of-course party with a themed buffet and personalised goody bags . . . Her NCT teacher, Tracey, had been open and frank

13

about the emotional side of new parenthood – she'd been pretty spot-on in fact. But Emily hadn't been ready to hear it. Not really. She was too busy fantasising about what her own image of motherhood would be like.

Nothing had prepared her for being this exhausted and guilt-ridden all the time. She just hadn't realised she'd be this emotional . . . Yesterday she'd had a complete melt-down because after a particularly yellow shit-storm from William whilst he was wearing a white babygro, Emily had given up on using cotton-wool balls and sterile water to clean him and moved to the dark side . . . Yes, she'd given in and switched to baby wipes. Which made her feel like an utter failure, and had her in tears for about an hour afterwards.

Her husband, Paul, had been there and had tried his best to make her feel better – hugging her and telling her she was being ridiculous and that it didn't matter, but it seemed to just make things worse.

She felt like she'd completely failed William because she hadn't stuck to her promise of using only natural products for the first three months. But she was already coming to the realisation that the promises you make yourself before you've become a parent are rarely realistic. What you think parenthood will be like, and what it actually feels like – are poles apart. Paul's reassurances were slowly sinking in and as much as she hated to admit it – perhaps he was right. It didn't matter.

She was doing her best.

That's what mattered.

She needed to give up on all the bullshit expectations she'd put on herself, and Paul, and even William, otherwise she was going to end up a sobbing wreck of a human in a matter of weeks. Making her own armpit cheese and dependent almost entirely on nougat-based confectionery. And processed-cheese slices.

Chapter 3

MARLEY DOES . . .

It was entirely possible that Marley was the perfect baby.

Molly actually felt like she had found her calling in life. Yes – she was tired. Very tired. And if she was honest, that slightly yeasty mushroom-y smell was probably coming from her, but she was loving being a mum so much she didn't care. It was like she'd never really loved doing anything before. She felt truly happy for the first time in as long as she could remember. It felt so liberating.

She honestly wasn't finding it that much of a change, she just wasn't finding it that 'hard'.

Life had changed but perhaps just not as much for her as it had for some other first-time parents – she'd spent her life to date completely winging everything anyway. She'd never really washed that much, she'd always survived living in a complete tip, and she'd always had pretty low expectations of herself. Some might find that a little sad, but actually it meant that she was rarely disappointed. She couldn't remember the last time she felt stressed or put herself under pressure to conform to someone else's ideal. Those words simply weren't in her vocabulary.

So motherhood hadn't been the same 'shock to the system' for her that it had been for her best friend Emily.

Their sons had been born only a week apart, but already their experiences and expectations of having newborn babies were so different. But then they were such different people. Emily was one of life's 'planners' – a career spent working in PR and events, and slightly obsessive-compulsive tendencies that led her to organise her shoes into colour order and alphabetise her spices meant she had tried to plan and organise herself into motherhood in the same way. But Molly was almost the polar opposite. She hadn't put any expectations on herself, she was going with the flow, doing what felt natural in the moment, and only owned about four pairs of shoes anyway . . . and apart from craving a good night's sleep and hoping things 'down there' healed up quickly so she and her highly attractive boyfriend Tom could get back to their overly active sex life as soon as possible, so far life had been pretty amazing. It had certainly been infinitely better than the pointless days spent with sweaty teenagers at the temp agency attempting to delay becoming a proper grown-up. Not that she had that much to complain about, temping had suited her – no ties, no commitment, every day different, full of new people and ever-changing scenery. She'd simply turn up in the morning and see what joyous adventures Blue Diamond Catering and Office Staff, and the unrelenting wrath of Busty Amanda's resting bitch face, had in store for her. Which was mainly photocopying in a mouldy Portacabin on an industrial estate, but still. A joyous adventure none the less . . .

Molly glanced down at her son sleeping on the sofa

17

beside her. Watching his tiny chest rise up and down with each tiny breath. She'd never been so happy that 'this' was what she was doing right now.

She located the twelve yards of blue material that was her sling, and got to her feet to begin wrapping it around herself.

'Hey,' came Tom's relaxed voice as he strolled into the living room and immediately planted a deep, loving kiss on her lips.

Molly kissed him back until a smile grew across her face, stopping her lips from connecting with his. It felt like he actually loved her even more now that they had Marley. He could be a little overprotective, it was slightly irritating that he couldn't let her get up from a chair without racing to help her to her feet, and was still insisting she only drank milk from fucking nuts, but he was a brilliant dad and partner. And that's all that really mattered . . .

'You sure you don't want me to come with you? Do you want some help down the stairs?' he said, sitting down carefully on the sofa next to his infant son and gently lifting his sleeping body up into his lap to get a better view of him.

'No. We'll be fine . . .' Molly said, trying to concentrate on tying her sling the right way – it was a lot to concentrate on, especially when your highly attractive boyfriend was sitting in front of you, cradling a newborn baby, looking like a walking, talking Athena poster. If it wasn't for the fact that her vagina muscles simply wouldn't allow her to right now – and that he'd placed a book down next to him entitled *Going Vegan Saved My Life* – she'd have pounced on him.

Molly eventually got the sling tied and gently took Marley from Tom, securing him in the little cradle she'd created on the front of her body. He barely stirred as she wrapped him in place, moved the material away from his face and took in his tiny, contented face.

'I'm just going to take him for a stroll and text Emily. I think she's finding it all a bit tough still . . . I just want to make sure she's okay. And not in some sort of Toblerone-induced coma,' Molly continued, as she located her keys and phone on the sofa arm.

'Okay. No worries,' Tom responded. 'I'm gonna get cleaned up here then. Get all the sheets changed and take out some green veg and tofu for dinner. It's important we keep your iron levels up,' he said with a little wink.

'Indeed,' Molly said, wrinkling her nose slightly at the thought of another broccoli-and-tofu-based dinner. 'And also important that we don't sleep in a bed that may contain several baby vom stains and skid marks.'

Tom smiled as he rolled his eyes a little, and gave her a nod before reaching for the vegan book and heading into the kitchen. Probably to begin massaging kale with moon water using the end of his penis or something.

On that note, Molly swiftly let herself out of the flat. She stepped carefully down the stairs, out of the main door, and set off slowly strolling along the pavement with Marley snugly secured to her front.

19

She soon reached a bench that she often sat on. It was set back from the road on a little patch of grass with a few trees and shrubs lining the border. Nowhere special, not even much to look at, but it was peaceful and fairly well kept so it made a nice stop on the way into town. She perched herself down gently, checking Marley was still asleep as she reached for her phone and opened up a chat window to her friend.

Molly
Hey sweetie – how are you?
How's William?
Any sleep yet?
Any chance of getting your tits back?

Emily
Hey you!
We're all good xx
And no.
There actually appears to be less
sleep . . .
I didn't realise that was possible but
he now has reflux too (yay).
So I spend most of the night frantic-
ally searching for muslins that have
camouflaged themselves in my fucking
sheets.
It's great fun.
Really.

Trying to find one in time just before
my newborn explodes and fires all the
breast milk he's just sucked out of me
for an hour straight back on to my
chest.
I love that.
LOVE IT.
(Sorry. I'm tired.)
How's you? How's Marley?

Molly
Oh poor you!
Can you give him anything for that??
Hope he gives you a break soon xx
We're both fine.

Emily
Just that Infacol stuff.
So far it's pretty much just made the
sick smell a bit orangey . . . but
seems to help sometimes.
So I'll take it!
Sometimes I do a shot of it myself.
Just to feel alive . . .

Molly
Pahahaha
Hey. He'll start sleeping for a bit
longer soon.
He's only two weeks old.

He's still freaked out about not being in your womb!

Emily
Well.
I'm pretty fucking glad he's not still in there I can tell you.
Not that my nipples or episiotomy scar agree but hey ;)
BEAUTIFUL TIMES.
Seriously need him to go longer than 45 minutes without waking soon though ☹

Molly
He will.
This isn't for ever.
You're doing an amazing job.
Keep telling yourself that.
Plus, Marley does, so it can happen!

Emily
Marley does what?
Sleep?

Molly
Yes.
Not through the night or anything but I only have to do two dream feeds at midnight and around 4 a.m. then he's through until about 8 most mornings.

Emily
I hate you.
Do you want to swap babies?
I'm sure they won't notice.
We'll just swap them back when
they're about four or something . . .

Molly
You're doing great sugar.

Emily
I don't feel like I am.
I keep having to milk myself after
drinking red wine in the evenings
because I start feeling guilty and get
terrified the baby will get shit-faced on
breast-Malbec.

Molly
lol x
That is exactly the kind of mental
imagery I want right now . . .
Please don't worry. Honestly.
YOU ARE DOING AWESOME.
We're off for a coffee in town if you
fancy it?

Emily
Thank you xx
I think I'm gonna get some rest before
the red wine milking starts again

23

tonight but thanks xx
Plus I just managed my first real-time
shit without laxatives.
So life is looking up!
Might celebrate with a nap.
Love to the boys from me.

Molly
Well. That was exactly the sentiment I
wanted to end this chat on.
Look after yourself sweetie.
Glad you had a nice shit.
Love to your boys too xx

Chapter 4

DATE NIGHT

It was Monday morning. It had only been forty-eight hours since Liz had discovered she was pregnant, but it was consuming her every thought. She knew she could easily hide it from her colleagues – she'd spent her entire working life meticulously keeping her personal life out of the office and had earned herself the reputation as quite the ice queen because of it. And right now she was thankful for it. The limited eye contact in the morning coffee room and the reluctance of anyone to approach her to make pointless chitchat about the weather or 'how her weekend was' had been a welcome bonus. There was only one person she was interested in speaking to today, and she was keen not to lose focus.

She knew she had to tell Gerald. And soon. It was unfair not to. Plus she'd seen how that scenario had played out for her friend Molly – Tom had completely freaked out after she'd kept it from him for weeks . . . Everything had worked out fine in the end, but it had been such a horrible, stressful time for everyone – and unnecessarily so. So there was no way she was going to make the same mistake. As much as she wanted to hide away in her office with her head down and pretend none of this was

25

happening, she couldn't. She was an adult. And it was time to do some proper adulting.

She was going to talk to him tonight. After work. In person. And tell him the truth – that she'd done the test and it said she was pregnant, and that she had absolutely no idea what this meant or what was going to happen from this point on. She would tell him that this was absolutely not the time for him to start asking her to marry him or showing her pictures of executive four-bed townhouses with good school catchment on Rightmove.

If she was honest, she already knew how it would play out. This was the man that confessed his undying love and proposed to her within a few weeks of knowing her . . . He was hardly one to hold back his feelings. He'd be elated. He'd kiss her. He'd smile and hug her and tell her this was the most wonderful thing that had ever happened to him.

And she should be elated by that too – by the fact that the man she loved would be nothing but supportive of their unborn child and do everything he could to make this work . . . But somehow she wasn't. Because she still didn't know if she wanted this. Certainly not now. Not for a while. Maybe not ever. Or maybe she did? Her mind continuously went round in nauseating circles.

Liz jumped and let out a little involuntary yelp as her desk phone rang abruptly, summoning her suddenly from her thoughts.

She placed a hand on her chest as her heart thumped quickly in her ribcage and took a deep breath to steady

herself, before looking at the caller ID on the screen . . .
it was external. Probably a client. Liz gently cleared her
throat and pulled herself back together.

She needed to get her game face on. Get through today.
And try not to obsess about meeting Gerald tonight.

Time for proper adulting. She reminded herself.

Then she lifted the phone to her ear and spoke smoothly,
'Elizabeth Milligan, Senior Family Law . . .'

It was 5.59 p.m. Liz knew this because every minute since
about five o'clock she'd glanced up at the time, feeling
more anxious with each moment that ticked by. Up until
then the day had flown by quite neatly – work had been
a welcome distraction, and with a big case dominating
their time, she and Gerald had barely spoken. There'd
been the odd tender glance across the board table, and
at one point he'd brought her a coffee as she sat at her
desk on a call, able only to mouth a silent thank you at
him, but in the final hour of the day the emails and phone
calls had dried up, and Liz's attention had turned to the
task ahead.

She knew that any second Gerald's smiling, unassuming
face would pop up at the door and it would be time.

Moments later, the familiar rap of a large set of
knuckles made her shift uncomfortably in her seat as
Gerald's broad, athletic, six-foot-three silhouette appeared
in the slim crack of her open office door.

'Ready?' he asked, pushing it open fully, looking
wonderfully handsome and relaxed.

'Sure,' Liz said, avoiding making too much eye contact with him, as though he might read her thoughts simply by looking into her eyes.

She quickly picked up her bag, and walked out ahead of him, hurrying to the lift.

'Everything okay?' Gerald said, catching up and striding along next to her, placing a soothing hand on the small of her back as he sensed her unrest.

'Let's just get to the bar,' Liz said self-consciously, as they stepped into the packed lift, stopping their conversation dead.

Liz took Gerald's hand as they scurried out of the building and down the street. She was keen to get to the bar and begin their conversation as soon as possible, out of the earshot of nosy colleagues. She wasn't one to mess around.

As they reached their regular haunt and sat at a familiar table, Liz placed her handbag down beside her, then removed her wallet and headed to the bar without delay.

Gerald still looked relaxed, though a little apprehensive when Liz returned from the bar and placed a large glass of red wine down in front of him, and a lime and soda in front of herself.

'So. What's up?' Gerald said, taking a small sip of his drink.

'I'm pregnant,' Liz said. The words had flown out of her mouth so matter-of-factly they'd almost taken her by surprise.

She said nothing more for a few moments, but simply

watched as Gerald's expression changed from that of surprise, disbelief then confusion, to utter delight, in slow motion in front of her.

He was reacting exactly as she had predicted. He was genuinely overjoyed. It was pasted all over his face. His sweet, smiling, handsome face.

'That's amazing!' he said after a few stunned seconds. And quickly rose to his feet, and came round the table to give her an all-consuming hug.

'When did you find out?' he said as he returned to his seat, maintaining her eyeline.

'I did the first test Saturday evening. And a few more yesterday . . . I just wanted to be sure before I told you.' Liz was still studying his face, but smiling a little herself now. It was hard not to when someone opposite you was grinning from ear to ear like a toddler who'd just found their penis for the first time . . .

'So . . . what do we do now?' Gerald said, still grinning.

'I don't know . . .' Liz responded, laughing slightly. 'I guess I make a doctor's appointment and we go from there. I'm still in a bit of shock. It's not really that brilliant timing, is it? But it is what it is . . . it just doesn't feel, well, real!'

'Hey, don't worry. I think that's totally normal. You just need to relax. I know work stuff is pretty intense at the moment for you, but we can figure it out, don't worry. I think I'd make a pretty amazing house husband while you bring home the bacon . . .' Gerald said, winking at her.

Liz laughed. He was right. She did need to relax. There were plenty of options once she'd had the baby, this was the twenty-first century after all. Neither of them had to give up on their careers in order to procreate. Liz was about to made partner at the firm, and whilst Gerald was still a senior solicitor – and a very talented one at that – it wouldn't be that hard for him to take some time off or drop down to part-time hours. He clearly wanted to . . . They could make this work. Perhaps she needed to be a little more positive about the whole thing.

'Wow,' Gerald said, still grinning wildly as the news sunk in a little further. 'We're going to be so happy, Liz. This is the most wonderful thing that's ever happened to me. You're the most wonderful thing that's ever happened to me.' He continued stroking her arm across the table and looking at her like he loved her more than ever.

'Have you told the girls yet? Ooh – we could send them a series of cryptic WhatsApp messages with a tiny pair of shoes next to ours, or spell something out in croissants, or something . . .'

'Erm. I think I'm okay for baked-goods messaging right now thanks. And no – I haven't told them . . . I don't think I'm going to just yet. They've got so much going on with William and Marley. Plus, I haven't even got my head round it myself, to be honest. I think I'll leave it another few days . . . let things sink in a bit more, if that makes sense . . . I love you,' Liz said, stroking his hand with hers. 'Tell me everything is going to be okay?'

'Everything is going to be more than okay. It's going

to be perfect. We are going to be perfect, Ms Milligan. And I think we need to sort me moving into yours sooner rather than later. I can be out of my place in two weeks. My landlord's pretty flexible. Seems no point delaying now!'

'No. I suppose not . . .' Liz said, realising she'd almost forgotten about asking Gerald to move in with her, given the events of the last couple of days.

'Why don't you start moving a few bits in this weekend? Between the two of us, we can probably get most of it done in a few runs.'

'Well, I don't think you should be doing too much running around and lifting things . . .' Gerald said, looking at her sincerely.

'Oh please,' Liz replied, rolling her eyes. 'I'm pregnant. I've not lost the use of my limbs. Besides, please don't turn into Tom. As much as he's a wonderful dad and boyfriend – I do not know how Molly copes with someone inspecting every item she eats, cleans and washes with to makes sure it's vegan, Fairtrade and grown by fucking pixies in accordance with the sun. If you go anywhere near my cleaning cupboard, make-up bag or start removing the milk products from my fridge, you'll be homeless quicker than you can say soya-based-dairy-alternative! Okay?'

Chapter 5

PATERNITY LEAVE IS OVER

Paternity Leave is over,
You think you're GOING TO DIE.
You don't know how you'll ever wash again,
All you do is eat scotch eggs and cry . . .

Paternity Leave is over,
How will you ever get out into town?
You smell like a zoo, and you still can't poo,
Let alone change out of your dressing gown . . .

Paternity Leave is over,
How the fuck are you going to survive?
Through the wind, the pain, and the epic baby-brain,
You'll need gin, wine and chocolate to stay alive . . .

Paul had finally gone back to work today.

He'd only been gone an hour, and Emily had already cried three times and eaten most of a box of Jaffa Cakes.

How could it have gone so fast?

She wished she'd been less tired so she could have enjoyed him being around more. She wished they'd done more. She felt so guilty all they'd really done for the past three weeks was look after William in shifts while Paul did all the cooking, cleaning and washing, and watched her cry whilst eating chocolate in between midwife appointments. It probably wasn't the way he'd imagined it either . . .

She didn't want to admit it – but she couldn't help the nagging sense of resentment she was feeling towards him right now. He got to go back to work, fall back into his old life, with its coffee breaks and showers and real-life human interaction that wasn't about what shade of shit your baby had produced that morning . . . Emily knew she was being a bitch, but somehow, she couldn't stop herself. Especially as in the short while he'd been at work, Emily had begun to realise just how much he actually 'did' do. And it was slowly dawning on her that this was it. This was how it was going to be now. Today. Tomorrow. This week. This month. Every day. FOR EVER.

How was she going to get out of the house by herself? How would she manage to eat, drink and dress herself without him there taking the baby for her? Who was going to pass her the TV remote and a glass of water as she began an epic breastfeeding session with everything just out of reach – again.

HOW WOULD SHE EVER HAVE A SHOWER?

The idea of leaving William alone for even a few minutes while she showered felt wrong . . . but how else would she do it?

She knew she needed to. She smelt like someone had regurgitated milky sick into a little lumpy pile on her neck in the middle of the night. Because that was exactly what had happened. And she hadn't even bothered to remove said lumpy pile, as that would impact on the already pitiful amount of sleep she already wasn't getting . . .

Stupidly, she'd signed up to start baby sensory classes today at 11 a.m. It had seemed such a good idea at the time. But right now it was the last thing she wanted to do. She was utterly exhausted, emotional and knew there was no way she could muster the energy to put make-up on or brush her hair. Molly had no interest in coming with her, but she'd managed to convince her NCT friend Rachael to sign up too – which was great for moral support but also meant she couldn't bail out. She had to go now whether she wanted to or not. It was slightly infuriating. She wasn't sure why she'd done this to herself. It was like when you signed up to exercise classes with a friend, and spent the next few weeks continually coming up with excuses as to why you couldn't make it that night – as you sat on the sofa in your pyjamas with some wine and a multipack of quavers, feeling incredibly guilty about letting them down. (But downing wine and Quavers until you felt better about it. Obvs.)

But she needed to do this. She needed to get out of the house, and prove to herself that she *could* do this.

She felt a bit like she'd forgotten how to be herself. It was strange. And scary. And a little overwhelming.

Emily heaved her weary body up from the sofa, and began to rack her frazzled brain for what she needed to pack in the change bag. It seemed so ridiculous that she'd organised huge press briefings and events for hundreds, if not thousands, of people in the past, yet this – the simple task of leaving the house with a newborn baby – seemed ridiculously hard. She just didn't seem to be able to engage her brain. If she started now, she could hopefully make it out of the door in the next hour and look quite convincingly like she had her shit together. Perhaps she'd even find her mascara . . . maybe a lipgloss . . . Although, probably not.

Nappies, babygro, spare babygro, baby wipes, muslins, nipple cream, Sudocrem, more spare babygros, breast pads, maternity pads . . . It was crazy. She was only going out for an hour or so. She gave the muslins a quick sniff and a squeeze to check they weren't too crispy with sick for use in public. Then realised she didn't give a shit and stuffed them in anyway.

She scraped her hair back into a messy bun, located her sunglasses, checked her T-shirt and leggings for any dubious stains, realised she didn't really give a shit about that either, and headed to the lounge mirror to inspect her face.

She looked so tired. So unhealthy. Her eyes looked heavy and troubled, with vivid dark circles underneath them. Her complexion was grey and lifeless, and her skin blemished and greasy. She really did need to stop surviving primarily on caffeine, chocolate, wine and Twitter.

William was asleep in the bouncer in the lounge, his tiny body looking even smaller, swamped by a baggy babygro that seemed like it would be too big for him for

ever. He slept so soundly as Emily moved around him, packing things into the change bag. He was probably knackered from a night of waking up every hour to regurgitate milk back in her face and generally fuck up her day so she was so exhausted she could barely function . . . but hey, it was hard to be annoyed at him when he looked so incredibly cute.

Emily decided to wake him for a feed. That way she could pump him full of milk, in the hope he kept it down and wouldn't spend the entire hour-long sensory class stuck to her boob under a muslin . . .

She lifted him gently from the bouncer and watched as he stirred and immediately began searching the area around him for a nipple.

As she started feeding him she felt a little triumphant. She was going to do this. Her plan was working. She was going to make it on time to her first-ever baby group, with a well-fed baby, reasonably puke-free muslins and leggings, and no actual shit in her hair.

She was actually beginning to look forward to it now – she'd have Rachael there for support, but she was looking forward to meeting some other mums too. She was sure they'd be lovely, and probably just like her. In fact, they'd probably all be just as fucking exhausted, wearing yesterday's clothing, and praying that the 'baby-sensorying' knackered their newborns out so they'd get more than two and a half hours sleep tonight too . . .

Emily began to feel a little better.

And relax a little, knowing she was well on her way to

getting back to being a real person who could leave the house on her own again.

This was going to be great. Better than great.

Just then. A thought struck her.

Shit.

HOW IN THE NAME OF ACTUAL REAL-LIFE FUCK DOES THE CAR SEAT CLIP INTO THE CAR?

Chapter 6

BABY-GROUP BANTER

Emily
OMG I MADE IT!
Is it weird that I'm almost as proud of
myself for making it to Baby-Group as
I am about releasing a human from
my vagina?
(I do have an overwhelming desire to
go to the pub now though . . .)
That's normal right . . .?!
I'm pretty sure Malbec has become
my biggest coping mechanism
(after Infacol)

Molly
Hey sweetie!
I think you've lost it! Lol
Well done for getting out of the house.
I knew you'd feel better if you got out
;)
How was it? Scary as it sounds?

Emily
Actually . . . yes.

It was sort of terrifying!
Rachael from NCT came with me
though so that made it a bit less scary.
There were some nice-looking mums
there too but everyone sort of keeps
to themselves really.
To be honest – most of them look as
knackered as I feel!
Which is kind of reassuring.
I could have happily dropped off halfway
through Twinkle, Twinkle, Little Star.
I probably would have done if William
hadn't started begging for a feed.
AGAIN.
There were a couple of women who
looked amazing though!
How do they do that?!
One was wearing lipstick.
And culottes.
Someone else had baked cookies that
morning for the class . . .
SERIOUSLY. WTF?!!
I haven't even put deodorant on since
Friday lunchtime . . .
And halfway through I found some of
William's puke in my hair.
At least I think it was puke . . .
Rach just got it out with a baby wipe
for me . . . lol

Molly

Sounds just charming . . .
Ah so it's 'Rach' now is it!
Looks like I've been replaced ;)

Emily

Don't be ridiculous.
You know I could never replace you.
You are a true one-off my sweet!
And you'd really like her! You should
come next week and meet her too.
See the crazy culottes people?

Molly

Well . . .
You have REALLY sold it to me.
But no, honestly I'm cool at the
moment.
I'll do some more stuff when he's a bit
older, but right now we're a bit too
skint to be chucking £7 an hour at
someone to sing nursery rhymes
at my newborn as he sleeps,
and turn the lights down
a bit . . .
;)

Emily

Ha!
It's so much more than that though!

It's amazing!
You'd love it if you came.

Molly

I know. I probably would.
But I'll leave it until my son can actually open his eyes a bit more if that's
okay!
Plus I'm not ready to see people in
culottes.
Is anyone?
Ever?

Emily

No. I think you're right.
Culottes aren't for anyone.
Except maybe people from the '80s
. . .
Why is Liz being so quiet?

Molly

She's probably working at her actual
real job . . . like you were only a few
weeks ago . . . remember . . . ;)
Much as she'd love to join you at your
post-baby-sensory piss-up instead, I'm
sure!

Emily

Well obvs.
Liz – I know you're reading this!!

41

Stop being boring and doing real-life lawyer crap!

Molly
Yeah.
Join in slagging off people who bake.
In culottes.
#Dicks

Emily
#CulotteDicks

Molly
#BakingCulotteDicks

Emily
Okay. She's clearly ignoring us.
So . . .
Pub?

Molly
Emily!

Emily
Okay fine.
I'm making a pot noodle instead then
☺

Chapter 7

MARLEY AND ME

Molly sat down in front of Tom's laptop and pulled up her emails.

She glanced over at Marley as he snored gently – sleeping soundly in his Moses basket a few feet away from her.

She couldn't help but smile to herself as she looked back at the screen and saw that the email she'd been waiting for was there. Waiting for her to open it. Waiting to be the beginning of a new era of her life.

Most people would probably think she was mad to even consider launching a new travel-business venture with a newborn baby in tow, but somehow there seemed like no better time. This felt right. The only other worthwhile thing she'd done in her life, outside of her starting a family with Tom, was to travel. If she were to have her way, she'd have as many babies as her body could phys-ically produce, as fast as she could, and spend her life travelling the world with them. She didn't care if that made her sound crazy; she couldn't think of anything more wonderful. So it made perfect sense to combine her two passions. She'd travelled on her own around most of Asia for three years after finishing university, and it had

been the best time of her life. There was a point when she wondered if she'd ever come home, or if this was her home now. Floating around Thailand and Bali in clothes she'd made herself, slumming it on beaches and in jungle huts had meant she'd seen all sides of the places she visited. Not just the touristy crap. She hadn't wasted much time socialising with teenage rich kids using their gap years to squander their parents' money on growing dreadlocks and getting drunk – she'd spent her time with local people, picking up work where she could and travelling to lesser-known villages and islands. It had taught her so much. And given her friends and contacts she'd never have made if she hadn't ventured off the beaten track.

Right now, she felt more alive than she ever had. Was she tired? – yes. Exhausted even. But she was so full of life and motivation. Something she couldn't remember feeling for such a long time. She'd spent every spare moment she had when Marley was asleep contacting friends and acquaintances from her travels to see who might be able to help her, or knew someone who could. If she was going to start a business sending families out to Thailand, she needed accommodation, facilities, travel, excursions, equipment; and all from trusted sources too. There was a lot to think about. And right now her Hotmail inbox was full of lengthy email chains, hopeful with exciting ideas and promises for the future. But there was one email she had been waiting for.

This one.

It was from a friend she'd stayed with in Thailand who

owned and ran a series of hotels on one of the slightly lesser-known islands. These struck a good balance between being authentic, whilst also being accessible and 'touristy' enough not to put off people with young children . . . Or so she hoped. It seemed he was interested too.

So right now, she was busy organising a date for her, Tom and Marley to head out on a scouting trip. Just a week or so to see how the journey was with a baby, what sort of facilities the hotel needed to offer for families and how they could use local businesses to create comfortable packages. It was so exciting. Molly felt like she was brimming over with ideas. The only problem was that she had no idea how they'd find the money to get out there . . . but that was a minor detail. Molly had never let things like cash flow bother her before. She was pretty sure if she wanted it enough, something would just sort of 'come up'. And it would probably all just be fine . . . right?

She couldn't wait until tonight for Tom to get home to give him a progress report . . .

Molly

Hey – I've got exciting news.
I heard back from my Thai friend with the hotels . . . It looks like he's up for it!
We'd need to head out in the next few months to give it a proper scope out, but I feel really good about this.

Tom

Hey gorgeous.

That's brilliant news.

Seems like it's all starting to happen.

I think we should sit down properly
and chat about it though.

I don't want to sound like a party-
pooper but I don't actually know how
we're going to afford all this Molly?

We're not exactly flush . . .

Molly

Oh details details . . .

You worry too much!

How about you bring me solutions not
problems eh ;)

Tom

Ouch. I think you need to work on your
comebacks ;) And we really do need to
plan this out properly that's all I'm saying.

We'll chat about it later.

How's my boy today?

Molly

Ha!

He's all good.

Sleeping right now.

And yes I know – we will. I'm just so
excited!

I've been thinking about the name too.
What about calling it . . .
'Marley and Me – Baby Gap-ventures.'
What do you think?

Tom
Isn't that a film where a dog dies
behind a tree?

Molly
NO!
Well maybe a bit.
But it's also the name of YOUR SON.
Which was more the angle I was
coming from tbh . . .

Tom
Ha. I'm not sure . . .
Perhaps something that reminds
people a little less about dead pets.
I'm going into a meeting.
We'll chat properly when I get home.
Love you.

Molly
Dick.
Love you too.

Maybe Tom was right. This probably needed a lot more thought. But she loved the idea of making the name personal. This was personal after all. If it wasn't for

47

Marley, she was sure she'd never have got the motivation to even start this. In fact, she'd probably still be in the queue at the temp agency, trying not to stare at Busty Amanda's more than ample, exposed cleavage, wondering where the teenage boys actually put their penises in order to squeeze their lower bodies into those skin-tight jeans . . . surely that level of restriction had to be unhealthy.

Maybe she'd try and use that for name inspiration . . . ? She could call it – *Temping, Tits and Thailand . . . Family Gap Year adventures*, or *No teenage erections here, just baby- and toddler-friendly travel across Asia*. . .

Maybe not.

Chapter 8

PARTNER

Liz had a very important meeting today.

The most important meeting of her career and possibly her entire life to date.

She'd received the email earlier in the week, telling her that the contract was ready and once the partners had given it the once-over, she'd be summoned to sign it on Friday afternoon.

So in ten minutes' time, that was exactly what was going to happen.

It was unusual for her to feel overwhelmed, but right now she couldn't help but feel emotional. Years and years of dedication, education and bloody hard work were finally about to be recognised. She didn't want to make this about being a woman. She didn't want to make this about being at least a decade younger than anyone else at the same level as her in the firm now. But she couldn't help but think that those facts made the moment even sweeter. Even more poignant. Even more really bloody awesome.

Knowing that she was about to sign on the dotted line to officially become the firm's youngest ever junior partner, and the first ever woman, was amazing. More than amazing. She felt like a fucking superhero.

She straightened her sharp, black designer suit and strode confidently out of her office, and down the corridor to the main boardroom.

She felt tall and strong in her expensive black court shoes, and kept her eyes ahead, ignoring any glances from open office doors or partitions.

As she reached the boardroom door, something strange happened. She felt a wave of intense nausea, and stumbled forward slightly.

She felt as though she might throw up. She made an immediate U-turn and took herself as swiftly as her legs would carry her to the ladies' room.

So far she'd had no identifiable signs that she was even pregnant. Other than two pink lines on a pregnancy test that is. But this felt like a stark reminder that things were going on inside her body that she had no control over. Liz steadied her breathing as she made it into the first cubicle, and soon the colour returned to her cheeks and the sickly churning sensation in her stomach faded. She could feel a slight pain for the first time too . . . if anything it felt like mild period pain, that familiar dull cramp that every woman knows, and certainly nothing she couldn't handle.

She felt uncomfortable though. Her mind was shouting questions at her. Was this normal? She remembered Emily being desperately ill for the first few months . . . perhaps it was just that?

She decided to quickly go for a wee while she was here. She'd already found she needed to do that more often.

She was a little startled by the small reddish-brown smudge on the toilet tissue . . . Surely that shouldn't be happening . . . It was only faint though . . . perhaps she'd imagined it. Maybe it was just the dim lighting in the cubicle. Her mind couldn't cope with this.

All she could think about was the room of people she'd just fled from, wondering where she was, what was going on. She didn't have time for this right now. She folded up a small wad of toilet roll and placed it in her underwear, before reassembling herself.

She needed to suck this up, get back in that room, and deal with this later. Her dream, her goal, her aspiration of being partner were all right there waiting for her, she just needed to go and get them.

Liz held her head up as she strode confidently out of the bathroom and back towards the boardroom.

She pushed all thoughts of anything baby-related to the back of her mind and locked them there.

The door was open when she arrived. She knocked on it gently with her well-manicured fingers as she walked into the room with a gentle smile of anticipation on her face.

'Liz!' Stanton's voice rang cleanly through the air above the chatter from the other people in the room. He was one of the senior, founding partners and had mentored and championed Liz from the outset.

He offered his hand out to her, and she shook it firmly. She hated weak handshakes. She especially hated it when men deliberately weakened their handshakes because she

51

was a woman. It was one of her pet hates. Limp, sweaty hands loosely gripping yours. Luckily Stanton was not one of those men. His grip was like iron. As was hers.

'Shall we get down to it?' Stanton continued, smiling with his twinkly eyes. Liz cast a look over the ready-seated panel of her peers that waited for her at the large board-room table.

'Yes. Let's,' Liz said directly, as she moved further into the room and took her seat opposite the panel, in front of a well-bound official document and very shiny pen.

She let her eyes fall on to the cover page . . .

Official Contractual Agreement
Hoare & Stanton Family Law Solicitors
and
Elizabeth Milligan
Junior Partner

Liz took her time reading through the pages, but not much of it was going into her brain properly. She was preoccupied with thoughts of what was going on inside her uterus right now . . . although you'd never have known it. On the exterior she was completely calm and demure . . . It was one of her talents.

When she was ready, she picked up the silver pen and smoothly scribbled her signature on the dotted line on all three copies.

She let out the breath she'd been unknowingly holding

as she finished the last signature, and allowed herself a triumphant smile, knowing this was it. It was done now.

Much hand shaking followed, and an expensive-looking bottle of Scotch was opened to toast her success.

Liz felt suddenly awkward as a tumbler of the potent, amber liquid was placed in her hand. The reality of her personal life flew back into her mind in a flash. She remained holding it and hoped no one would notice her simply place it down on the table again without it touching her lips.

There were a hundred conceivable reasons why someone wouldn't be partaking in an alcoholic drink at work on a Friday afternoon, but she didn't want to be forced into a situation where she'd have to lie . . . or be questioned.

No one noticed.

Why would they?

It was Liz.

There was absolutely no way this strong, career-focussed woman in a fledgling relationship with a fellow solicitor, having just been made partner at a law firm, was about to announce she was up the duff.

No. That would be absolutely ridiculous . . .

Chapter 9

HEY GIRLS

Liz

Hey ladies

Sorry I've been a bit MIA

Had so much on!

Been totally swamped at work for one.

But can now officially announce I am
an ACTUAL PARTNER IN AN
ACTUAL LAW FIRM.

How amazing is that!!

Signed the paper work just now.

Woohoo!

Also . . .

Had a bit of shock news actually . . .

I'd ask to meet you in person to tell
you this but considering you've both
just had babies – that seems a bit
unfair!

Anyway . . .

Seems Gerald and I will be joining the
parenting club.

I know it's probably a bit of a surprise.

Trust me, it was for me too!
But it's happening!
Arrgggghhhh!

Emily
Oh. My. God.
Are you joking?!
This is amazing!
Totally unexpected and completely
freaking me out, but AMAZING!
And also amazing on the partner front
too obviously!
I cannot believe you are having a
baby!!
Have you just found out?
This is insane!!
How is you being made partner going
to work with you having a baby??
Have you told them?

Molly
Seriously WHAT!!!???
Liz – I can't actually believe I'm
reading this.
When did you find out?
How far along are you?
THIS IS NUTS!!
And yes – huge congrats for the
promotion!
What did work say??!

Liz

Honestly. No one is more surprised
than me that this is happening.
I still can't get my head around it!!
But I've done about 10 tests.
They all say yes.
So it's real. Really, really real.
Only found out last weekend.
So literally a few weeks along.
I guess.
Haven't told work.
Too terrified to right now.
It'll come out soon enough but I want
to have a plan in place first!
I have not worked this hard to get so
far, only to go backwards because of
having a baby . . .
Gerald's already joked about being a
house husband but to be honest – I
think that may be the reality for us!
Childcare and Daddy going part-time.
It's too much to take in though.
I nearly fainted at work today.
Think I've been bottling it all up and
then stressing about it all night on my
own.
I'm glad you girls know now.
Feels like a weight has lifted to be
honest!

Emily
Wow.
I can imagine it's all a bit stressful.
I think Gerald would make an excel-
lent house husband though!
Plus – having a baby doesn't mean
giving up on your career Liz.
Aren't you in family law?!? Lol xx
Aren't there laws to protect parents
from that sort of stuff?

Liz
Well yes.
Although a different part of the law.
But I get the irony ;)
I think I'm just freaking out and over-
thinking this because I didn't exactly
plan it . . .
If you know what I mean.

Molly
Everything will be okay Liz.
Trust me x
Having a baby was the best thing that
ever happened to me.
I know it will be for you too.

Emily
Me too.
Much as I whinge and joke about

some of the crappy bits, I wouldn't
change it for the world.
Although . . .
I would like to poo more than once
every three days.
And not the width of a toddler's arm
each time!
Seriously. My poor bottom.

Molly
Your poor toilet system.

Liz
Okay. I'm less looking forward to that
part . . . perhaps you could keep the
poo-talk to a minimum for me until
I've fully come to terms with
everything thanks!

Emily
Will do.
Congrats all round again sweetie.
We're here for you.
Whatever you need.

Molly
We are.
You'll be fine.
We love you.

Liz

Thank you.

Love you both too xxx

Look – it's my birthday next weekend so we should all get together round here.

Gerald should have moved most of his stuff in by then too so it'll be a three-way celebration!

Bring the boys and the babies.

I'll cook.

And can't promise it'll top Molly's pesto-pasta and vegan-cheddar EXTRAVAGANZA at her old flat with the sticky carpets, but I'll rustle some-thing up!

Molly

We'll be there xx

Emily

Us too xx

I will be drinking a lot of wine though.

Just to warn you.

But I'll keep the poo-chat on the down-low and try not to use your toilet.

Chapter 10

TOLLY TIME

Friday nights were always Molly and Tom's night.

In a life-before-baby, they would go out for some food then drink, laugh, dance and kiss all night in sticky-floored high-street pubs before heading home for a night of passion. Passion mostly fuelled by vodka-based cocktails and burger-van noodles.

How things had changed. Not in a bad way . . . they'd just changed. Life had become instantly different, and the memories of how things used to be seemed so distant now.

Molly felt a little flutter of happy excitement as she heard Tom's key turn in the lock.

She was always so glad when he got home.

And that Friday nights were still their night. Tom seemed to have no interest in heading out with his mates and drinking the night away like they used to. Molly would never stop him. She wouldn't even mind if he wanted the odd night to let loose . . . but she loved that he didn't. She loved that he looked forward to the 'new' Friday nights as much as she did . . . He would plan a meal, and stop at the Tesco Express on the way home to pick up the fresh ingredients to cook for them both, maybe grab a few bottles of alcohol-free beer, and arrive home ready to settle down on the sofa to dote on his son and girlfriend.

Even if he'd had a shitty, stressful day, he was nothing but grins when he walked through the door. His face would light up as soon as he saw them both.

Sometimes Molly would just sit and watch him doting on his infant boy as he kissed his forehead and breathed him in after a day away from him. Oozing with pride and love.

Yes, Fridays were clearly different now – but in so many ways they were better.

She didn't even miss the booze – she'd promised Tom she'd steer clear of alcohol whilst she was breastfeeding, but in truth she would have done anyway.

Perhaps she'd go crazy and have a glass of something at Liz's birthday thing on Friday, but it was surprisingly easy for her to give up the vodka. Albeit temporarily. She was so focussed on Marley – nothing else mattered apart from him.

Besides, for the most part Tom had been sympathy-sober throughout her pregnancy and the last few weeks with a new baby in their life.

He still had the occasional drink, but Molly loved how much he was into parenthood alongside her. Even if she did have to eat tofu or nod appreciatively along to an article he'd found about new mothers eating different seeds in accordance with the lunar cycle . . . It came from a good place.

61

Tom came and sat next to her on the sofa, tie loosened and face beaming. He planted a deep and loving kiss on her lips as he stroked her cheek, and then gently lifted his son from Molly's lap into his arms. Molly sat and stared at the side of his face. She loved every curve, bump and texture of it.

'I think we should do it again,' Molly said, almost unaware that her thoughts had turned into actual speech.

'Do what?' said Tom, a gentle puzzled frown on his face.

'Have another baby . . .' said Molly, feeling confident she meant it.

'What! Like now? Really?' said Tom, slightly taken aback and checking her face to make sure she was serious.

'Well, not right now – obviously! But soon, I mean. Start trying in the next few months,' Molly said, laughing a little. 'Why not? This is the best thing that's ever happened to us . . . I don't really see the point in delaying, to be honest. I'm not saying we get down to it right here, right now in between *Poirot* episodes, but honestly, I think I'd like to start trying again after Christmas – I definitely want to be pregnant before he turns one . . . I think eighteen months or so apart is a nice gap. They'll be so close. In every sense. I think it'll actually be easier getting the baby stage out of the way at the same time. What do you think?'

'Wow. I guess you're right . . . I hadn't really thought about it, if I'm honest, but if it's what you want, then it's what I want too . . . so long as there aren't any risks with having two babies close together or anything? For you, I mean?'

Molly rolled her eyes a little. It was typical that that would be Tom's first thought. But she knew it was just because he loved her. When it came to baby stuff, he had an incessant need to research everything to make sure he knew all the risks, advantages, pros and cons, and could make an informed decision. He'd probably come at her with a PowerPoint presentation before the end of the week . . .

'Plenty of people have babies close together, Tom. I'm sure it's completely natural and fine.'

Tom looked at Marley and then back to Molly with a soft smile across his face.

'And what about Thailand? I thought we were off out there soon and looking at getting the business off the ground . . . Are you sure you want to start all that if you plan on being pregnant again early next year?'

'It'll be fine,' Molly soothed, wondering for a moment how she might actually manage that. And then deciding that winging it, like she had everything else in life, had worked out pretty well so far, so she'd just do that again. 'Once it's set up, it can run itself. I can be here overseeing everything from the comfort of the sofa, just eating pumpkin seeds and breastfeeding . . . It'll be fine!'

Tom threw his head back and laughed, before bringing his gaze back to Molly's. 'I love you, Molly. I can't imagine anything more amazing than completing our little family. I just think we should enjoy having one baby for the next

few months, and then see how you feel. But I'm up for whatever. And I'm definitely up for our Wednesday-night naked-bedroom-Twister to start up again whenever you're ready . . .'

Molly smirked and took in his face. God she fancied him so much. She had been terrified that having a baby would affect their sex life. That he'd look at her differently. She was so scared he'd stop seeing her as sexy, and start seeing her as a slightly funky-smelling baby-feeding machine. . . but he hadn't. He hadn't pushed her, but she knew he couldn't wait to be intimate with her again. The way he kissed her, the way he looked at her, the way he stroked that bit of her waist that made her want to explode inside . . . she knew he wanted her more than ever. He was just being patient – waiting for her cue.

Molly felt a surge of tingles move up her body.

She glanced over at Marley, fast asleep in Tom's arms. She gently took her sleeping boy and placed him down in the Moses basket without him so much as stirring. She knew he'd be out straight until midnight now, when he'd wake for his feed . . . so they had time . . . plenty of time . . .

She leaned in towards Tom, looking into his eyes and inviting him to kiss her as she paused with her lips only an inch away from his.

He did.

Fully and passionately. His arms wrapping around her body and moving it close into him.

Molly pulled her face back slightly from his and maintained eye contact, before putting on her best husky sexy voice . . .

'Tom. I think it might be time for that naked-bedroom-Twister session . . .'

Chapter 11

SLEEP IS FOR THE WEAK

If she was honest, Emily felt a little bit like she was losing her mind.

It was the eighth of September, and William was over a month old now. She craved sleep so much it was making her life a complete blur. She walked around like a zombie most days, managing only to get dressed when she needed to be somewhere, and even then she'd arrive at least twenty minutes late, and looking like she'd slept in a skip, being groomed by foxes for most of the night.

Plus, being so tired was making things tense between her and Paul. They'd never been like that before – they were always the couple that people envied, they rarely argued or disagreed. They had always been so in tune with one another. But recently it felt like everything he did irritated her. It wasn't that he wasn't supportive, he was great in fact, but she was exhausted. And desperate for sleep. And she didn't seem to be able to help but take it out on him. It was making her sad. She just wanted to get a little bit of 'them' back. But right now she couldn't see how . . . And what made it worse was that everyone else around her, her new-found NCT friends and Molly included, seemed to be managing it all just fine.

How did everyone else look so much better than her? How did they all seem to be coping so much better? And why did she seem to be the only one whose baby literally never slept? Was this some sort of karma? If she was honest – she'd begun to feel slightly resentful towards any parent she met whose child slept more than twelve minutes in the average night. Plus it didn't help that Marley was a week younger and seemed to be the most placid, easy, sleepiest baby ever constructed in a womb. Molly looked almost radiant last time she saw her. She'd even washed her hair. Emily didn't want to admit it to herself, but she felt jealous. Molly was her best friend, but Emily couldn't help but feel a little deflated by how well she seemed to be dealing with everything, when despite her own careful planning, preparation and organisation, Emily felt like she was drowning in it all. It just wasn't fair.

She'd also barely touched her blog in the last few weeks. She'd started blogging when she was pregnant and once she'd begun voicing the true realities of what had been a pretty tough pregnancy for her and all involved, she'd gone viral. And even got herself a collaboration with iCandy . . . but right now she wasn't sure she could even string a sentence together, let alone pull something witty and relatable out of her head for the army of Facebook mums that was inevitably waiting for her. She needed to write something soon. She missed it. And aside from that, the mum-army might think she was dead via Hobnobs and sleep deprivation, if she didn't pop up and say hi soon.

Anyhow – she didn't want to think about any of it right now. Today she was meeting her mum in town for a granny-mummy-baby date. And afterwards they'd be heading to John Lewis to buy every single item, regardless of cost, that even suggested it might make newborn babies sleep through the night.

Emily lifted William gently into the car seat, careful not to wake him. Although, right now he was so drunk from milk he'd probably sleep through the apocalypse. Which was as cute as it was irritating, considering he'd spent three hours from 2 a.m. crying almost non-stop because he just didn't fancy sleeping and would rather just look at her or something.

Emily dragged her fingers along the puffy skin beneath her eyes, willing herself to wake up a little more. She knew her mum wouldn't care how she looked. She'd been there herself, right? In fact, Emily had thought more about that the last few weeks since William had been born. She actually felt a deeper connection to her mum, appreciating that she'd been through all of this with her and her sister. It was so bizarre to think of her mum at this age, going through the exact same things she was going through now.

Her mum had been so brilliant, especially since Paul had gone back to work and Emily had felt a little lost. She'd brought food round, bought her magazines, and offered to sit with William for an hour or so in the afternoons so Emily could have a nap, change her clothes, have a shower, brush her teeth.

It made her feel guilty for every bad word she'd ever

said to her mum, especially during those tough hormonal years as a teenager. It's natural, she guessed, to have a phase where you feel like you don't want to be around your parents, pushing them away and mostly wanting to sit on park benches drinking Diamond White and smoking Marlboro Lights, with far too much eyeliner on. But the idea that William would grow up and say anything other than *I love you* was soul-destroying . . . and it must have been for her mum and dad too.

Emily knew she couldn't dwell on it. The teenage years had been short-lived at least, and seemed an age ago now . . .

And one way she could definitely make it up to her mum was with a bowl of pasta and an accompanying glass of expensive white wine in an Italian restaurant in High Wycombe while she cooed over her grandson. That would gain her some daughter points for sure.

Just then, the familiar beep of her mum's little Ford Fiesta shook her from her thoughts.

Emily opened the front door and waved, before heading back inside to check her face and hair in the mirror one last time, before deciding there wasn't much that could be done. She lifted the car seat up in front of her and struggled out of the door with it. She was glad her mum had offered to pick her up. She was too tired to drive. Certainly too tired to park. And she wanted wine.

'Hello darling!' her mum called enthusiastically from her wound-down driver's window. 'Do you need a hand?'

'Hi, Mum. Don't worry, I'm fine,' Emily said, smiling,

as she stepped around the car and began fastening the car seat in place on the back seat.

After about twenty minutes of quite frankly medal-worthy seat-belt wrestling, Emily wiped the sweat from her hairline and jumped into the passenger seat. Finally he was clipped in and they could go.

Emily felt slightly wobbly and light-headed as she raced around the baby department of John Lewis, somewhat frantically grabbing at products and chucking those that made the cut into a trolley. She could feel the lunchtime wine pulsing through her temples as she attempted to tick off the items on her list.

'Right,' Emily said firmly, trying not to lean against a stand that contained a lot of stuffed toy rabbits. 'I still need a black-out blind, a Gro-clock, a Gro-egg, a microfibre pillow, a temperature-regulating mattress protector, an amber teething bracelet, a new mobile, a dehumidifier, and one of those little machines that makes womb noises . . .'

'Wow. Okay,' her mum responded with her eyes wide and unblinking. 'Darling, are you sure you need all this? He is only a month old . . . chances are he'll settle down soon. Don't you think? You could spend a fortune and it make no difference whatsoever!'

Emily sighed deeply. Her mum was right. There was hundreds of pounds of stuff on her list and she had no idea if any of it would make the slightest difference. She just felt like she needed to do 'something'. Even if that something maxed out the joint credit card and meant they couldn't make the mortgage payment this month.

'Okay. I might have gone a bit overboard . . . I'm just so exhausted, Mum. I feel I'm walking around in fog, and if one of these things just helps me get five per cent more sleep – right now, it's worth it. I'm about to lose the plot.'

'I understand, sweetie. I really do,' her mum responded, rubbing Emily's arm supportively. 'I think you should just pick a couple of things that you really think will help and then I'll treat you to a nice piece of cake in the cafe. What do you think?'

'Okay. You're probably right . . . I know you're right, Mum,' Emily said, rooting through the mountain of products in her trolley, before selecting a few and clutching them to her chest. 'I think we should get the Gro-egg, a new pillow and this sheep thingy. Above all else, I need that sheep. I've read the reviews. I think he's the one to do it . . . If that woolly purple bastard can't make my baby sleep, then nothing can! Let's go pay. And also absolutely, yes. I fully accept your offer of cake.'

Chapter 12

GERALD'S MOVING IN

This might be my flat,
But I want it be 'our' home.
You catch the spiders,
And we'll share the entry phone.
I have just one request though –
When you're using the loo.
For wees you can keep the door open,
But keep it shut for a number two . . .

Liz heard the key go in the lock. She smiled. Gerald was the first person to ever have a key to her flat. With the exception of her, of course. And the lady across the hall who fed Jasper the cat when she went away, but that didn't really count.

Gerald was actually going to live here. Properly. Not just sleep over and top up the Go-Cat when she had an early meeting, or head over to watch box sets on the sofa on a Sunday.

She'd had a key cut and presented it to him last week at work, leaving it on his desk when he nipped away to make coffee so she didn't have to watch him open it. She wasn't ever one for sentimental moments and emotional gestures . . . She'd much rather hide behind her office door, spying through the crack as he unveiled it. Especially as she was now regretting that she'd bought the tackiest key ring she could find to mount it on – some hideous 'BIG-G' ring on a fist-bump emoji. She'd felt dirty just ordering it. And it wasn't even the worst one.

But she knew he'd laugh and love it all the more knowing it made her cringe a little. And she wanted to show him that this was not just about him living at 'her' flat. She wanted this to feel like 'their' home from day one. It was important. Even if it was a little daunting for them both.

And even though he'd been going backwards and forwards a few times this week, this was the first day he'd be here with all his things, without somewhere to 'go home to' the next day. This was really it. The first day of the rest of their lives. Together. Living together. Being together. All the time. Becoming parents together . . .

'Hello . . . ?' came Gerald's cool, calm voice as he let the door swing closed behind him.

'In here,' Liz called back from the bedroom, as she finished making space in the wardrobe for the rest of his clothes.

He had boxes of things everywhere. She had no idea where it was all going to go. But she was clearing as much space as she could, none the less. She'd even cleared out a few pairs of shoes . . . mostly the cheaper ones she never wore any more or those that had needed re-heeling since about 2011. She always wore the same four or five pairs anyway – the rest were mostly just for show these days. She'd even bought him a new toothbrush. And given him an entire shelf to himself in her bathroom cabinet. This was serious shit.

The cat looked pretty happy about the whole thing too. Jasper's little kitty eyes had lit up as Gerald strolled into the bedroom and planted a kiss on Liz's lips, before triumphantly placing a final suitcase on the bed.

'That's the last of it!' Gerald said, chirpily gesturing towards the case. 'Sorry if there seems a lot. It's amazing the stuff you find when you have to pack it all up, isn't it? I may need your advice on how many plain white work shirts is too many, to be honest . . . I look like I'm starting some kind of export business.'

Liz laughed. He always made her laugh. He was silly and buffoonish at times but it was so easy to be in his company. Right now, she couldn't really imagine ever arguing with him. Not in a serious way – having blazing rows and needing space . . . it didn't seem possible to get angry enough at him. And she was fairly sure he didn't get angry about anything. Ever.

He was wonderful really. He put up with all her mood swings and never complained when she was frosty or inattentive towards him. She needed to let him in a little more now. She needed to simply give in when she wanted to hug and kiss him. It was stupid the way she still overthought silly little things.

As if reading her mind, Gerald pulled her gently into

his arms and for a moment Liz allowed herself to be consumed by his embrace.

'I love you, Liz,' he whispered softly above her head.

'I love you too . . .' she responded. Allowing herself to smile and sink into him a little.

'So this is it then . . .' he continued, his heart thumping gently in Liz's left ear as she rested on his broad chest. 'I'm here. Despite you rejecting my advances almost non-stop for six months, turning down a marriage proposal that I'm still quite literally paying for now, removing the Rightmove app from my phone and barring me from discussing the fact we're having a baby together in front of anyone other than your cat . . . somehow I'm here.'

Liz laughed again. He really had been quite persistent, considering how she'd relentlessly turned down his advances. It was completely crazy to think he had actually proposed to her after only knowing her for six months. She'd said no, of course. It was ludicrous to think he'd have thought she'd say anything but . . . Yet somehow, they'd come out the other side. And she knew that she loved him, in her own way. It seemed silly that she'd resisted him for so long now, but perhaps they'd never have got here if she hadn't . . . and she did still need to exercise what she liked to call GDL, or 'Gerald Damage Limitation'. Given half a chance, he'd have a blimp outside the flat and have taken out weekly ads in the paper to announce the pregnancy to the entire world.

'But we are here,' she said eventually. Breathing in how

wonderful he smelt. 'And there's nothing wrong with playing a bit hard to get . . .'

'Perhaps that should be "almost impossible to get", but I hear you! And what a lovely start to your birthday weekend it will be, having your very-persistent boyfriend fully moved in, toothbrush and all,' Gerald said, planting a kiss on top of her head before gently breaking their embrace.

'Well, indeed,' Liz said, smiling up at him. 'Although, I hate the word boyfriend – makes me feel about sixteen again, about to go on a date to Pizza Hut wearing a Kappa tracksuit.'

'Ha,' Gerald laughed, throwing his head back a little. 'So can I get my beautiful pregnant life partner a cup of decaffeinated tea, and get her sat down with her feet up while I organise our shared wardrobe by colour, size and hanger variation?'

'Wow. You most certainly can. And can I just say you absolutely know exactly how to turn a girl on . . .'

Chapter 13

BIRTHDAY BUMPS

Today was the ninth of September and Liz's thirty-first birthday. And she felt slightly odd.

It was such a strange feeling to long for an ordinary, uncomplicated life for such a long time. And then to suddenly get it. And realise that even though she should be the happiest girl in all the land right now, she couldn't shake the uneasy sensation that this was all happening a little too quickly. And was a little too out of her control.

In the space of a fortnight she'd got her dream promotion, she'd had the man she loved move in with her, and she was going to start a family with him.

She should be skipping down the street singing, with a selection of cartoon woodland animals at her feet clearing a path for her . . . But somehow? She wasn't.

It was all too much.

This time last year, she'd been a complete wreck – in love with a terrible man who destroyed her trust and confidence, and working hard but seemingly getting nowhere because she was so worried about letting anyone get close to her. Plus her social life had been close to non-existent. She'd had her heart ripped from her chest and broken in two after discovering the wife

77

of the man she loved was heavily pregnant, that he had absolutely no plans to leave her, and her life was one great big shit-stained lie. It hadn't been that great, if she was honest.

But here she was – a law-firm partner, in love with a wonderful, kind man who couldn't stop kissing her, whilst she carried his unborn child, about to enjoy a night with her best friends in her newly shared home – and she was still picking holes in everything . . . What was wrong with her?

Why couldn't she be grateful for how wonderful her life was becoming? How wonderful it already was.

Liz began to get annoyed with herself. She needed to stop over-analysing everything and trying to find fault in every little thing. It was just so hard to relax and enjoy it when you'd been treated like shit for so long.

She huffed at herself irritably as she began placing homemade canapés on to perfect white plates, as Gerald unpacked his pants into the drawer space she'd cleared for him in her dresser in the bedroom. She let her eyes flick around the kitchen and into the open-plan living room as she worked, becoming aware of the picture frames and foreign possessions slowly appearing on surfaces as his life infiltrated hers.

It was going to take a little getting used to. But she didn't want him to feel like a guest in her home. And to make it feel like both their homes, he needed his things there too. It was just odd. After living alone for so long, there were suddenly someone else's things in the bathroom cabinet, someone else's clothes in the wash-bin, and pictures of someone else's university graduation on the bookcase. Plus the loo roll seemed to disappear virtually overnight – what the fuck was he doing with it all? Eating it? Hiding it? Or do men actually have twelve secret late-night epic shits they never tell anyone about . . . ?

She was thankful for the knock at the door interrupting her thoughts. She knew Gerald would get it. It was his front door as well now, after all.

She heard the familiar voices of her best friends and their other halves. And felt a little happier knowing they were here and the celebrations could begin now. She'd decided to keep tonight just for the six of them – she wanted to relax, and as she wasn't ready to announce her pregnancy to the wider world just yet, it felt simpler having only Molly, Tom, Emily and Paul there to celebrate with her and Gerald.

She washed her hands quickly and removed her cooking apron ready to greet them properly.

Before she even turned around, she heard Emily squeal in delight – delight which quickly turned into gushing uncontrollable tears and she flung her arms around Liz's neck and sobbed into her collarbone.

'Everything okay . . . ?' Liz said slowly, hugging her friend back and laughing a little.

'Fine! It's all fine!' Emily said, releasing her and frantically wiping her tears away as she fought to get her breathing back under control. 'I'm just so happy for you! I can't believe how wonderful it all is. Gerald, the job,

the baby . . . who would have thought it . . . I mean. It's just amazing. I'm so so happy for you, Liz.'

'Oh, come on. I've got a good job. And a boyfriend whose penis works effectively . . . Stop acting like I've just been made queen of the known universe,' Liz said smartly, rolling her eyes. But she knew that Emily knew how much she appreciated it. She just found it easier to be sarcastic in emotionally charged situations.

'You had me at "penis works effectively". . .' Molly said, strolling between her two friends with a dry smile pasted on her lips as she tried not to laugh at her own joke.

She hugged Liz tightly and kissed her on the cheek. 'Well done, sweetie. I mean it. You've got it all going on now. I think you might actually *be* queen of the known universe. You definitely have an excellent enough fringe for it.'

The three friends laughed, and Liz exchanged kisses and hugs with Tom and Paul as she stood in the entrance to the kitchen watching Gerald organising everyone and fetching drinks, as he laughed and chatted. Just as he should be. It was their home now. And they were a team.

The two babies were fast asleep in the car seats they'd been carried into the flat in. Molly and Emily gently lifted their sons out and placed them on a large soft blanket to the side of the table. Liz allowed herself to watch them, feeling happy but odd that that would be her soon. She became aware she had unconsciously moved a hand on to her stomach and was gently rubbing her belly.

She snapped out of her thoughts quickly at the sound of the oven timer pinging behind her and headed swiftly back into the kitchen.

'Is it okay if I leave this in here?' Emily said hurriedly, as she walked in behind her and placed a breast pump down on the side. 'I really need to drink alcohol like a normal person tonight! So my plan is to pop in in between courses and syphon off the excess wine as I help you load the dishwasher . . . that way I get to have a drink, be a brilliant and helpful guest, and I can't be accused of force-feeding my baby tit-vino.'

'Tit-vino?' Liz said, raising her eyebrows and laughing at the slightly chaotic nature of her friend. She wondered if this what was sleep deprivation did to you . . .

Emily laughed. 'Well. You know what I mean. I'm not going to go mad or anything, but I just want to have a couple of glasses of wine tonight. It's so hard when you're basically a giant on-demand milk-tap for a tiny boob vampire! It just feels relentless – sometimes it's every two hours all day and night! To tell you the truth I've started giving him a bottle of expressed milk once a day just so I can get a rest, and let Paul do one of the feeds. I felt like I was going insane . . . and I didn't even want to tell anyone I'd started doing it because I felt really ashamed. I know that sounds stupid but it just feels like everyone else I know who's breast-feeding seems to find it so much easier than me . . . I'm

81

scared I've let him down but I just needed a break. Do you think I'm terrible? It's just so hard, Liz!' The exasperation was clear in Emily's voice as her eyes became damp and intense.

'Hey, of course not!' Liz said, reaching out to squeeze her friend's hand reassuringly. 'I think you know what's best. You're exhausted, sweetie. How can one feed of expressed milk in a bottle, if it helps you get some rest and feel better, be a bad thing. You're not letting anyone down. You're doing an amazing job. You don't need to question that and you never need to feel guilty, okay?'

Emily let out a long sigh and let her shoulders drop as she relaxed and smiled back at her friend. She'd needed to hear that. She felt instantly better.

'I know you're right. Thank you. It's just hard when it seems like everyone else is managing so much better. But the truth is they're probably not. It's all just perception, isn't it? I think I need to get off Instagram. It's fucking with my mind!' Emily said, laughing.

'I hope there's not some kind of secret meeting going on in here . . .' came Molly's voice as she entered the kitchen and joined her friends.

'Not at all,' Liz said, smiling as Molly bypassed them both and headed straight for the canapés.

'I thought you were all hippy and vegan now?' Emily said, laughing, as Molly began stuffing a couple of bacon topped scallops into her face without much regard for chewing.

'What? No!' Molly managed, swallowing the last of

her mouthful. 'I might be wearing a necklace made out of my own dried placenta, but the vegan thing is all Tom, thanks! I'd happily go and wear my freeze-dried-fanny chain the whole way through a super-size Big Mac meal but Tom won't let me! Truth is, it's driving me a bit mad . . . I'm having meat dreams . . . I think I'm going to start staging a tofu protest and Deliveroo-ing myself meat pasties throughout the day from Greggs . . .'

'Fuck, I've missed you . . .' Emily said, before the three friends fell about laughing. 'And seriously? Greggs is on Deliveroo? How did I miss that! I think you just made my life!'

'Come on,' Liz said, gently taking her friends' by the arm. 'Let's take you and your secret meat-eating, and you and your tit-vino, and get back to the party. The boys will be wondering what the hell we're doing in here.'

The women re-joined the table, where Gerald had been busy sorting out glasses of prosecco for everyone, and fizzy elderflower for Liz and Molly, who was staying sober, possibly as much for Tom as for the baby, but she clearly didn't mind either way. She didn't even miss drinking alcohol. Bacon, on the other hand, was a bit of a different matter . . .

Liz brought out the plates of canapés and placed them on the table, before sitting to join her friends.

'Speech!' Emily shouted playfully.

Liz glared at her and rolled her eyes a little.

'Yes! Speech!' Molly called out, dinging a well-polished knife on the side of her glass.

Liz sighed, but knew she wasn't going to be left alone unless she said something.

'Okay. I'll keep this brief,' she said, lifting herself to her feet and coughing gently to clear her throat. 'Thank you for coming, everybody. Tonight may not quite be up to the exemplary culinary standards set by our wonderful Molly at her last dinner party – pesto, slightly out-of-date cheese cubes and some dubiously bendy Bombay Mix, if I remember rightly? You really know how to set the bar high, sweetie . . .' Liz let the tittering laughter die away before starting talking again. 'I don't want to sound corny but I'm so grateful to have such lovely people in my life. A life which is pretty awesome for me, and every one of us right now. Two beautiful baby boys, born to two sets of amazing parents. Something I'm now going to be experiencing myself. With this wonderful man who moved into my flat and my life today. I'm the happiest I've ever been. I really am . . . So happy birthday to me. Happy promotion to me. And cheers to you all. Now. Please feel free to get pissed on my behalf, and make me a promise, ladies, that for tonight, at least . . . NO POO, WEE OR VAGINA TALK – me and my fanny want to stay ignorant for as long as we can, thank you!'

Everyone laughed and raised their glasses, before getting stuck into the tantalising treats in front of them. Liz couldn't help but smile broadly as she watched her friends eating, chatting and relaxing. Her eyes met Gerald's across the table, and he winked at her and smiled. He loved her. She loved him. And she'd meant every word of everything she'd just said. She just needed to keep believing it . . . Especially as the canapés would soon be finished and it would be time for Emily's first round of dishwasher-stacking and tit-vino.

Chapter 14

THE THAI LIFE

A night spent with your best friends is like having therapy you didn't even realise you needed until you get it.

Molly had missed them so much. Even though they were right there, living only streets away, and she chatted to them most days over WhatsApp and Facebook – it wasn't the same. It wasn't the same as hugging and touching them, and looking into their eyes as you all laugh hysterically at rubbish jokes only you find funny, and are reminded again of all the history that binds you . . .

Liz's birthday meal last weekend had been a wonderful night of reminiscing about *Just Seventeen* magazine quizzes, Impulse O2 body spray and singing along in their teenage bedrooms to badly-edited mix-tapes they'd recorded from the radio. It had been marvellous. No awkward silences, no subjects out of bounds – just love and laughter and great times.

They'd also chatted about now. Molly felt so inspired. Her friends were completely behind her venture. She'd told them all about her plans at the meal – her friend with the hotels in Thailand and her ideas for the baby- and toddler-friendly trips and holidays. They'd nodded and asked questions and it had felt so wonderful to have

the answers. Even if it was only some of the answers . . .
Molly wasn't really known for her planning and cautious-
ness – she was more of a 'fake it until you make it' kind
of girl. Details had always seemed a bit overrated to her
. . . But considering this was potentially the start of a
new business, a new life, a new everything for her and
her family, perhaps she should look into things a little
more in-depth than just 'Googling stuff' whilst she was
breastfeeding, and asking her dad . . . After all, she wasn't
making a lasagne or something, she was starting up a
travel company. (And incidentally, the last lasagne she'd
made was absolutely fucking terrible so probably best not
to base her research skills on that.)

She'd come back from Liz's with new ideas and new
questions of her own, but a lot of them she simply couldn't
answer sitting on her arse in front of a laptop, with her
infant son latched on to her left tit. Which was exactly
what she was doing at the moment.

It was amazing how much 'stuff' needed to happen,
but also how many friends of friends came out of the
woodwork once you needed to find people who knew
about stuff you didn't. Everyone had been incredibly
helpful at putting names in the hypothetical hat of Molly's
future – graphic designers, brand conceptualisers (whatever the fuck they were), someone who'd done PR for the
Gap Year Show, another someone who had their own
travel insurance business and could offer some advice,
and a mate of someone's cousin's friend's housemate who
could set her up with a domain name and holding page.

It was pretty far from her comfort zone, but Facebook was proving incredibly useful – Molly wondered if Zuckerberg had considered that his multi-billion-pound social enterprise would mostly be used for people continually asking if they knew any cheap web designers who liked to work for free and pretty much not get paid except in smiles and hugs and the occasional cuddle with a cute newborn baby . . . perhaps not.

She was beginning to realise just how big a task this was going to be. Especially without any actual money. It was all well and good feeling creative and fired up – she was brimming with ideas and enthusiasm, but that didn't pay the £150 domain and hosting fee. Or the five hundred quid she'd just been quoted for a 'cheap' website design. Plus it didn't even begin to cover the costs of actually getting out there to Thailand with Tom and Marley in tow . . . Her head was starting to spin a bit.

It had certainly been easier when all she had to do was make wonky photocopies and do binding for £7.50 an hour, cash in hand . . . This was clearly going to take a bit more thought than she had first envisaged.

Tom had a pretty good job, he worked in sales and marketing for a regional radio station, but he was currently their only real 'income'. His wage covered the bills, their food, their day-to-day living, but there wasn't much left over at the end of each month . . . plus Christmas was coming up. What little they did have would mostly go towards that.

The fact was, if she was going to do this properly – she

needed cash. And she needed to begin a plan of 'how much'. Then she could work backwards from there.

Molly huffed at herself as she grabbed her notebook and turned to a fresh page. Which was a bit awkward to manage over Marley's head but it was amazing how dextrous you became at reaching for stuff around a feeding infant when you needed to.

STUFF I NEED TO DO/PAY FOR

She wrote matter-of-factly in capitals on the top of the sheet. Before drawing a slightly wonky line down the middle of the page, and starting to jot down all the 'stuff' line by line on the left-hand side.

Now the real hard work started. She needed itineraries, lists, trip ideas, a website, and most importantly a name . . . Everything she'd come up with was so crap!

There was no faking that – time to switch boobs and get planning . . . which still wasn't really her strong point.

Smiles and hugs and cuddling a cute newborn baby were.

Chapter 15

SLEEP IS STILL FOR THE WEAK

William was nearly eight weeks old now.

And absolutely none of the baby gadgets that Emily had bought with her mum the other week seemed to have much effect on his sleep.

In fact, they may have actually made his sleep worse. Something she hadn't previously believed was possible . . .

Emily was at the end of her tether. She was delirious from the tiredness. It was even beginning to affect her and Paul's relationship. She felt angry and irritated all the time. Everything he did annoyed her. He got to go to work – be a normal person, speak to other humans about subjects other than piss, puke, poo and how exhausted he was. He got to sleep for longer than forty-five minutes at a time before being screamed at by the hungriest baby known to man. It felt unfair. To be honest, she was jealous. Although, she didn't really know what she was jealous of. He looked almost as exhausted as she felt most days.

Not that she'd say that to him. She was too knackered and hormonal to have sympathy for anyone but herself at the moment.

Right now, it was a drizzly September morning and if

she was honest, she just couldn't face baby-group today. She'd be back on it tomorrow. Especially as all the NCT mums were meeting for lunch, and she definitely didn't want to miss the chance to catch up with everyone and line the babies up in size order for a new photo. Obviously. But today she needed a day at home without anyone. Without changing out of her pyjamas. With a Netflix marathon and a range of sugary snacks, lying on the sofa and not caring about anything else. She texted her NCT friend Rachael to let her know she wasn't going to make it, being completely honest about why. She felt horribly guilty as she pressed send, but when a lovely supportive message came flying straight back, she realised that Rachael completely understood. In the same way Emily would have completely understood, if it had been the other way round . . . all new mums have days like this. And that's okay. It was really lovely to know she wasn't alone. And that everyone had the 'just can't do it today' days.

William began to stir from his sleep in the bouncer by her feet, crying to be fed again. Emily sighed. And readied herself on the sofa for another breastfeeding stint. As she pulled William up on to her and began feeding, she looked to see the TV remote just out of reach and her water glass empty. Again.

She sighed irritably at herself. But she had her phone at least – she'd take the time to chat to Molly. It'd stop her from feeling guilty about missing this week's 'Under the Sea' themed baby sensory class, which William probably

gave as many fucks about as last week's 'Space' theme. Which he'd slept through. Entirely.

Emily
Hey x
You there?

Molly
No.

Emily
Funny.

Molly
Okay. I'm here ;)
How's things?

Emily
Okay. Although I'm being naughty
and skiving off Baby Sensory today.
I'm just too bloody knackered.
Decided box sets, jaffa cakes and
trying to get a decent brelfie for my
blog Instagram page are my main
goals today . . .
You okay?

Molly
Ha! I feel you ;)
We all need a day like that every so
often x I'm cool – just waiting for

the rain to stop so I can head into
town.
What the fuck is a brelfie?

Emily
A breastfeeding selfie.
You know the ones.

Molly
Err . . . no?

Emily
You must have seen them?
On social media and stuff?
Women sharing really lovely photos
of themselves feeding their
babies . . .?

Molly
Not really . . . but okay.

Emily
Well I tried to do one yesterday,
but it was HORRENDOUS.
How do they make them look so
beautiful and serene?
I took about ten shots with my
iPhone and every single one looked
like I was either smothering my
baby with a giant stilton-veined puffy
boob, or he wouldn't keep still so

his face was all blurry.

I gave up on the final shot after he regurgitated his entire feed back on to my tit.

Possibly in protest.

I don't know.

And then I cried.

Perhaps I should just give up.

In fact now I've recalled all that and seen it written down I officially do give up.

Molly

Honestly, you need to stop putting all this weird pressure on yourself sweetie.

Who gives a shit that you can't get a picture of you breastfeeding to look like the ones on the internet . . . it doesn't matter.

Stop beating yourself up over pointless shit.

The Netflix and jaffa cakes I am totally down with though. Obvs.

Emily

You're right. I know you're right.

I just feel like I'm going a bit mad sometimes . . . do you?

Molly

Sure I do.

It can all be a bit monotonous and strange at times. I think some of it is down to the lack of sleep, and the rest is hormones and just how over-whelming it can be sweetie. We all feel it. Some more than others. But we all do.

Let's meet soon.

When you're not doing tit-selfies.

Emily

I'm so glad you said that.
Makes me feel so much better knowing it's not just me!
Earlier on I spent about an hour searching for my phone . . . after I'd torn the entire house apart, cried, punched the sofa, cried again and tidied it all back up again . . . I found it.
In my hand.
I just feel like that sums up my life at the moment!
Moments of brilliance, mixed with moments of finding the shit you're looking for in the palm of your fucking hand.

ANYWAY . . .
I miss you guys.
Maybe we can meet this weekend?
All of us I mean – Liz too ;)
Last Saturday Club . . .?
Feels like we haven't done one for
AGES.
And I love you sweetie.
Thank you for having a baby at the
same time and making me feel like
less of a complete loon.
Even if your baby is really easy and
mine is rubbish and broken and it's
not fair and I slightly hate you a little
bit . . .

Molly
Hey! You love me really, and your
baby is not broken x you'll get there I
promise.
This weekend sounds good.
Love you too. xxx

Emily did feel a little better. Last Saturday Club always
cheered her up – it was the name they'd given to the
meet-ups the three of them had been doing since they'd
left school . . . no matter what, they'd make time for
each other on the last Saturday of every month. It didn't
always happen – but it was definitely time to make this
one happen. And brelfies aside – she really did want to

post something on her blog. It had been ages since she'd written anything. Other than an announcement to say the baby had been born, she'd neglected her blog page almost entirely. She'd been too tired to be funny, or witty, or anything other than a bit teary and angry and worried about the future of her labia.

But even though the fog of new motherhood was still very much hanging over her, she really did feel a little better today. After chatting to Molly and discovering she wasn't going quietly insane and that everything she was feeling was normal – she felt a little restored.

It was just the sleep thing. If she could just get more sleep, she would surely return to being nice, sweet, kind-although-slightly-high-maintenance-and-a-bit-bossy Emily with the big hair and smiley face.

Emily decided it was time to get back to blogging. Sleep was undoubtedly the topic of the moment. So she'd start there. She was sure other new mums would be able to relate to that, right?

So she reached for her laptop in its usual spot down the side of the sofa, and in no time at all she was tapping away quite ferociously, and starting to feel a lot more like her old self:

11 Things All Parents Have Done When Their Babies Won't Sleep (contains crying, mine)

1. Got out of bed as noisily as possible so your baby knows you really shitting mean it this time.

2. But then crept out of the nursery like a frickin' ninja. On tip-toes. Backwards. One boob hanging free. Balancing a Sophie-the-bastard-Giraffe on your head. Holding your breath. Without blinking.

3. Begun checking Amazon for Perfect Prep machines. Ewan the Dream Sheep. And boarding schools.

4. Decided that slightly crusty cot-sheet will be fine . . . They're in a bloody babygro . . . It's not like they're rolling around naked in their own filth.

5. It's 5 a.m. You haven't been to sleep since Tuesday. (Last Tuesday.) Your baby is piping liquid yellow shit into their sleeping bag like they're squeezing banana porridge out of an

Ella's Kitchen pouch . . . You leave them rolling around naked in their own filth.

6. Taken to Twitter. To call your baby things you literally can't say to their face. Because you're too scared your 7-week-old will somehow understand you.

7. Reminded yourself that the 4-month sleep regression can happen in months one, two and three as well. Along with month five. Upwards. For ever. Until you're dead.

8. Been truly at the end of your tether, after finally getting your baby to sleep, then real-ising . . . shit . . . You can't remember if the black-out blind is down and your baby is wearing a POLYESTER BABYGRO. CODE RED. CODE RED. I repeat CODE RED. *(Now repeat points 1 through to 7 again . . .)*

9. Become inconsolable after not being able to locate the muslin *that you left RIGHT F@*KING THERE FOR F@*K's F@*KING SAKE.* The bedding is white. The muslin is white. You can't turn the light on . . . What do you do . . .? That's right. Cry. Until your husband wakes up and finds the muslin instantly without even opening both eyes. Twat.

10. Accidentally entered the nursery naked. (*You're too exhausted to recall how to clothe yourself. Or use eyes.*) So sat there freezing your tits off, (*quite literally if you're breastfeeding*), then realised that your shivering seems to have provided some kind of sleep-inducing vibration, and that this is it now. You're here for the night. Time to get on Twitter.

11. After exhausting all the useful advice Google has to offer, you've begun begging. Using your best truly-pathetic-desperate voice. So your baby knows you really shitting mean it this time.

#gin

Chapter 16

SOMETHING'S WRONG

Something was wrong.

As Liz sat awkwardly in the women's toilet cubicle just down the corridor from her shiny new partner office, she stared down at the vivid red smear of blood in the gusset of her knickers. She knew this wasn't normal. She knew this wasn't something she could just ignore. Even though part of her desperately wanted to – she knew something was really really wrong.

By her calculations she was around ten weeks pregnant now. She was supposed to be seeing a midwife for the first time later this week, after what had felt like a fairly pointless appointment with her doctor where she'd had her blood pressure checked and then been told not to eat pâté, go kayaking or get pissed. She probably could have worked those ones out for herself really . . .

But she knew, looking down at the fresh red colour of the blood, that there was no way she could wait days before telling someone she was bleeding like this. This was nothing like the small brown smudges that had appeared intermittently in her underwear before. She'd googled those. They were quite common – apparently.

'Old blood leaving the body', the forums said. 'Unlikely to be anything to worry about'. So she hadn't.

But this was different.

Liz knew Google wasn't going to give her the answers for this. Not any real ones anyway – the Internet just gave you the answers you wanted, didn't it? While you mentally filtered out all the ones you really didn't . . .

She got her phone out.

> Can you meet me at my office now?
> I think something is wrong.

Gerald must have literally sprinted from his desk the moment he received her text, because he was already hovering in the doorway as Liz turned the corner to return to her office. He looked painfully worried. But was trying to keep a face of strength. For her. She appreciated that. But she couldn't help thinking the worst right now.

'What's going on? Are you okay? Has something happened? Is it the baby?' Gerald's questions were flying at her as he followed her into her office and closed the door behind him. She wasn't sure which one to tackle first. Not that she could tackle any of them really – she didn't have any answers for him.

Liz composed herself and turned to face him. 'I don't know . . . I called 111 from the toilet and they put me straight through to a doctor – they've made me an appointment at the hospital for 2 p.m. today. They want me to have an emergency scan. I've been bleeding. There's not that much actual blood, but it's constant. They won't say it, but I think something is very wrong. Will you come with me? I don't want to be alone . . .' She'd been holding it together right up until the last sentence. A choking lump appeared in her throat as Gerald embraced her intensely.

'Of course. Shit. Look – we don't know anything yet. We need to let them look at the baby and tell us what's going on. We can't let ourselves think the worst. Let's get out of here. You can change into something comfy at home and we'll get there with plenty of time.'

'I love you.'

'I love you too.'

Liz hated that the sonographer wouldn't turn the screen around.

It felt so tense. So inevitable. She was just waiting for her to say the words.

'Do you know how many weeks you are?' the sonographer said gently but without inflection, her eyes remaining on the screen.

'Just over ten,' Liz said purposefully. Trying to read her reaction. She didn't have one.

After a few moments she passed Liz some blue paper-tissue to clean up with, and they were taken into a small waiting room, where they were told to wait for the midwife.

Liz and Gerald took a seat on the low, spongy, plastic-lined

chairs quite automatically without speaking. Liz couldn't look at Gerald. He was holding her tightly – one arm around her shoulders, the other in her lap clutching her hands. She was so glad he was there. She didn't want to do this by herself.

There was still a small glimmer of hope that everything would be okay, but it was dwindling. The table in front of them was full of leaflets about miscarriage and handling loss . . . Fuck, this was horrible. It all felt so inevitable.

There was a polite tap on the door and a kind-faced, middle-aged woman with short hair came in. She was clearly the midwife the sonographer had mentioned.

She led them to a small room nearby, closing the door behind them. The room was arranged with two hard plastic seats facing a desk topped with files and leaflets and all sorts of paperwork.

Liz quickly recognised her own pregnancy notes in a purple folder laid out in the centre of the desk.

The three of them took their seats quickly as the short-haired midwife introduced herself before getting straight to the point.

Liz had immediately forgotten her name. It had been overpowered by the words that came next. She tried to listen to them, but it seemed like they didn't all go in . . .

'. . . baby stopped growing at five weeks . . . no heartbeat . . . body taken a while to realise the pregnancy is no longer going on . . .'

It was almost like an out-of-body experience. She could feel Gerald's grip on her hands and shoulder get stronger.

Her eyes were fixed intently on the midwife's but the words and her vision seemed muffled. She became aware of her hairline becoming sweaty, her throat closing up, the back of her neck becoming clammy and uncomfortable. She was trying quite hard not to throw up.

'Are you okay? I know this is devastating to hear. I'm so sorry . . . You look very pale, would you like to take a few moments? Do you need to lie down?'

Liz zoned back in on the midwife as she passed her a small cup of water. She seemed to have lost the power of speech. It was all she could do to nod and take a few sips of the cold liquid, which she forced down past the stiff lump in her throat.

The midwife talked about all the next steps. Gerald asked a few questions. They were given leaflets and phone numbers in a brown envelope. They were standing up now and leaving – it seemed like they'd been in that room a long time, although the entire conversation was probably over within ten minutes.

For a moment Liz thought how awful it must be to have that job. To deliver that news to desperate, broken couples over and over. Perhaps only made easier when sometimes the news wasn't bad . . . but for them it was. It was fucking horrible.

She needed to get out of there. She just wanted to go home.

After what felt like for ever – working their way through a maze of corridors, lifts and turns – they finally made it out of the hospital and into the car park.

Liz didn't remember if she'd said goodbye or thank you . . . she wasn't sure she had any energy left to care. She thought she probably had. Or at least Gerald would have, on behalf of them both.

It was an overwhelming relief to reach Gerald's car and hear the dull thud of the door closing, blocking out the outside world. Suddenly – all the emotion she'd been holding in burst from her as the tears streamed down her face and she sobbed uncontrollably into her open hands. Gerald gripped her shoulders and pulled her towards him. She was vaguely aware of him crying too.

This was terrible. Horrible. Just the worst and most unexpected moment she could possibly imagine.

Her sadness slowly changed to anger and confusion – she was annoyed at herself for being so cavalier and selfish about it all. Was this her fault? Did this pregnancy not work out because she didn't want it enough? Liz choked on the thought that she'd somehow made this happen because all she'd done was question how a baby would fuck up her career plans. How could she have been such a selfish bitch?

She was also angry at herself for telling people. So many people. A knot formed in her stomach as she began thinking about how she'd have to text around everybody to tell them what had happened . . . Fuck, she couldn't think of anything worse . . . Having to contact everyone to let them know her body had fucked it all up. That she was no longer having a baby.

The tears were flowing now. Hot, ugly tears of guilt

and anger and overwhelming sadness were streaming from her eyes without relenting.

All she could do was hug Gerald and let her tears soak into his shoulder as her mind raged with terrible thoughts and questions she was struggling to stop.

They sat there together for a long time. Crying, hugging and letting their emotions pour out of them in the front seat of the car as it sat stationary in a cold, concrete hospital car-parking space.

It was raining now.

And everything around them was grey.

Chapter 17

THAI-SPIRATION

Molly
Ladies!
I need your help!
Trying to think of a name for my Thai
stuff is killing me . . . feel like I'm
continually going round in circles!
Can you tell me if you like any of
these??

Emily
Molly it's 3 a.m.

Molly
But you're replying.

Emily
That's because I haven't slept in 73
days.

Molly
Wow. Saying it in days defo makes it
sound worse . . .

Emily
I know.

Molly
But hey, you're already up so you
might as well make yourself useful
right?!

Emily
I guess so . . .

Molly
Okay – just say the first word or
feeling that comes into your head as I
send you my company name ideas
. . . okay?

Emily
Okay.

Molly
Here goes . . .
Family-Travel-in-Thailand

Emily
BORING

Molly
Thai-Family-Gap-Travel

Emily
Yawn . . .

Molly
Fam-Thai-Trav

Emily
WTF?!

Molly
Thai-Babes

Emily
Brothel

Molly
Thai-Babies

Emily
Infant trafficking

Molly
Eastern-Escapes

Emily
Prison

Molly
Eastern-Infant-Escapes

Emily
Infant prison trafficking

Molly
Far-East-Families

Emily
Witness protection

Molly
Emily!! I don't feel like you're taking
this very seriously . . .

Emily
It's 3.09 a.m. And I've been angrily
keeping a tiny human alive with only
my tits for over two months . . . I'm
not sure I'm the best person to ask.

Molly
Fair point.
I am beginning to lose the will to live
though! Nothing sounds right!

Emily
There must be something . . .
Perhaps you're over-thinking it! I'm
sure it'll come to you. You just need
something a bit less brothel-y and a
bit more family-travel . . .
How about something like 'Thai-
Travel-Tots'

Molly
I hate you.

Emily
Why?!

111

Molly

I've been trying to think of a name for WEEKS and getting nowhere, and you just come out with something perfect at 3 a.m. after 12 seconds thinking about it with a baby stuck on your nipple. I HATE YOU.

Emily

lol. You're welcome.

Molly

I'm nicking that and taking all the credit by the way.

Emily

I wouldn't expect any less.

Molly

Thanks though. Love you.

Emily

Love you too.
Now piss off and hopefully we can both get some sleep!

Molly

xx
And I know you're reading this pretending to be asleep Liz! THE BLUE TICK NEVER LIES . . .
Liz . . .?

Chapter 18

iAMBASSADOR

It was an ordinary day.

Not cold, not warm. Just dull and grey and full of clouds, and a reminder that it was the end of September and summer was a distant memory now, with autumn here to stay.

The weather was predictably mundane, and daytime TV was slowly mushing Emily's mind into some kind of vegetative state. Not that she minded all that much – watching a reality TV show about a bunch of wealthy American women who enjoyed arguing, having plastic surgery, and generally being complete dickheads to one another actually made you feel a little bit better about sitting up all night with one tit waggling around in the dark by itself, while your baby decided he'd only sleep if he was in contact with your skin AT ALL TIMES.

Emily actually had felt better over the last week. She'd been a bit kinder to herself. She'd started blogging again and it had felt amazing, like a release of emotions she hadn't found another outlet for. There'd been so many responses to her post about her never-sleeping son – it'd been like a virtual hug. She'd put something out there at a moment of weakness and desperation, and the Internet had responded by shouting 'ME TOO!' on behalf of exhausted parents everywhere. It had actually been a huge relief to know she wasn't alone.

It wasn't like she was simply whingeing and whining about new motherhood – writing something funny was therapy. If she could laugh about it, and make others nod along in agreement whilst laughing too, then it kind of felt like a public service. For herself as much as others. Even though she hadn't been blogging that long, it was already hard to imagine ever not doing it . . .

She'd not checked her blog stats yet – William had been such a pain with feeding the last twenty-four hours, she'd not done much other than tend to him. The few brief stints he had slept, she'd dozed on the sofa dropping in and out of *Real Housewives* and occasionally piling some Doritos into her face. Whilst thinking quite relentlessly about how if she had a time machine, she'd head back and have a stern word with her former self about NEVER taking sleep for granted ever again.

Now William had finally decided on a longer nap, Emily took the chance to get on her laptop. She'd check her blog, and have a quick scroll through her emails – hoping there'd be something there other than fake PayPal notifications, newsletters about holidays she'd never go on, houses she'd never afford and Amazon nappy-order confirmations.

Emily lifted the laptop to her knees and began logging in. She popped it to one side on the sofa, and lifted herself wearily to her feet to go and make herself a hot cup of tea. (Another thing she would be adding to the list of things not to take for granted.) Even if she only managed a few sips of it while it was still warm, it'd be worth it . . . There's only so many times you can microwave tea before it starts to taste like pond water. Although, she'd had worse things in her mouth during the last twelve weeks of new motherhood, if she was honest about it . . .

She'd also perfected the art of making hot drinks as fast as possible. No filling the kettle to the brim. Milk ready and waiting. This shit was serious. Hot tea was a treat and luxury now. HOT TEA WAS LIFE.

Emily quickly removed the squeezed teabag from her cup and strolled back to the living room, cradling it with her palms and sipping it even though it was still boiling. The first layer of lip-skin was a worthy sacrifice when your sleeping baby could wake at any moment.

Her laptop was all fired up now. She let her eyes gently scroll down her emails . . . Boring . . . Spam . . . Eye test . . . discount voucher I'll never use . . . holidays I can't afford . . .

Emily stopped scrolling abruptly and set her tea down quickly next to her. She felt a little flutter of excitement in her chest as she read the email subject line:

"Official iCandy Blogger Programme Invitation"

As Emily opened the message, she let out a small squeal of delight. This was wonderful. It was what she'd wanted for so long – just after William had been born she'd

115

accepted a free iCandy pram, in exchange for publicity through her blog, from the PR team and it had pretty much made her life (at that time she wasn't yet quite as in need of hot tea and sleep). Her blog had clearly caught iCandy's eye again, as it was going from strength to strength – her honest, no-nonsense posts were gaining her more and more of a following – and now they wanted her to become an official iCandy Ambassador for the next twelve months . . . It was a little more than Emily's pelvic floor could handle. Who knew getting no sleep for three months, and surviving primarily on corn snacks and cold tea could get you a gig as a professional blogger . . . WHO. KNEW.

She'd be receiving a high-chair in a few months, a new change bag and a whole host of colour-coordinating accessories so she could style her buggy ready for winter, as well as a friends-and-families discount and VIP access to their new launches . . . this was actually her dream. HER ACTUAL DREAM.

Move over, Chris Hemsworth, Tom Hardy and the slightly obsessive crush she had on Cillian Murphy as Mr Thomas Shelby . . . THIS was the new Mum-Porn for the modern woman – coordinating iCandy hoods and foot-muffs, and a free VIP ticket to The BabyShow.

Total. Bliss . . .

Chapter 19

JUST US

Liz felt strange.

She was trying so hard to keep it together, but it was so odd to know something was over, yet have your body try to trick you into thinking it wasn't.

She still felt pregnant.

Even though she absolutely knew that she wasn't.

It felt so cruel. So unnecessary.

It was just over a week since they'd been to the hospital and found out she was going to miscarry the baby.

And it had happened now.

She was thankful it had occurred naturally. And quickly. While she was at home with Gerald there to support her. And that it was done. Over. Time to begin getting back on with their lives . . . Liz couldn't bear the idea of everyone feeling sorry for her. She hated that she felt so weak, so helpless, so not-in-control of anything. She couldn't wait to be back to 'normal'. If she was honest with herself – she just wanted to pretend none of this had ever happened. She could see Gerald was struggling with how cold she was being about it all . . . but she didn't know how else to be. It was just her way.

They'd said she could go back in for another scan to

confirm everything was over if she wanted to. But she didn't. Everything had occurred exactly as they said it would, and going back through all of that just to confirm what she already knew felt pointless.

She hadn't told work what was really happening. She'd simply said she had needed emergency hospital treatment and needed the week to recover. They hadn't batted an eyelid. Especially as she'd promised to dip into her emails and deal with anything important that came up. Much to Gerald's dismay and protest. But it was another focus and a welcome distraction from what had really been going on.

Liz felt awkward and guilty that she'd still not told any of her friends and family what had happened . . . Every time she thought about it, it made her feel sick. It brought the sadness and the shame back. She'd insisted Gerald let her tell her own friends and family. She wanted it to be her. She didn't want to hide behind him. But she was struggling to be able to do it. She felt embarrassed that for eight entire days she'd been hiding away from the reality of it all. It wasn't that unusual for her to go off radar for a week or so when she was swamped at work, but she knew if she left it much longer her friends would be worried or at least suspicious. If they weren't already, judging by the number of unread messages she had on her phone.

What she needed to do now was stop hiding and tell everyone who knew she had been pregnant. She didn't really know why she hadn't . . . But she just hadn't had the strength to say or type the words up until now. See it written in a message. Logged. Real. Not able to be ignored . . .

Liz finally switched her phone on.

Messages flooded in.

She'd deal with those later.

Right now . . . it was the last Saturday in September and she was already half an hour late to meet Emily and Molly in town and they'd be worried about her. They'd know something was up – she was never late for anything.

She needed to tell them she wouldn't be making it. And she needed to get the strength together to tell them exactly why . . .

She pulled out her phone and typed the horrid sentence she'd been dreading writing, before hovering over the send button as a familiar fat painful lump appeared in her throat.

Liz
I can't come today.
I lost the baby.
I'm fine. Just really sad.
Not ready to talk yet. I'll be okay
soon.
xx

She pressed send.

And cried.

And waited.

Chapter 20

LAST SATURDAY REVIVAL

Emily sat waiting in the little cafe off High Wycombe high street, just as she had so many times before, waiting for her friends.

It was no shocker that Molly was yet to appear, but she was surprised Liz hadn't already been here – she'd barely heard from her in the last week or so, but she'd reasoned that wasn't that unusual if she was busy with work and had a big case on . . . But being here before Liz was a little odd. In fact – she wasn't sure it had ever actually happened before. Emily decided she was being paranoid and shook her thoughts aside as she tended to a now increasingly wiggly William stirring in his pram.

As she gently rolled the pram back and forth on its wheels, her thoughts crept back to Liz. It had taken all of Emily's strength not to continually message her with a hundred questions about the pregnancy – how she was feeling, was she excited about the scan, had she begun planning anything yet or bought any tiny tiny shoes that she sniffed and cried into whilst hugging at night . . . Not that anyone would ever do that, right. That'd be weird. Right . . . And also very much not Liz's style. And Emily knew that. It was just that finding out Liz was expecting had brought back so many memories of all the excitement and anticipation Emily had felt when she first found out she was pregnant. It brought a smile to her face, and possibly a tiny weeny amount of jealousy, dreaming back to that sense of unassuming optimism you got when you first saw those two little lines . . . Even if she did first discover William existed in the unisex loos at work whilst Brian from accounting was coughing himself through a rather pungent episode of IBS. But still. Shitty Brian aside – she remembered how insanely happy it had made her feel to watch those lines appear vividly in front of her eyes.

Emily continued to grin to herself as she effortlessly swiped the muslin from inside her change bag and mopped up the spluttery pile of phlegmy white sick William had just brought up into the hood of his padded suit. She'd become quite a pro at spotting his pre-puke face now.

She knew she'd have to drag the information out of Liz when she saw her, and force her to begin to get a bit excited. Yes. She'd show her all the Pinterest boards she'd been putting together in her honour so that she could begin picking out nursery themes, baby shower ideas, pram collections . . . she'd LOVE IT. Well she wouldn't . . . but Emily would.

Emily laughed a little to herself at how different they all were. Three best friends – but three completely different people, and inevitably three completely different types of parents. Concerned thoughts crept back into her mind again as she glanced down at the time on her phone – it was now almost twenty minutes past when they were supposed to meet. It really was strange for Liz to be this late for Last Saturday Club. In fact it was strange for Liz to be late for anything. Normally she'd be here perched in front of a latte, tapping her watch and rolling her eyes at everyone else as they arrived late. Or in Molly's case – very late.

Emily checked her phone again – no messages.

William was becoming increasingly restless now. She'd feed him again now before the others arrived, that way with any luck he'd sleep through the rest of the cafe-date and she'd actually get to catch up properly with her friends, without sitting in front of them like a giant sweaty udder.

Emily lifted William gently out of the pram, and arranged herself into a feeding cloth as he began impatiently moving his head back and forth. He fussed around a little, but soon latched on and let her relax into her seat. She smiled again. It didn't seem so long ago that they were all meeting in this exact spot when she'd just found out she was pregnant. She'd had to throw up in the bin outside . . . Such beautiful, precious memories.

'Oi, oi!' came a familiar voice across the cafe, and Emily looked up to see Molly beaming in her direction with Marley strapped to her front in his sling. Probably fast asleep. And not feeding.

Molly planted an exaggerated kiss on Emily's forehead and sat down on the seat opposite her with a relaxed sigh.

'No Liz?' Molly said, scanning the counter area before turning back round to look at Emily with a mildly puzzled look on her face. She placed her phone and keys on the table and checked on Marley as she sat down opposite her friend.

'No actually,' Emily replied, trying not to frown. 'Which is a bit weird, isn't it? Have you heard from her this week? She's been very quiet. I'm trying not to get worried but it's strange she hasn't texted this morning to let us know she'd be late . . . don't you think?'

'Yeah. I know what you mean,' Molly said, seemingly not as concerned as Emily was, and now attempting to locate her baby somewhere in the several metres of material she'd wound him into before she left the house. 'And no . . . I haven't heard from her. She's probably just busy with work stuff. You know what she's like.'

Just then, both their phones buzzed at the same time. Emily couldn't quite reach hers, but Molly took hers off the table instantly.

'It's Liz,' she said, frowning at her phone as she swiped to load the rest of the message. 'She not coming . . . she's . . . Oh my God . . .'

Molly's hand went immediately over her mouth as her eyes instantly moistened. She looked up at Emily, her eyes wide and serious, turning her phone around so Emily could see the full message.

Emily gasped, her eyes wet now too. She was stuck with her arms around her son as she fed him, else she too would have flung her hand to her mouth.

123

Neither of them could believe it. They just sat in silence for a few moments and let a few tears out in sympathy for their poor poor friend and the baby she'd lost.

They'd be there for her now, just like they'd always been.

Liz was strong and she had Gerald, but girls needed their girls.

And that was that.

Chapter 21

WE'RE HERE

Molly
Hey are you there?
Liz?
Look you don't have to answer.
You can just read without responding
and that's fine.
We totally understand.
We just want you to know that we
love you.
We know you're strong. You're the
strongest person I know.
But you don't have to be strong for this.
You don't have to do this by yourself.

Emily
We want to let you know you can
talk to us as soon as you're ready.
We're worried about you.
We miss you.
I want to give you the biggest hug
ever, and chuck wine down your neck
and let you do that weird crying you do

125

when you're really upset where little
bubbles of snot come out of your nose.
Because real friends don't care if their
friends get snot on them.
We secretly love it.
We love you.
Please let us know you're okay?

Molly
It's fine if you don't want to see us
yet.
But when you do we'll be there when-
ever, wherever, as fast we can.
We promise.

Emily
Everything is going to be okay.
Keep hugging Gerald until we see you
next.

Molly
We love you so much.

Emily
We're here.
xxx

Molly
Yes.
We're right here.
xxx

Chapter 22

THE CHAT

Liz felt okay.

Not good.

But okay.

The tears had stopped.

Life had started up again.

That's what she'd wanted. To get back to 'normal'. To get back on with everything and try to forget about what had happened.

Gerald, Emily, Molly, her family . . . they'd been so wonderful. So supportive. The messages and texts they'd all been sending her had helped so much, even though she'd barely responded to any of them. It was so nice to know that everyone was thinking of her, without feeling the pressure of having to get back to them just yet.

She had missed people. It had been a bit intense having only herself and Gerald for company. But she hadn't quite been ready to see people. Not yet. Her sister had repeatedly offered to drive all the way up from near Winchester just to bring her homemade lasagne and a hug. And although she couldn't stomach béchamel sauce and human contact just yet, it had meant so much to know she was

there thinking of her . . . she hoped her sister knew that. She hoped everyone knew that.

Gerald had been wonderful. Which wasn't surprising – he *was* wonderful. Almost too wonderful . . . He'd been there for her, but without smothering her. Supported her, but made no assumptions. He'd cleared life to one side and allowed her space to heal. It was exactly what she'd needed.

And now she was beginning to feel better, Liz was aware of how strong he'd been. It had been his baby too. She was aware of that. Now when she looked at him – really looked at him – he looked as sad as she felt. In fact he probably looked sadder.

It had all just been so horrible.

And even though they'd been around each other so intensely since it happened, they'd actually hardly spoken about it. Liz was not good at opening up at the best of times, and now was no different. If Gerald had even begun to bring it up, she'd brushed it to one side. Quite plainly – she didn't want to talk about it. What was the point? She was fine. She was going to be fine. It was time to get on with life.

But Liz knew, looking at him now, that Gerald needed her to open up a little. She needed to talk about it for him if she couldn't do it for herself. She had to, for them. She knew 'the chat' was inevitable at some point. The one where they spoke about what happened next – Gerald would want to know when they would try again. Of course he would – he had wanted this so much. Much more than she had. When he'd found out Liz was pregnant it had been like a scene from a Disney movie – it was a wonder he managed to restrain himself from breaking into song. She could see how much he desperately wanted to be a father, and she knew how wonderful he would be at it. And as guilty as it made her feel, what they'd been through, what they were still going through, everything that had happened had told her she wasn't ready to do this right now.

She needed a little while. Some time to adjust back into life, and concentrate on the things that she'd worked so hard for . . . She just wasn't sure if Gerald would feel the same.

Liz had decided to go back to work tomorrow. She felt ready. She hated the idea of being 'office gossip', and if she left it any longer she knew tongues would start wagging. They probably already were.

She felt good that they were spending a lazy Sunday together, knowing that life would be beginning properly again tomorrow. It was time.

'Something smells amazing,' Liz said, sniffing the air as she wandered into the kitchen, and watched as Gerald stirred a large steaming pot of something on the hob.

'As it should. That's my mum's stew right there. I was brought up on that stuff! She sent me the recipe. Good for the soul, she always used to say.' He smiled gently at Liz with big twinkling eyes.

'Yum, I can't wait. It's making my mouth water,' Liz said, licking her lips a little and brushing a slightly

129

unkempt fringe away from her eyes with her finger tips. She was trying to ignore the state of the kitchen – how on earth he'd managed to use every knife, pot and utensil available she wasn't entirely sure . . .

'Well, it'll be a good hour yet. But well worth the wait. And don't worry, the kitchen will be back to its gleaming Liz-standard clean state in no time. I can see you developing a mild tic looking at the potato peelings in the sink,' Gerald added with a little wink. It felt good to be more normal around each other.

Liz laughed. He knew her too well.

He poured them each a small glass of wine and tipped his head in the direction of the sofa.

Liz followed him, and sat in her usual spot. As he sat in his.

He seemed relaxed. They both did, considering what they'd been through in the last week.

'Thank you for all this. Thank you for everything. You're actually pretty amazing, you know . . .' Liz said, smiling but with heavy eyes. Anticipating the tough conversation she knew was coming.

'Hey. You don't need to tell me that. I'm just looking after you. You should let me do it more often,' he said, leaning in towards her and holding her gaze.

'I know,' Liz said. And she did. 'I don't want to dampen the mood, but I think we need to talk. Not about what happened so much. But more about what happens now . . .'

Gerald looked a little unsettled. Liz realised she'd made it sound slightly ominous.

'Look. I don't want anything to change. I love you. I love us. The thing is – I just don't think I'm ready to be more than us just yet. I just want to . . . wait a while. Are you okay with that?'

It was clear he wasn't. But what could he say? He looked crushed, though he was trying to hide it. Liz felt that awful sensation of guilt returning – sometimes it honestly felt like all she did was let him down . . . she didn't mean to. But she had to be honest.

'Of course. I understand,' Gerald said eventually, with a sincere frown on his face. A little tear rolled down from Liz's eye. A tear of relief as much as anything. 'I don't want to put any pressure on you, or us, or anything, at the moment. I want you to know I'm ready to be a father, whenever you're ready to become a mother. I'm here. I'm not going anywhere, Liz. I love you.'

'Thank you,' said Liz. Meaning it so much.

'I love you too.'

Chapter 23

THE THREE-MONTH-A-VERSARY

Dear little man . . .
When will you fucking sleep?
I can't remember the last time I laid down my head,
Without dreading the next night-time feed.

Dear lovely boy . . .
It just doesn't matter what I do.
Gro-bag, no bag, hot, cold, light or dark . . .
Remember I ruined my vagina for you?

Dear gorgeous chap . . .
I love you, but enough is enough.
Just sleep through the night, so I won't be so uptight,
Or top my cornflakes with Pinot Grigio Blush.

How was October almost over?

How was William twelve weeks old?

How, how, HOW?

Emily actually felt pretty proud of herself for surviving the last three months, and keeping both herself and her baby alive up to this point, if she was honest. But also a little sad she'd been too exhausted to enjoy it properly

. . . It had flown by. She wasn't entirely sure where the last twelve weeks had gone. But they had gone. Just like her previously taut labia and her ability not to wee herself a little bit when she sneezed.

The Internet seemed to deem the three-month stage as some kind of important milestone . . . it seemed to think this was the point at which your child miraculously started sleeping through the night. Why? What happens when they reach twelve weeks old that would suddenly mean they went to bed one night, slept for twelve hours and stopped waking up just to look at you whilst smiling a bit at 4.30 in the morning because they fancied it. Again. After doing it at 10.30, 12.30 and 2.30 a.m..

It made Emily feel like shit. She'd started to switch off at baby-groups when mums she'd just met began talking about how their three-month-olds slept through from seven to seven. It made her go a bit stabby and want to swap babies for twenty-four hours in some sort of infant smash-and-grab at the end of 'Incy Wincy Spider', just so she could remember what it felt like to sleep uninterrupted for an entire night . . . Emily wasn't capable of being rational about it any more. She was too bloody knackered. She knew none of the mums were saying it to taunt her – they weren't horrible people. They were just lucky. LUCKY. And she was jealous of them and their magical sleeping infants and their ability to put mascara on before 9 a.m. They'd simply lucked out – when they were dishing out the ones that slept, they'd made the cut. It had nothing to do with the routine, the products, the

133

advice, the fucking moon rising through Venus and setting up camp in a rainbow with some leprechauns . . . because if it did, then every fucking baby would sleep through, wouldn't they? . . . But some of them, just don't.

And William, just didn't.

It had made her feel slightly better seeing the group WhatsApp messages from her NCT friends. The chats seemed to focus primarily on pooing, sleeping, nappy prices, under-eye concealer and longing quite desperately for a night away in a hotel without any other humans who needed you to sustain their lives with your breasts. AKA – THE DREAM. Last night at 3 a.m., Rachael had posted a four-page-long rant about how she'd been so exhausted this week, she'd fallen asleep in the feeding room at Mothercare, and had to be woken up by the till staff because they needed to close the shop. It had actually given Emily some comfort that she hadn't yet passed out in a changing room. A small win. Sort of.

Emily knew she had spent far too much time in the last three months beating herself up about things she couldn't control. The toughest part had been continually feeling like she was always being the mum whose baby 'didn't' or 'hadn't yet'. Parenting a tiny human being was exhausting enough without feeling guilty too. Plus, she was a quarter of the way through her maternity leave already, and that seemed an utterly depressing thought. She had already begun to panic about how she'd cope with things once she got back to her Senior Account Manager role at Angel PR – in truth she already felt a bit out of touch with everything. She wondered how her maternity cover was doing. Did the clients long for Emily to return? Or did they prefer shiny-haired Charlotte and her baby-sick-free shoulders? Was her dickhead colleague Matilda still brown-nosing management, trying to worm her way into Emily's main accounts and being a general dick around the office with her dickheadedly dickish behaviour? (Probably. Thought Emily.) And was this just hormonal rage or did she really care . . . ?

Well, actually yes a bit. Emily had been ignoring the messages she'd had from her boss Natalie about dropping into the office to catch up and meet William. She'd also asked if Emily fancied doing a 'keeping in touch day' – a sensible idea, Emily had to admit. But the thought of becoming a functioning adult human who did work again for an entire eight-hour day straight seemed a little beyond her at the moment. Especially considering she'd had the same pants on since Tuesday, and had started hiding Mini Cheddars under her pillow for 'easy access'.

Emily knew sooner or later she was going to have to start adulting again. It would probably be really good for her to have a few hours away from William – she could express a couple of bottles and give her boobs a bit of a rest – she'd probably enjoy it, maybe she'd even enjoy Matilda's company now she'd not seen her for a few months . . . Although, probably not.

She'd email Natalie later and arrange a half day or something; her mum could take William, and she'd get to wear clean pants, lipgloss and a real bra again . . . But

for now she'd get back to more pressing matters – it was almost Halloween, and she was in the process of scouring eBay for the perfect padded-pumpkin baby-costume for him to wear. She'd already planned it. She and William would attend baby-group with the NCT gang, head back to hers for a coffee afterwards, and get all the babies in a line on the sofa in their scary costumes ready to Instagram the shit out of it later that day. It would be brilliant. And certainly entirely original. She was absolutely sure that no one else on social media would be doing anything like that on the same day, at all. Ever.

Chapter 24

WE'RE STILL HERE

Molly

Hey.

I know you probably still aren't ready to talk but we're right here waiting when you are xxx

And we just want you to know it's okay to be sad.

You're amazing.

You're strong.

You're a brilliant friend.

You're a wonderful girlfriend and daughter and sister and auntie and friend.

And even though you pretend you don't care, I know you love your cat Jasper more than most humans and bought him his own special cat bed made from Madagascan yak's wool that you hide in your wardrobe.

You're the only person who sends a taxi for me just to make sure I'm on time for stuff because you know I'm useless.

137

You're a brilliant cook and do that posh slurpy thing with wine that makes everyone apart from you look like a total dick.

You're an amazing career woman and work harder than anyone I know.

YOU LITERALLY HAVE THE BEST FRINGE OF ALL THE HUMANS.

And I promise to never ever tell anyone outside of the three of us about that time we went to Reading Festival when we were 18, and you were really drunk and didn't know how to use the She-wee. And instead of weeing through it . . . you stuck it up your fanny and pissed all over your trousers!

Emily

OMG I remember that!

Literally amazing.

Are you okay Liz?

Will you let us know how you're doing?

We miss you xx

Liz

Well how could I not respond to that . . .

I love you girls.

Thank you for cheering me up.
I'm doing better I promise. I'm back at
work this week so getting back to
normal now.
Sorry I haven't been in touch. I'm not
good at that stuff . . . But I can't wait
to see you both soon x I miss you
too!
And Jasper loves that bed by the way
you cheeky cow.
And if you ever tell anyone else that
She-wee story I will literally fuck you
up.

Molly
Fair play.
Love you too xx

Emily
xxx

Chapter 25

THE ARSE FROM THE PAST

Liz was quite amazing at portraying the image of being perfectly fine.

Certainly, at work, she found it easy to tune out her emotions and play the part of the 'ice queen' without much effort at all. It was an act she'd fine-tuned over many years of fighting her way to the top of a male-dominated industry and dealing with arseholes on a daily basis. One arsehole in particular, if she was honest. Once you'd been in a relationship with someone who wore you down to nothing, lied to you, and made you feel utterly worthless . . . you got used to pretending. You were constantly hiding behind a façade.

Besides, Liz didn't have time to be anything other than fine. She just had so much to do. So much work. So many people looking up at her. She'd worked so hard to get where she was, she didn't feel like there was any other choice than being 'fine'. And she certainly wasn't going to jeopardise everything she'd worked so hard for.

She knew there was chatter around the office. It was inevitable. People loved gossip — it was human nature. But she wasn't going to feed the rumours. As far as she was concerned her personal life was no one's business but hers and Gerald's.

She had no intention of letting anything that had happened affect her work – she just needed to get her head down, get stuck into her cases, and not let anything distract her. This would all be a distant memory in no time. Just as she wanted it.

Liz's phone buzzed in her bag. It was most likely Gerald, she thought, as she reached into her handbag beside her feet, her eyes remaining forward on her computer screen. She located the phone and brought it up towards her eye level.

As her eyes flicked on to the screen, Liz felt every ounce of strength she had left drain from her body in an instant. It was like the air had been punched from her lungs, and she'd forgotten how to suck breath into her body to make them work again.

Liz felt a ball of anger rising up from inside her. She couldn't believe it. She couldn't believe that 'he' actually had the nerve to contact her. That he would have kept her number all this time. Why? It sent spiky prickles down the back of her neck to think about people she worked with feeding him private information about her. And not just her – her and Gerald. About her losing a baby. She felt sick. How much did he know? Why would he be doing this? Contacting her. Probably because he knew she'd be weak. He knew she'd be vulnerable. Of all the disgusting things he'd ever done, all the crippling and exhaustive manipulation he'd subjected her to – this felt the worst.

Liz couldn't take her eyes off the text. There it was. Just sitting there. Glaring back at her. She hated that even after all this time he could have any effect on her . . . yet he did.

Hey.
I hope you don't mind me texting you Lizzie.
I heard what happened.
And I just felt like I had to say something. I'm so sorry for what's happened to you.
If you ever need anything, I hope you know I'm here for you.
xx

It was the way he'd assumed they were still on friendly terms. Friends even? The familiar tone in his message enraged her. What an arrogant bastard. How dare he? As though he'd ever actually cared for her. Ever actually wanted her. In a second – it was almost like she was right back there. Like the entire last year had evaporated and she was right back to being someone so worthless and easily walked over. She'd hated herself for that. And now with the guilt of what had happened, she could feel that sense of self-loathing flooding back. It was like a disease. It was choking her.

She felt consumed by rage and emotion. Perhaps it was the swirling mix of feelings she'd been concealing and ignoring since the miscarriage, perhaps it was just him – the hate she still felt for him. But she knew she needed to get a grip. This wasn't who she was now – she needed to remind herself of that. She needed to scream it at herself.

If she responded to him now, she'd be letting him back in. That's how he got to people – he found a way inside, and before you knew it, he was there. Infecting you.

Liz felt big hot tears squeeze out of her eyes. She didn't think she'd ever cried at work before. Not since that one time in the boardroom – because of him. When she'd found out his wife was pregnant and that everything he'd ever told her had been a lie. It had been the worst and most humiliating moment of her life. She hated that she was struggling to hold it together. She had been doing so well up until now, suppressing all the hurt and anger she felt about losing the baby – but it was all bubbling to the surface uncontrollably. And it was all because of him.

How could he do this when he wasn't even part of her life any more? She had to find her strength again. She couldn't give in to her emotions. She had to be strong.

Liz blew air slowly and purposefully out of her mouth, trying to calm her pumping heart and steady her mind. She wouldn't cry any more tears over him. She would never let him have the satisfaction.

Slowly she began to feel better. Her strength seemed to be returning – she could see sense again. It took everything she had left not to respond.

Liz took a deep breath and quickly deleted the message. It was done.

She shook her head, as if shaking out the dark thoughts

that had been creeping back into it. Memories she thought she'd buried. Feelings and emotions she never wanted to have again.

She couldn't let those feelings come back. She knew she wasn't strong enough to deal with them on top of everything else right now. She had to get a hold of herself.

She turned her phone off and tossed it back into her bag, sitting up straight.

She was stronger and better than this. She kept repeating that to herself in her head. She had Gerald, she had her career, her wonderful friends and family – she had a wonderful life. She wasn't going to let anything or anyone fuck it up again.

Liz knew she was okay again. She was holding it together. She felt slightly triumphant.

The text was gone. He was gone. No one needed to know about this.

She'd done it.

That arsehole had been sent back to the past where he belonged. And she promised herself, she'd never let him back into her life in any way ever again.

And she hoped she really meant it.

Chapter 26

PRIME TIME

Emily

Hey x

You guys awake?

Sorry I know it's late!

I just needed to get something off my chest

(Other than William that is. Who's been lying on my chest for about four hours now refusing to be put down . . . JOY.)

Anyway.

I think I have a problem . . .

I'm addicted to ordering stuff online!

I know it sounds stupid but I honestly can't stop.

I get so bored sat up feeding and rocking him most of the night I start searching through Amazon and stuff, and before you know it

BAM!

Next morning.

Fuck ton of Prime boxes.

I. NEED. HELP.

Molly

Hey you . . .

What are you on about?

I'm sure you can stop by just stopping.

Do what the rest of us do and just

fantasy shop without actually buying it

. . .

Isn't that what the ASOS basket is

for? . . . lol

Emily

I can't!

Sometimes I don't even know I've
bought it until it shows up the next
day.

But then it's like getting a little present
isn't it – makes me feel nice.

Like a big Hermes-delivered-hug.

Even if it is twelve pairs of Havaianas
and a toddler picnic bench . . . IT
STILL FEELS NICE.

Molly

Havaianas? As in flip-flops?

You do know it's November, right?

Emily

Yes.

And that's why they were cheap.

God you sound like Paul now!

Molly

Yes. It's clearly US that's nuts.

Emily

Well ANYWAY.

What should I do?

I've started destroying the evidence each time it happens by taking the cardboard and shoving it straight in the recycling bin out the back . . . if ours gets too full, I use the neighbour's. Do you think that's weird?

I'm weird aren't I.

This must be how addicts feel!

Molly

Yes . . . I'm sure it's exactly the same . . .

Emily

Okay. Well, maybe not exactly like that but can you see now that I have a problem?

Molly

Yes. Your problem is you are MENTAL. And you need to delete all your shopping apps and stop texting your best mates at 11.37 p.m. on a Friday night about Brazilian-branded fucking flip-flops.

147

Emily
Okay.
You're right.
Sorry.

Liz
Ha! I can always count on you ladies
to make my Friday nights a bit more
exciting.

Molly
Hey you! How are you? How has
work been the last couple of weeks?

Liz
Actually great. It just feels good to get
stuck back in and feel normal again.
Sorry I've been a bit MIA – I've
honestly just been so busy with work.
Which I KNOW is rubbish, but I'm
honestly good. We're good. Honestly.
(I don't know why I just said honestly
so many times.)

Molly
I'm really glad you're okay – we've
been worried about you!

Emily
Hey you!! Yes we have. Are you sure
you're really okay? Like really okay?

It is all right to say you're not, you know. No one expects you to be fine sweetie . . .

Liz
You know me. I'm a fighter. And yes – I really am okay now. Honestly.

Emily
Okay. Well you know where we are. Let's meet up soon! I need to hug you so hard you die.

Liz
Well I can't say no to that now can I? Death and hug in one . . . you're spoiling me.

Molly
She's all give, that one ;)

Liz
We'll meet soon I promise. I'm just so swamped with work (yes, yes, I know still a rubbish excuse but it's true). Maybe the first weekend of December? Things should have calmed down a bit for me by then.

Molly
Good for me.

Emily
Me too.
But please look after yourself Liz.
Don't work too hard.
And anytime you need us you know
where we are.

Liz
It's a date then. And I do. And I'm still
fine.
Honestly.
(I'll go and stop saying honestly now.)
Xxx

Chapter 27

WHEN REALITY STRIKES . . .

Molly looked a little vacantly around the area formerly known as their living room, which now looked like some kind of pop-up jumble sale.

Marley was fast asleep in his crib in the nursery. She knew he'd be out for the next hour or so, so it seemed the ideal time to begin getting organised. But she couldn't even work out how or where to start. There were boxes and 'stuff' literally everywhere.

This was Molly's attempt at tackling her cash-flow problems. She needed to fund the start-up of her travel business. So she needed money. And quickly. In typical 'act-now, think-later' Molly style, she'd come up with several harebrained schemes, which naturally she'd spent very little time researching and had simply leapt into, feet first, hoping one of them would take off. Because that was how she pretty much tackled everything in life – hope, luck, and just working it out as she went along. So she was tackling her business finances by throwing what little money they did have at a series of quick-fix solutions, which mostly consisted of eBay tat and some stuff she found going cheap on Gumtree, with no consultation, assistance or guidance from anyone except herself. Given

her track record of managing to successfully do 'anything', she was now beginning to wonder if this had really been the best idea . . .

Molly felt a sinking sensation in the pit of her stomach, as she cast her eyes around the front room and tried very hard to ignore the nagging voice at the back of her mind telling her she'd been a bit of a dick. She wasn't sure she could even remember everything she'd ordered.

And her attempts to organise things over the last few hours had seemed to only create more mess. She didn't even know how that was possible.

Tom had been very specific that she should sit down, work out exactly what she needed to do, how much it would cost, and that they'd formulate a plan of action together to raise the funds. He had about £500 in savings they could use to begin financing something, but that was it. So they needed to be smart with it. And not waste it on a load of useless crap that would take for ever to pay them back and see them worse off than when they started.

Molly had listened and nodded along. She had every intention of planning and researching and doing all the things he'd said, but before she knew it – she'd spent the money. Quickly. She'd barely even thought about it. Until now. When the reality of it all had begun to hit her.

Standing in front of a mountain of plastic toys and party-bag fillers that she intended to sell as 'pre-filled' party bags, she suddenly began to doubt her choices a little. She'd also bought a huge box of trade-price Christmas decorations, which she planned to sell on eBay, and – the thing she was most excited about – an absolutely enormous roll of beautiful hand-weaved Thai fabric she'd purchased from a UK importer. She'd had to ask the neighbours downstairs to help her up the stairs with it. But this was the one she felt could make the biggest profit. She'd found a slightly rickety old sewing-machine on Gumtree, and had grand plans to make scarves, baby slings, and throws . . . I mean how hard could it be?

Surely if she just used the patterns and templates she'd downloaded, cut and pinned the fabric, and learnt how to use a sewing-machine, and also sort of learnt how to sew . . . it'd probably be EASY. Right?

Molly felt the sinking sensation worsen a bit. Tom was due home from work any minute, and she knew that, now all this stuff had arrived and was invading their entire living room, she was going to have to come clean. She'd spent the money. It was done. And she was sure she could make Tom see how amazing this could all be. He loved her. He would surely love all this . . . Wouldn't he . . . ? The sinking feeling was actually making her feel quite sick now.

Molly decided a different approach might work better. She'd consult her notebook and make him see the numbers could work . . . yeah. That'd do it.

Molly found her notebook amongst some plastic singing Father Christmases on the sofa. She leafed through until she found her workings from the other day, and let her eyes flick down the page.

According to her fairly rough calculations – she needed

in the region of £3,000 just to get the business off the ground.

Three grand. Shit.

Based on making a realistic profit each week, taking out material, postage and overheads, she could hope to make that money in approximately . . . two years.

Double shit.

Okay, perhaps numbers wasn't the best approach. She'd let the quality of the products do the talking . . .

Molly picked up a Rudolph bauble with a light-up nose and sighed at it. The sinking feeling really wasn't getting any better.

She heard Tom's key go in the lock. She waited, unsure how this was going to go.

'Hey, babes, you—' Tom stopped dead mid-sentence as he entered the living room.'

Molly didn't say anything for a moment, she simply watched as his eyes flitted over the boxes and piles of festive tat she'd been attempting to organise into bundles.

'Surprise,' Molly said slightly weakly.

'What . . . is all . . . um, this?' Tom gestured towards the various piles and boxes. He was frowning. This wasn't a good start.

'Look. Don't go mad,' Molly said, putting her hands up to show her palms and taking a couple of paces towards him. 'I know you said we'd do everything together and that I shouldn't leap into anything without researching it, but I found some great opportunities, and waiting just didn't seem like the best tactic, and I know you probably think I'm an idiot, but I'm going to prove you wrong. I can do this. Honestly. Are you angry? Do you hate me?'

Tom hadn't answered, so Molly had begun waffling. She hated waffling. But she felt uncharacteristically nervous.

Tom let out a deep sigh. Then let his eyes meet hers. The moment felt tense.

'Oh, Molly.' He said her name slowly with another exasperated sigh. She watched as he rubbed his face and eyes with his palms and waited painfully for him to speak again. She felt for a moment like she'd been transported back to secondary school and was waiting for a detention to be dished out, after once again skipping PSHE in favour of smoking a few Marlboro Lights in a skirt that barely skimmed her bum cheeks behind the bike sheds.

'I just can't believe you've done this,' Tom said, shaking his head. His tone was uncharacteristically strong. 'We literally spoke about this the other day and you promised me you weren't going to do anything reckless or stupid. You promised me you were going to plan this out properly. But you just can't help yourself, can you? Can you? For fuck's sake, Molly!'

Molly wanted to interrupt him and tell him he was wrong, but everything he was saying was right. She had been reckless and stupid, and he had every right to be angry with her. She just didn't think she'd ever seen him angry like this. It was horrible. She didn't know how to respond.

Tom sat down on the sofa, rubbing his face again, as

if trying to ease away some of the stress. He met her eyes with his. He still looked angry. Molly hated that she'd made him feel this way. She felt like she wanted to cry.

'Okay,' Tom said eventually, his face pained. 'Can you at least tell me you haven't spent everything we had on all this . . . crap. I mean what the fuck even is this stuff, Molly? Please tell me you haven't wasted our entire savings on plastic reindeer and party poppers. Please?'

Molly cleared her throat before answering. Then let her head droop down as she spoke. She felt too ashamed to look him in the eye right now.

'I don't know what you want me to say, Tom . . .' she mumbled.

'I want you to tell me that you haven't spent every penny of our savings on this.'

'Well . . . I can't. Because I have. I'm sorry.'

Molly felt like she was shrinking into herself. Her voice was getting smaller and smaller.

Tom didn't reply. He simply looked up and sighed loudly.

Molly wasn't sure what was worse. Being told off, or watching the painful look of disappointment on her boyfriend's face as he struggled to even face her in agonising silence.

Tom sighed again and let his head fall back into a natural position. His face softened slightly, but he still looked angry.

'Do you hate me?' Molly knew it was a childish thing to say but it was all she could manage. She and Tom had never had an argument like this before – she'd never known him be so disappointed in her. She didn't know how to take it.

'Of course I don't hate you,' Tom said, frowning at her. She could see he was calming down a little now. Or perhaps he just didn't have the energy to carry on fighting with her.

'I can send some of the Christmas bits back, and most of the party bits I can get a refund on anyway. The fabric would be harder as I'd have to re-sell it . . . but I can probably get most of the cash back if I hunt around for a buyer. I can make this right. I promise. I really can.' Molly couldn't stop her voice quivering. She felt really sad and really stupid.

Seeing her struggling not to cry, Tom rose to his feet and took her hand. Molly looked at him – his face was still full of anguish and frustration, but he seemed less angry now at least.

'Look, I don't want to upset you. And I don't see the point in losing even more money trying to flog this stuff quickly . . . I'm really annoyed that you've done this, Molly. But it's done now. You'd better have a plan – that's all I'm saying. Because we've got nothing now – no savings, no fall-back, and no bloody carpet space left in our own living room.'

Tom gestured towards everything with a swooping arm and almost smiled. But Molly could see he was still annoyed with her. It wasn't time to laugh and joke about it just yet.

'I know,' Molly said, her voice still small. 'And I know I've fucked up. Honestly I do. I'm going to make this work though. I'll work hard and I'll get the money back as soon as I can. I promise.'

'I hope so,' Tom said, the exasperation still lingering in his voice. 'I just wish you'd talk to me about this stuff. You don't have to make these decisions on your own, Molly. You know that, right? We're supposed to be a team.'

Molly smiled gently at him and nodded.

'I know. I know. I'm so sorry – I honestly am. I just can't help myself. I won't do anything without chatting to you about it first again ever, okay?'

'Yes. I think that needs to be a general life rule from now on. And please tell me, as we're pretty much stuck in this mess now, that you do have some kind of plan for flogging all of this.'

'Of course,' Molly said, trying to sound convincing. 'I've got YouTube tutorials and everything. It'll be fine. Probably.'

Tom frowned, but allowed himself a small laugh at the same time. 'Molly – you are incredible. I really mean that.'

Molly laughed back. It was a welcome relief. She knew Tom was still annoyed, but it was true they were resigned to this now.

'So does that mean you forgive me?' Molly pulled herself in closer to him, biting her lip a little.

'No,' Tom said, allowing his arms to move around her. 'This means I've accepted that my girlfriend is a huge liability and I now have to share a living room with five hundred plastic reindeer and there's pretty much nothing I can do about that, because unfortunately I happen to love her.'

'Well that is very lucky for me. And the reindeer.'

'Yes it is,' Tom said, a flicker of conflict still registering on his face.

Molly leaned in and kissed him. 'I really do love you,' she said firmly as she held his gaze for a moment.

For a few moments they stood and hugged. Molly didn't really want to let go of him. She could feel he didn't want to fight any more, maybe because he didn't want to upset her any further, but she also knew he'd lost a bit of trust in her, maybe even a little respect for her. And she was determined to make it up to him. And to herself.

She'd got them into this shitty situation and created a horrible underlying tension between them. And now it was up to her, and several hundred light-up Rudolphs, to make it right again.

Chapter 28

DIRTY LITTLE SECRET

Liz wondered what in the name of fuck she was doing.

How she'd ended up here.

Again, after all this time.

Back in a shady dark corner, in a half-empty bar, in an unfamiliar part of town, with that same unpleasant sensation at the pit of her stomach. As she sat in front of a drink. Waiting for 'him'.

She had no idea why she was doing this, no idea why she was here.

The sickening guilt she felt at lying to Gerald – sweet, amazing, completely innocent, trusting, wonderful Gerald – was all-consuming right now.

But still – she'd come.

It was disturbing how easily the lies came out. She'd simply told Gerald that she had a late meeting, so she'd be home after him, and off he'd skipped. None the wiser. Like it was any other Tuesday in the life of Giz . . . but it really wasn't.

And even though she knew this was an utterly terrible mistake that could never come to any positive end – somehow, she was here. Waiting.

She already hated herself for it.

She was so disappointed in herself for being so 'easy', so uncharacteristically weak. She'd known from the moment he'd started messaging her again that she'd be coming here tonight. He'd told her exactly where he'd be and at what time, and even though she hadn't responded – she'd known she was coming. And so had he. In the strange sadness and shame that she felt for everything that had happened to her recently, she'd accepted that a part of her wanted to be here. Even though she couldn't quite put her finger on why . . .

'You got my message then, Lizzie,' said a smooth voice from behind her. A chill ran down the back of her neck. It was like she'd been instantly transported back in time.

It was hard to look at him directly. At the face she'd once loved. The one person who had such a devastating hold over her that even after everything he'd done, everything they'd been through, she'd still come here to meet him. She felt overwhelming guilt that she'd even entertained his messages and come here at all.

'You look so beautiful,' he said, the words rolling off his tongue far too easily. They made her feel sick.

'Why did you invite me here?' Liz said, ensuring there was just enough disdain in her voice to let him know she wasn't here to kiss and make up. She was trying very hard to believe that.

'Why did you come?' he responded instantly. She hated that she couldn't answer the question, even if she tried.

'I don't know,' she said, her voice small and honest, letting herself look at him now. It annoyed her that he was looking good. He looked healthy, he had a new shorter haircut, and he was wearing a suit she'd never seen before. There'd been a time she knew his entire wardrobe – clearly not any more. It felt so odd seeing him. Unsettling. Was she still attracted to him? She hated that her mind was saying these things. She hated that he'd been able to get back on with life so easily, as if she'd never been there. No doubt he was happily playing the perfect father and husband. No doubt he'd replaced her and found someone else to fuck about with by now. He looked almost smug. She hated it. She hated him. But she was still sitting here.

'It's okay, Liz. I don't really know either – I was worried about you . . . I know it must have been so hard. I know things didn't work out with us but it doesn't mean I don't care what happens to you. We loved each other once, Lizzie, didn't we? I still care about you. You must know that.'

Liz felt like her blood was about to boil out of her body. He made it sound like they were teenage sweethearts who'd drifted apart . . . not that he was a lying, manipulative bastard who cheated on his wife and liked to pretend he was a respectable human being.

'No. That's not what I remember. I remember you fucking me. Whilst fucking your wife. And me only leaving you because you knocked her up and I found out about it. Hardly a Disney movie,' Liz said, trying to contain her contempt. Breaking eye contact, she waved at the barman to refill her martini.

'Hey, potayto, potahto . . . I wasn't trying to drag up the past, Lizzie.'

Liz hated that he could make jokes about it so flippantly. She hated that he called her Lizzie. He'd almost ruined her life, and she'd barely dented his. That was the truth. That was why he could let her come and go so easily, and she had so much anger towards him. She was weak now. The impact of the last few months had ravaged her more than she had admitted to anyone . . . much more than she'd admitted to herself. She knew she shouldn't be here. She knew everything about this was wrong. But she still was. He still had some kind of hold on her. She wanted to get up and leave. But she couldn't.

'Look, if there's something you want, just spit it out. I think I'm done here. I don't even know why I came,' Liz said, sipping on the fresh martini that had arrived in front of her. She wasn't sure how many she'd had. Three . . . Four maybe? She'd barely drunk alcohol in months – the effect was pungent. Clearly her tolerance had gone down. The room was beginning to spin a little. Her hair-line was beginning to feel uncomfortably moist. She knew she should probably slow down, but she didn't care.

'I just . . . I miss you, Lizzie. Do you miss me?'

His words punched into her like bullets. The room seemed to be spinning even more now. She was perched on her seat, yet it felt like she was moving.

He suddenly seemed a lot closer to her. She could feel his breath on her face. He smelt so familiar – a musky mix of aftershave, cigarettes and 'him'. That smell evoked

so many memories. A sense of familiarity she hadn't realised she'd been craving until now. She needed to get a grip.

'So your wife knows you're here?' Liz said quickly, and as spitefully as she could manage. She could hear her words were slightly slurred now. She wished they weren't. Then maybe he'd take them more seriously. Maybe she would too.

'I doubt she cares where I am, Lizzie. Our marriage is loveless. We just stay together for our son. That's it. You know that . . .'

His face was right there. Liz couldn't quite bring herself to turn her head. She felt like crying and screaming and hitting him. All at the same time.

She felt his hand come up and gently stroke her cheek, then move to the opposite cheek. He applied just enough pressure to gently turn her face towards his. She wanted to fight him. But the martinis, the confusion . . . everything that had gone on . . . she just didn't have any fight left.

His lips touched hers. Just for a split second, before he pulled his head back and looked into her eyes as if seeking approval to kiss her again. She felt frozen. Why wasn't she stopping him? Why was she allowing him to do this?

He let his hand slip down on to the top of her arm, pulling her in towards him as he kissed her harder this time.

Liz felt his lips hard on hers. Her lips kissed back almost automatically. Like they had done a thousand times. The rough texture of his top lip and the taste and feel of his mouth were so familiar and strangely comforting. Even though she knew she needed to stop this now, she couldn't. Not just yet.

Eventually she forced her face away from his, trying to process what was happening. The martinis seemed to take hold of her body and she slipped awkwardly out from his arms, falling clumsily from the bar stool she'd been perched on. She was struggling to get her legs to work and her thoughts clear, but she knew she needed to get away from him. Before her mind had caught up with what her body was doing, she was scooping up her things and practically running out of the bar.

She didn't turn around to see if he was following her. She stumbled out into the brisk November air and sucked in long cool breaths, attempting to clear her head enough that she could get herself out of this situation. There was a black cab over the road with its light on. She moved as quickly as her limbs would take her, scared that if she looked back he'd be there. And she wouldn't get in.

As she moved around the car, she felt her body freeze on the spot. There he was. Holding the door open for her – the perfect gentleman. How laughable that was.

'Lizzie,' he said smoothly, his eyes piercing into hers as the world waved around in front of her and the alcohol pulsed in her ears. 'Look, I'm sorry about that. At least let me help you get home. I can't leave you like this. We'll buy you a coffee on the way.'

Liz seemed only to be able to nod, as she clambered into the back of the cab and tried to focus. She wasn't interested in talking any more. She was staring ahead of her, aware of his hand resting on her thigh so comfortably, yet somehow not doing anything to remove it.

Perhaps everything from the point she'd made the decision to go the bar tonight had been inevitable. Perhaps she was more to blame than him in all of this. She was a grown woman. A strong woman. She knew what she was doing, and she knew what she was about to do. She didn't know why she felt so helpless to stop it, but it was happening and she wanted it. She couldn't deny it.

Before she knew it – they were in a hotel lobby, a strong black coffee bringing her back to her senses. Moments later they were on their way up a grand staircase, then entering a dimly lit hotel room, with a perfectly made bed, curtains drawn and a familiar yet stifling sense of inevitability.

There was kissing, fumbling, touching, undressing . . .

It didn't last long. But it was done now. Whatever itch she'd felt she needed to scratch, it had been well and truly scratched. Her head was beginning to pound with the fix of caffeine and vodka, her mouth tasted disgusting, and the nauseating smell of sex hung in the air. She needed to get out of here.

Now wasn't the time for goodbyes, she simply got dressed and left. Noting that he seemed to be doing the same. She clutched her coat to her shoulders, and swiftly made her way back out of the hotel to hail a cab. She had no idea what time it was . . . Late – but not that late. Maybe eleven. The city was still jumping. But all she could think about was running away from here. The night air was clearing her mind. She felt sick. And guilty. And couldn't make any sense of what just happened.

What she'd allowed to happen.

She could barely let herself think about it. She knew that when she got home, Gerald would be there, innocently sleeping. And that she could never tell him, or anyone else for that matter, about what had happened here tonight.

It would for ever be her dirty little secret.

Chapter 29

FANNY-CHAT

Emily
Molly? You there?

> **Molly**
> For you – always ;)

Emily
Okay.
I know this is a bit TMI but honestly –
the first time you and Tom had sex
after having Marley were you a little
bit slightly
ABSOLUTELY TERRIFIED YOUR
FANNY WOULD NOT WORK ANY
MORE?
Or anything?

> **Molly**
> Well – a bit I guess.
> But it was fine.
> And we've done it loads since then. Obvs.
> Have you and Paul not had sex since
> you had W then?

Emily

No! I've wanted to.

But I'm scared.

I know I'm being an idiot, but I just
feel a bit differently about everything
'down there' since a baby busted out
of me head first . . .

My vagina has stage fright!

I'm paranoid it's got all stretched out
or wonky or something?

Molly

Wonky?! You do make me laugh
Emily!

You just need to go for it.

The first time it does feel a bit
daunting, but you soon realise you
had nothing to worry about!

You're just building it up too much in
your head.

Emily

I know.

You're totally right.

And Paul's being great but I know
he's really frustrated.

There's been no P in the V for a while
tbh.

(Or should it be in P in the E?)

169

Molly
Haha!
Look – you'd be amazed how
quickly it all goes back into place
down there. It's been nearly four
months since W was born lady!
Trust me – it's all working like it's
supposed to be. Is everything okay
with you guys??

Emily
Well if I'm honest we're just a bit shit
at the moment – is it like that for you
and Tom?
Everything he does seems to piss me
off!
I know I'm being a dick and it's all
down to hormones and lack of sleep
but we just seem to snipe at each
other all the time.
Or I snipe at him and he just sucks it
up so we don't have a row . . . which
is sometimes actually MORE
ANNOYING.
I think I'm jealous he gets to sleep
and go to work and be a normal
person.
Then I get really upset because I
know I should be enjoying my

maternity leave, not wishing it away.
I don't know what's wrong with me!!

Molly

There's nothing wrong with you x it's
tough this mum-stuff.
And yes me and Tom get at each
other sometimes too.
Except I think I'm the one pissing him
off more these days!
You probably just need to take some
time for yourselves.
Remember how to be Paul and Emily,
not just Mummy and Daddy xx

Emily

Ha x I know you're right.
Okay. I'm going to sort it out.
Before my husband leaves me for
someone who isn't a mental cow
that's scared of their own vagina.
Plus if I don't give things a good trim
down there soon I might not actually
find it again anyway . . .

Molly

Get on it lady!
Pretty soon you won't be able to keep
your hands off each other again.
Or your penises out of one another!

Emily

Well.

I'm not sure we were ever really like that.

Plus I'm pretty busy being the Udder of All Life most days and nights still.

But it'd be nice to know everything still works properly!

Also – that makes no sense. Lol

Molly

Ha!

Get that fanny trimmed lady!

Emily

I will.

And thanks for constantly listening to all my crap.

I love you. xx

Molly

Love you and your big wonky fanny too.

xx

Chapter 30

THE FOUR-MONTH FUCK-YOU SLEEP REGRESSION

I'm four months old, with a permanent cold.
All this snot is just for you.
I'm wriggling around, to a familiar sound,
That's right – I'm up to my hairline in poo.

I'm always awake, it's for your own sake;
I use the daytime to practise not sleeping . . .
Routine's a farce, stick your 'shush-pat' up your arse,
Only another year or so of teething . . .

You've bought ENOUGH toys, including hundreds
*   that make noise,*
Don't you know we've just come out of
*   recession . . . ?*
Oh, and don't bother with bed tonight, coz I've
*   forgotten how to sleep at night,*
Welcome to the 4-month fuck-you sleep regression.

Even though she knew deep down inside it was probably a mistake – Emily had once again consulted the Internet for sleep advice.

And amidst all of the smuggy-mc-twatty judgy mummies whose babies had slept through the night since leaving the uterus and were now proficient in using the iPad and putting themselves to bed at sixteen weeks old, were quite a lot of desperate, and clearly slightly manic mothers in Facebook groups talking about the 'four-month sleep regression'. Emily actually took a lot of comfort from this . . . knowing that for once, nature had made it so her baby wouldn't sleep and it wasn't simply because she was really shit at babies.

But right now, she finally had something to look forward to . . . it was Friday night. And she and Paul were about to go on their first night out together. Just the two of them. Without a baby attached to one of her nipples or inside her body. For the first time in what seemed like for ever.

Emily was not leaving anything to chance – Paul's Valentine's attempts earlier in the year had essentially involved a curry house and a pair of slippers. With faces on. And that had NOT gone down well with his excessively hormonal pregnant wife, so tonight she was taking control. She didn't want to be a bitch about it – but she was angry, exhausted and completely incapable of handling disappointment. So it was just best all round if she managed the arrangements.

She'd booked a posh restaurant, organised for her mum to baby-sit, planned a nice bar to visit afterwards, and most importantly she'd purchased new underwear, put on lipstick for the first time since a human tobogganed through her cervix and SHAVED HER NEWLY AMPLE VAGINA.

She'd only managed it by propping William up in the Bumbo on the bathroom floor, surrounded by toys, where he could see her the entire time. And was seemingly entertained by the 'real-life human-woman-shearing' that Mummy was athletically performing on herself whilst blocking the plughole with pube debris, and reminding herself this was not 'sexy-information' she should share whilst attempting to seduce Daddy later.

Sexy-pubic-hair drain-unblocking aside – she felt epic. Like a new, hair-free, real-underwear-wearing woman again. Even if there was likely to be severe chafing and the world's worst shaving rash by the morning, for tonight, she was smooth and ready to pop her post-birth-sex cherry (totally a thing). If Paul could fight his way through the Spanx to get there in the first place that was . . .

Emily stood in her bedroom in front of her wardrobe mirror admiring herself. She turned her body from one side to another, one hand on her stomach, pushing it in and prodding it a little. She wondered if she'd ever have a flat stomach again – or if she ever really wanted to? That little paunch around her tummy was a reminder she'd carried life. She needed to remember that. Crop tops and six-packs were hardly the fucking priority . . . her baby was four months old. She looked fabulous for that, she reminded herself, pouting a little and holding her head up confidently. And for everything else – there was Spanx, girdles and support tights.

William stirred a little on the bed behind her. He was sleeping contently on top of the duvet with a pillow either side. Which had actually given Emily a chance to get ready. It was all working out quite marvellously in fact . . .

Emily glanced down at her phone – it was 6.09 p.m. Her mum would be here any moment, and Paul had promised he'd be back for 6.30 as he'd had a late meeting. The taxi was booked for 7 p.m., and the table ready for 7.30. She needed to feed William once more now, and then there were two expressed bottles waiting in the fridge for her mum to give him later. It should buy them at least four hours, but Emily was secretly hoping for a bit longer . . .

She'd written lists, colour coded items, laid things out ready for any possible situation, and pretty much done everything except provide her mum with some kind of haka to perform for William.

She was trying to concentrate on getting ready – but it was hard to ignore the niggling voice at the back of her mind telling her not to go, making her feel guilty, making her feel like a terrible human and an awful mother for wanting a few hours away from her darling sweet baby.

Emily heard the doorbell go. Thank god her mum had arrived. She'd begin letting her read through the notes and instructions as she gave William his last feed . . . and if all else failed, she'd start thinking about that haka . . .

It felt so strange to be out. In a lovely restaurant, full of lovely adult-only people. Even though only a year or so ago this was their life. All the time. What else would they be doing on a weekend . . . ? It was amazing the things you took for granted.

'Relax,' Paul said smoothly, smiling and giving her a reassuring glance.

Emily had insisted on leaving her phone on the table in front of her in case her mum called. But it had only served to make her more agitated, clicking the home button every few minutes to check she still had wifi and full service . . .

'How about you put your phone away for twenty minutes, just while we have dessert – nothing is going to happen. Your mum knows what she's doing. She did a pretty good job with you, didn't she . . . ?' Paul said, smiling gently. 'And if she needs to know anything she can consult the colour-coded William manual complete with 3D diagrams and flow charts that I saw you'd left her . . .' Paul continued, reaching out and squeezing Emily's hand from across the table.

Emily smiled. He was right. Of course. Not that she'd ever fully admit that to him. She dropped her phone into her handbag and released a deep breath as she rolled her shoulders back. She'd feel it buzz anyway if a message came through.

'There. It's gone. Sorry – it just feels so strange being away from him. I'm sure every new parent feels like this the first time . . . it'll get better, I'm sure.'

'It will,' Paul said, pulling the dessert menus into view so they could choose. 'I'm having the lemon thing. I'm guessing the chocolate brownie for you . . . ?'

177

Emily liked that they were predictable sometimes. Felt a bit like the good old days for a moment. 'Hey. You know me. I'm a sucker for anything with the word chocolate in!'

'Indeed, I do. Thanks so much for organising this tonight, sweetie. You look amazing. Not that you don't always look amazing to me . . . but tonight . . . you look so stunning.'

Emily blushed. It seemed a long time since she'd had a compliment. One which wasn't about her parenting abilities or her baby . . . one which was just about her.

'Thanks. You don't look so bad yourself . . .' Emily said, admiring Paul's rugged handsome face and realising how much she'd missed having time to look at him.

'So, what shall we do after this? What time is your mum going to stay until, do you think?' Paul said, trying to disguise the yawn that crept up on him as he finished his sentence.

'Oh, I think she's fine for another hour or so . . . we could go to that new bar? Have another drink here . . . I don't mind really . . . ?' Emily said, catching Paul's yawn and trying hard to disguise her own.

Paul laughed. Emily did too.

'You know – there's no shame in admitting we're knackered and just can't be arsed . . . I've had a crazy week at work . . . I'm honestly fine with just heading home to snuggle up on the couch with our boy after this. I mean – only if you are?'

'Well, I'm sorry you've had such a crazy work week

– perhaps you'd like to swap, and you can be sucked dry twenty-four hours a day by a miniature human that fell out of your arsehole, and I'll go to meetings and get to have coffee breaks with real humans who don't talk about infant shit and reflux all fucking day!' Emily snapped without even meaning to. She suddenly heard herself . . . it was very hard to not make every conversation a 'who's more tired' competition. But she did feel like a bit of a dick for doing it right now. During their first evening out together since they'd become parents. The last thing she wanted to do was totally ruin what was left of it.

'Hey,' said Paul. His voice calm and sincere. 'I know you're shattered. I know your job right now, looking after William, is a million times harder than mine. I do. Honestly. I don't want to row. But it doesn't mean I'm not tired too. I'm working fifty-hour weeks and arrive home to a pissed-off wife who seems to hate me and only wants to thrust my son in my face so she can go for a bath every evening and ignore me. I do actually want to see you too, you know? I miss you both while I'm at work – I'd love to be around more but I can't. No matter what I do it's wrong, Emily. And you seem to want to punish me for it every day.'

Emily could hear how exasperated he was. She didn't know what to say. It was difficult to hear, but she knew everything he was saying was right. She was unreasonably angry all the time, and it was clear she'd been taking it out on him more than she realised.

179

'Well. I didn't realise you felt that way,' Emily mumbled, feeling a little wounded from his words.

Paul softened his face and took her hand across the table. 'Look. I didn't mean for it to come out that way. I just meant I miss you. And I want you to be as happy to see me at the end of each day as I am to see you when I come through the door.'

'I am.' Emily said, letting his words sink into her. 'I'm sorry if I made you feel like that. I'm just so shattered and angry. I suppose I've been taking it out on you more than I realised. I miss you too.'

'It's okay. It's natural for you to take it out on the person closest to you. I get that. But we need to make time for each other too. I just want my wife back.'

Emily smiled back at him. Somewhere between happy and sad. But she didn't want to row either. She was glad he'd got this stuff off his chest. They both clearly needed to make more effort.

'Sorry. I know. I don't think I'd really thought about how things have been for you since William came along. I know we need to get back to us. I've just been too tired to see anything but myself these last few months,' Emily said, feeling a little choked, but determined not to cry. She squeezed his hand a little harder. 'I love you, you know. And even if I haven't said it before – I really appreciate everything you do for us.'

'I think we both need to start being a bit kinder to ourselves. And each other,' Paul said, smiling and looking into her eyes. 'We have a beautiful family, we love each other, and we're bloody knackered but that's okay. I don't care about Fridays in the pub, wild nights out and hungover Sundays any more, I just want to be with you guys. In fact, I can't think of anything I'd like to do more right now than sit on my sofa with my boy and wife and eat chocolate brownies . . . So, let's get the desserts to go and take the rest of the evening home. What do you say?'

'You know what – I'd really like that,' Emily said, smiling back, 'because honestly – I really need to get these pants off. I'm not sure thongs are for me any more . . . My perineum just isn't the same . . .' Emily said, letting herself laugh a little to break the tension.

'Well, I love your perineum just the way it is. And I love you too,' Paul said, laughing back. 'Although, I am a bit worried that you think the baby fell out of your arsehole. I mean, I was in the room. And I can one hundred per cent confirm that that was not how it happened . . .'

The couple laughed together, enjoying these few moments before they left more than the entire rest of the evening put together, if they were honest.

Emily felt slightly disappointed that she didn't have the energy to go drinking, and dancing, and post those slightly smug 'I'm having an amazing time' photos on Facebook that make everyone comment with how jealous they are, but Paul was right – she just couldn't be arsed. The exhaustion of new parenthood had got the better of them, and there was nothing wrong with that.

He was right about it all; she needed to stop focussing on the things she missed because of having a baby, and start appreciating some of the good stuff. She felt like she was having some kind of epiphany.

Right now it was 9.37 p.m., Emily's inner thighs felt like they'd been sanded, she desperately missed her baby, and her boobs were heavy enough to be used as weapons. She was ridiculously uncomfortable, and frankly couldn't wait to cut herself out of her Spanx, slap some baby lotion on her poor sore fanny and get into bed.

And to top it all off – she was pretty sure her fucking period had just started up again for the first time in just over a year. Which really was the perfect slightly disappointing shitty end, to her slightly disappointing shitty evening.

Chapter 31

NEVER AGAIN

Liz knew she couldn't tell anyone about what happened the other night.

No one.

Ever.

When she'd got home, Gerald had been asleep and she'd managed to sneak into bed without having a conversation. She deleted all trace of 'him' from her phone and blocked him on everything – any possible contact method. From now on she wasn't taking any chances – she needed him erased completely from her life, for ever. Something she should have done a long time ago.

She'd been sick when she got in. Perhaps from the guilt. But four large martinis on an empty stomach, after being sober for several months, was not a good idea. But then clearly the entire night had been full of utterly terrible ideas.

Liz still had no idea why she'd done it. Why she'd gone. Why she'd stayed there when he'd started spouting all the crap she'd heard a hundred times. Why she hadn't stopped him before he tried to kiss her, why she'd let him get in the cab with her, and gone to the hotel with him . . . The moments kept replaying in her mind. It made her want to throw up again.

She couldn't believe she'd risked everything. Everything she had with Gerald. Wonderful, kind, and not-at-all-an-arsehole Gerald. The life she'd built up with him – their future, everything . . . simply for a drunken shag with an arsehole from her past.

Liz stood in front of her bathroom mirror, inspecting her face. Prodding her cheeks a little as if to check the guilt wasn't seeping through. She hoped she could handle this on top of everything else, but she couldn't deny she was feeling a little broken. Losing the baby, and now this. It was taking so much to keep up the act of being 'fine' now.

The last few days had been hard. She'd struggled to look Gerald in the eye. She was sure he'd be able to tell she was hiding something if she did. So she'd mostly avoided him. Gone to bed early – said she'd had a head-ache. Taken lunch at her desk to keep herself distracted . . . She didn't feel close to him at all right now. And she knew he must feel that too.

It was horrible. She didn't know how much longer she could keep it up. But she knew she couldn't tell him either. With everything that had gone on the last few months it would kill him. She just couldn't do that to him.

Gerald had shown her nothing but love. He'd been so wonderful and supportive as they'd begun trying to get back to normal after losing the baby, but all she'd done was shut him out, and now this . . . Liz knew she didn't deserve him. She was disgusted with herself.

And she couldn't work out whether it was better or

worse that he suspected nothing. That he'd never know. That she'd 'got away with it'. Fuck – she felt terrible.

Liz felt like she might cry. She was struggling to cope with all of this. She had to talk to Gerald. This couldn't carry on.

Liz jumped a little as Gerald knocked gently on the bathroom door.

'You okay in there?' came his kind voice.

Liz coughed to clear her throat a little and dabbed the corners of her eyes with a tissue. It was time to face him. She turned and opened the door.

Gerald face was smiling but tinged with concern. She could see it in his eyes.

'I'm fine,' she said, placing a hand gently on his arm.

Gerald breathed out heavily. There was clearly something he wanted to say. 'Can I be honest with you, Liz? You don't seem fine. If anything – it feels like things are getting less "fine" each day. Has anything happened? I don't want to sound paranoid but I feel like you're pushing me away . . . and I don't know what to do.'

Liz instantly felt the tears returning. She needed to pick her words carefully now.

'I know. I'm so sorry,' Liz said – choking on hot tears, panicking as she racked her brain for what to say next. She had to tell some truths, but she couldn't tell all of them . . . 'I think I've spent so long pretending I'm fine about everything to do with the miscarriage that I just lost my way a bit . . . I don't really know how to explain it better than that. I know that probably sounds really selfish. But the last few days – the guilt has just all felt too much. I can't help feeling I've let you down. That all of this is my fault. And that . . . I don't deserve you. I don't deserve us . . .'

Liz's voice was getting smaller with every sentence. She was scared of what she might say next. It was so hard lying to him. But telling him the truth would be even harder. She knew that.

'What do you mean?' Gerald said, his voice soft but confused. 'Why would you ever think you didn't deserve me, and us? I don't understand, Liz? You need to stop blaming yourself. A really terrible, shitty thing happened but we're going to get through it and we're going to be okay. You have to believe that.'

'I know,' Liz said, her head hanging down. 'I want to believe that. But I know I'm fucking this all up. I don't know how to be, and even though I don't want to push you away, it's like I can't help it. It's just happening anyway out of my control. Everything is just so fucked.'

'No, it's not,' Gerald said firmly, lifting her chin gently so she was forced to look at him. 'It's not fucked, Liz. Not if you don't let it be. We need to start moving forward now – it doesn't mean we have to pretend everything is perfect, but you've got to start talking to me. Tell me when you're sad and we'll cry. Tell me when you're angry and you can punch me in the face if it makes you feel better. But the only way we're going to get through this is if you open up to me. Okay?'

Liz nodded at him with fresh tears still pumping from

her eyes. Trying as hard as she could to suppress the blurry memory of lying naked on a sweaty hotel-room bed with 'him' thrusting away on top of her. It was all she could do not to be physically sick.

She coughed her thoughts away and pulled herself together, wiping her eyes with her sleeve.

'I will try. I really will,' she said eventually. 'I don't want to lose you. I can't . . .'

'Why would you think you'd lose me?' Gerald said, frowning slightly and stroking her hair.

Liz sighed loudly, it was becoming increasingly hard to talk without saying too much. 'Because of the things I've done, the person I am. I'm not a good person, Gerald. I feel like that's why this has happened to me. Because I don't actually deserve to be happy or to have anything nice in my life. Every time something good happens to me, I ruin it . . . I don't even know how I do it, but it all just turns to shit . . .' The words and tears just kept pouring from her. Liz was terrified of what might pour out of her next, but the words kept coming.

Gerald cut her off. 'Liz, you can't keep doing this to yourself. What happened has nothing to do with your past or who you are as a person. I know you, Liz – I know who you are. You are not a bad person. To me you're actually pretty fucking amazing. I wish you could see that. We've all done shitty things in our past that we're ashamed of. If you beat yourself up about them for the rest of your life then how are you ever going to be happy?'

Liz shrugged. The tears were choking her now. His kindness was killing her.

'Look,' Gerald said firmly. 'I'm not going anywhere. And everything is going to be okay.'

Liz tried to believe him. He meant it.

She also tried hard to ignore the guilt that was infecting her every thought right now. She had to find a way to hold it together because she had meant what she'd said – despite what she'd done, she loved him. More than she'd ever loved anyone. And she knew she couldn't lose him. Maybe if she could do that then everything really would be okay. She allowed herself just the tiniest glimmer of hope as she held him close and breathed him in.

'Okay,' she managed to repeat back to him as she got her tears finally under control. Maybe everything eventually would be okay.

Chapter 32

GASH RASH

Liz

Hi ladies.

How are your weeks going?

How was your date night last Friday Emily?

Hope your fanny was up to the task!

Lol x

Emily

Very funny.

Fanny didn't get any action I'm afraid.

Mostly fanny just got back into some comfy PJs, regretted having all its hair shaved off and decided it didn't really fancy penis any more, so it would just start having a period again instead.

Excellent.

Liz

Okay well that was probably a bit more information than I needed but sorry to hear that!

Hope you still had a good night
though?

Emily

Yes – not quite the way I planned it!
Was tucked up back in bed by 10
p.m.
Which is pathetic.
I think William might have actually
broken me.
As a person.
Inside and out.
I could barely keep my eyes open!

Liz

Oh sweetie don't beat yourself up.
He's only tiny – and he doesn't sleep
through the night yet!
It's totally understandable you're
knackered. There'll be plenty of
chances for nights out.
Don't put pressure on yourself.

Molly

Yep. And plenty of chance for fanny
action! (and hopefully without the gash
rash this time. Ouch!)

Emily

Can't actually believe any mature
human above the age of fifteen

would say the words gash rash, but I appreciate the sentiment! Lol

Liz

Jesus Molly. Thanks for that image. I'll enjoy having that etched into my brain as I brush my teeth.

ANYWAY. Just checking we're still on for this weekend?

Molly

You're welcome.

And yes defo still on for this Saturday.

Emily

Me too! Can't wait to catch up.

Liz

Me neither. And I'm sorry I've been so rubbish at staying in touch recently – it's just been really hard trying to juggle everything. Work, personal stuff, Gerald, me, mostly me . . .

Emily

We know sweetie. We understand and you're doing amazing. Is everything okay between you guys?

Liz

Well – it wasn't. I had a bit of a wobble. About us I mean.

I'm not very good at opening up – I think I was driving him away. Shutting him out and throwing myself into work. Typical me really.
But we had a chat and I think we can start to get back to where we were.

Molly
Hey, you've had a lot to deal with – you can't beat yourself up about not knowing how to cope with it all. But I'm glad you're trying to sort things out.

Emily
Me too. And I know I've said it a hundred times but you guys are great together. I know you've already had so much shit to go through, but I know you'll be okay.

Liz
Well thank you Jeremy Kyle, I don't actually need you to sell my own relationship to me but I get what you're saying. We'll be okay. Don't worry xx

Emily
Okay, okay! I'll shut up. Can't wait to see you.

Molly

Me neither. Can't wait to see you both
on Saturday! Feels like FOR EVER.

Liz

Me too.
See you soon ladies.
Hope your fanny feels better by then
Emily!
Xxx

Emily

Me too! I know! It has been for ever
xx
And thanks – I think all this fanny chat
has given me some inspiration for a
blog post . . . lol
xxx

Molly

#yourewelcome
xxx

Chapter 33

MUMMY-MAINTENANCE

Emily couldn't wait to see her friends. Their chats were what kept her going some days. Catching up on WhatsApp with Molly and Liz, and her own Friday night self-preparation – which had led to her sitting on her sofa, legs spread, with nappy cream pasted on her bikini area – had given her more than enough material for a blog post.

Feeling about as glamorous as she ever had, Emily located her laptop, and placed it carefully on her lap being careful not to get Sudocrem all over it. And began to type. . .

THURSDAY 30 NOVEMBER

'Mummy-Maintenance'

It's hard not to 'let things go' a little as a new mum.

It's to be expected that trimming your pubic hair into a perfect pineapple is not going to be high up your priority list, when a human being you grew in your body just head-butted their way

out of you via your vagina a few weeks ago . . .
BUT a little bit of pampering in the right places, a
neaten up, and a bit of 'Mummy-Maintenance'
could be just what you need to feel a little more
like your old self again . . .

(And I can say this confidently as I sit here –
legs akimbo, with a fanny full of nappy-rash
cream after trying to hack my vagina hair back
with a blunt razor I found at the back of the bathroom cupboard . . . I SHOULD HAVE TAKEN MY
OWN ADVICE.)

So, here's my guide to a 'Mummy-Maintenance'
now you've had a baby:

1. Under-arms: Shave them quickly. Over the sink.
   In ten-second intervals so you don't have to
   look away for too long . . . as the baby escapes
   the Bumbo on the bathroom floor and begins
   trying to suckle something you hope is only
   dry toothpaste or toilet roll (unused toilet roll).

   If you make it through without severing an
   arm you can take this as a #win.

2. Legs: Shave as little of your legs as possible.
   Don't worry about the backs or anything above
   the knee. F@*k it. Just do the front of your
   ankles and be done. Remember to remove the
   rust from the blade and failing that get the
   kitchen scissors on the case for the clumps. Try

not to sit down next to anyone you know without at least 90-denier tights or long leggings . . . except your other half. He's over it. Trust me.

3. Bikini line: Just trim it back to the point you can wear pants without looking like you're smuggling tobacco in there. Take the time to reminisce . . . Let's go back about a year to your pre-baby self and try to remember what it was like to neaten up the old fanjo without having to physically fold bits of yourself out of the way first . . . *sobs*

4. Eyebrows: Pluck from below not above . . . And by 'below' I mean your chin and/or nipples too . . . (And toes.)

5. Hair: Dry shampoo is now your best friend. And yes – you can do your roots while still wearing your messy-mum-bun and yesterday's mascara . . . #phew

6. Sunglasses: It doesn't matter that it's November and there's no sun . . . GO BIG. To hide the past five months of vertical sleeping and general despair . . . LAUGHS MANICALLY WHILST KNOCKING BACK WINE, ROCKING AND SUCKING OWN THUMB.

7. Skincare: Why cleanse when you can use your own tears to self-moisturise each evening . . .? Also try to avoid deepening your scowl lines by simply ignoring your partner while he uses a new cup EVERY BASTARD TIME HE MAKES A CUP OF TEA. Or something.

8. Makeup: Invest in a decent powder and a really nice lip gloss to join the crispy muslins, used baby wipes, and whatever that weird yellowy-brown stain is at the bottom of the change bag . . . it'll make you feel good about yourself. *flinches a bit*

9. Underwear: Remember thongs and underwired bras . . . Well, you shouldn't. They're not for you any more. Take a moment to mourn them while picking out some giant pants and a nursing vest in H&M as you cry into one of those crispy muslins and wonder if you'll ever be able to have or wear any NICE THINGS EVER AGAIN. EVER.

10. (The answer is no, you won't.) (And/or wine.)

Chapter 34

A FESTIVE FIRST SATURDAY CLUB

Technically it was the first weekend of December. So Last Saturday Club had become First Saturday Club this month, but Emily didn't really care about the finer details.

Life had been so hectic for all three of them the last couple of months. All that really mattered was that she was on her way to meet her two best friends. To hug them. And laugh with them. And drink, and chat, and set the world to rights with them. And do all of it ON HER OWN. As today Paul was on daddy-duty, and thanks to a well-spent morning milking herself into Tommee Tippee bottles, she was very much looking forward to having both hands (and boobs) free for an afternoon.

Although, as she strolled through High Wycombe town centre, she realised how very odd it felt not pushing a pram or holding an infant. Even not having the change bag – in fact not having any bag that wasn't the size of a suitcase and didn't contain enough equipment to sustain life, was odd. Her small shoulder bag with her wallet, keys, phone and a few nipple pads felt like nothing compared with the sack of baby crap she was used to lugging around the South Bucks area . . .

Emily wasn't quite sure what to do with her arms. But considering it was freezing cold and drizzling, she kept them stuffed inside her big padded coat with her hood up, firmly keeping her curly blonde mane from the elements. And diverting as much rain off her freshly made-up face as possible.

Emily picked up the pace as she walked, head down, along High Wycombe high street. She was keen to get there now, set her hair free, and distract herself from the urge to WhatsApp Paul every three or four seconds, just to check how William was.

She'd left him two large bottles of expressed milk so he'd have more than enough for the couple of hours she'd be out. And he was William's daddy. He was just as capable of looking after him as she was . . . she knew that. It wasn't that that was bothering her. But it just felt so strange being away from her baby. It was now that she was beginning to realise just how intense her relationship with William really was.

But she needed a little time away. She'd done her hair, done her make-up. Layered enough contour cream on her face to disguise a llama. She felt good. She honestly did. She wanted to feel like more than 'just a mum' for a short while. She needed the conversation to not be about babies, or sleep, or parenthood in any way. Else she'd never relax. Especially as she could already feel the spiky tingles of the milk filling back up in her boobs. Why on earth she'd worn an underwired bra she wasn't sure . . . she'd thought it might make her feel more like

199

her old self, but actually she felt like she'd created her own personal chin-ledge that was highly likely to leak if she applied any more pressure to it . . . It was probably still worth it though, just to not be wearing a bra that had those clicky little clips at either side . . . She was sure she'd started to hear the clicking noise in her dreams . . .

Emily was happy to have finally reached O'Neill's pub just off the high street, which was their chosen meeting place for the day. It was large and comfy, they'd have no problem getting a seat, there was food if they wanted, and the wine was perfectly gluggable. She wasn't sure she cared about much else.

She spotted Liz immediately as she stood in the doorway, taking her hood down and removing her now wet-through coat. She wasn't late, but Liz had been early – of course – and was sitting comfortably on a large leather sofa to the left – a glass of red wine in front of her, carefully reapplying a slick of red lipstick in a compact mirror. She looked as immaculate as ever. Emily tried not to feel emotional seeing her. She'd not seen her since before all the horrible things had happened. She had promised herself she'd wait for Liz to bring things up if she wanted to talk about losing the baby, but seeing her in the flesh only made her more desperate to make sure her friend really was okay now. She could already feel her eyes getting damp in the corners. She needed to hold it together.

At that moment Liz spotted her. An understated smile

spread across her face, as she remained seated and packed her lipstick away in her handbag. Emily wasn't going to let her get away with not hugging her – she practically mounted her friend, wrapping both her arms around her tightly. Perhaps a little tighter than usual. Liz might not be a hugger – but Emily was, so Liz had no choice in the matter.

Liz broke away first. 'Well, hi . . .' she said, smiling a little more now.

'Well, hi, yourself,' Emily said, getting back on to her feet and dumping her soggy coat on the back of the sofa. It felt so amazing to see her friend. There was emotion ready to burst out of her, but before any bursting occurred she was going to get a glass of wine, sit down with her already-quite-enormous pushed-up boobs in front of her and enjoy a child-free afternoon like a REAL GIRL. With lip gloss on and everything.

'Grab a drink – I opened a tab,' Liz said, as if reading her mind.

'I will. I'll get a bottle of red, shall I? Molly's not drinking obviously, but I'm sure you and I can polish one off! It's nearly Christmas so it doesn't count anyway, right . . . ?'

'Absolutely. Both Father Christmas and Jesus would absolutely want that,' Liz said, smirking a little and brushing her fringe back into place after the mounting.

Just then the door swung open again, letting a rush of cold damp air in, as the familiar shape of Molly wandered through, shaking off a large umbrella.

201

Molly looked breezy and relaxed as always. It was hard to imagine her in any other state, thought Emily.

'Ladies . . .' Molly said, grinning widely as she approached them both. She quickly hugged her two friends in turn and took a seat next to Liz.

'I'm just going to get a drink if you want something . . . ?' Emily said, edging towards the bar.

'Oh. Something incredibly exciting like an apple juice, I guess . . .' Molly said, rolling her eyes a little, as Emily turned on her heel and kept her eyes fixed on the twenty-something barman, who looked quite put out to have to tear himself away from whatever he was watching on his iPhone.

Emily was back with a tray of drinks within a few moments. Molly and Liz had been making small talk in her absence.

'Here you are . . .' Emily said, unloading the tray, before taking a seat herself.

'It feels so nice to be here without the babies, doesn't it? Weird . . . but nice. How are you feeling, being away from Marley for the first time? Are you anxious? I'm feeling a bit strange, if I'm honest . . . I know Paul and I went out the other night, but because it's the daytime it feels a bit surreal. Don't you think?' Emily was rambling a bit, so she poured herself some wine.

'Not really . . . It's only a couple of hours,' Molly responded with a shrug of her shoulders. 'He's only with Tom, after all. I've not left him under a rainbow, guarded by a pack of wolves in a forest somewhere. He's in Staples.

Tom's getting a new printer. I'm pretty sure it's safe in there.'

Liz laughed a little more than Emily did.

'Wow. Staples. Parenting really has taken you to new heights, hasn't it, ladies . . .' Liz said, still laughing and reaching for the wine to top her own glass up.

'Absolutely,' Emily quipped. 'And I know you're right. The dads are obviously more than capable of looking after the boys, I didn't mean that . . .' Emily could feel herself getting irritated, even though she didn't really know why. 'I just feel weird being away from him. Even though I've been looking forward to this all week! I know I sound mental. It's probably hormones. I think I need some more wine.'

'Then some more wine you shall have,' Liz said, winking at her friend. 'Sure we can't tempt you to half a glass, Molly? Vegan-Sober-Sergeant Tom isn't here . . . we could ply you with breath mints afterwards and exfoliate you before you leave . . . he'd never know . . . just saying!'

'Honestly I'm fine. I was never that big on wine anyway. Just tastes like fruity vinegar to me! I don't even miss the booze these days. The only thing I can't deal with it the lack of MEAT. I find myself sneaking pepperamis when he's at work . . . I'm a secret meat-eater! So actually if you wouldn't mind grabbing me some pork scratchings next time you're at the bar, that'd be awesome. Give me my meat-fix for the day!'

'You do make me laugh, Molly!' Emily said, throwing

her head back. 'And how are *you* . . .' Emily said, sensing the automatic change in her tone of voice as she directed her question at Liz.

'I'm fine,' Liz said, trying very hard to mean it. And ignoring the nagging sense of guilt that was rising up again. As much as it felt weird keeping something from her best friends – she knew she had to. It was the only way to make sure it stayed buried. She just couldn't risk anyone knowing. It was easier to just keep the attention on them. 'So how does it feel knowing it's the boys' first Christmas? I'm sure it makes this one a bit different!'

Liz had seamlessly changed the subject. Emily knew she wasn't going to get anything out of her. But she knew she'd tried. And perhaps Liz genuinely was fine and didn't want to talk about that stuff any more . . . it just felt like there was something she wasn't saying, but perhaps she was just going to have to accept that not everyone was a sharer like she was.

'Well – we're not really doing anything, to be honest with you,' Molly said after slurping her drink. 'I'm pretty sure, at four and a half months old, Marley won't be that arsed either. We're pretty skint with trying to set the business up, there's been way more stuff than I anticipated . . . I think I just thought it'd sort of happen. But turns out you need all kinds of insurances, and then there's websites, company names, marketing . . . it's been a bit of an eye-opener. I think even I need to admit that it's not quite as simple as I originally hoped! So everything's on hold for a bit until we can begin raising the funds – it'll be a cheap one for us this year. I don't really care what we do, so long as we're all together anyway.'

'Ha – well, I think you're right. As long as you're together,' Liz said, nodding a little. 'And I'm glad you're still moving the business on though. I'm sure all the hard work in the beginning will pay off in the long run. Frustrating as it is . . . Are you still going out there?'

'Yeah – at some point. I think we're going to delay for a while though. We just don't have the money for it. I'm doing everything I can to try and make some extra cash but it kind of feels like I'm getting nowhere, to be honest. I still just seem to be spending money, and nothing's really coming back. It's driving me a bit mad. I know I wanted my own business but it's just so frustrating . . . I've got an eBay business starting now, selling Christmas bits, and I've started making custom breastfeeding cloths and stuff. It's keeping me busy while we're waiting to get out there, so I can't complain. I know that all sounds a bit nuts but I know somewhere that supplies this amazing Thai fabric for way less than you'd pay anywhere else, so I can make a decent profit once I get going properly. Not that I've actually made any sales yet . . . I'm struggling a bit with how to get the sewing machine to go in a straight line . . . they've looked less like feeding cloths, and more like weird giant bunting, if that makes sense?' Molly looked like she was a bit confused by it all herself for a moment.

'Well. Not really. But I think it's great you're trying. You'll get there. If it's hard, it means you're getting somewhere. Like a real adult. I'm proud of you, sweetie!' Liz said, laughing. 'And hey – like you said, you're only delaying things a bit, it's not like you're giving up on it completely. Reality gets in the way sometimes!'

'It sure does,' Emily said, nodding in agreement and sensing she might need to replace her nipple pads sooner rather than later. 'Sounds like you're a proper grown-up making proper responsible decisions there, Molly . . . watch out! Next you'll be buying brown trouser suits and going to council meetings.'

The friends laughed. Probably a little more than they'd meant to. But the pub was empty, and it felt so nice to giggle like idiots together . . . even if it did mean the barman was forced to look up from his iPhone again. Poor love.

'And how about you, Em? I bet you've had Christmas organised since about July, haven't you . . . ?' Liz said, wiping a few tears of laughter out from the corners of her eyes.

'Very funny,' Emily said exaggeratedly. 'But yes. Pretty much. I've not completely finished the gift shopping yet, most of it's in the spare room in bags and boxes, and the last few bits I need to grab in town at some point. Paul's being a bit of a dick about some of it. He doesn't seem to understand why William needs a Jumperoo and a walker. I mean . . . isn't it obvious?'

'Err . . . Well. Not really,' Liz said, with her perfectly

shaped eyebrow raised sarcastically. 'He's five months old. He'd probably be happy with a shiny bit of wrapping paper and the TV remote to play with, wouldn't he . . . I'm not sure he'll know what's going on anyway!'

Molly sniggered as Emily resisted the urge to explain herself. She knew she'd gone a bit over the top with gifts . . . but she was happy with her decision to spoil William regardless of whether he knew it or not. She knew who she was.

'And what the fuck is a Jumperoo?' Molly added, once she'd got her sniggering under control. 'Sounds like some kind of friendly torture instrument . . .'

'A-NY-WAY.' Emily decided changing the subject was easier. 'So tell us what you're doing for Christmas? It's your and Gerald's first one together, isn't it – I love first Christmases! There's something so romantic about waking up together on Christmas morning for the first time . . .' Emily suddenly panicked that she might have overstepped the mark. With everything Liz and Gerald had been going through, she had no idea if they'd even planned to be together this Christmas.

'Well, I'm not much of a Christmas person, to be honest, but maybe you're right . . .' Liz looked thoughtful for a moment. 'In fact, I wanted to run an idea past you girls. I was thinking about doing something a bit crazy, for me, and maybe planning to spend Christmas away, just me and Gerald. I haven't thought of any of the details yet, but I think we need it. Some time away from everyone and everything – I think it's what we need to get our

207

relationship back on track. Do you think I'm being selfish and stupid?

'Not at all! I think it's a brilliant idea,' Emily gushed immediately. 'I'm already jealous and I don't even know where you're going yet!'

'I totally agree. Everyone will understand – sometimes you need to be a bit selfish. You guys deserve some time away. You should just do it!' Molly added.

Liz smiled a little awkwardly. 'You know what, I think you're right. I might just do it anyway.'

'Oh wow! Who are you and what have you done with our Liz?' Emily jested. 'It's like you're a new person.'

Liz felt her cheeks flush momentarily at Emily's question. She wasn't ready to admit to anyone, even her best friends, that the overwhelming guilt from meeting up with her arsehole ex and having sex with him in a London hotel room was probably the main motivation for her sudden change of life attitude. She had to start moving past that. She needed to make everything she did from now on about her and Gerald. She had to.

She topped up her and Emily's wine and lifted her glass in a little toast to herself.

'Then here's to the new me,' she said, as she took a small sip and smiled at her friends.

'Well. I'm super pleased for you both,' Emily said eventually, trying not to think about how much her boobs were aching now.

'You'll be jetting off somewhere – flouncing about with your god-like boyfriend, while I spend Christmas Day in my living room, eating Quality Street, wearing a bad Christmas jumper, while Paul constructs the jumpy-ring-of-neglect . . . but it'll probably be just as glamorous . . . right? Right . . . ?'

Chapter 35

JUST ABOUT GIZ

December had arrived, and Christmas had thrown up everywhere. Every advert, every shop, every house, every window – everything was gold and red and tinsel-y, and came with a Slade soundtrack and a handful of glitter . . .

Liz wasn't a massive festive fan. Not a Christmas hater – just not that bothered. She simply didn't feel the need to purchase novelty earrings and blast out Wham! at every possible moment. She didn't even bother putting a tree up most years, as she spent the majority of the festive period staying with her sister Holly and brother-in-law Dan, spending time with the whole family. And of course, especially enjoying the intense yet wonderful company of Clover and Isla – her two little nieces.

She'd always bring her best 'Christmas game' for them – who couldn't be Christmassy when presented with an overexcited toddler dressed from head to toe in a home-made snowman costume (some empty cereal boxes, squashed a bit and covered in glitter glue and cotton wool, with a badly attached carrot that had been partially eaten and held on with approximately four metres of Sellotape) accompanied by a grumpy-looking baby with reindeer ears.

Perhaps she was a bit of a Scrooge because Christmas had never really been about her. Before Gerald, there hadn't been much to celebrate in her own life. She'd just tagged along with her sister's Christmas – made polite conversation with her parents, eaten and drunk too much, and diverted most of her attention on to her nieces. It had been easier – making it about the children. Gerald had joined her at her sister's last Christmas too – the first time she'd ever introduced a 'boyfriend' to her family. Which had been just as awkward and embarrassing at times as she'd dreaded. And rather like arriving with a prize pony to be judged, inspected and questioned by a panel of people who really thought they knew everything about which pony was the best for you, even though they really knew fuck all about you or ponies . . . It had helped that Gerald happened to be a blond, six-foot-three pony-Adonis. Who spoke fluent Tombliboo . . . apparently.

Liz felt horrendously guilty at the idea of not spending time with her two nieces this year. Clover was three now, and 'baby Isla' was in fact fourteen months old, and not really a baby at all. Liz knew she wasn't the best auntie. She didn't have a huge amount of time for them, work had always dictated that. And they lived a bit too far away for her to be an active part of their lives. She tried to FaceTime them all a couple of times a month though – more her sister Holly's idea than hers, but she couldn't deny it was often the highlight of her week. Even if it did remind her how fast they were growing up, especially baby

Isla who was now climbing furniture like a circus acrobat, was entirely proficient with an iPad, and apparently old enough to find Arnee Lizzee boring and head off to look for some Happyland figures to insert into a nearby plug socket if she attempted to strike up a conversation with her . . .

Clover's face always lit up when she saw her, though. She clearly missed Liz. And Gerald. And told them both repeatedly each time they spoke. Which only served to make her feel like an even more terrible aunt and usually resulted in her buying them things they didn't actually need or want, but which made lots of loud noises and made her feel slightly less guilty about not spending much time with them. So, the thought of explaining to her that she and Big Uncle Geeraaa wouldn't be there for Christmas morning this year was giving her little guilt-laden stabbing sensations in her chest whenever she thought about it.

But she needed to do this. She needed to be selfish for once. A little reckless, even. It had been such a shit few months, and for the first time since the miscarriage and all the stupid crap that followed after, she'd begun to sense a glimmer of hope that things really would be okay. She knew there was still a long way to go, but in the last couple of weeks she and Gerald had begun talking more, smiling a little more often, and she'd started to feel like she could relax in his company again. And now she needed to do something that was just for them.

And hope that everyone, including the Tombliboos, understood.

Anyhow – Liz had ordered Holly's entire Amazon wish-list for the children, and had it gift-wrapped and sent over to them to try and relinquish some of the guilt. It would be there in the next couple of days, so she'd text her later and let her know a lorry-load of Christmas was about to arrive and throw up all over her doorstep. She was entirely sure that a four-foot Iggle Piggle and a drum kit would make Clover's entire year – although, in hindsight, Holly and Dan might not be quite so thrilled . . .

But right now, on a fairly boring Friday evening in December – Liz was sitting with her laptop open in front of her on the sofa, a freshly poured glass of red wine in hand, as Gerald had a shower and freshened up after work.

He'd be in there a while, Liz had come to understand that in the short time they'd been living together. People think that women take their time in the bathroom – well that is nothing compared to the length of time a man can string out a post-work shit, shower and possibly another shit. It was a thirty-minute operation at the very least. She didn't even know how it could take that long . . . she wasn't sure she really wanted to think about it that much, to be honest.

And she wasn't complaining about it today. Gerald's bathroom habits would mean Liz had plenty of time to get the trip she'd been researching all week booked. She wasn't really sure why she hadn't booked it yet – she'd found the flights, the hotel, researched the transfers, some things to do, places to eat . . . she was meticulous when

213

it came to organising that sort of thing. The only thing that usually stopped her from doing this kind of thing was work, and her inherent lack of spontaneity.

She had no doubt, once she did click 'book now' and announced her plans to Gerald that he'd think she'd lost the plot. He'd certainly never expect it. It was the last thing anyone would think sensible Liz with the immaculate fringe would do . . . Her plan was to wait until the last minute to surprise him. It would be brilliant.

Because if the last couple of months, the last year, and in fact the last few years of her life had taught her anything – it's that no matter how much you planned things and tried to organise every detail of everything you did, life was still going to totally dick you every so often. So sometimes you should press the fucking button and worry about the consequences later.

So that was what she was going to do.

She let her eyes flick over the details on the screen – two adults, flights to JFK airport on the 24th of December, taxi transfers, and accommodation in a junior suite, breakfast included . . . It was all there. Ready. Waiting.

Her finger hovered over the 'book now' button for just a second. Oh, fuck it, Liz thought to herself and pressed confirm. She felt a flutter of excitement rumble in the pit of her stomach. It felt good. Really good. It seemed a long time since she'd had something to look forward to. She began to gain confidence that she was doing the right thing.

'Hey . . . what you up to?' Gerald said coolly, as he

strolled over from behind her and planted a kiss on her forehead. Liz snapped the laptop shut with a smile on her face.

'Wouldn't you like to know . . .' she said, winking and trying not to smile. Which wasn't really working. She felt like a naughty schoolgirl hiding secret notes about boys she fancied.

Gerald moved round to sit next to her. His face suddenly seemed a little more serious. Liz could tell there was something on his mind.

'Everything okay?' she said, placing a hand reassuringly on his knee as she sat down.

'Well. You tell me,' Gerald said, the seriousness she'd sensed on his face now in his voice. Even though he was trying to speak gently. 'Is everything okay? I know we're trying to get back to a good place, and in many ways we are, but I feel like there's something you're hiding from me, Liz . . . Are you?'

Liz felt paralysed by the stifling sensation of guilt that flooded into her chest and body. Her mind raced. She knew she was hiding something from him – that one horrible thing. That stupid fucking night. Just one drunken, stupid, ridiculous night. With him. But it would be enough to break Gerald's heart. She knew it. She knew she could never tell him. She could never tell anyone. She just needed to bury it so deep that it never came back again.

She also knew there were blocked emails and deleted messages – none of which she'd read. She'd deleted and

215

blocked him out as much she could, but he was still finding ways to get through. Mostly via different email addresses . . . it wasn't rocket science, after all. She blocked each new one in turn, refusing to even allow herself to read them. No doubt he'd thought their night together was the start of rekindling their affair, but if she just kept ignoring him he'd get the message sooner or later. He had to. He wasn't one to make a fool out of himself. And his attempts to contact her were dwindling, so she had taken that as a sign he was getting bored of her lack of response.

Liz suddenly became aware she'd been scowling. She let her face relax and she smiled at Gerald as best she could. She hated that she'd made him paranoid – perhaps sneaking around and booking this trip had not been the best idea after all. But at least it might be the excuse she needed to ease his mind. It was still the truth after all . . . just not quite all of it.

'Hey – there's nothing to worry about. I promise you. I know I'm still a bit vacant sometimes. But we're getting there – just like you said. We're slowly getting back to being good. I'm just as frustrated as you are, but I can absolutely promise you that there's nothing wrong. If it's felt like I've been sneaking around, it's because I've been trying to organise something really special for us. Something to help us get back on track properly – that's all. I promise it's a good surprise . . . I need you to trust me on that. Okay?'

Gerald let out a heavy sigh. But it sounded like one

laced with relief more than frustration. 'Okay,' he said simply. 'I believe you. Sorry. I just want to get back to the way we were, is all. I can see you do too. I think I've just been overthinking everything. I couldn't stand to lose you, Liz. Sorry for being an idiot. I'm sure whatever you're organising will be great.'

He looked more relaxed now – clearly she had put his mind at ease. Liz felt relieved too.

'It's fine – and don't be silly, you're not an idiot. Far from it. Everything will be great. Just you wait,' Liz said, smiling at him as he moved closer to her and rested a large muscular arm around her shoulders, before engulfing her into a hug. His wet hair slightly tickled her face as he went in for a gentle kiss.

'What are we actually doing for Christmas this year anyway? Is Holly hosting again?' Gerald said, smiling at her.

'Well, you'll just have to wait and see now, won't you . . .' said Liz playfully, glad he had changed the subject, before kissing him back. It had felt like a long time since she had. It felt amazing just to breath him in for a moment and squash all the bad thoughts out of her head.

She needed to keep focussed on their trip. She was doing something wonderful for them, and it would be the beginning of the next chapter of their lives. Where she could leave all the shit from this year behind her, and they could get back on track. Back to being about her and Gerald. Back to being just about Giz.

217

Chapter 36

AGAIN . . .

It was suddenly the third week of December.

Christmas was only a few days away.

And it was suddenly absolutely freezing.

The maisonette was full of those slightly pitiful night storage heaters, which seemed to only wimpishly piss out lukewarm heat if you sat with your entire body pressed full-frontal up against them. And considering there wasn't any form of heating at all in the small bathroom between the bedrooms of their Victorian-converted home, the idea of sitting on a ring of ice with your bare bum was not an appealing one. Sometimes Molly would take a blanket with her – although that didn't seem the most hygienic solution . . . she wasn't sure she really cared.

But Molly wasn't here just because her pelvic floor wouldn't allow her to hold a wee in any longer. No – she had something else she needed to do. Another question she needed answering. A thought that had crept into her head a few days ago and wouldn't go away. And despite being freezing from the fanny down, she couldn't help but grin as the answer she'd been looking for revealed itself rather quickly in front of her . . .

Her grin quickly faded though . . . How the hell do

you tell a friend who's just lost a baby that you're pregnant?

How do you find the words, when you're at the beginning of a wonderful journey that has just ended so utterly shittily for them? How? How do you do that?

Molly stared down at the positive pregnancy test in her hands, and mixed with the elation of realising she was having another baby – her thoughts just kept returning to Liz.

How could they not? It was so hard not to think about her and everything she'd just been through. Even though Liz had kept insisting she was completely fine. It was hard to believe her – it was almost strange how well she'd dealt with everything and simply swiped it to one side as though it never happened, and thrown herself back into her work and her life. Molly was sure it still hurt, but it was impossible to get her to open up. It always had been. But that didn't mean it wouldn't hurt finding out someone else, your best friend, now had what you'd just lost . . .

Molly huffed deeply. She knew she couldn't let what Liz had going on impact how she felt about having another baby, but it was so hard not to feel for her. She knew Liz would be devastated if she thought she was affecting her friend – she'd tell both Emily and Liz later, once she'd told Tom. That was definitely the right thing to do.

Molly felt a little better. As she should – this was wonderful news. She needed to get out of the arctic bathroom and warm back up in the living room under a

blanket, so she could check on Marley and let Tom know he should hurry home tonight.

It was a Friday afternoon, so he'd be in a meeting, no doubt . . . but she wanted him to know there was exciting news waiting for him. She couldn't wait to see his face when she told him he was going to be a daddy again. It would almost certainly go about a thousand times better than it did last time, that was for sure. It was crazy how far they'd come – from that horrible dark time when Molly had fallen pregnant with Marley, and Tom just hadn't been ready to accept it. He'd left. It had been terrible. Molly hadn't known if he'd ever come back. But he did. And while it may have taken him a little while to come round to the idea of being a father, it had ultimately made them stronger. She wasn't going to dwell on the shitty past. They were a family now. And he was a wonderful, happy, doting daddy. Three were about to become four. And everything was going to be perfect. She could feel it.

Plus, she had other plans for when he got home. Plans of the more adult nature – she'd just dug the Twister board out, and had planned to put her sexiest underwear on underneath his favourite band T-shirt. He loved that. It never failed to get results . . .

She made her way back into the living room and set the pregnancy test down on the coffee table on a piece of tissue. She'd let Tom see it when he got in. He'd like that. (In a different way to the sexy pants under the Metallica tee. Obviously.)

AGAIN . . .

Marley was still fast asleep on a blanket on the carpet. Molly had propped him up with a few cushions, but he'd still managed to snuggle into a gap between them. Still – he wasn't going anywhere. He looked completely content.

A sudden grin filled her face again, as she realised her baby boy was going to be a big brother. It didn't seem possible with him still so small himself, but it was happening. She'd work the dates out properly later, but there'd only be around a year or so between them – it'd be perfect. They'd be best friends. She could already see it . . .

Molly didn't have any siblings of her own, so the idea of a little ready-made playmate only a year younger than you seemed like an amazing idea to her. And she wasn't even sure she wanted to stop there . . . the idea of a big family was so appealing to her. She remembered always feeling a little lonely growing up – watching all her friends with their brothers and sisters . . . she'd never had that. And it wasn't until she'd started her own family that she'd realised how desperate she now was to make sure they had it. She wanted a tribe.

She couldn't imagine anything more perfect that growing old with Tom, surrounded by their brood of children. She could home-school them. They could live in the countryside, maybe on a farm, maybe in a caravan – they could travel round the world together . . . or certainly South Bucks to start with. But then they could hop around as the travel business in Asia grew – sleeping on beaches, in huts and in jungle dwellings . . . perhaps they could all run it together as the children grew up – it could be so amazing!

Molly realised she was getting a bit ahead of herself. Tom's words and their money issues suddenly sprung into the front of her mind. Her dreams seemed so far out of reach again. And perhaps she should be concentrating on looking after the two small people that currently did exist – one the size of a grain of rice, just starting its journey, and the other very much on the outside now, but still so small and in need of her. She rubbed her stomach and looked lovingly down at Marley as his warm little body occasionally twitched and moved in his sleep.

Molly put any thoughts of finances and business worries out of her mind. She was so happy about being pregnant – she wanted to focus on that, although she could barely believe it was real yet. It had all happened so fast, much faster than she'd imagined, but she didn't care – it was wonderful, and she couldn't get the grin off her face. She looked up at the clock on the wall – it was almost 4 p.m. now. Not long until Tom could finish and get back to them. All of them.

Just enough time for her to get things ready – locate the T-shirt and her skimpiest (and hopefully clean) knickers, and jump in the shower to give things a bit of a celebratory trim (always sensible with a thong – side-pube overspill is not the one).

Tom didn't know it yet, but when he got home tonight, life would change again – and even though they had no money, no real plan, and Christmas was just around the corner, tonight they wouldn't think about any of that. Tonight they'd simply be happy and spend it celebrating. At least twice in the living room and once more for luck over the kitchen counter, if Molly had anything to do with it.

Chapter 37

NOOO BORK, NOOO BORK

Liz had managed to keep her surprise trip to New York a secret from Gerald for the last three weeks without much trouble at all.

She felt quite smug that he had literally no idea what was going on. She hadn't needed to lie to him – she'd simply needed to not tell the truth. Which she'd found quite easy, if she was honest, and it had distracted her nicely from all the other things she'd been feeling guilty about lately. If Christmas plans had come up in conversation she'd just changed the subject or brushed over his comments. Gerald was an only child and his parents lived abroad so there were no obligations there. And without actually saying it, she'd allowed him to think they were going to her sister's house to spend Christmas and Boxing Day with her nieces as they had done last year. Which had made her feel a little uncomfortable, but it would all be so worth it when she got to see his face when she told him. She couldn't wait for that bit.

And she really did hope the disappointment of not seeing Clover and Isla (and becoming their personal festive-toddler-ride-on toy for forty-eight hours) would be swiftly replaced with joy and surprise at what they were really doing.

The logistical parts had been fairly simple – now they lived together, she'd been able to locate his passport and sort their visas. And bearing in mind she was now one of the bosses – getting holiday time approved hadn't been an issue. The office was practically shut down for Christmas anyway.

But right now it was the day before Christmas Eve and Liz thought it was time to let the cat out of the bag. It was a Sunday afternoon, Gerald was in the lounge reading a newspaper, and sipping on fresh coffee. Liz was feeling a little less relaxed and was currently printing off the booking confirmation in the spare bedroom, willing it to go faster for fear Gerald might come looking for her at any moment.

The printer finally spat out the newly inked sheet, and Liz let her eyes flick over it one last time. She had an understated grin on her face as she pressed a little festive present bow on the top right hand corner of the paper. She felt a little surge of excitement and nerves as she suddenly began to wonder if she'd done the right thing. That was normal in this situation, right? She wasn't good with surprises herself, so honestly she had no idea . . . she certainly hoped she hadn't gone to all this trouble for him to say no . . . Oh god. What if he DID say no . . . ?

Liz decided she was being an idiot and composed herself. He would love it. Because he loved her.

She strode into the living room and sat down next to him, the paper confirmation clutched firmly in her hand, as her palms began to feel slightly clammy.

225

'Sooooo,' Liz began, letting the word roll on a little longer than usual.

Gerald finished off whatever he was reading and gave her a slightly suspicious sideways glance.

'So?' he said, smiling now and letting his newspaper sink down to his lap as he waited calmly for her response.

'You know how you've been asking me about what we're going to do for Christmas, and I've just sort of not really said anything, and kind of just let you think we'll be going to Holly and Dan's again . . . ?'

'I guess,' said Gerald, shrugging his broad shoulders a little. A slightly confused frown appearing between his eyebrows.

'Well. There's a reason for that . . .' Liz said, feeling her stomach beginning to do those fluttery little loops again. She found it strange that she felt so nervous. She wasn't used to it.

'The reason for that . . . is this,' she said, passing him the confirmation and unconsciously nibbling the side of her lip as she waited for his eyes to take in the information.

Gerald's face slowly changed from one of concentration, to one of complete shock and ended up brimming with utter joy. He didn't seem to be able to find words for a moment. It was incredibly touching, sweet and funny watching as he glanced at her, his eyes so wide they might pop out of his skull, and then back at the paper, then back at her again repeatedly.

Liz seemed to have lost the power of speech too. She

couldn't do much other than look at him and laugh. Hoping he'd talk first so she didn't have to.

'This is . . . I mean . . . I just never . . .' Gerald stuttered – letting little snippets of sentences fly out erratically as he shook his head. His frown had deepened a little. Liz was sure he still hadn't been able to blink. He finally managed to get his composure back. 'Liz, I can't believe you've done this. Thank you so much. I'm just so shocked! This is not like you at all! I can't believe you've managed to organise a trip to New York for us and I had no idea . . . this is crazy!'

Liz laughed again, more loudly this time – as much out of relief, as out of happiness that he was so happy. This definitely wasn't a no.

'I know,' she said, blotting away a few happy tears with her jumper sleeve. 'I just thought we could do with having something amazing to look forward to. And I've always wanted to go to New York at Christmas . . . and I can't imagine anyone else I'd rather do it with.'

'Ah, so you just booked what you wanted and thought you'd take me along for the ride, eh . . .' Gerald said, winking at her playfully.

'I can still go on my own, you know!' Liz said, jabbing him gently in the ribs and he grabbed her arm and pulled her in closer to him.

'You make me so happy, Liz,' Gerald said, suddenly more serious. 'I am so touched you've done this. You are a wonderful, kind, amazing person, you know . . . even if you do hide it well sometimes, with your sarcastic comments and that fringe that manages to look immaculate even when

you've just got out of bed . . . I know you're a just big softie really . . .'

'Well, I wouldn't go that far,' Liz said, laughing again, 'but I really wanted to do this for you. For us. I love you so much . . . You make me so happy too . . .'

Gerald smiled at her, his face close to hers now. He bent his head forward and planted a deep, loving kiss on her lips. It felt amazing. She felt amazing.

'So, I know you've only just found out about this, but it's probably time we got packing. We're leaving in the morning,' Liz said – the reality of their trip sinking in for the first time.

'Wow. Yes. I suppose we'd better,' Gerald responded, casually nodding, his eyes still fixed on Liz's.

'There is one thing though . . .' Liz said, holding his gaze. 'I promised Holly once I'd told you, we'd FaceTime the girls and tell them in person that Uncle Geeerraaa and Arnee Liz won't be there for Christmas this year. Holly's already said something to them, but we'd better call and say Happy Christmas now in case we don't get a chance while we're in Nooo Bork. As Clover is now calling it apparently.'

'Absolutely. I'll make sure she knows that Father Christmas will still be able to find us. Have you sent some gifts?'

'Oh yes – I ordered the whole of Amazon. Apparently it all arrived in a huge van last week and is now taking up the entire spare room AND the garage. Holly loved it. LOVED it.'

'Ah well, if you can't spoil them at Christmas, when can you? I'll miss being with them on Christmas Day but I honestly can't wait to be just me and you, in an amazing city – the skyline, Central Park, the restaurants, stunning scenery . . . Nooo Bork is going to be pretty spectacular.'

'Yes,' Liz said, breathing in deeply, feeling happy that everything seemed to be working out exactly to plan. 'Yes, it is.'

Chapter 38

#TOLLY-JOLLY CHRISTMAS

We don't need much for Christmas,
We just need you and me.
Some silly hats and last year's crackers,
And a spot on a battered settee.
We'll laugh and not care about presents.
You'll open yours, and I'll open mine.
We'll cuddle, and eat, and watch rubbish telly.
And as I'm pregnant, I'll be in bed by nine.

Molly was more than happy to keep Christmas simple this year. She preferred it, if she was honest.

It was just them, Molly's dad, their slightly beaten-up couch, and a marginally improved feast this year of Chinese duck pancakes, Molly's new pregnancy craving. Even though she'd only found out she was pregnant a few days ago and wasn't even sure it was possible to get cravings yet, that was what she was telling Tom, and he seemed to be buying it. It was Christmas after all and even Tom, the King of Soya-Alternatives could let the veganism slide for today. Whilst Molly didn't put her foot down about much, today festive pregnant girlfriends were getting what festive pregnant girlfriends wanted.

It wasn't the most conventional of Christmas Days. They couldn't all fit on the couch, so Tom was sitting on a fold-down office chair. Intermittently swapping with Molly's dad when his bum started to ache. They didn't actually have a dining table either. There was a tiny breakfast-bar area in the kitchen, but it could only fit two and didn't really feel the right setting for Christmas dinner. Especially with one of them not only newly pregnant but intermittently breastfeeding too.

So, in true festive fashion – Tom had instead got the ironing board out to rest their feast on, and the rest would be laps and balancing drinks on the little side table they had. They had a small tree up in the corner next to the TV, but they hadn't gone mad with gifts. They didn't really have any money – Molly had made and sold a few slings now, but it provided just a bit of pocket money at best, it was hardly a full-time income. And Tom's wages mostly went on bills and day-to-day living. They had nothing left of Tom's savings, and the small amount Molly had made so far was to use towards the start-up costs and their Thailand trip when it did finally happen. Costs she still kind of had no idea how they would afford right now, especially as they'd just discovered there'd be another mouth to feed in approximately nine months' time. But hey, it was nothing they couldn't handle. She was sure they'd find a way. But it did mean Christmas was a slightly frugal affair in the Tolly household this year.

231

They'd set a £20 limit on each other, decided they'd buy something small from both of them for Marley. After all – he wasn't even five months old. It's not like he knew what was going on. Molly had been sensible and picked up a bag of second-hand clothes at a nearly new sale, plus a couple of toys she'd found on eBay, which meant there was a conservative but amply festive display of presents beneath the tree.

Molly rested Marley down in his bouncer for a sleep. She felt like she could sleep herself, if she was honest. She had a stomach delightfully full of duck pancakes and hoisin sauce, and their little home was feeling unusually warm and cosy today.

'Hey. I've got something for you,' Molly's dad said, stirring her from a dozy moment.

'Oh thanks, Dad. You didn't need to get us anything. We're just happy having you here,' Molly said, fighting a yawn.

'I know,' Molly's dad said, smiling at his daughter. 'It's not really because it's Christmas . . . there's just something I want to give you. Both of you. Well. All of you really,' he added, looking down at his grandson. Molly thought his eyes looked a bit moist as she smiled back at him.

He passed her an envelope. Thinning his lips a little in anticipation of her opening it.

Molly ran her hand along the back and tore it open gently. She pulled out a card, and carefully opened it out as a piece of paper dropped into her lap. She could now see it was a cheque. She lifted it up and let her eyes scan over it.

'Dad!' Molly said, trying to suppress her voice a little as Marley stirred slightly. 'Dad, what is this? This is far too much!'

The cheque was for £1,000. Which was a huge amount of money to Molly and Tom. And a lot to her dad too.

'It's been in a rainy-day fund for a long time. Think of it as a gift from your mum too. She had a little bit in an account when she died. I decided not to touch it, unless I really needed to, so that I could give it to you one day to do something with. Use it to start your business, use it for your children. It's what she would have wanted . . . what we both want, I suppose.'

Molly couldn't help but let a few tears squeeze out of her eyes. She knew her dad didn't have a lot. None of them did. She placed the card and cheque to one side and gave her dad a huge hug.

'Thank you,' she said simply, looking at her father and feeling so much love and gratitude. It meant so much that he had done this for her.

'Thank you from all of us,' Tom added. Not wanting to step on the moment.

Molly looked up at Tom and let a slightly teary laugh out. The money would really help them. They suddenly seemed to have a lot going on . . . She was so thankful to have such wonderful people in her life. Cheesy at it sounded – even without that money, she felt like the richest girl alive right now.

233

And this Christmas was working out perfectly.

It was small, and awkward, had an ironing board as a table, and probably looked quite ridiculous to everyone else, but to them – it was perfect.

Chapter 39

THE #PEMILY FESTIVITIES

Emily had been sweating a lot, swearing a lot and stirring things. Angrily. A lot.

And was wondering exactly WHY in the name of festive FUCK she had offered to cook and host Christmas dinner at theirs this year, considering she had spent the last twenty weeks as a giant sleep-deprived emotional udder. (Which was, on the whole, contributing to her not feeling that Christmassy.)

She was mostly feeling the sweat patches forming underneath her boobs from a sparkly glitter-infused, but polyester jumper she'd bought from Primark at a weak moment, and which she was intensely regretting wearing every time she needed to breastfeed.

It was supposed to be a beautiful coming-together Christmas for both sides of the family to spend with the first grandson, but Emily had been way too ambitious. On top of that, Paul's sister had decided she now couldn't be bothered to come and would instead go and spend the day with her new boyfriend. Also Emily's own sister was working abroad and couldn't get the time off to come back, which had entirely let down the 'Auntie-front'. Although, perhaps having a few less mouths to feed wasn't

a bad idea, considering nothing was going to plan. Nothing looked the way that Pinterest had said it would look. And she was very close to checking if Deliveroo were still taking orders on Christmas Day. And serving everyone something in a crispy coating from Chicken Cottage . . .

'Are you sure I can't help you with something, sweetie? You look a bit, erm, flustered. I'm sure we don't really need all this stuff, do we?' said Paul. Wandering calmly into the kitchen looking quite annoyingly relaxed and gesturing with an empty prosecco glass towards the area formerly known as their kitchen work surfaces. He was trying to help. But realised quickly by the eye daggers Emily had just stabbed him with, that he probably wasn't. He was being a dick.

'Can you just not touch anything, please, Paul,' Emily snapped whilst still glaring at him intensely, then she quickly turned back to the task in hand, irritated by how irritated she was becoming at how much her turkey did NOT look like the one on the *Good Housekeeping* website . . . 'I'm trying to make parsnip and potato mash to create these little swirly duchess thingies and I can't find the lid to the mini food processor, and the turkey's drying out, and I haven't even started on the smoked salmon starter, and my fucking hair's dropped out, and my make-up has smudged everywhere because it's the temperature of the bastard sun in here, and everything is just totally shit. TOTALLY. SHIT.'

Emily hadn't meant to, but she'd started to cry. She

cried a slightly pathetic, snotty weep that sent loose tears cascading down her cheeks, which she wiped away with the back of her hand, trying not to let them drop into her parsnip and potato mash – or slightly squished-up lumps as it was at the moment. Parsnip and potato lumps. Parsnato . . . ? (Maybe not.) Paul had gently put a re-assuring hand on the back of her neck and was lightly massaging the tension out of it.

She was sad that she was shouting at him. It had nothing to do with him, it only had to do with her and her ridicu-lously over-ambitious plans and refusal to let anyone help. It was so frustrating that she knew that, yet still over-stretched herself every time.

'Hey – don't be upset,' Paul soothed. 'Why don't you let me help you? I can chop things. Baste things. I can see the lid of the processor there under the potato peelings for a start . . . William is having a ball being passed between the grannies. He's basically in a giant granny-love-sandwich and loving every second. The grandads are chatting. Everyone's drinks are topped up. No one is going to miss me for a while. Let me do something? Please, sweetie?'

Emily paused and turned to face him for a second. He was so right. She was already beginning to feel better. And a little stupid for getting so worked up.

'I suppose you could whip up that veg in the sink in the processor then . . .' she said, smiling at him. And wiping some parsnato out of her hair.

He nodded dutifully and got on with his task. Once

237

he'd done that, he tidied up, loaded the dishwasher, and chopped, and basted. And showed her that they were a team. And that Christmas might actually be on again, after all . . .

Emily had managed, with Paul's help, to create a quite spectacular feast. Maybe not the vision of Pinterest-perfect perfection she had in her mind's eye, but a festive spread she could be proud of, none the less.

She'd not had time to fold her napkins into swans. She'd not had time to create the sparkler-laced, floating centrepiece she wanted for the table, but she didn't really give a shit now.

She'd made an epic roast dinner – turkey, all the trimmings, a wonderful fish starter, and a healthy mix of homemade and shop-bought condiments, after her plans to make chutneys had not quite worked out . . . Five months of pandering to the needs of a child who would happily be Velcro-ed to her tits permanently had seen that off. Along with the parsnato – which was a step too far for her hormones. And was currently parsnating away alone in the bin.

But now looking at the empty plates, and the faces of her husband and their families laughing, wearing tissue-paper crowns and telling jokes that at no other time of the year anyone would find remotely amusing, yet today seemed beyond hilarious, was a wonderful sight. And right now it seemed quite ridiculous that she'd spent so long stressing about how she rolled up the smoked-salmon pieces, and that her carrots weren't cut on a perfect forty-five-degree angle . . . There was something about having a baby, and being so physically and mentally tired, that had made things that really weren't that important at all into a big deal. She could see that now. Now that she had a glass of prosecco in her hand and a belly full of Christmas dinner, she had finally begun to relax. She could barely manage to have more than two showers a week, so rolling up pieces of pink fish with lump-fish caviar and a blob of Philadelphia into perfect-pissing-parallelograms had nearly popped a blood vessel.

Emily was ready to laugh at herself now, at least. And was incredibly thankful that William had slept through the entire meal. So she'd got to sit down and actually eat a plate of food, with both hands, in real time, whilst it was hot. That in itself seemed like a Christmas-Bloody-Miracle . . . And now it was time, finally, to start opening the presents.

This had been the part she was really looking forward to. She couldn't wait to spoil her little man. He already seemed so far from the tiny scrunched-up newborn he was just a few months ago. Emily could see him changing so quickly as his chubby cheeks filled out and his body grew so much that it felt like clothes that fit him one day, were too tight only days later. Really it was quite sensible that she'd bought him everything a five-month-old baby could ever desire . . . wasn't it?

Right now it appeared all he desired was a snooze in his bouncer, while the adults filed into the snug living

room and made the most of the limited seating options around the enormous pile of gifts that engulfed half the available floor space.

As she sat herself in front of the present-mountain, Emily actually began to feel a bit silly and was starting to have that weird shopping-guilt sensation you get when you've bought that ridiculously overpriced handbag, and thought fuck it, and slung in the matching shoes too . . . except it wasn't handbags and shoes. It was at least thirty medium- to large-size gifts all with William's name on. And a partly erected Jumperoo with an enormous red bow on it, which looked like it needed its own planning permission.

It'd probably be fine, Emily thought as she began dishing out William's gifts amongst the adults so they could begin opening them for him . . . And in any case – she had new iCandy colour packs to put on her buggy in the new year, and a nifty little cup-holder to attach with its own refillable cup that would actually keep her tea hot, so frankly she was winning at not only Christmas but all of life and parenting in general.

Chapter 40

GIZ-MAS

It felt so odd being away from everyone and everything you knew on Christmas Day.

It almost didn't feel like Christmas – not in the way Liz was used to anyway.

Her and Gerald's time was actually their own – they'd had a lie in, woken up naturally rather than by a troop of tiny toddler-folk having broken into their room and jumped on the bed screaming, 'He's been, he's been!' at a time any rational human being would normally consider to be the middle of the night. They'd eaten a stunning five-star breakfast in the elegant five-star breakfast room of a hotel which looked like the setting for a movie, and now they were strolling through the streets of an enormous city at their own pace without a care in the world. It was bliss.

It was true that New York didn't ever sleep – even on Christmas morning, it seemed. Liz had been twice before, but never in the winter, and Gerald hadn't been here since a brief visit during his university days. The city buzzed and hummed with life as they strode along the wide pavements and took in the scale of it all. Christmas was prominent on every corner and down every street – the

241

shop windows were bursting with it, decorations were everywhere and if you listened, it even sounded like Christmas. America certainly did it bigger than the UK, that was for sure. There was no escaping it here – even if it felt a little over the top and commercial for most British tastes, you couldn't deny it was a sight to be marvelled at.

Liz felt the chill winter air pinch her cheeks as she walked arm in arm with Gerald. He had his iPhone out ahead of him – checking Google maps every so often to make sure they were headed the right way. New York might appear a huge concrete monster on the face of it, but its grid-based layout meant everything was easy enough to find. Liz wasn't sure she really minded getting lost anyway . . . strolling without a commitment to be at any one place at a certain time felt refreshing, something she rarely got the chance to do back at home. She couldn't remember the last time she felt so relaxed and carefree.

They'd reached Central Park now. Liz had so wanted to see it on Christmas Day. There was fresh snow all around them, the footprints on the paths were new but sparse. Some small areas had been cleared of snow, but others had been left with their soft white blanket, looking unspoilt and inviting.

Liz clutched Gerald's arm tightly as they slowly made their way into the park and padded gently down the path, their breath puffing out visibly in front of them.

Liz couldn't help but smile. Even though the cold was

biting at her teeth a little as she did so. But she didn't care – she couldn't imagine a more perfect Christmas Day. She couldn't imagine a more perfect day, full stop.

Looking back at the New York skyline and its amazing height and stillness – Liz thought how much it engulfed the sky. It was all as huge and impressive as she'd hoped. More so.

'You warm enough?' came Gerald's voice, interrupting her wandering thoughts.

'Mmmhmm,' Liz said, nodding a little. Not wanting to stop taking in the sights around her.

'Let's walk up to the little lake where the restaurant is, I like the sound of that spot,' Gerald continued.

Liz nodded again and nuzzled into his upper arm. The air was bitter and the snow was so glaringly white she needed to squint to see properly. She was very happy to have his arm to link on to. Mostly because of a bad choice of footwear in the treacherous conditions, but also because she was enjoying being near him, being in contact with him. And it feeling so comfortable again.

They continued to amble down the paths, watching their footing, before they came to the pretty lake. Which was really more of a pond, but lake sounded nicer. The restaurant was closed, but the tables remained neatly laid inside. They walked around the water, and paused for a moment as they reached the centre of a little bridge. The view was enclosed, but was so pretty.

Everything was frosted, and every branch and horizontal surface was heavy with little shelves of freshly piled snow.

Liz became aware of Gerald unlinking his arm with hers. She didn't mind. She was quite happy to lean on the wall and take in the picture-perfect scene in front of her.

'Liz?' Gerald's voice had lost its usual relaxed tone.

Liz turned to face him straight away. Finding him directly behind her. Below her, in fact. Bent on one knee . . .

Liz took a sharp intake of breath. Felt her heartbeat quicken. She felt momentarily frozen. Confused by what was going on, even though really – she knew exactly what was happening . . .

'Liz,' Gerald repeated, more firmly this time. Intent on getting his words right. 'I can't imagine a more perfect moment than this one. I can't imagine anyone more perfect than you. We've been through so much already . . . I don't want to waste any more time. I love you, Elizabeth Milligan. Would you . . . would you make me the happiest man alive, and do me the great honour, here in New York, in our own perfect Christmas Day wonderland, of agreeing to become my wife . . . ?'

Liz could no longer feel the cold. She felt her blood pumping hard under her skin across her entire body. But she knew what she was going to say. She'd known it from the moment she'd spun around and seen him down on one knee. If she could just find the power of speech again to actually tell him . . .

'Yes,' she blurted suddenly. Feeling the need to laugh and cry at the same time, as she felt an intense rush of emotion and happiness.

'Yes of course I will, Gerald. I love you too.'

Chapter 41

WHAT LIZ SAID

Liz
Ladies? Are you there?
Are you awake?
HAPPY CHRISTMAS
Sorry if it's a bit late! I just had to
contact you RIGHT NOW!!!

Molly
Hey. Happy Christmas! I'm still up.
In a kind of duck-based coma, but I'm
still just about
awake.
What's up?
Everything okay??

Emily
Hey you guys. Happy Christmas to
you both too!
Been meaning to text all day, but
literally been working my tits off to
create the CHRISTMAS
EXTRAVAGANZA OF THE DECADE.
Although I've mostly been sat around

eating Quality Street for the last hour,
so still winning.
(and by that I mean I've eaten all the
purple, green, and toffee ones)
What's going on Liz?
SPILL!

Liz

Well – I couldn't wait any longer to tell
you!
And I know we've sort of been here
before but . . .
GERALD PROPOSED.
AND I SAID YES!!!

Emily

OH MY GOD!!!
That's so amazing!!
I'm so so happy for you x
It must have been so romantic.
Please tell me about it immediately!
(I'm just milking myself into a bottle so
Paul can feed William in a bit. But you
can pretend I didn't say that if it's
ruining the moment . . . lol)

Molly

I'm so happy for you Liz!
It's not a massive surprise though –
you guys are perfect for each other.

247

Always have been.
So made up for you xxx

Liz
Thank you!
I'm smiling like a lunatic!
(Even with the mental image of Emily
milking herself . . .)
I don't think I've ever been happier.
And yes – it was so romantic.
I never thought I'd go in for all that
but it was like a film. Honestly. I had
no idea he was going to do it! Think
that's what made it so amazing!
We were walking through Central Park
in the snow, and we reached this
lovely spot, and there he was on one
knee . . .

Emily
Wow. That is literally the dream . . .
I'm actually crying just reading it!
Couldn't be more happy for two more
wonderful people.
Love you both! So so much!

Molly
Has Gerald been created in a lab? I
swear he is actually the perfect man.
And he also lets you eat meat

whenever you want. Sigh . . . Lol x
But so happy for you – welling up
here too.

Emily

I want the full story when you get
back!
DO NOT SKIMP ON THE DETAILS.
Can you send us a picture of the
ring?

Liz

Ha ha x you guys make me laugh so
much!
Thank you xxx
I'll tell all in great detail I promise.
We're going to choose the ring
together while we're out here.
I know some girls wouldn't like that –
but I love it. I want us to choose it
together x
I've got to wear it for the rest of my
life after all!

Molly

Well actually as we're all here sharing
news – I've got some too.
Wasn't sure whether to say something
but it feels weird not to, and I hate
keeping anything from you ladies you

249

know that. It's just with you being
away Liz, and it's Christmas and all
that. You know. There's not really
been the right moment and all that.

Emily
Spit it out lady! What is it?

Molly
OK! Here goes. I'm pregnant again. It
was a bit of a shock, but it's definitely
happening! All the tests say positive!

Emily
Wow that's amazing!
Huge congrats!
What an awesome Christmas present
for you guys xx so happy for you xxx

Molly
Thank you!
I know it's probably a bit hard to read
Liz, but I couldn't not tell you. I
wanted to wait until you got back but I
just couldn't hold it in any longer.

Liz
Don't be ridiculous.
I'm over the moon for you!
I don't ever want you to feel like you
can't tell me anything. It's just a

double celebration now! Huge
congrats to you, Tom & Marley xxx
Anyway – I've got to go ladies. New
York calls.
Hope you've had wonderful
Christmases!
Love to the boys and the babies xxx
See you soon!

Emily
And to you!!
Love to Gerald too!
GIZ IS OFFICIAL NOW.
#GIZFOREVER
xxx

Molly
And tell him well done on finally
getting you to say yes!
#Gizforever
xxx

Chapter 42

NEW YEAR, NEW JUMPEROO

All hail the magical Jumperoo,
The mystical ring of neglect(-eroo).
The giver of time, the taker of stress,
Circumference of confinement that creates no mess.
It traps all the babies with its rainforest joys,
Fuck knows why I bothered with any other toys!
It lets you sit down, use both hands, and
    pretend,
You've got your shit together, Jumperoo's your best
    friend.
Who cares if it takes up more space than your settee,
When you get to drink an ACTUAL REAL-LIFE HOT
    CUP OF TEA.
Yes, all hail the wonderful Jumperoo.
Respect it or fall victim to the Jumper-poo.
Love it and cherish your infant-restraining device,
Knowing the Jumperoo SAVED YOUR LIFE.

There'd been no swanky New Year's Eve party this year. No canapés and endless bottles of champagne and party poppers, and certainly no chance of Tom and Molly showing up with another 'Unexpected Dale', or any unexpected guests whom they planned to set Liz up with . . . How things had changed.

It was crazy to think that a year ago, on New Year's Eve, Emily was pregnant, Molly was, quite literally, finding out she was pregnant in her bathroom a few moments before midnight, and Liz had just got out of a terrible relationship and was flirting away with Unexpected Dale and his bizarre face tattoos . . . It was fair to say that Molly's taste in men wasn't quite on the same level as Liz's, but if a shameless bit of flirting with a thirty-year-old man who lived in his parents' garage and whose job was being in a band, by himself, made her feel good, then hey, no harm done.

Everyone, including Molly, was very happy that Unexpected Dale had made a swift exit that night, and within a few months Gerald was on the scene and Liz had never had to look back.

Emily smiled as she reminisced about the year past and was glad that for once she had actually listened to Paul and decided that this New Year was not about glitz and glam and trying to impress anyone. Christmas had been amazing, but stressful, and messy, and hard work, if she was honest. She was more than ready for this New Year's Eve to be about comfy clothes, a posh bottle of champagne, some Christmas leftovers and a night on the sofa with her wonderful husband and son. If they lasted until midnight they'd toast in the New Year with some fizz, if they didn't (and to be honest, right now Emily would be quite happy passing out at about 10 p.m. with

253

a prawn spring roll and a bit of Toblerone stuck in her face) then it really didn't matter. It felt wonderful to not have to spend her night feeling the need to impress anyone.

She was so happy for her friends – Molly was having another baby next year, Liz had said yes to marrying Gerald and had all the fun of planning a wedding in the coming months. They had so much going on . . .

For a moment, she began to wonder what she had going on? It was hard not to. She was due to return to work in June at the latest. That sounded so far away but bearing in mind how fast the first six months of maternity leave had gone, it would flash by. She wasn't sure if that made her happy or sad . . . one part of her longed to get back to 'normal'. Get stuck back into her career again and have a purpose other than just being 'Mummy'. But then another part of her couldn't imagine not being with William, leaving him with someone else every day, and also how she'd ever wear heels again . . . Even thinking about returning to working life began to give her uncomfortable feelings, even though she knew she couldn't avoid thinking about it for ever.

But she wasn't ready to think about it right now.

She had a blog post ready to go up, and she was actually really looking forward to a night of snuggling in her PJs with her boys.

MONDAY 31 DECEMBER

Realistic Resolutions for Knackered Mums & Dads

Christmas is dead.

And now, the depression of January with its lack of Quality Street breakfasts and 'dryness' of alcohol looms. Stupid sober bastard boring sober January.

So, for all the owners of tiny folk out there – here's my list of realistic New Year Resolutions for you all to enjoy with your last glass of guilt-free festive-fizz. (Until February that is. Obvs.)

1. Go on social media less. Okay – only whilst drunk. All right – don't actually post anything, turn all your settings to private and pretend you're not on Facebook whilst stalking everyone and laughing at their lives while you cry into some tofu. (But the drunk thing still stands.)

2. Buy a Spiralizer. And then Spiralize your own fucking face off for actually using the word Spiralizer. Then put it at the back of the cupboard with the juicer, the smoothie maker, the soup machine, all the pencils, batteries and

255

hairgrips, as well as the last dying memories of your pre-natal vagina.

3. Shout at your husband less. Then remember you EARNED THAT GODDAMN RIGHT WHEN HE STUCK A BABY IN YOU WHICH THEN TOBOGGANED THROUGH YOUR CERVIX AFTER MAKING YOU CLINICALLY OBESE FOR 9-MONTHS (or something).

4. You will not wear leggings every day. Okay. You will not wear the same leggings every day. All right. You will only wear the same leggings for three days and you will Febreeze your fanny in between. Win.

5. Go to sleep an hour earlier . . . by cutting out all non-essential tasks like eating, washing, dressing, undressing and balancing at least twelve mouldy, grey, almost-full cups of congealing tea on your side table in the lounge. Also – what's sleeping . . .?

6. Never go to bed on an argument . . . So . . . never actually go to bed then . . .?!

7. Leave only positive people in your life and cut out the twats. Or see point 1 and just secretly Facebook-stalk them. Only resurface if you

think it'll result in an invite to a wedding. As you plan on attending simply to look fabulous (and drink all the alcohol whilst judging them).

8. Take more time for yourself . . .
   Ahahahahahahahahahahahahahahahahahahahah ahahahaha.

9. Stop writing blog posts under the influence of an entire tub of festive Mini Cheddars washed down with an entire tub of wine . . . Shit.

Happy New Year Parent People!

Emily x

Chapter 43

MOLLY SAY, LIZ I DO

Molly

Happy New Year Bitttcchhhheessss!
I know it's 9.37 p.m. . . . but as I'm
newly pregnant, Liz is being all
swanky and romantic and eating
pastrami with her highly attractive
FIANCE in a different time zone,
and Emily is absolutely no doubt
throat deep into a Toblerone whilst
breastfeeding the eternally hungry
William – I just wanted to say I
LOVE YOU.
This will be our year ladies!
We can do anything.
We can do everything.
We're pretty much like the Justice
League. But with less lycra, more
boobs and way better super powers.

Emily

Okay firstly . . . Toblerone – guilty.
(Obvs)

And if you're counting super powers
as two of us being able to keep
actual human beings alive with only
our tits (and for me just the
occasional formula top
up ;))
Then yes.
100% we are totally like the Justice
League.
Way better in fact.
And Liz is our wing-woman.
She's there to awesome lawyer the
fuck out of life with her case-winning
vagina!
(or something)
We're pretty formidable to be fair.

Liz
Well I'm not sure I've had my legal
career described in quite that way
before but thanks . . . I think!
Happy New Year you two wonderful
women. Couldn't be prouder to call
you my best friends.

Emily
I think you'll find we're your joint maid
of honour best friends . . . right?!
wink wink nudge nudge

Liz

Well you don't beat about the bush do you Emily!

We haven't even begun to make any decisions yet. It hasn't even sunk in that I'm engaged tbh! Apart from this big fat diamond which I'm absolutely looking forward to flicking around smugly at every opportunity when I get back – obviously.

But OF COURSE if we do the whole big wedding thing then you guys will be a big part of it. Okay?

Emily

What do mean 'if'?

How could you NOT do the big white wedding thing! You only get to do it once – (hopefully) so make the most!

GO CRAZY I SAY.

You'd better come down the aisle riding a unicorn shitting glitter or I'M NOT EVEN COMING.

(Just kidding please don't un-maid-of-honour-me)

And I cannot wait to see the ring in person!

Molly

Give the girl a break Emily! Jeez!

We're happy for you whatever sort of
wedding you have lady. Even if you
disappear off to an exotic beach and
get married alone on the sand . . .
so long as you skype us in later,
we'll be there with you in spirit
anyway xx

Liz

That's so sweet. Thanks ladies. I
honestly haven't even had a chance
to think about it. I just want to enjoy
being engaged and sort that out when
I have the headspace.
Look – I've got to go.
Hope you're feeling okay still Molly.
Can't wait to see you both when I get
back!
Happy New Year you two beautiful
ones!
I will see you next year! Literally!

Emily

You too. Thanks for making me sick
with jealously again btw! Bet you're
about to swan off to some gallery
and eat sushi. I'm going to get back
to leaking breast milk in two big
round patches on to the inside of
my new fleecy pyjamas and not

261

giving a shit about it. Lol x
Happy New Year ladies!
Love you both so much xxx

Molly
Happy New Year x
Love you both too xxx

Chapter 44

OFFICIALLY #GIZ

Liz had spent quite a lot of the morning twisting her hand one way then the other. Watching as the diamond in her engagement ring caught the light, and admiring the way it looked on her hand.

The ring that she and Gerald had picked in New York was stunning. A simple platinum band, with one large emerald-cut diamond, so clear and icy it almost didn't look real. It was elegant and classy. Not overwhelmingly huge and bling-y, but big, beautiful and sparkly enough to capture attention. Liz was utterly in love with it.

She had never imagined this would happen to her. And certainly never imagined she'd be that gushing girl, ring on her finger, planning a wedding, and actually being excited about what the future held.

They'd made no big announcement, they'd told her closest friends and family straight away, but she certainly wasn't one for pasting news on social media or barking her personal business around the office. She had no doubt that people at work had begun to notice anyway. Office gossip spread faster than wildfire in her experience. But this time she didn't care who knew. There's no shame or embarrassment in letting Pauline from floor three, who

263

makes terrible cups of tea that are somehow the colour of hummus and have bubbles in them, see your huge Tiffany engagement ring as she passes you the file for the Jenkins case now is there . . . ? It was somewhat satisfying seeing the slightly stunned look on Pauline's face as she glimpsed the big rock on Liz's hand. Yes, Pauline, breathe it in. Stuck-Up-Elizabeth-Milligan with the impeccable fringe, good shoes and red lipstick is getting married. Yes. Someone actually wants to marry me. ME. MEEEEEEEEEEEEEEE.

The feeling was almost euphoric. Liz was positive that it was beaming out from her, just as she could see it beaming from Gerald.

It was probably the first time most people had seen Liz crack a smile in the office. But for the first time in a long time, she just couldn't help herself. She was happy. And excited about the future. And it was impossible to hide.

It was already the second week of January, it was crazy how busy she'd been at work, and how rapidly the days seemed to be sucked away, but she was pleased to see it flying by. Last year felt like a distant memory already. It was amazing how long ago Christmas, the proposal, New York, everything, felt, when it had been only three weeks ago.

She wasn't sure she minded anyway. Just like Molly said – this year really was going to be her year. She'd settled into her new role at work now, she and Gerald were stronger than ever, and she now had a wedding to plan. Who would have thought it? Lizzie with the good hair, the girl who put her career above everything, the girl who swore she never needed anyone or anything, was getting MARRIED.

Liz sighed happily and allowed herself another ring-ogling moment.

She felt bad she hadn't yet seen Molly and Emily this year but after spending Christmas away, the last couple of weekends had been dedicated to visiting family. And the weekdays were packed with work. They'd messaged each other of course, but she really couldn't wait to meet up for the first Last Saturday Club of the year in a couple of weeks.

As much as she never thought she'd be 'that girl', she honestly couldn't wait to see her friends, hug them, show off her ring and re-tell the engagement story for them in person, as demanded by Emily continually, possibly even daily, since they'd arrived back from New York.

'You ready to go?' came Gerald's familiar voice, as he leaned his broad frame against the doorframe of her office, interrupting her wandering thoughts.

'Almost,' Liz said, her voice muffled as she held a pen between pursed lips and raced to finish off the last few emails of the day.

'Hey – you're the boss,' Gerald jested. Although it was clear he was keen to go and leave work behind him for the weekend. They'd both been flat out since returning after Christmas. Friday evening, and the prospect of a lazy weekend on the couch, flicking through wedding magazines and absolutely not venturing out into the

265

freezing wet January weather, was a very welcome prospect.

Liz took the pen from her mouth, and pressed a quite triumphant 'send' button, whilst swiping her notepad shut and quickly replacing a few bits of paperwork into files on her desk. 'That's it! I'm done! We can go,' she said, shutting her computer down.

Liz picked up her coat and bag and strode out next to Gerald. As they walked down the corridor together, she allowed herself to place her hand into his and intertwine her fingers with his.

It seemed crazy, but this was the first time she'd allowed herself to publicly display any kind of affection for him at work. For so long the façade had mattered so much that they'd been leading almost double lives, leaving any emotions at the front door as they left for work together, and communicating only as colleagues until they left again in the evening. But now, the line seemed quite happily blurred.

Liz decided hand-holding wasn't exactly risqué; it wasn't the fifties, and she was hardly about to get caught with her knickers round her ankles in a compromising position with her fiancé in the photocopy room. That was probably more Molly's style than hers!

No. She and Gerald were the real deal. They were engaged. They were going to get married and start a family at some point. Avoiding eye contact and deliberately not sitting next to him in board meetings seemed a bit pathetic now.

Liz tightened her grip on his fingers and smiled up at him as they reached the lift. He smiled back, releasing his hand momentarily to press the lift call, then swiftly replacing it around hers as they waited together amongst a few colleagues, grinning at each other like a pair of loved-up teenagers.

Chapter 45

TOLLY TAKE TWO

A bump and a tiny baby
At the same time . . .
Oh hey, it'll be easy!
Well it'll probably be fine*.

(*It probably won't)

Molly turned the key in the door and heaved herself into the flat. Everything ached, and she felt completely exhausted.

Why on earth she'd decided to walk the entire way to Tesco in the rain in late January with a baby strapped to her front, to pick up 'a few bits' that had become two rather large and heavy shopping bags and a new shower head bought on impulse, she didn't know. It had seemed like a good idea at the time . . .

This was the first time she'd become aware of the exhaustion that comes with early pregnancy. She couldn't remember feeling it with Marley – but then being pregnant when you already have a baby to look after is knackering in itself. Her body felt so heavy – just putting one foot in front of the other felt like such hard work – that by the time she'd walked back home, her legs were like lead. The shower head was way heavier than it looked . . .

But having now finally made it the twenty-minute walk back to the flat (which had actually taken about forty minutes with two bags-for-life cutting painfully into the grooves of her fingers), with Marley now very much awake and wondering why the hell he didn't have a nipple in his mouth, she was very ready to sit down and not have to put shopping away, or do anything that wasn't just sitting down.

She hadn't noticed as she'd walked in, but now the bags were on the floor at her feet and she was taking a few moments to stretch out her back and tend to Marley, it occurred to her that something seemed different.

She slowly became aware that the lights were on, and there were noises and smells wafting towards her. It was 4 p.m. on a Friday, Tom shouldn't be home yet but she was sure she could hear music, and smell something quite wonderful (and quite possibly non-vegan for once, thank fuck) wafting towards her from the kitchen.

Molly left the bags where they were and headed towards the tiny kitchen off the lounge, where she was instantly presented with the back of Tom's thick jet-black hair in front of her. Molly didn't know how, but even the back of his head was highly attractive.

'Hi . . .' Molly said, with a friendly note of confusion in her voice as Tom spun around slightly startled, before planting a few soft kisses on his son and his girlfriend in turn.

269

'Hey,' he said smoothly. With it sounding much more suggestive to Molly than he had probably meant it to be. She guessed that was the pregnancy hormones returning . . . not that she needed any hormonal help to want to rip Tom's clothes off. Although, that was probably not advisable with her infant son, who was becoming increasingly impatient for a feed, still strapped to her boobs.

'I wasn't expecting you home yet. Or this . . .' Molly said, gently frowning and letting her eyes flick around the kitchen surfaces for a moment at the pots and pans, and things that were being chopped and prepared, as she begun unwrapping a now mildly irritable Marley from her front.

Tom threw her an inviting smile.

'I wanted to surprise you. We never did this last time . . .' he said, nodding his head down to a now-visible Marley. 'Well, you know – I never let us do this last time because I was an idiot. But having now become very much a non-idiot – I'm giving us the baby celebration we should have had last time, this time. If that makes sense.'

'Oh right,' Molly said, allowing a broad smile to spread across her lips, trying not to re-visit the memories of how her first pregnancy announcement had gone down when she'd discovered she was expecting Marley.

She'd blocked that out since it had happened and she avoided giving much thought to it at all. Tom had freaked out. He'd left. She'd thought she might never see him again and it had been a terrible time; definitely not something she ever wanted to think about or go through again.

But now she knew she wouldn't ever have to. He wasn't going anywhere. She trusted him entirely. He was a wonderful father, a wonderful partner, and had even put up with her turning the entire flat into a festive-jumble-sale-cum-sweatshop for the last couple of months. Not many people would have put up with that, especially given she'd only made about £200 in profit for her efforts so far . . . She'd worked so hard, and had so wanted to prove to Tom that she could turn things around, but the truth was she would have made more money if she'd temped for a day, and it certainly would have been less stressful.

It was lucky that he loved her – festive eBay tat and all. And she loved him. And it helped really quite a lot that they could barely keep their hands off each other. Which, to be fair, was exactly what had landed them with bump number two a little earlier than either of them expected . . .

'Well, please carry on then. I need to feed this little man before he chews my hand off!' Molly called back as she stepped into the lounge and finally freed a now fairly desperate Marley from his sling-based-prison.

'Go for it. I'll bring you some water and a snack,' Tom called after her.

'And there's a load of shopping in the hall. Sorry. I couldn't carry it any further. It's mostly non-fridge stuff anyway,' Molly said, organising herself on the sofa, and beginning to feed her son.

'No worries,' said Tom casually, filling a glass of water from the tap, and placing it and a little tray of parsnip

crisps next to her, and planting another kiss on her fore-head.

'I'll sort it. I'll sort everything. You just sit there and feed our baby. Both our babies . . . technically.' His voice was laced with pride. Molly loved that.

'And is that something non-vegan I can smell . . . ?' Molly said, trying not to sound too hopeful.

'Not quite. I found this amazing place near the office that does these incredible mushrooms . . . they're huge, and really do taste like meat if you stick them in a curry. Loads of texture. And a few cubes of tofu to bulk it out . . . you won't even notice the difference!'

'I fucking will,' Molly said, laughing. Or just about.

Tom laughed too. 'Well. It's only the best for my little tribe. You'll love it, trust me. They're an aphrodisiac apparently too . . . so later on . . . you might just get lucky . . .'

'Wow. Mushroom curry and a shag before *The Crystal Maze* starts – you seriously do know how to make a girl feel lucky on a Friday night, don't you.'

'Well, before any of that I think it's time we sat down and discussed exactly where we are with our finances,' Tom said, his voice suddenly a little more serious.

Molly groaned a little. She couldn't think of anything worse, although she knew this conversation had to happen sooner or later.

'Okay,' she managed unconvincingly, as Marley relaxed into her, and she felt him beginning to drift off into a milky-slumber.

'I've made some notes, jotted down the projections –
but I think we need to look at what you've projected for
business costs and decide how best to use your dad's
money. And we should definitely agree absolutely no
spending outside of the plan – okay Molly?' Tom's voice
was stern and direct.

Molly could only nod. It felt like Tom was taking over.
She knew she only had herself to blame for that, but as
he pulled out figures and facts and used words she wasn't
even sure she knew the meaning of, she began to feel like
she was being lectured.

She tried her best to listen, but the gist of it really was
that they had only a fraction of the capital they needed,
and for the meantime she was to leave the money her dad
had given them well alone. She felt a little patronised that
Tom would think she'd make the same mistake so quickly
again anyway. Even she had to concede she'd learnt her
lesson. For now at least.

She felt tired again. And hungry. Right now, she was
more interested in getting stuck into her dinner, before
getting stuck into Tom – anything to stop him from talking
to her any longer about calculated risk, and profit-and-
loss schedules . . .

273

Chapter 46

THE FIRST OF MANY

At first, Emily just hugged and hugged them both.

Then she'd look at Liz's ring, and then at Molly's stomach, and then cry a bit. Then the hugging would recommence.

Both Liz and Molly knew it was easiest to just let her get on with it. Emily was a gusher. Unashamedly. She could gush professionally. It was one of her main skills.

'I'm just so happy for you both!' Emily managed between slightly snotty sobs. Finally breaking her embrace and taking a seat.

They'd met at the little coffee shop off High Wycombe high street, as they often did, for the first Last Saturday Club of the year. The weather was positively yucky outside and there weren't that many people around on a dreary January morning, but they had cake, hot drinks, currently sleeping infants and more than enough to catch up on.

'That ring is nothing short of spectacular, Liz. Seriously. It's beautiful. You are one lucky lady. Although, Gerald is even luckier in my opinion of course,' Emily said, dabbing her eyes and seemingly having herself back under control as the fresh tears stopped.

'Thank you, sweetie. We're lucky to have each other.

I'm just so happy I booked that trip! I think it did us the world of good. I feel like a new person, I really do. I'm a bit worried that I now have an actual real-life wedding to plan though. I'm not sure when exactly I'm going to have time to do that . . . I'm completely rammed at work and if I'm honest, I have no idea where to start! Perhaps I'll just leave most of it up to Gerald. I think he's probably better at that sort of stuff than me anyway,' Liz said, wondering if that could actually be the best course of action.

'What? You can't do that! What about the cake, the flowers, the dress, the venue you've been picturing yourself in, walking down the aisle of, since you were a little girl . . .' Emily said, looking quite genuinely horrified.

'Well – I guess I haven't ever really done any of that. I didn't even think I'd get married until I met Gerald. I want to now, of course I do, but I'm just not one of those women who's got it all planned out obsessively. I wasn't ever that bothered about marriage – if you're not religious it's just a piece of paper and a party, isn't it? I think Gerald is more bothered about it than me,' Liz said calmly as Emily's face continued to emit her feelings of horror.

'Hey – I'm sure whatever you do it'll be wonderful, Liz,' Molly interjected whilst Emily composed herself. 'I totally understand that feeling – I'm not bothered either, to be honest. Reckon Tom and I will wait until our kids are older and run off to some beach somewhere . . . certainly wouldn't go in for the big white wedding with all the formal stuff. You should just do whatever you both

want. Besides – Emily's probably created you a sequence of animated mood boards and a PowerPoint presentation by now . . . it's been over a month, after all!'

Liz and Molly laughed. Emily didn't. She managed a weak smile and decided that perhaps now wasn't the time to start showing Liz the Pinterest boards she'd been collating for her . . . probably best left for another time . . .

'Well, actually, I agree,' Emily said, realising she had been coming on a little strong. 'You should totally make it about you. And if you're worried about researching it all, we can help you! Or I certainly can, I've got plenty of time during feeds and baby classes where I can begin creating mood boards for you.' Emily winked at Liz. She wasn't completely above taking the piss out of herself. She knew who she was.

Liz paused before answering – she needed to be careful not to commit to something here, or before she knew it, it would be Emily's wedding . . . 'Well . . . Thank you. At some point I could definitely do with your advice, but I think Gerald and I need to first decide what, when, and where we're going to do this. I definitely don't want anything big. Just something understated. A nice country pub perhaps, close friends, nice garden . . . honestly. I think low-key is the way forward. I'm not even sure I want to wear an actual wedding dress. I like the idea of wearing blue or yellow or something . . . I don't know. It's hard to know where to start, isn't it.'

'Don't worry – I'll lend you my wedding spreadsheet,' Emily said competently, getting her phone out, and tapping into her Hotmail account as though it was the most normal thing in the world to have it readily available on email.

'Okay . . . thanks,' Liz said. Knowing she'd be getting a copy of the spreadsheet whether she liked it or not.

'And how are you, how've the last few weeks been?' Liz continued, turning to Molly. Not wanting to hog the limelight with her news.

'Oh, not too bad,' Molly said, suddenly looking a little defeated, which was not normal for her. 'I'm definitely feeling more tired already. I don't know if that's normal with a second pregnancy, but I'm having a mid-afternoon nap every day at the moment! Which means I'm getting a bit behind on making my feeding cloths and stuff, but I'm just so shattered. If I'm honest, I'm a bit worried I've bitten off more than I can chew. The Christmas stuff didn't make that much money, and we've still only got about half the cash we need to fund the business, and most of that is thanks to my dad. Plus, instead of getting on with the stuff that can actually make us money, I'm passing out on the sofa most days. I seriously hope this passes by the next trimester!'

'Hey, you can't beat yourself up. If your body is telling you to rest – you've got to do it,' Emily said, reaching out and stroking her friend's arm to comfort her. It was unusual to see Molly rattled this way. 'And this is coming from a woman who threw up almost every day of her first two trimesters and became the width of a sofa. So, trust me. I know that when your body wants to do something while

277

you're pregnant, it's going to do it regardless. And that includes indulging in all carb groups. Obvs.'

'Ha. She's right,' Liz said reassuringly. 'Give yourself time to rest and do what you can. You've got a little person in there that needs you to be strong. That's what matters.'

Molly nodded and allowed herself to smile a little. Clearly her friends' pep talk had helped. 'And what about you?' Molly said, nodding her head at Emily. 'Any more thoughts about work stuff? Have you spoken to your boss now?'

'Actually yes,' Emily said, taking a sip of her coffee and placing it back down in front of her. 'I emailed Natalie after the Christmas break – it had been bugging me so much, and we've decided I'm going in for a keeping-in-touch day next week hopefully. It's nothing major – I just feel a bit lost, like I'm losing touch with my career and all that. I think I need to go back in for the odd day here and there just to remind myself I've still got it, if you know what I mean. Or to discover that I haven't and decide what I want to do next . . . I don't know. I do know that I want to take the full year off either way. And if I'm honest I am totally paranoid that that bitch Matilda will have stolen all my accounts and sabotaged my career prospects. I need to get back in there just to check how much of a dick she's been the last six months in my absence!'

'I'm sure nothing like that's been going on, Emily,' Liz said reassuringly. 'But I totally understand you wanting to keep a handle on things. That's natural. You're good at your job and you give a shit. You can't completely turn that stuff off. I think it's a really sensible idea.'

'Me too,' Molly added. 'You'll probably really enjoy it. And either way you get a bit of a day off from being a mum, don't you? Who's looking after William? How are you going to cope with the feeding and stuff?'

'My mum and Paul are taking him. I haven't worked the exact details out yet. And I'm a bit worried as we've never spent more than a couple of hours apart before – I have no idea how it's going to go! I might take him in to meet everyone first thing, then get Paul to pick him up. My mum will probably take over at lunchtime and bring him for a boob feed if he needs it, and the rest will be bottles. He takes formula fine now, so I don't need to panic about her running out of expressed milk or anything. I do feel weirdly nervous about the whole thing, though.'

'You'll be fine,' Molly replied. 'You're probably just building it up in your head – once you're there, it'll be great. You'll see.'

'I hope so . . .' Emily said, trying not to think too hard about Matilda's twatty annoying face and how shiny-haired and not-at-all-exhausted her maternity cover, Charlotte, had looked last time she saw her. 'I really do hope so.'

Chapter 47

DECISIONS, DECISIONS

Emily

Are you awake?

Ladies?

I know it's gone midnight but I'm panicking!!

I'm due to go into work tomorrow for the day and can't find anything to wear!

Seriously. NONE of my old work clothes fit.

They're all a size 10.

I can't believe I ever used to think I was fat. I was tiny. I actually went in at the waist. WHY DID I TAKE THIS FOR GRANTED?

All my pencil skirts and trousers are ridiculously fitted. The only way I'd get away with it, is if I wore one black skirt on each leg and coloured my vagina in with a fucking sharpie.

And don't even get me started on wearing heels.

Oh GODDDDD this is terrible!
Why have I left it until the last minute.
I haven't got time to buy anything.
Please help!
Girls??!!
I can't wear my maternity stuff.
Can I?
Oh God. What's happened to me?
I used to love wearing nice stuff.
Reckon I've lived in manky leggings
and feeding tops since W was born. I
don't even wash them that often. I just
sniff the pile of clothes by the bed and
put on whatever doesn't have chunks
on it/doesn't smell too bad . . .
I CANNOT GO TO WORK SMELLING
LIKE A USED FOOT.
The only thing I can think is to wear
one of my black maternity dresses
with a belt and try to not to walk too
far.
This is so depressing.
Ladies . . .? LADIES!!!??

Chapter 48

TWATTY MATILDA AND THE KEEPING-IN-TOUCH DAY

February was supposed to be a little less dark and dreary than January, but right now, at 9.05 in the morning on her first keeping-in-touch day at work, Emily felt nothing but dark and dreary.

The office of Angel Public Relations looked the same yet different. Like when you revisit somewhere you once went on holiday, or visited as a child, and the proportions seem off . . . It all felt a bit odd. It didn't help that the weather was depressingly miserable and really quite twatty – which was ironic really, as it was exactly how Matilda's face looked to Emily right now as she looked at it for the first time in over six months. It was just as irritatingly smug as Emily remembered. Possibly even more so . . . and seeing Charlotte, her maternity cover, sitting at her desk was like a stab in the stomach. She looked great. Her hair was just so fucking shiny. It might have been her hormones and several months without sleep, but Emily began to feel weirdly territorial. The little pen pot she had placed to the side of her Mac screen had disappeared. And for some reason Charlotte had shifted her out-tray from the left-hand side to the right-hand side of the desk

– which made absolutely no sense at all. WAS SHE COMPLETELY MENTAL?

Emily realised it probably wasn't a good idea to voice her concerns about Charlotte's out-tray placement. She was maybe overreacting ever so slightly about the whole thing, to be honest – but she'd barely slept in the last two days. Mostly because of the human milk vampire she had intermittently stuck to one breast throughout the night, but also because she was so desperately nervous about re-visiting her old life . . . It was strange, she felt so out of touch with it. She was simultaneously desperate to run in and reclaim her desk and out-tray screaming 'It's mine, you bitch, and what have you done with my little pen pot? It's all mine, MINE, MINE!!!', and also to get the hell out of there, back to her Hobnob-laden sofa-pit, vowing never to return . . . It was hard to explain.

Clearly, right now she wasn't going to do either. It was the second week of February. It was freezing. And she'd got out of bed at 5.47 a.m. just to begin applying copious amounts of exhaustion-covering make-up, because it somehow seemed so important to look like she had her shit together, even though she felt like she absolutely didn't right now – she was not going to waste this much contouring effort for nothing.

She'd brought William into work for the first half-hour and then Paul would pick him up and take him for the rest of the day. He was owed a few days in lieu, so it had worked out well. Natalie, her managing director, had insisted she bring William in; she wanted to meet the little

man and thought it'd be a nice distraction for the office for a while.

Emily had probably changed his outfit at least twenty times. Twice because he'd thrown up on it, and the other eighteen because she just wanted him to look his absolute best. She wanted to show everyone how amazing he was. And how amazing she was. Even though inside she felt like a barely functioning pile of flesh – held together by Berocca, Toblerone and an unhealthy addiction to Pinterest – whose breasts were clearly no longer made for under-wired bras.

Emily looked on as a little crowd formed around her and her son, and various colleagues came for a cuddle with William and to ask her how new motherhood was. She smiled and watched carefully as he was held for a few moments by each of them, suppressing the urge to tell them they were doing it wrong, or to step in like some strange overprotective mother and grab him back. She was not enjoying the way Brian from Accounting was holding him like a brick. She was keen for Paul to arrive soon.

'So how old is he now? Is he sleeping through yet?' Matilda mused, clearly not that interested in the answers, whilst gently taking William from the last person and cradling him slightly awkwardly in her arms. It was like she was trying to hold him without getting any of him on her cashmere cardigan.

'He's six months now. And no. Unfortunately it looks like he's not going to be sleeping through any time soon!'

Emily said, aware she was probably laughing a little bit too much at her own words, especially given that they weren't actually funny.

'Oh right.' Matilda began to frown. Twattily. 'Shouldn't he be by now? Sleeping, I mean? A few of my friends have had babies and they were all going through the night by twelve weeks . . . perhaps you should talk to someone?'

FUCKING. BITCH. Emily felt her blood pressure rise a little as she resisted the urge to launch across the desk and snatch her baby back.

'Well. They're all different. Unfortunately, they don't come with an instruction manual, eh . . .' Emily's laughter was getting weird and a bit manic now.

'Sure,' Matilda responded, laughing a little herself with her stupid smug stupid face. 'He's quite big for six months, isn't he? Chunky little monkey.'

FUCK. YOU. Emily willed her baby to produce some kind of epic, gravity-defying spew, right up and over that ridiculously beautiful and expensive-looking cardigan.

'He's on the ninetieth percentile. Perfectly healthy.'

'Sure . . .' said Matilda, trailing off as though she'd run out of any fucks to give, now that Emily wasn't giving her the satisfaction of letting her know she bothered her. Deeply.

'Anyway. I'm so busy. Better dash. Good luck with the sleep and everything. I'm sure it will happen eventually for you,' Matilda said, practically tossing William back into Emily's arms.

I. WILL. FUCKING. CUT. YOU.

'I'm sure you are. Have a great day.' A lot of Emily's teeth were showing. She should probably work on that, if she was going to talk to real life adults again. Undoing her bra and pulling it out of her armpit probably wouldn't be the best move either.

'My turn for a cuddle!' came Natalie's voice from over her shoulder.

'Sure. Hey Nat – how are you?' Emily said, smiling – it felt nice to pass William to someone who actually gave a shit about meeting the human she'd grown for nine and a half months inside her body and had now managed to keep alive with only her breasts . . . Or at least someone that was convincingly pretending to.

Natalie gently positioned Emily's son on her forearm and smiled down at him, gently stroking his head.

'Gosh he's beautiful, Ems – well done you! Don't worry about how I am. How are you? I bet it's all been a rather exhausting fog, hasn't it? How are you feeling about everything? You look amazing.'

'Yes that's a fairly accurate description, to be honest!' Emily said, laughing a little. 'But I'm fine. Just tired. Really, really tired. And only looking okay right now due to about £12 worth of MAC contour cream on each cheek. And three double-shot caramel lattes . . .'

'Ha! Well, you'd never know. And hey – everything is working out here brilliantly with Charlotte, so there's no need for you to worry about work stuff. We've got it all covered until you're ready to come back, so you can concentrate on looking after this handsome little chap.'

Emily smiled. That weird jealous, slightly unknowing feeling was creeping back in, but she suppressed it.

Paul would be here any moment, and she could spend a few hours chatting with her old colleagues, seeing how her accounts were doing, and going out to lunch with Natalie . . . so it wasn't all bad. She might even ask Charlotte what she used on her hair.

Emily began to feel a little better. Although she couldn't ignore the uncomfortable sensation that she didn't belong here any more. Everything and everyone seemed so foreign to her now . . . she was probably just being silly, maybe everyone feels like that when they begin visiting their old life again. She was fairly sure, if she could avoid having to talk to Matilda again for the next few hours, she'd be fine. All she had to do was keep busy enough that she didn't have time to miss William and soon she'd be out to lunch with real-life food she could enjoy whilst it was still hot, uninterrupted, and eaten with not only both hands, but both boobs free at the same time. That alone was worth it.

Chapter 49

FIRST PREGNANCY VERSUS SECOND PREGNANCY – THE SHIT YOU NEED TO KNOW

Molly had been feeling a little less 'raring to go' than she'd hoped, throughout the first part of the year.

February was almost over now. But it was still so cold. And gloomy. Snow was even being forecast for the weekend. And she was several weeks pregnant with a six-and-a-half-month-old baby to look after at the same time, and although she didn't enjoy admitting it – it wasn't quite as easy second time around.

She wasn't sick, or in pain, she just felt TIRED. So tired she was struggling to function. She had barely any appetite – she was forcing herself to eat when and where she could. And if she was honest, she was beginning to feel a bit lonely and overwhelmed by everything . . . She couldn't remember it being this way with Marley. She only remembered feeling pretty normal – but slowly being able to do fewer of her jeans buttons up.

It was the first time she began to wonder if avoiding doing baby-groups and NCT classes had been a mistake. She'd been to the odd one with Emily and her NCT chums, but it was clear they had a tight little mummy-friend group going on. They weren't trying to exclude her, they just didn't know her. Other than Emily of course. Plus none of them were pregnant – they all had their entire attention on their first babies. Not a luxury Molly could afford right now. And it seemed whenever she mentioned that she was pregnant to people, they'd cast their eyes down to Marley and back to her with slight horror on their faces and begin jibing at her about how crazy she was having two so close together. Or asking how she'd cope with two sets of nappies to change, and how she'd literally have 'both hands full' for the rest of her life . . . None of it was meant maliciously, but Molly couldn't help but feel a little excluded. A little judged. And all of this was beginning to make her question her choices a little. Especially with her cash-flow pressures nagging her at the back of her mind all the time.

Molly simply didn't have the money to do all the various groups and courses that Emily and her friends went to every week. And now she had to bring some money in, most of her spare time was spent either working in the front room or sleeping. She suddenly wondered if she was really doing the right thing by Marley – perhaps she did need to take a step back from her business goals and be more of a mum for a while. The guilt was eating her up. And it was hard to tell if it was down to pregnancy hormones or if she really did feel like she was failing a bit at everything right now . . .

She had her first scan later this week and she was

looking forward to that – it had been hard to know exactly 'how' pregnant she was because her periods had never actually returned since having Marley. But she'd get some answers at the hospital, at least. And she should be past the first trimester pretty soon with any luck, so hopefully the tiredness would fade. The idea of doing anything other than surviving right now was a struggle.

Molly had actually begun to get quite busy with her feeding-cloth-making business. Nothing that was going to change the world, but slowly the orders were dripping in, and she'd booked herself a stall at a local baby show in a few weeks' time to drum up some more interest. It was dawning on her how quickly it was coming around, and that she had to arrive complete with ready-made products to trial, fabric samples and promo material. They'd suggested a banner and some business cards too, but Molly wasn't sure she had the time or the money to organise that now. She huffed at how exhausting it all felt suddenly – it was like every time she began to turn a small profit, there was something she needed to spend money on. It was a never-ending cycle of being continually skint.

Tom was adamant that they played it safe for the meantime and that they invested in slowly building up funds as and when they could, but it was just so frustrating. And now that she knew they had another baby on the way, it felt like there was even more pressure to make money right now, before the next child was born. She just wished she could find something that could help her make money faster, a lot of it. And ideally without her having to physically do anything. But so far it had eluded her – perhaps she needed more skills at her disposal than Facebook, Google and just wishing really hard . . .

She was happy to be having a little break from it all today and meeting up with Emily though. She was looking forward to seeing her friend and was glad they were meeting at Emily's house today instead of out at a cafe or a baby-group. She needed to not spend any money, and could do with a nice relaxing environment where, if need be, she could have a little judgement-free nap on the sofa in between decaf teas . . . And Emily had every baby toy, gadget and gizmo going – she was certain there was enough there to keep William and Marley entertained until they were ready to start school. Plus she needed to see this Jumperoo contraption for herself . . .

Judging by the photos Emily had sent her – it was a giant piece of plastic scaffolding that took up at least a third of her living-room floor and came complete with a harness in the middle for containing infants. She wasn't sure how Marley would react to it, but hey – it would be nice to catch up with her friend with both hands free and the option of a little snooze at any time.

Molly realised she was already ten minutes late and hadn't even begun preparing to leave the house. Plus it was a good fifteen-minute walk. In the rain. Carrying a baby and a large pot of Tom's homemade vegan soup. She'd better let Emily know.

Molly

Hey – just leaving. Do you want me
to bring anything?

Emily

Just yourselves.
I'd already guessed you'd be late.
Why change the habit of a lifetime eh!

Molly

I think late is such a restrictive
word . . .
I prefer time-challenged.
What can I say, I'm a free spirit!

Emily

Well, I have barely managed a single
event, class or meet-up since W was
born where I haven't arrived late.
With a pile of sick on my shoulder.
And some human shit smeared on my
clothing somewhere, so trust me, I am
not one to talk!
(but hurry up as I might eat all the
biscuits if you don't arrive soon!)

Molly

Right. I'm on my way.
I'm coming to save you from the
Hobnobs.
I have soup. I have a baby. I have a

giant coat on. I'll be there quick as my
preggo-legs will carry me.

Emily
Excellent. See you soon!

When Molly arrived, she couldn't help but stare in awe as she walked through Emily's front door. The area formerly known as her friend's living room appeared to have been turned into some kind of Fisher-Price shrine.

Molly had no idea how a not-even-seven-month-old baby could possibly have need for all of that 'stuff', but she also knew her friend. She was 'all or nothing'. And this was her doing 'all'.

'Get in quick,' Emily said, pushing the door closed behind her friend. Her front door led directly into the living room of her little terraced house. Which was not great when it was blowing a winter blizzard outside, as it tended to blow a blizzard straight into the front room.

'Hey – how are you? How are you feeling? I think you're doing pretty well to be pregnant, with a baby strapped to you, wandering around in this! I haven't got out of my pyjamas for at least two days now. I'm not even sorry. I'm enjoying the musk.'

'Oh, the musk . . .' Molly said, laughing as she removed her enormous sleeping-bag-esque coat and placed it across the back of the armchair in the bay window. 'And I'm okay. Ish. It's just this tiredness. It's really getting me down. That fifteen-minute walk has almost finished me

293

off! It's really frustrating – I had such an amazing pregnancy first time round, this time it's not feeling quite so . . . breezy? I feel like I need to sit down constantly. And no matter how much sleep I get, I never stop feeling exhausted. It's horrible.'

Emily twitched slightly at the idea of sleep. But decided now wasn't a time to comment on that. It wasn't a 'who's more tired' contest, after all. And she could remember that sensation in pregnancy of barely being able to get through a day without a nap. God she missed naps . . .

'Oh, hunny – I can only imagine what it's like when you've already got a baby. I really hope the second part is a bit kinder to you. Sit down and let me get you a nice cup of tea. Are you on decaf?'

'Yep. Life on the edge. I might even go with a real tea just before I leave. Should give me the energy to walk home! Just don't tell Tom. He'd probably shit himself if he thought I was having caffeine and biscuits containing gluten,' Molly called after her friend as Emily headed to the kitchen to make them hot drinks.

Molly unwrapped Marley from his sling. And gently placed him next to William on one of the many multi-sensory floor mats Emily had laid out. Marley was awake. Just. He vaguely made an attempt to grab at a black and white dangly penguin, then, after deciding that was a bit too much, lay still and closed his eyes again. He was possibly the sleepiest baby alive.

Molly began to take in the sights of Emily's living room. She really had transformed so much of her house to accommodate all the 'stuff'. It was impressive and overwhelming at the same time. Molly barely had anything – a bouncer and a small box of toys in the living room, but other than that their home had remained fairly 'adult'. Her shelves were piled up with DVDs, books and various photos and mementos from travelling. Emily's was a feast of wooden and plastic toys, sensory surfaces and baby-based gadgets. It was like her and Paul's life had been swiped to one side to allow William to take over every surface. Molly smiled at how different they were. She knew she couldn't live like this, and that Emily would have some kind of fit if she were forced to parent in Molly's awkward, slightly cluttered and not entirely clean flat without the presence of the sacred Jumperoo . . .

Molly stirred herself from her thoughts and smiled down at William, letting her head tilt to one side and sticking her tongue out playfully at him. He smiled back at her. Then promptly shoved a well-gummed Sophie the Giraffe back in his mouth. Now that the babies were lying together, Molly could see how much bigger William was. It was clear Emily wasn't lying when she said he spent his entire waking life feeding. He looked gorgeously chubby, in comparison to Marley's petite slim body. Marley's babygro swamped him. Whereas William was wearing a flat cap and tiny baby loafers with a bow tie and cord trousers . . . Molly didn't know why, but she'd also learnt to simply accept and not ask. It was easier that way.

'Here you go . . .' Emily said, strolling into the living room and handing Molly a steaming hot cup of tea.

'So how was your keeping-in-touch day? We haven't caught up properly yet – did it go okay?' Molly asked, sipping the hot liquid and wrapping her palms around the cup to warm up from her walk.

'Yeah. It was okay,' Emily said, as both ladies took a seat on the sofa amongst the toys. 'I don't know what I expected really. It's clear that Charlotte's doing a great job. It felt good to know I don't need to worry about anything on that side. Matilda's still a dick, but that was no shock. Natalie is still lovely. And she's being great and really flexible about when I want to come back and stuff, it's just . . . I don't know. It felt strange being there. Like it wasn't really "me" any more. I don't know how to describe it really. I know this might sound like a terrible idea, but I'm not really sure I want to go back to work. I mean – of course I will one day. But I'm not sure I want to go back now – while he's still so little. It just doesn't feel right . . . Does that make sense? Am I being ridiculous?'

'Of course you're not being ridiculous,' Molly said, touching Emily's hand reassuringly. 'You can't help how you feel. I would say don't make any hasty decisions and see how you feel in a few months . . . you might change your mind as he gets older. I think the best thing you can do is not put any pressure on yourself. You'll know what's right when the time comes.'

'Do you think? I'm scared I'm going to make the wrong

decision. On one hand I'm terrified that if I'm "just a mum" I won't feel fulfilled and will miss work, but then on the other hand – whenever I think about getting back into working five days a week away from him, it just feels wrong. I don't want to go. I've tried talking to the NCT girls about it but they're all doing completely different things – most are heading back to work, some full-time, some three or four days a week, but then a couple of them are going to do the mum thing for a bit longer. But then that's not an option for everyone, is it? . . . most of it comes down to finances, I guess. And what you actually want. Everyone's different, right . . . It's impossible to make a decision! It's tearing me up. Plus I can't stop thinking about what a judgemental dick I was before I had kids – I pretty much used to look down on the mums in the office just because they had to leave early, or didn't work Fridays, or had to drop everything when one of their kids was ill. I feel horrible about that. I totally get it now!'

'But how could you understand? You had no idea . . . you can't understand something you have literally no idea about. But now you do. I think it's called growing up! Having children makes you do that. You're supposed to be a dick when you're young. It's sort of the point, right?' Molly said, laughing. 'Besides, what about going part-time? Is that an option?'

'I know you're right. And yeah – I might be able to do four days, but I'm not even sure that's what I want. The blog is starting to take off more and more, so I have got a small income from that, and I keep thinking that if I

297

push it a bit more I could make enough to justify staying at home with him. I don't know.'

'Well, it sounds like you've got it as an option. That's quite exciting. I think you need to relax, enjoy the next few months, and see how you feel. Only you can make the decision after all. What has Paul said?'

'Much the same as you, to be honest – that I need to decide what I want and we'll find a way to make it happen. It's just going so fast, I'm starting to panic already. It's made me realise how tough it must be being a working parent. I definitely didn't appreciate that until now. Anyway. Let's talk about something else, how's the business stuff going? Are you still on track to set up the travel company before baby number two arrives?'

'Well, I don't know, is the truth. I know what I want to do – that part I've been thinking about a lot and I've been spending loads of time emailing my contacts in Thailand. I have two hotels interested and the idea is to run baby- and toddler-friendly week-long active holidays – all travel, meals, accommodation and activities included, with personal guides for the trips. All the baby stuff is there at the hotel so you can pack light, and enjoy a holiday where you actually get to see stuff, but in an organised and safe way. To be fair, that part has been pretty fun and interesting. I've also found someone who'll design and host the website on the cheap for me. What I really need to do now is get out there and road-test everything. Which is the hard part because we don't have the money to do that. It's so frustrating and boring! And

Tom is making me do all these spreadsheets and projections and stuff that sort of make me want to die inside a little bit. If only a giant parcel of cash could fall out of the sky, it would solve all my problems!'

'Ha – mine too. I promise to share if it happens to me, if you promise to share too.'

'You're on.'

'And you'll get there. I know you will. It sounds like you're getting it all worked out. You'll just have to exercise a bit of patience, Molly – I know that's not your strong point!' Emily said, nodding her head towards Molly's tummy and laughing.

Molly looked down and laughed too.

'Hey, patience is for dicks anyway. Where's the fun in that . . .'

Chapter 50

WEANING WAS SENT TO TEST US

Weaning was sent to test us,
And make us want to scratch out our eyes.
All the pureeing, and potting, and pissing about,
So they can spit it in your face while you cry.

Weaning was sent to try us,
And show us we can no longer have nice stuff.
All the smearing, and throwing, and flinging it about,
My poor pre-baby furniture's had enough.

Weaning was sent to show us,
That cooking makes us wish WE WERE DEAD.
All the mess, and the waste, and the effort
*   it takes,*
Now you just stick to pouches instead.

Weaning was actually a lot harder, and a lot more disgusting than Emily had imagined.

She'd so been looking forward to it. But as with many things in motherhood it hadn't been quite as expected. And even though she'd been attempting it on and off for a few weeks now, it really wasn't going to plan . . .

especially as she couldn't ever look at bananas or broccoli the same way again.

Suddenly, it felt like there was an entire new level of pressure. And so much washing-up. She seemed to be endlessly steaming, food processing, blending and portioning out tiny little pots of brown, green and beige gloop . . . not to mention how nervous she was becoming about the cream carpet in her dining room.

The only thing that was making her feel better about the whole thing was her amazing new iCandy high-chair – the MiChair; it was putting the rest of her dining-room furniture to shame. In fact – it was putting all her furniture to shame.

To tell the truth, Emily was beginning to feel a little differently about her sweet little Victorian terraced cottage. She knew it sounded a little selfish, but it really was beginning to feel a bit small.

She didn't notice so much when William was just a newborn, but slowly as the toys and the Jumperoo, and all the other stuff appeared, her home seemed to shrink under the mass.

It seemed quite ridiculous that someone so tiny could warrant so much space. When it was just her and Paul living here, she never considered she wouldn't have enough space to house a seven-month-old baby in addition. She loved that it was small and characterful: the fireplaces, the wonky doorframes and the narrow staircase . . . now they seemed to say DEATH, AWKWARD and oh-fuck-I-nearly-clipped-his-head-on-the-banister-again.

301

And the next natural stage was him crawling, then cruising, and walking and she really wasn't ready for all that. This house was simply not suitable for a small person who could move. Was it? But then perhaps once the Jumperoo and floor mats had gone, they'd actually get some living-room space back. Emily was in that weird place between desperately wanting him to move on to the next phase, whilst simultaneously wanting him to stay a tiny stationary baby FOR EVER. It was a strange contradiction.

But right now she needed to concentrate on this phase. Getting William – the ever-hungry milk monster – to start enjoying real food, so that he might enjoy a little less boob and a little more broccoli. Especially as the magical Internet fairies (or Facebook baby forums as they are better known) seemed to think that once she managed to get three meals a day into him, he'd been so carbed up he'd begin sleeping through the night . . . finally. And she was more than ready for that to start happening, regardless of how much steam-mopping she had to do, and how many baby wipes it took to bring her beautiful MiChair back to its former glory each time she attempted banana.

Although, her patience for creating purees was beginning to wear thin, and she was on the verge of bulk-ordering a load of baby-food pouches from Amazon whilst intermittently throwing the odd bit of cucumber on to his high-chair tray.

That's what Molly was doing – she simply sliced off a bit of what she was eating, and Marley sucked on bits of fruit and veg quietly on her lap. But then this was Marley – the perfect baby. The constantly sleeping, non-crying, ever-content, 'ooh I'll just eat a bit of that and make your life easy, Mummy' baby . . .

Emily took a look at the state of her kitchen. And back to the state of her son. Who was now wearing his smashed blueberries as some kind of hat/facemask.

Yep. It might be time to try something else.

Chapter 51

TOLLY DD

Molly

Hey ladies! How are you all?

Thought you'd like to know I've just had my scan, and luckily I'm not too far along – about 13 and a half weeks now.

And the due date is 1st September! How awesome is that? My babies will only be 13 months apart! Eek!

Emily

Aww that's brilliant!

Wow so close. September really doesn't seem that far away does it?

I think it's completely awesome and insane that yours will be so close in age.

I don't think I could hack it!

I'm actually considering not having another one until William is at school. Seriously.

I can barely cope with one child!
I seriously take my hat off to you
   sweetie – you are super mum!
(I am exhausted-in-a-pile-of-sick-and-
   faeces-whilst-crying mum.)

Molly
Don't be silly. You're an amazing
mum.
I just wanted mine close together is
all ;)
Although it was a little unexpected to
have them quite this close. But hey
I'm embracing it – got no choice now
anyway! Haha!

Liz
Hey ladies just checking in!
That's wonderful news Molly. Big
congrats. The time will fly by! Can't
believe it's March already?! What has
happened to this year? I blinked and
it was almost spring!

Molly
I know. I feel like every year I get
older the years go even quicker.
Remember when the six-week school
holiday seemed like a lifetime?
Crazy . . .

Emily

I know! I feel like I'm wishing my life away in 6-month chunks. Adulting sucks really doesn't it? I'd much rather be sixteen again floating around in halter neck tops from bay trading and my biggest problem being whether to buy Charlie Red or Charlie Blue body spray this month . . .

Molly

Ha! Or Impulse o2. Don't forget o2 body spray! That one was the best. Do bodysprays even exist any more?

Liz

Who knows? I reckon teenagers are too busy buying vape pens and iPhones, and putting pictures of their genitals on SnapChat . . .

Emily

That is sad but probably incredibly true!

Molly

Ah well. Times change. I can sense you're both jealous you don't have pictures of your willies floating around the Internet.

Emily
Naturally.

Liz
Devastated.

Emily
So enough about teenage penises . . . How's the wedding planning going Liz? Have you used my spreadsheet? I can send you some of the Pinterest board links I have if you want some inspiration . . .

Liz
Well I haven't really started. I'm just so busy. I'm just so busy. I know I should make time for it but it's hard. I'm knackered when I get home from work! Gerald is really bugging me about getting going on it. I've promised him I'll sit down this weekend and we'll start searching for venues. And I'll print off your spreadsheet and start using that too. Okay.

Molly
Hey don't beat yourself up. It should be fun, not a chore. I reckon once you get into it you'll enjoy it.

Emily

You'll love it! I loved doing mine. And as soon as you have the date pinned down we can begin looking into the hen doooooooo!

Liz

Okay okay, let's not get too far ahead of ourselves! I'm really not sure I'm a hen do kinda girl. Giant inflatable penises and Jägerbombs are not that high on my list of priorities. But you'll be the first to know once we've found somewhere okay?

Molly

Take your time hunny. This is about you (not Emily). ;)

Emily

Hey! I'm not making it about me. I'm just offering friendly encouragement

. . .

(and obvs I'll never let you get away without a hen do. Just so you know. I'm googling inflatable penises as I type).

Liz

We'll see . . . And thank you for all the encouragement ;) Look I've got to

run. Congrats again Molly. Looking
forward to seeing you ladies soon!

Molly
Thanks! Yes, let's meet soon. xxx

Emily
xxx

Chapter 52

THE WEDDING WITHOUT A PLAN

Liz began to wonder if it was weird that she'd been engaged for two and a half months and not actually started to 'plan' anything yet.

The thing was, she didn't feel weird about it but she could tell from everyone's reactions when they asked how it was going, and she said that so far it wasn't, that they thought it was weird. And there's only so many times you can get a raised eyebrow, a wrinkled nose and concerned frown as a reaction before you begin to wonder if it's you . . .

She knew that it wasn't because she didn't want to get married – she had every intention of marrying Gerald. She loved him. She knew that. She wouldn't have said yes if she wasn't confident this would end in a wedding of some sort.

But that was the thing – Liz just wasn't up for the big white wedding extravaganza. The huge performance. She honestly did not want some tacky hen do. She didn't see the point. Perhaps that's why she was putting it off – every time she dared flick through a wedding magazine, there were endless pages about table plans, favours, where to sit people, speeches, meal options . . . it all just felt a bit over the top. And seemed to be almost entirely up to the bride. She wasn't sure she wanted to do it all. She wasn't sure she had time to organise a wedding alongside a career that barely let her get home before 9 p.m. most evenings, and on weekends she wanted to de-stress, drink wine and sit on the sofa with her marginally overweight cat, enjoying the company of the man she loved. And not be responsible for making decisions. About anything really.

She wasn't religious, so churches were out, and she certainly didn't have enough friends and relations, or people that she liked enough for that matter, to fill up some enormous stately home or a barn conversion. She could probably count how many people she genuinely wanted to be there with her on both hands and she couldn't decide if that was a good thing, or a little bit sad . . .

She was beginning to wonder if she was really bride material. She didn't seem to give enough fucks.

Perhaps she just needed to come at it from a different angle. What did she and Gerald actually want from a wedding? Because if it was simply to get married with a small pool of their closest friends and family there then surely it needn't be a huge fuss and performance. And definitely no white doves released over a crop of llamas set against the background of a jewelled waterfall hand-crafted by virgins . . . or something.

She wondered for a moment if she'd be quite happy just going to the registry office with their nearest and

dearest, and heading off for a nice meal afterwards. Would that be so terrible? It could all be done with class, and great food, and she certainly didn't need to wear a big white meringue to feel beautiful. In fact she had her eye on a stunning navy evening gown, simple lines, to flatter her long, lean figure, and Gerald in a suit to complement. Just because it wasn't 'traditional' and couldn't be found on a double-page spread in a glossy magazine didn't mean it wasn't right. It was supposed to be about them, after all, wasn't it? Not about Emily's Pinterest boards and biodegradable table decorations.

For the first time Liz began to actually imagine how the day might work – she felt far more relaxed and happy at the idea of something elegant and understated with only those she loved. Her nieces Clover and Isla might make the elegant and understated part a little harder to achieve if they were feeling boisterous, but that would just make it personal, wouldn't it? She'd take an excited toddler telling everyone she needed a poo during the speeches over a flock of doves and llamas any day . . .

She'd promised Gerald they'd talk about it today. It was Sunday morning. She was up, bright-eyed and reasonably bushy-tailed despite the red wine they'd consumed last night, and had left Gerald to have a lie-in as she pottered about, lost in wedding thoughts, considering things for a cooked breakfast, which might be a remedy for her slightly fuzzy head.

She put the kettle on, pulled some bacon out of the

freezer to defrost and counted out some eggs on to the side. She'd make it once Gerald was up, so they could eat together.

Last night she'd sent Emily's wedding spreadsheet to the printer and left it there ready to study this morning. She'd not opened it before printing it. It seemed wise. There were quite a few pages but she knew it was time she showed some willing.

Liz made herself a cup of tea and headed to the sofa, placed the steaming hot drink down next to her on the side table and located her laptop.

She pulled it up on to her lap and opened Google: 'Wedding Venues South Bucks'

Liz watched as hundreds of results flooded back. Perhaps she was going to have to be a bit more specific.

'Old Pubs Wedding Venues South Bucks'

Liz allowed herself a small smile now. Gone were the grand halls, stately homes and huge marquees, and instead a few pages of lovely old country pubs with beautiful interiors and intimate bars. She could even have the ceremony at some of them. One had a stunning conservatory extension leading out into an orchard. Private and natural and beautiful. She felt a lot more comfortable now. In fact, she'd felt a shift. Even her red-wine headache seemed to have lifted a little.

She'd gone from not wanting to do this and putting it off for so long, to feeling an uplifting hum of excitement at finally knowing what she wanted.

Suddenly, she couldn't wait for Gerald to get up. She

313

had things to show him. Ideas to present to him. And she'd be doing all of it with a freshly grilled bacon sandwich and a twelve-page-long wedding spreadsheet, which she was no longer scared of, from her best friend Emily.

Chapter 53

POUCH-CHAT

Emily
Okay. I've just ordered about 400
Ella's Kitchen pouches of the Internet.
Is that terrible?
I feel like it's saved my life.
And my kitchen.
And my dining-room carpet . . .
I'm still doing the odd bit here and
there, but this is just so much
easier.
Especially when we're out and
about . . .
Do you think I've failed?
Most of the NCT girls seemed to have
turned into Annabel Karmel clones.
One of them is talking about starting a
baby food blog ffs!
I wanted to home-make everything but
it's just so much!
It's making me feel so guilty.

Molly

Hey you x Don't be silly you nutter —
you've no reason to feel guilty.
Pouch baby food is basically as good
as the homemade stuff now anyway I
reckon! So stop stressing xx
Ideals are great until real life takes over.
I could not be dealing with all that
chopping and pureeing. That's why
we're doing the baby-led weaning . . .
although I'm not sure how much he
actually eats of it TBH
He just sort of sucks on stuff a bit.
But he seems to like everything I've
given him so far.
Some of the nappies have been fairly
spectacular. So I suppose that proves
it's going in!

Emily

Oh god I know.
I've gone up another size in nappies
to try and contain it more. And if it's
too awful I just chuck the clothes in
the bin! I know that sounds bad but it
can be horrendous! I have no idea
how someone so small can produce
something so terrible . . .
When he's eaten blueberries it's like

comedy purple slime.
PURPLE SHIT SLIME.
We don't wear pastels any more. And white is completely out. For both of us. FOR EVER.

> **Molly**
> A lovely image for me to take away thank you.

Emily
And I know you're right about the pouches. I swear if anyone told me I'd spend more of motherhood feeling guilty about stuff than any other emotion I'd have been a bit better prepared!
It drives me crazy.

> **Molly**
> You were always crazy.

Emily
Thanks.

> **Molly**
> But I get exactly what you mean.
> You're doing great though.
> Every mum and every baby is different.
> You've just gotta do you.

317

Emily
I know you're right.
I feel way better about it now.
Hope you're okay?

Molly
Still feeling pretty shattered, but I'm
ploughing on.
Lots of naps.
Still struggling to get much done
outside of existing right now!

Emily
Poor you.
Don't work yourself up.
You're doing the right thing resting
when you need to.

Molly
I know.
But resting won't pay the bills.
And definitely won't pay for Thailand.
Just wish I could make it all happen!
It's so frustrating!
I had to cancel my stall at the baby
show I was on about. I couldn't
afford the marketing stuff, and there
just wasn't enough time to get it all
done! Plus the idea of standing up
all day talking excitedly to strangers

is totally beyond me
right now.
To be honest I wish I'd thought it
through a bit more before I'd booked
it!
Total waste of the £30 deposit ☹

Emily

Well I'm sure it's the right decision
hunny – don't be hard on yourself.
Perhaps you just need to stop being
so impulsive Molly! And look after
yourself a bit more.

Molly

Yeah, yeah, yeah.
You sound like Tom now! Lol x
Anyway – being impulsive has got me
the best experiences of my life so far
. . . Not sure I know any other way to
be ;)
And hey, on that note – do you think
if you saw a way to get cash, and fast
– you'd go for it?
I mean – if you had an opportunity
presented to you that seemed a bit
too good to be true, but if it went well
– could solve all your problems . . .
Would you do it?

319

Emily

Hmmmm – I'd say if it seems too good to be true, then it almost certainly is!
Has something happened? What opportunity are you talking about?

Molly

Oh nothing. I'm sure you're right. You know what it's like when you're feeling a bit low and like you can't get anywhere. I think I'm just searching for the quick way out!

Emily

Well I'd say there never is a quick way out. Please don't do anything crazy. I know it must be so frustrating but the hard work will pay off. Even if it takes a while. Honestly xxx

Molly

Yes I know you're right. And don't worry I won't. Although I might . . .

Emily

Molly!

Chapter 54

LIFE BEFORE MUMMY

It was the last day of March.

In two days, William was going to be eight months old.

Emily was finding it increasingly hard to remember what life was like before him. It felt like a blur. The things she took for granted, the things she missed, the things that were now so wonderful about life with him . . .

She now completely understood what people meant when they said that becoming a parent was the hardest thing you could ever do. It wasn't because the day-to-day things were 'hard' necessarily – it was the constant emotional toll, the loneliness, the love, the tiredness, the guilt, the way your life shifted so instantly and dramatically that you barely had time to comprehend it, before you realised you felt differently about every single thing in your world now. AND SO MUCH OF THE GUILT.

And no matter how many people said that to you before you had a child, it just never made sense until you were there, experiencing it for yourself and saying it to other people and registering their slightly vacant expressions as you tried to tell them that parenthood would be the most wonderful, yet the most challenging thing they'd ever do.

And even though it seemed like William had been a part of her life for ever, the months had whipped by.

He was so far from that tiny tot that she cradled preciously in her arms eight months ago, terrified she might break him. He was a chubby, smiley, little boy now. An unruly tuft of thick blond hair that ended in a curl on top of his head, plump little legs that pumped away when he got excited, and a dribbly little mouth full of gums ready for teeth. Emily really couldn't imagine his smile with teeth in it but she knew they were coming. She could see and feel the little nubs beginning to appear below the surface, which was a little disturbing, and there were no doubt more sleepless nights in the future because of them.

Emily worried that she might be becoming a bit of a baby-bore. William was so much of her life, it was hard not to be. Sometimes she found herself actively trying to steer the conversation away from teething, and nappies, and the-slightly-snotty-lady-from-NCT's cottage-pie-for-babies recipe, just so she knew that she still could.

Now that most of the NCT babies were between eight and nine months old, the chats between the mums had turned to returning to work, costs of childcare, and the juggling of life now that maternity leave was close to an end. It was clear that life would vary a lot for each of them, and that whilst some of them had formed firm friendships, others not so much. They'd all met up so enthusiastically in the beginning when they were pregnant and when they'd just had the babies, but slowly the numbers had dwindled and now Emily found that she was really only 'proper friends' with Rachael, and friendly with two of the other mums. They even had their own rebel splinter WhatsApp group away from the main group now. One lady (the snotty-cottage-pie-recipe lady) was a bit of a judgemental competitive cow – if it wasn't all natural, organic, pressed and rolled with the tears of Himalayan yaks, she turned her nose up at it. When Emily pulled out a ready-made pouch of baby puree at a recent lunch meet-up she'd had some kind of physical convulsion and begun a ridiculous rant about how she'd never give her child processed food. This had done nothing for her popularity and had made Emily crave a Big Mac, which she'd eaten smugly in the drive-thru carpark afterwards as William slept, and she decided to give literally no further fucks about that. If anything, Emily felt a little sorry for her. It was sad that she felt the need for her baby to always be the first at everything: already crawling, eating three meals a day, sitting, babbling, doing Rubik's Cubes with his nostrils whilst reciting the Taiwanese alphabet. Emily simply avoided speaking to her now. She didn't have time for the bollocks.

One lady had moved away, another lived quite far out and found it difficult to meet up, and another clearly just didn't have any interest in being friends with any of them,

323

which was a little sad, especially as gaining a few mummy-buddies was surely a big part of doing the NCT classes for most people, but Emily supposed that no one can be friends with everyone and some people simply aren't that sociable. Not something Emily had ever personally experienced, but she could sympathise with not wanting to always be surrounded by people when you've been up all night and can't remember when you last changed your pants.

It is certainly the case that you tend to gravitate towards those whose parenting ideals are most similar to yours, and stick where you feel the least judged and most comfortable. She was firm friends with Rachael, and also Sophie and Julia, who all seemed very relaxed and realistic. Their husbands had met and got on well too. Emily found herself sometimes sharing things with them that she hadn't with anyone else. It was strange that after only ten months of knowing each other, a group of strangers, flung together based only on postcode and pregnancy, would have seen each other cry, laugh, be desperately angry, discuss their marriages, their fears . . . and probably spend an above-average amount of time talking about poo. But hey.

The real test would be when they all did head back to work. They'd soon see whether they'd be able to maintain their fledgling friendships once 'real-life' had started up again and they weren't simply meeting at baby-groups and cafes to chat about their fannies and intermittently lining the babies up for group photos.

Emily felt a bit sad that the end of it all was in sight.

She still had over three months left before she had to return to work, but that seemed like nothing. There were things to be organised now, the baby-days would soon be over, and she'd be back in the company of Matilda-McTwatty-Dickface on a daily basis. Perhaps she could introduce her to Twatty-NCT-Cottage-Pie-Lady – they'd probably get on like a house on fire.

Emily knew she had some big decisions to make in the next three months. Important decisions that would affect the rest of her life. Their lives – hers, Paul's and William's. The days of thinking about just herself were well and truly over.

Emily decided a blog post was in order. It always made her feel better to articulate her thoughts on there. Especially as every time she did, she was so happily amazed at everyone out there who felt the same . . .

SUNDAY 31 MARCH

Life Before Mummy

There are things I miss from my *life-before-mummy* . . .
Like sleeping, bladder-control, and a less
    scrotum-like tummy.
I miss wearing clothes without Spanx underneath,
And not thinking that a good day is when I've
    managed to brush my teeth.

325

I miss having breasts that stay up and round the
    front,
I miss getting drunk and acting like a total
    cough *idiot*.
I miss walking in high heels and being convin-
    cingly thin,
And not having a vagina that flaps in the wind.

I miss matching pants with actual 'under-wired'
    bras,
I miss leaving the house without Sophie the
    fucking Giraffe.
I miss eating food in my own time while it's hot.
Not one-handed forking from the Noodle-of-
    the-Pot . . .

I miss using the sofa rather than sat on the
    floor,
I miss not having a buggy that doesn't fit through
    ANY CAFE DOOR.
I miss Saturday nights and their random
    gin-fuelled adventures,
And not living a secret life as a twatty nappy-
    price inspector.

Yes, there's so much I miss from my life before
    kids,
There was less crying, more sleeping and
    certainly less skids.

But this is my life now – with my boy and his beautiful curls.

And I wouldn't bloody change it for anything in the world.

(Except maybe a lie-in . . .)

Chapter 55

THE FESS-UP

Molly's stomach was churning.

She felt as though she might throw up. Her palms were sweating, her throat felt tight and raspy, and she couldn't shake the overwhelming sensation that she'd just done the stupidest thing she'd ever done.

Because she almost definitely had.

Before her life with Tom and Marley, she'd only ever had herself to worry about. If she fucked it all up, she only fucked it all up for herself. So nothing had ever really mattered that much before.

But it did now.

It mattered more than her mind had ever allowed her to realise.

Her brain kept hopping from one emotion to the next – anger at her own stupidity, fear of telling Tom what she'd done, sadness and loss of hope at how the hell she was ever going to fix this.

Because it was her job to sort out this mess. She'd been reckless, impulsive, and stupid, and the risk had not paid off this time. Her luck had run out. Her mindless optimism and misplaced trust had bitten her back in the worst way.

And now it was time to come clean.

And tell Tom what she'd done . . .

She wanted the world to swallow her up so she didn't have to do this. But as that was unlikely, she'd have to get on with telling him what had really happened. Despite how terrified she was.

Tom was due home any moment.

He was probably expecting a nice calm evening on the sofa with his pregnant girlfriend and infant son.

But unfortunately, that was definitely not going to happen. Not now. Because once she told him. He'd know that everything was fucked.

Molly's heart rate elevated as she heard the familiar sound of Tom's key in the front door.

Suddenly all the words she'd practised, the sentences she'd been repeating in her mind all afternoon that might somehow make light of the situation, make it sound more reasonable, they all escaped her.

Her mind was a blank pit of nothing.

'Hey, babes. What are you standing there like that for? Everything okay?' Tom said breezily as he strolled in and placed his work bag and jacket down by the sofa. Molly was standing in the middle of the lounge. She didn't know why. Standing up seemed better than sitting somehow. She was too uncomfortable to sit.

Molly didn't seem to be able to find words right now. Instead, fat tears suddenly appeared and began falling relentlessly out of her eyes. The pregnancy hormones were in full force now, and she felt completely consumed by emotion.

'Hey, what's going on? Has something happened?' Tom said, his voice full of concern as he quickly rushed to hug her and gently guide her to the sofa to sit down.

Molly sat, her body angled towards him, and stared into his eyes for a moment. They were dark and full of sympathy. It must be horrible to see her crying like this. She took a few deep breaths and steadied herself. She had to tell him. She knew she did.

'I've . . . I've done something really stupid,' Molly managed, her voice noticeably shaky.

'Okay,' Tom said slowly, maintaining eye contact, his expression changing from one of sympathy to one laced with concern.

'I've . . . I've . . . lost all our money.' The words suddenly flew out of Molly's mouth and the tears began again. Harder this time. She let her head flop forward on to Tom's shoulder as she sobbed at the reality of her confession. She wasn't ready to look at him again yet.

For a few moments, Tom didn't move or say anything. Molly had anticipated him shouting, leaving the room, throwing his hands up in the air in exasperation, but his silence seemed worse.

Molly lifted her head slowly and allowed her eyes to meet his again. She'd expected to see anger. But there wasn't any. He looked sad. Confused perhaps, but not angry.

'Okay,' he said – the disappointment oozing from his every word. 'I think you'd better start from the beginning and tell me exactly what's happened, Molly.'

Molly nodded. It felt strangely difficult to know how to start explaining everything. But this was important. She had to tell him everything now. And hope he loved her enough to not hate her for it.

'I just wanted to help, you have to believe that,' Molly began, feeling the need to justify her actions. 'I was getting so bogged down – I'm exhausted, the feeding cloths were taking so long, the profits so pitiful . . . Every time I made money I had to pay for something else. It just felt like I was getting nowhere, and I couldn't handle it.'

Tom nodded, but his face remained expressionless. Molly knew she needed to get on with it.

'And then, this email showed up. At first I thought it might be too good to be true, but then a part of me just thought there'd be no harm in investigating it, at least. This guy said he could take our money and double it within a few days. That he was a broker and the risk was minimal and worst case we'd end up with our original amount back. So I checked out the company, the reviews, it all seemed so legit. And, I just thought I'd get it all back in a few days and you'd be so pleased. I thought I could surprise you . . . So I did it. I gave him our all money.'

Molly paused for a moment to allow a few new tears to fall, as the reality of her confession hit her again. Tom's head fell into his hands.

'And . . . well, you can guess the rest. He stole it. Disappeared. And slowly I began to realise what he'd done. And then I found others who'd been duped the

same way. And I knew that was it; it was all gone. For ever. And I'm just so ashamed, Tom. And so sorry. I know you told me to slow down and not do anything without discussing it with you. I know that. I know you're angry with me. But I really thought it would be okay this time, and that I'd come to you with all this money and it . . . It . . .'

Molly broke down again. It felt a relief to get it all out in the open.

Tom hugged her. He was breathing deeply. She could feel his heart thumping in his chest as she pressed her face into his shoulder. She wanted him to say something now. She needed him to. He pulled away from her and sat looking at her.

'I don't even know what to say, Molly,' Tom said eventually. He sounded broken. 'I can't believe that you've done this. I honestly thought I'd got through to you after all the crap we went through before Christmas, but you've really surpassed yourself now. We were just getting back on track. All we had to do was sit tight and go steady for a few months and everything would have been okay – don't you understand that?'

The anger was coming out of him now. His words were cutting into her. Along with the feeling of overwhelming stupidity.

'Why do you have to do this?' He was getting more worked up as he processed everything she'd just told him. 'Are you telling me that every penny we had, everything your dad gave us at Christmas is gone?'

Molly nodded, unable to speak. His words were venomous now.

'I just can't believe you wouldn't talk to me about this. It's like you want to punish me. All I do is support you and our family, and all you do is try to fuck it up! And then make it my problem to try and sort out . . . I don't even know if we can sort it out this time, Molly. You've really fucked it this time.'

Molly couldn't respond. She just couldn't find any words. She felt crushed.

'You know what – I can't do this,' Tom said, suddenly getting to his feet and leaving the room.

It was all Molly could do to sit and listen as the front door slammed shut and she heard Tom's footsteps quickly patter down the steps to the main door.

She tried to reassure herself that he'd just gone for a walk, he was just clearing his head, he'd be back soon, and they'd talk when he was calm and they'd sort this out . . . But as she sat there in the painful silence, tears still rolling down her face, it didn't feel like that at all. It felt like she really had fucked it this time, and she'd lost him. And she'd never felt more alone.

Chapter 56

FOUND IT . . .

Sometimes you just knew.

And Liz just knew.

Perhaps it was the balmy late-April weather putting a shine on everything, the sun gently warming their faces and telling them spring was here, and nature was thriving again. Perhaps it was how unassuming she'd been on the drive over, thinking she wouldn't like it, thinking she'd have to settle, let Gerald decide for them as she felt quite unfussed about the whole thing . . .

But how wrong she'd been about that. Her stomach was fluttering delightfully as her eyes took in the sights before her, and she unconsciously gripped on to Gerald's hand, willing him to feel what she felt.

She couldn't tear her eyes away from the beautiful tall windows, the view over the apple orchard, and the immense light that flooded the large conservatory they were standing in.

It was amazing that this was a pub. It was out in a little village the other side of High Wycombe, and it was a complete gem. And calling it a 'pub' simply didn't do it any justice whatsoever. The Olde Bell was disguised as a quirky eighteenth-century tavern at the front, but once entering, the low ceilings and wonky door frames only lasted a few feet before it opened out into a stunning glass-box extension complete with a Michelin-starred restaurant to one side, a gin and champagne bar to the other and a view over its own private enclosed orchard, complete with pretty arbours, blossom trees and the gentle hum of nature hanging in the air. It was like stepping through the wardrobe into their own private Narnia. But no snow queens and talking beavers, just some vintage gins and cheese soufflés that came with tiny polished silver spoons instead.

They could do the ceremony, food, drink, canapés, rooms for the immediate family and could accommodate a wedding for up to forty people, with a few more in the evening if they wished.

It felt something like perfect. Liz couldn't decide whether it looked more wonderful in the summer, or if its quiet decadence would be better suited to a frosty winter wedding.

She didn't want to get her hopes up before discussing the price, but frankly – with both of them in very well-paid jobs in the city, and with no dependants, money wasn't really an issue. And up to now, they hadn't really had much to spend it on.

Liz turned to look at Gerald, trying not to convey any emotion in her face, he might hate it after all, and there was no way they could get married somewhere only one of them felt happy in.

But she needn't have worried; his face was brimming

with child-like excitement. Unlike Liz, he was an open book. What he was thinking seemed to be permanently conveyed on his face, something Liz loved him for all the more, possibly because she was almost the exact opposite when it came to expressing feelings.

As she looked up at him, she allowed herself a small smile in return. How could she not? Being in this place, together, feeling the same about it . . . it felt cheesy thinking it, but it really did feel like it was meant to be.

He leaned in closer to her ear. 'I love it,' he said briskly. His voice full of excitement.

'Really?' Liz said coyly. 'Because we both do have to love it, don't we. And honestly, if it's not the one then we need to be honest about that. We can keep looking, but this seems beyond perfect to me. I can picture us here . . . the light streaming in, the champagne waiting, saying "I do" in front of the garden with our friends arced around us . . . Can you see it?'

'Liz,' Gerald said, almost sternly, 'I said I love it.'

Liz allowed herself to grin like a schoolgirl for just a moment before composing herself. If there had been no one else around, she might have allowed herself a triumphant little squeal.

'Okay,' she said, her lips tight across her teeth from smiling. 'I never thought I'd fall in love with a place this much, but the pictures didn't even do it justice. This is the one, Gerald. This is the one.'

A man referring to himself only as Simon had shown them around. He was the events manager, and looked like

he was probably into yachts and skiing. He had a wea-
thered tan and floppy hair that went smartly with his
crisp Ralph Lauren shirt and chinos. He'd explained a
few bits about the food, the set-up, and the ceremony
options but had mostly let the venue speak for itself.

'So what do you think?' Simon said from a few paces
behind them. 'Would you like me to look into availability
for you?'

Liz glanced quickly up at Gerald. His face was screaming
yes quite ferociously. 'That'd be great. We really like it.'

At the sound of the word 'availability' Liz had gathered
herself completely, ignoring how fast her heart was thud-
ding in her chest. Her business head was back on; finding
and loving this place was only the first hurdle, now it was
in the hands of tanned Simon and his 'availability'.

'Okay . . .' Simon said, pulling out an iPad and tapping
at it a few times. 'So do you know which year you're
looking at?'

Liz felt her shoulders physically drop a little. That was
not a great start. Liz hadn't really considered that it would
be 'years' until they could get the venue.

'Er . . . not really. How many years in advance are you
taking bookings for?' Liz was remaining calm but she
began to feel a little deflated. She daren't look at Gerald
right now, he probably looked like a kicked puppy.

'Well, usually we run two years ahead for weekend
dates. Friday weddings are almost as popular but we might
have a Thursday or a Monday. It really depends what time
of year you're looking for?'

337

A Thursday or a Monday? It had never occurred to Liz that she wouldn't get married on a weekend. Clearly there were many things she didn't know about organising a wedding.

'Well, I think autumn might be nice?' Liz said, looking up at Gerald, who shrugged and nodded at the same time. But had deflation pasted agonisingly over his face now.

'Hmmm,' Simon said, tapping a little more furiously now. 'September is probably our most popular month, funnily enough. I think the next weekend date I have would be in two years' time for a September or October wedding, unless you'd look at week days in which case there's one Thursday left next year, but that's about it.'

'Wow,' Liz said audibly. She felt incredibly disappointed. The initial elation and Narnia-like tiny-soufflé vibes were replaced with frustration at having found something they wanted so instantly, yet were now being told they'd have to wait years for.

Simon had clearly sensed their turmoil. Liz was thankful that he spoke next. She wasn't really sure what to say.

'Look, you don't have to make a decision right now. Why don't I email you with the available dates and once you've looked around at any other venues you're seeing, and made some more decisions, you can let me know? Plus – there's always a chance of a cancellation. They don't happen that often but we've had the odd one. We could just agree to stay in touch? What do you think?'

Despite how incredibly charming Simon was, it was obvious that he was letting them down gently. She didn't want to wait over two years to get married, and getting married on a crappy Thursday in February when everyone had to work the next day just seemed wrong. It wasn't how she'd imagined it.

'Of course,' Gerald said, stepping in and shaking Simon's hand firmly. Liz shook it in turn and tried hard to not let her disappointment show.

There'd be other places. Ones that were just as perfect. She said this to herself slightly unconvincingly as she walked out of The Olde Bell, hand in hand with Gerald, and decided she didn't want to look at him right now.

Yes, there'd be other places.

Places just as perfect.

Just as wonderful and enchanting.

Places with their own gin bar and orchard and complete with their own charming, well-pressed 'Simon'.

But as they reached the car and she looked up at Gerald's face again, she could see that he didn't believe any of that for a second.

And if she was honest, neither did she . . .

Chapter 57

COME BACK, TOLLY . . .

Tom had barely spoken to her since the other night.

It had been agony.

Wanting so much to make things right, but not being able to find any words. Molly knew she'd gone too far this time. He could barely look at her. And found any excuse not to be in her company for too long. She knew she needed to wait until he was ready to talk again, but it felt like this might go on for ever. And it was killing her.

It was Friday evening and the prospect of a weekend of him ignoring her in a series of awkward silences was not a welcome one.

Molly sat on their battered sofa struggling to feel comfortable, while Tom was putting Marley to bed. Normally they did it together, but Molly could sense that wasn't the right thing this evening. She was allowing him some time with his son. He was the one thing that might put him in a slightly better mood perhaps . . .

They needed to talk. They couldn't carry on like this.

Tom eventually appeared. Molly watched him as he walked into their living room avoiding looking at her – he looked tired, worried, broken.

She said nothing as he fetched himself an uncharacteristic beer from the fridge and sat down next to her. It was progress at least. They were sitting in the same room within touching distance of each other for the first time in four days. Molly desperately wanted him to say something now.

'I don't want to do this,' Tom said, his head hung low as he stared into the neck of his beer bottle.

Molly's heart sank. Do what? Be with her? Was he leaving her? Was he saying he couldn't be with her any more? Her mind was racing.

'Don't want to do what . . . ?' Molly said after a few moments, her voice small.

Tom sighed before responding. 'Do this – fight with you. We need to find a way to sort this out, Molly – for both our sakes. For the sake of our kids.'

Molly felt instant relief. He wanted to sort things out. She could burst into tears. It was what she wanted as well.

Tom took a swig of his beer and turned to face her.

'You make it really hard to love you sometimes, you know,' he said, his eyes slightly damp. 'But look. I can't change who you are. You are reckless and annoying and you do stupid fucking things, but I guess those are some of the reasons I fell in love with you in the first place, Molly.'

Molly sat silently. Simply listening.

'You drive me crazy, but there's no point me shouting at you because you fucked up, and making you feel bad

341

about it for ever isn't going to help either of us. Obviously I'm devastated we've lost the cash, but it is just cash. We've still got what's most important, haven't we? There's a slim chance the police might catch this guy, but as that's highly unlikely I think we just need to write this off. The money is gone. There's no point dwelling on it. We start over from now. New plan, new timeframe, and we never make the same mistake again. Okay?'

Molly couldn't talk. She simply nodded. And felt a huge relief. Tom was right, screaming and shouting wasn't going to get their money back, and there was no point letting it destroy their relationship. It was time to look forward and learn from their mistakes. Or rather — for her to learn from her mistakes.

'You need to understand that whilst I love you, I don't know if I can trust you right now. With money and stuff, I mean.'

'Okay . . .' Molly kept listening but shifted uncomfortably. She knew she'd brought this on herself, but she couldn't help but feel like Tom was treating her like a child.

'The truth is, I've closed the joint account, emptied it completely. And from now on I'm going to handle all the finances. I'll draw cash out and you'll have an allowance for groceries and stuff, but any big purchases you'll need to come to me. I'm sorry, Molly, but I just don't see any other way. You're going to have to suck it up for a few months until we get right again.'

Molly nodded slowly but felt a little shocked. She'd

massively messed up – yes. But she was a grown woman and a mother. This felt wrong. But what could she say . . . ?

Tom didn't seem interested in discussing it further. He changed the subject fairly quickly. 'And I've had good news. There's an opportunity for a promotion at work. I wasn't sure whether I'd go for it, because it potentially means a bit more travel, slightly longer hours, and with the new baby coming along I didn't think it was the right time, but given recent events, perhaps it's the exact right time. We need more money. There's a bonus scheme attached to this because it's a step into junior management too, so we could recoup our losses in no time. Provided I hit my numbers that is, but my boss thinks it's perfect for me. I think I'm going to go for it.'

'Umm . . . Well, yeah. I think it actually does sound like pretty perfect timing,' Molly said, still feeling unsettled but realising she was resigned. It was clear that she had no plan to get them out of this mess, so for the meantime she simply needed to let Tom take over, and in a few months they'd be okay again. She needed to believe that. 'I suppose it's what we need,' she added, attempting a small smile.

'I reckon so too,' Tom said, his demeanour relaxing again. 'Now, it's time for you to look after yourself and our babies. All the pressure is off – I think that's what we need right now. The travel business can wait, we'll spend this year planning and saving, and before you know it we'll have it all. Honestly. Sometimes it takes something

343

really shit to happen, before you get to the good stuff. That's all.'

'Okay. I think I can agree to that too. No more stupid decisions. We're in it together and for the long term now,' Molly said, nodding and trying to feel positive that Tom had it all worked out in spite of her actions.

Tom finished his beer, and for the first time in days they sat on the sofa together and things started to feel a little like they were getting back to normal. Even if it was a new normal . . . and one that Molly wasn't entirely sure she was comfortable with.

Chapter 58

SHIT. HE'S MOVING.

Remember when you'd just sit in cafes,
As your tiny baby slept in their pram?
Remember how quiet and still they were?
Well, now the Universe don't give a damn.

Remember when clothes looked so tiny,
And everyone commented 'how cute'?
Remember when your carpet wasn't 90% rice cake
And nappies didn't contain whole chunks of fruit?

Remember when your house wasn't a death trap,
That resembled a neon plastic squat?
Remember your coffee table was used for actual
* drinks,*
Not another cornered object to maim your tot . . .

Well, remember those days with great fondness,
As you remove another breadstick from your hair.
Then crack open the wine, tell yourself all will be
* fine,*
At least they still can't understand you when you
* swear.*

It felt like the end of an era.

It looked so odd, like he was too small to actually do it, but William was crawling around the carpet, gaining speed and momentum on what felt like an hourly basis.

Not only that, he'd begun crawling up furniture and lifting himself into a standing position within days of mastering his four-limbed mode of getting around.

It was weird how every great milestone seemed to be tainted with a bit of sadness that you were saying goodbye to the last stage. Saying goodbye to a stationary baby. Saying goodbye to just leaving him in the pram. Saying goodbye to going to cafes and actually sitting down EVER AGAIN.

Emily decided to be thankful that it had taken him until he was nearly nine months old to work it out. Two of her NCT friends had babies walking at nine months, who had been crawling at six. She'd had an extra few months of still having some nice things in her home. Although, it had dawned on her that she may not be able to have anything in her house that was valuable or break-able below waist height for the foreseeable future, considering what William was currently doing to Paul's collection of PlayStation games . . .

A welcome sacrifice, if she got to sit down for a few minutes – Emily decided. He'd barely played the thing in months anyway. He'd not really been allowed to.

In a moment, she was going to attempt some mascara and under-eye concealer in the living-room mirror and she might even go really nuts and put some lippy on. She was meeting Molly and Liz in town shortly for Last Saturday Club, and, given William's recent need for speed (and need to prevent his mummy from sitting down with a glass of wine and catching up with her friends), she'd taken the executive decision to leave him with Paul for a boys' day. The weather was good – they could play in the garden and enjoy the spring sunshine, as it inevitably wouldn't last.

Emily couldn't wait to see her friends. The year was flying by. She was supposed to be back at work in ten weeks, which was a terrifying prospect she wasn't mentally ready to confront yet. Every time the thought crept into her head she began to feel anxious, despite the few keeping-in-touch days she'd had, which had done nothing for her anxiety levels. Or ability to wear an underwired bra again.

She really wasn't sure she wanted her old life back now. Paul was completely supportive, and had said they'd find a way to get by financially if she wanted to try and make a career out of blogging. She really did. And all her friends were telling her to go for it. But making that final commitment, and letting go of everything she'd worked for in her career up until now, was not coming easily. She was still scared she'd take the plunge and regret it. It was such a big decision.

Emily shook thoughts of thongs and Public Relations proposals out of her mind.

She had lippy to apply and an afternoon with her best

friends ahead, time to concentrate on enjoying that instead.

Molly looked more than a bit dishevelled as she arrived. Late, of course. But it was an unusually warm weekend for the end of April, which was strange when you considered that only a few weeks ago there was snow on the ground. It did mean that nobody quite knew what to wear though . . . You'd pass people on the high street dressed in T-shirts and shorts, swiftly followed by couples zipped up to their chins in winter coats with boots on. This was what spring looked like in the UK.

But one thing was for sure, having a nearly nine-month-old baby strapped to the front of a rapidly expanding baby bump in the muggy spring heat was enough to exhaust anyone. Even the ever-breezy Molly, who had been seeming increasingly less breezy as her second pregnancy had gone on.

Liz immediately got to her feet and let Molly squeeze past to join her on the sofa. They were back in O'Neills in High Wycombe. The beer garden to the front of the pub was rammed, but inside was lofty and empty as everyone else poured on to pub benches to soak up the limited rays. At Molly's request, the three friends had picked a table inside. Emily remembered the sweaty joys of pregnancy in the sunshine, so she had every sympathy.

'You okay?' Emily said, waiting for Molly to unwrap her son and assemble herself into something close to a comfy position next to Liz.

'Urgh. This heat is killing me. I massively underestimated how hot it was, so I wore my big coat and put Marley in a fleecy suit. It's literally been like having a hot-water bottle strapped to me whilst completing some kind of epic journey. Look how much I'm sweating, I feel like I've taken the fucking ring to the centre of Mordor. I started getting paranoid he might be too hot, so I walked even faster to get here. So now I'm not only boiling but also soaked in sweat and feel like I've done a hundred lunges, so yeah, I'm great!' Molly said, laughing at herself by the end and placing a sleeping Marley down on the sofa beside her, unzipping his fleecy suit to release some heat.

'Oh, I don't envy you at all. If you'd just said, we could have shared a cab! Why don't you let us help you, sweetie? It's okay to ask for a lift when you're five months pregnant with a baby to carry about in the meantime, you know,' Emily said, looking sympathetically at her friend.

'Hey, you know me. I like to walk and I'm fine usually. The heat just caught me by surprise is all. Anyway,' Molly said, not wanting to dwell, 'I'm here now. And in desperate need of some ice water, if you wouldn't mind watching Marley for a sec?'

'I'll get it,' Liz said, standing up abruptly and heading to the bar for her sweaty pregnant friend.

'You okay otherwise, though?' Emily asked, clearly concerned for her friend.

'Yeah, soldiering on. I'm actually feeling so much better now that I've slowed things down on the business front.

349

I'm still doing bits here and there but now Tom's got this promotion at work I can relax a little on the finances and concentrate on being sweaty and exhausted most of the time, like every mother dreams . . .'

The two friends laughed as Liz headed back with a pint of ice water for Molly.

'Share the joke, ladies,' Liz said, smiling, as she retook her seat and watched in awe as Molly downed the water she'd just been passed, like a hungover teenager.

'Molly was just saying she's slowing the business stuff down a bit while she's pregnant,' Emily said on Molly's behalf, as her friend glugged down the last of her drink.

'Oh right . . .' Liz said, seeming a bit confused. 'Last time I spoke to you, it was the exact opposite! You were raring to go, is everything okay?'

Molly paused for a moment. She hadn't told her friends about what had happened to the money she lost. It was hard to relive it, if she was honest.

'Well . . .' Molly began. Not quite knowing where to start with it all but wanting to get it off her chest. 'I fucked up a bit.'

Both Emily and Liz raised their eyebrows at her.

'Fucked up how . . . ?' Liz said, picking up her wine and taking a slow sip.

'Nothing much . . . I just, erm, lost all our money and the savings my dad gave me, on some scam on the Internet . . . and stuff . . .' Molly flicked her eyes between her two friends to monitor their reactions. She was very much hoping she'd be able to brush it under the carpet without much discussion, but judging by the wide unblinking eyes that were staring back at her, maybe not.

Emily gasped slightly as the words she'd just heard sank in, and appeared to develop a slight stammer which prevented her from talking temporarily.

'Wow,' Liz said, slightly taken aback. 'That's so awful for you. I did not expect you to say that, but okay, when did this happen? Can you get the money back? Have you reported it?'

'Yeah. A little while ago now, I guess. All reported and the police say it's unlikely but they'll do their best,' Molly said, shrugging like she was talking about something totally unimportant.

'I . . . I just can't believe it. I'm so sorry. You seem so okay about it? Are you?' Emily said, regaining the power of speech but not the power of blinking just yet.

'I am now. It's been a pretty shitty few weeks. Tom stopped talking to me, and even though it's getting better, he's become really controlling now. We've closed the joint account, and basically all the money is his . . . so he gives me cash when I need it, but I've got little to nothing coming into my own account, so I'm totally beholden to him. It's weird. But then his promotion could not have come at a better time. So we're taking a bit of a step back and I have promised to absolutely not go into a career in finance any time soon.'

'So, are you okay with that?' Liz said, her face full of concern.

'How can I not be?' Molly said, shrugging. 'I lost all

351

our money. And now we're reliant on his wages for everything and I've got no way of financing or starting a business, so I'm stuck.'

'That's awful, sweetie. I don't know what to say. I know you'll come through this, but it must have been so horrible. You should have told us sooner, maybe we could have helped . . .' Emily said, trying to reassure her friend.

'I know. It'll be okay eventually. Anyway – I don't want to talk about it any more. It's been a bit of a downer for me, as you can imagine . . . Sorry I didn't tell you sooner. I just felt a bit ashamed, if I'm honest. I know you've probably not had this – but it's really hard when you've done something really stupid that you know you should fess up about; it feels easier to just pretend it never happened . . . but then it feels like this huge weight you're carrying round with you, which you constantly need to unload, but you can't, do you know what I mean?'

Liz felt disconcerted by Molly's intense eye contact. She knew that feeling only too well, but she'd never be telling her secrets. They were dead and buried and would never see the light of day. It had to be that way. She suppressed any feelings of guilt she felt rising up from within, and managed a weak smile.

'We understand,' Emily said. Able to blink again now. 'Let's change the subject, then. I want to hear about the wedding planning, Lizzie-pants! How's it all going? Have you picked a theme? A colour scheme? How many ushers and bridesmaids are you going to have? Have you decided your menu? The cake! Ooh, are you having a live band?'

Liz wasn't sure which question to tackle first . . .

'No, no, none, no and no?' Liz answered slightly sarcastically.

Emily looked a little deflated.

'But actually . . .' Liz continued, unsure whether she wanted to share her trip to The Olde Bell with her friends, before remembering it was unlikely she'd ever get married there anyway so what difference would it make.

'We did kind of, find somewhere . . .'

'Really?' Emily eyes became so wide it looked as though her eyeballs might pop out.

'Yes . . .' Liz said slowly, casting her mind back to how perfect it was and feeling a little sad about it. 'But unfortunately, it's not available until the moon rises in Venus and cats rule the world, so it's a no.'

'Oh, that's so annoying for you,' Emily said, looking genuinely devastated for her friend.

'Just means it wasn't meant to be and you'll find something better,' Molly added, smiling and finally looking a little less hot and sweaty, Marley still fast asleep next to her.

Liz wanted to believe her. But she wasn't sure that was true. She didn't see the point in dwelling on it any longer, though.

The friends sat and chatted for a long time, laughing and talking about anything and everything. Their lives suddenly seemed packed full again; so many decisions and wonderful things to look forward to in the next few months.

353

Not least another baby, career changes and a wedding. And apparently, according to Emily, who had collated a very interesting set of options for Liz to peruse throughout the afternoon, she could also now have a wedding cake made entirely out of cheese. Who knew?

Chapter 59

ANGEL NEGOTIATIONS

Emily

Girls. I've made a decision.

I think.

I know you probably think I'm being a bit hasty here but I've decided not to go back to Angel PR.

I know I used to love my job – but I just don't feel like it's me any more!

I think chatting it through with you both the other day at the pub helped me realise that.

I'm terrified but I think it's the right decision.

I've talked it through with Paul and he's 100% behind me.

I've had some really amazing opportunities come up through the blog and actually, if I do it properly I can make a decent wage.

Obvs it won't match my PR salary but it's enough for me to contribute to the bills and more importantly I won't

have crazy childcare costs!

Over half my salary would go on just paying for nursery otherwise, how crazy is that? I don't even know how people do it!

So fuck it.

I'm waving goodbye to the PR world and hello to being a professional blogger!

What do you think?

Am I mad?

Fuck – you think I'm mad don't you?

This is not just because I don't want to wear proper bras any more.

Honestly.

Girls?

Molly

I think that's great hunny but it's 4.23 a.m.

Can we talk about this when it's time for humans to actually be awake?

I was having a really nice dream about Tom Hardy and you totally ruined it . . . lol

Emily

Okay point taken.

I'll chat to you when the sun's actually up.

I was just so excited about it I couldn't
hold it in!
Apologies – I'll let you get back to
Tom.
And Tom.
Both Toms.
I'll go now.

Chapter 60

WINNER, WINNER – BIRTHDAY DINNER

Birthdays felt different now.

When Emily thought back to her last birthday – the barbecue, the sweating, the need she always felt to throw a big party and host everyone, the sweating again – she began to wonder where that girl had gone.

There'd been a shift in her over the last few weeks. Over the last year really, if she thought about it. Whether she'd just grown up a bit – perhaps motherhood really had changed her and made her see where her priorities needed to lie – or maybe because she'd finally made the decision not to go back to work in PR, and instead use her blogging as a career, she didn't know, but she felt so much more relaxed about that kind of thing now. The girl who used to sulk when she didn't get her own way, who had every part of her life so perfectly planned all the time, who was far too quick to judge others around her, and wouldn't dare leave the house without perfectly plucked brows and matching handbag and high heels on – well, that girl was a bit of a dick really. And Emily felt slightly ashamed that that used to be her.

She'd got a bit of perspective now. Handbags and shoes were still lovely (obviously), and there was nothing like a fresh haircut and new lipstick to put a smile on your face, but it was all insignificant in comparison to her little family and the new life they were carving out.

A life that she was slowly learning to appreciate and embrace more and more, as the party girl faded and the sweaty nights in smoky nightclubs became nothing more than sweaty, smoky memories.

She wanted her birthday to only be about her little family this year. There were so many years she'd partied and drunk and danced the night away, and those times would be back again at some point in the seemingly distant future, but right now she couldn't think of anything worse. The idea of squeezing herself into something so restrictive it was impossible to go to the loo in, in heels she could barely balance in, to drink shots of awful things that would make her feel just as awful, to music she no longer related to, in places she was made to feel old and flabby, was just not her idea of fun.

She was thirty-one, and it was okay to say that she'd partied for over a decade, had some amazing times and that now she was over it, and ready to concentrate on her baby boy and her husband for a while.

She knew she could do something low-key like go out for a nice meal or something, but that didn't float her boat either. She'd see Molly and Liz for a few glasses of wine at some point, and she'd already met up with her mummy friends earlier in the day for cake and the

germ-filled, slightly sticky, don't-look-too-closely-between-the-cracks delights of soft-play, which had been a true celebratory treat and required a lot of hand sanitiser afterwards.

But now it was Friday evening, Paul was due home any moment and she couldn't wait to see him, hug him, and spend the weekend just the three of them.

William was busy gurgling to himself in the Jumperoo in the living room as Emily inspected her clothes in the mirror for any signs of human seepage, and quickly scraped her hair back into a slightly neater messy bun. She dabbed on a little lip-balm and smiled back at her reflection, taking a moment to really look at herself; she actually didn't look so tired now. A few months ago, the bags under her eyes were so dark she looked ill, her skin looked grey and she hated her reflection most of the time. She didn't feel that way any more. Even without much make-up, the colour was back in her cheeks, her eyes sparkled again, and she looked happy.

Her smile widened as she heard Paul's key turn in the front door.

As he walked into their little lounge, he smiled back at her, placing his bag and suit jacket on the chair, and immediately scooping her into a hug and planting a sweet kiss on her lips, as he let his eyes flick over her face for a moment.

'Hey, birthday girl. You look happy,' he said finally. 'How's your day been?'

'Good actually,' Emily said, realising she probably didn't say that enough. It was easier to reel off the parts of her day where she'd been late, tired, hungry, pooed, puked or weed on etc. etc. . . . She could easily spend the next few minutes relaying the story of how she was fairly sure she'd spotted an actual human turd jiggling its way to the top of the ball-pit during today's soft-play extravaganza, but she didn't want to. She just wanted to focus on the hopefully turd-free weekend that lay ahead. 'Today was fun, but now I'm just really looking forward to a nice chilled birthday weekend with my boys.'

'Great. Me too,' Paul said, taking a deep satisfying breath. 'Now are you sure you aren't going to change your mind and suddenly tell me tomorrow that I should have planned a surprise party, or a cruise down the Thames, or arranged a sky-dive with some dancing ferrets at the finish line or something?' He was laughing, but with an undertone of suspicion.

'Ha. I know it's not like me to want to do nothing, but I'm a new woman, Paul. I've got everything I need right here. So you can save the sky-dives and ferrets for when I'm back to getting eight hours sleep a night and can be arsed to get my roots done, okay?'

'Well, I'm glad to hear it. I thought we could get a takeaway tonight and tomorrow we'll head out for a nice walk and grab a pub lunch or something. Or we can just play it totally by ear, it's your weekend after all.'

Emily smiled again broadly. 'That sounds perfect. You

361

go and have a shower and I'll get Deliveroo up on the iPad. And as it's my birthday, let's go crazy and order an Ebi Katsu each with our mains instead of sharing. We are living life on the edge tonight, husband . . .'

Paul kissed her again and rolled his eyes playfully at her before heading upstairs.

Emily smiled to herself as she sat down on the sofa and looked lovingly at her son, who was still blissfully bobbing around in the Jumperoo.

Yes. Life was working out pretty blissfully; she was in her early thirties with everything she wanted. She probably needed to remind herself of that a little more often. She was married to a wonderful, kind man, she had a brilliant, happy baby boy that they both adored, she was about to embark on an exciting new career in blogging, which she loved, and she had brilliant people in her life. And for everything else she had a wicked sense of humour, a cupboard packed with gin and chocolate, and a Deliveroo app that would bring hot noodles right to her door at the press of a button, so yeah, right now life couldn't get much better.

And she just about had time to publish a little blog post she'd been brewing during the early hours before she ordered their dinner.

Happy Birthday to Me

It's my birthday today. And I'm celebrating it with family, alcohol, a hugely overpriced new lipstick and some ramen, which I thoroughly deserve.

So for anyone celebrating a birthday soon, with a small person in tow, I thought you'd like to know what I'm expecting from my birthday celebration today. I've provided a copy to my husband in advance. Obviously. And please feel free to print out if you wish to do the same:

1. For the first time in nearly ten months, I would like to wake up after the fucking sun does. Someone else can be on porridge and Octonauts duty until then. Thanks.

2. I would like to have a bath, not a shower, but a long languishing soak in the tub, from which I will emerge when I bloody well feel like it, without conditioner stuck in my ear and razor burn under my armpits.

3. I would like to wear underwear without nursing clips and reacquaint myself with my hairbrush.

363

4. I want to have a conversation in the morning that isn't about who Wendy the Wide-Mouthed Frog spoke to next in the jungle, and talk using my normal adult voice for an entire day.

5. I would like to eat with BOTH hands.

6. Just for once I want to enter my living room in the morning and not feel like I've been punched in the face by Toys'R'Us. 24 hours in a neon-plastic-free zone is not that much to ask. Clearly, the Jumperoo will have to be dismantled throughout the night by a team of trained professionals and stored in an appropriate facility.

7. It's MY day – so no nursery rhymes, no farmyard noises and no In The F-ing Night Garden. Iggle Piggle can suck it.

8. I will happily put the pureed sweet potato into the baby, but I'm making it someone else's responsibility when it comes out the other end.

9. I will be drinking at lunchtime. Sorry, FROM lunchtime. In abundance. Until a time of my choosing.

10. I need everyone to tell me I look young.

11. I need to everyone to tell me I look thin.

12. I need a lot of cards in which people tell me how young and thin I look.

13. I need gifts that help me get drunk, thin and younger – the first person who presents me with a Mothercare gift card and some nipple cream will be asked to take care of the sweet potato nappy and politely be escorted out.

#thatisall
#happybloodybirthdaytome

Chapter 61

GETTING THERE

Liz
Girls. I've done something crazy!

Emily
Did you decide to get the cheese
wedding cake?? I knew you'd come
around once you'd seen my collage!

Liz
Well it was a tough decision but no
. . . it's even more risqué than that.

Emily
Shaved your head and had a full body
tattoo?

Liz
Close. But no.

Emily
Fostered a family of travelling rabbits?

Liz
That doesn't even make sense.

Emily

I know. I'm too tired to be witty.
I'm all out now. So you may carry on.

Liz

Thank you.
Okay. So . . . I've booked the wedding
venue.

Emily

WHAT!!??
That actually is a bit crazy (for you)
(no offence!)
How exciting!
That was seriously fast work – last
time I spoke to you, you'd given up
and were using wedding magazines
as coasters . . .

Liz

Well yes.
I still am.
But I got a call earlier from the venue
we found that we loved but was
booked up until the end of time . . .
and they had a cancellation! Can you
believe it? I'm still pinching myself a
bit, but I had to take it because
there's just nowhere else that
compares!

Emily

Wow. That's brilliant news – so happy
you got the place you really wanted.
When is it?

Molly

Oh wow – that is amazing news Liz! I
knew the universe would listen ;)

Liz

Thank you ladies.
And well that's the thing . . .
It's the second weekend of
September. Which I know is really
close to when your baby's due Molly
– so I'm hoping it's all going to work
out because I want you to be there
more than anything. But I also
wanted the venue more than anything
too . . .
I'm sorry it's so close! I didn't really
have any choice . . . I hope you're not
angry with me.

Molly

Hey – don't be silly! You absolutely
did the right thing and I'm sure we'll
be there. Even if I have to squat down
and give birth as you walk down the
aisle I am not missing it! OK?

Emily

Ooh how romantic . . . that's even better than the cake made of cheese.

Liz

Obviously I'm totally hoping for this scenario, but if you could have the baby a week or so beforehand that would be lovely too.

Emily

Spoil sport.

Molly

Ha. Well okay. I'll do my best xx

Emily

Wow – September is so soon! Are you going to have enough time to organise everything?? It's June already – that's literally weeks away!! It took me years to plan mine!

Liz

I hope so. I'm sure it'll be fine.
We're going very low-key.
There's not much to organise to be honest – there's a wedding planner at the venue so that's all sorted.
I'm just going to message everyone to

save the date and the rest seems
pretty straightforward to me.
Do not worry Emily.
It's all under control.
And I'm still not having a fucking cake
made of cheese so please stop
asking.

Emily

Ha. Well when you say it like that I'm
now kind of wondering why I stressed
for 24 months!
(And okay. No more cake of cheese
chat. I promise.)

Liz

Because it wouldn't be your
wedding if it hadn't been wonderfully over the top and stressful. It
was perfectly you. But mine will be
almost boring in comparison! I just
want everything really simple and
understated.
So just save the date and don't worry
about it. Okay?

Emily

Okay. I'm sure it'll be perfect too. And
consider the date well and truly
saved.

Molly
Ditto. Can't wait. I'm off for a nap now
– all this talk of aisle-births has knackered me out!

Liz
Ha. Thanks ladies.
Have a nice nap Molly. xxx

Chapter 62

THE WEDDING RUSH

June had flown by.

Liz had barely stopped to think about her wedding, she had been so busy at work. And when thoughts of her imminent nuptials did creep into her head, they weren't smiley happy relaxed ones – they were *'oh fuck I'm getting married in literally a few weeks and haven't a clue what's going on because I don't have time to think about any of this shit'* ones.

It had actually begun to make her feel really quite annoyed when people asked her about it in conversation now – questioning her on whether she'd sorted her flowers, had her dress fitted, picked the food and music, decided what centrepieces and favours she was going to have . . . she would have loved to have had all the answers for them, but she didn't. She wasn't your typical blushing gushing bride she supposed, she was mostly working fourteen-hour days, juggling an insane high-stress workload and really rather hoping that the wedding planner she was paying a rather large amount of money for, who kept leaving her slightly panicky voicemails, would just do all that stuff for her. Because she quite frankly didn't have the time.

She was only just managing to eat and sleep and maintain the life of a cat, let alone decide whether she preferred peonies or roses in her bouquet. She didn't see that as very fucking important, if she was honest. She thought that was why she was hiring Claire with the flicky hair and grey suit, but it was clear it didn't really work like that. And at some point, she was going to have to make time to have some input and get back to one of her 'polite yet firm with an undertone of desperation' emails before flicky-haired Claire had some kind of flicky-haired breakdown.

Liz was beginning to feel a bit overwhelmed by it all. She was currently sitting at her desk, swamped by paperwork, her inbox overflowing and her lipstick in desperate need of reapplication; she had a habit of pursing her lips tightly together when she concentrated – or was trying to ignore pissy emails from the increasingly anxious flicky-haired Claire. Liz took her eyes away from the screen, took a few sips from her water bottle and rubbed her temples.

She needed to get a grip on everything. She knew that. This wasn't fair to Gerald. This wasn't fair on anyone. She couldn't blame everything on work. She could make time if she wanted to, she knew that. She just needed to get on with it and focus her mind.

It was eleven weeks until her wedding. Two and a half months. And she didn't even have a dress. She began to wonder for a moment if they were messing this all up – rushing to get married just because they wanted so much to do it at The Olde Bell. Was she being an idiot about this? Wasn't this supposed to be fun? Right now it felt like a chore, frankly. Were they making a mistake putting all this pressure on themselves?

Liz pondered her choices for a moment. She couldn't work out if she was just stressed because there was so much going on right now, or if she was genuinely doubting whether she was doing the right thing. A weak but familiar sense of guilt began to rise up and sit in her chest. It was normal to begin questioning things just before you got married, wasn't it? Surely it was, she thought to herself, and hoped she was right.

Liz jumped slightly as a firm tap sounded at her office door.

She sat up straight, cleared her throat and straightened her clothes slightly, running her fingers through her fringe automatically before summoning her intruder.

'And how is my beautiful fiancée this fine afternoon?' Gerald said smoothly, as he let himself into her office and pushed the door closed behind him.

It was a strange relief that it was Gerald. Although that niggling sense of guilt was still lingering.

'Ah the case files I asked for. Thank you,' Liz said, noticing the clearly labelled box file in his hand.

'Indeed. You okay? You look a bit tired. Perhaps we could call it a day early and grab some food after work?'

Liz wanted to, she really did. But she just had so much to do. 'I'd love to, but I'm swamped. And exhausted – thanks for noticing.' She managed a small sarcastic smile. But she really was exhausted.

'Hey, the offer is there. Sometimes it does us all good to knock off early and come back fresh the next day, is all I'm saying. Perhaps a few hours out of this office will do you good?'

Liz felt slightly irritated but she knew he was right. She was so used to powering through, it was the way she did things. But now she thought about it, she'd skipped lunch, and actually felt weak because of it. Maybe escaping to eat something wasn't such a bad idea.

Liz allowed herself to smile again, a friendlier one this time. It felt good to know he was looking out for her. It felt good to have someone who cared.

'Okay,' she said suddenly and a little triumphantly.

'I expected more of a fight than that from my feisty future wife. I think you might be going soft,' Gerald said, winking at her with a grin that could only be described as 'goofy' pasted across his face.

'I'm too tired to fight. And plus, I am in serious need of carbs and a cold beer, and you are just the person to accompany me.'

'Now that I won't argue with,' Gerald said, softening his eyes as his gaze met hers.

'Everything is okay though, isn't it? I mean, I know work is crazy, but everything else is okay? I keep getting messages from the wedding planner saying she can't get hold of you. I'm sure I'm just being paranoid but you're not putting it off, are you? I keep thinking you might be having second thoughts . . .'

Liz felt awkward for a moment, like he could read her

375

mind, but the feeling passed quickly. Like hearing him say all that out loud only confirmed to her what she already knew – that she loved him. That she wanted to marry him. And that she needed to take a break from work and get back to flicky-haired Claire before she totally lost her flicky-haired shit.

Liz allowed herself a bigger smile now. 'Of course not,' she said eventually. 'I've been so busy I just couldn't find time to come up for air. But I promise you we will call her together over dinner and answer all her questions, and finally get this wedding started. Okay?'

Gerald looked visibly relieved. His goofy grin was back. He didn't say anything, but simply leaned in, took her hand and squeezed it.

Liz felt herself relax a little for the first time in as long as she could remember. The old Liz was behind her now, and she didn't need to look back ever again. She had the perfect venue, the perfect man, and the perfect life all ready and waiting for her.

Right now, she was going to text her sister Holly to arrange a day to go dress shopping, email flicky-haired Claire to say they could talk in a few moments, and head out for noodles with the man she loved whilst they discussed centrepiece options.

Wedding planning was easy, right?

Chapter 63

MOLLY DOLLY

Sometimes I'm happy, sometimes I'm sad
Sometimes I'm lonely, sometimes I'm mad
Always I love him, but sometimes I need space
(Just one poo on my own would be ace)
Some days are amazing, some days only fine
Some days I think I might lose my mind
Every day I'm grateful, but sometimes I need to cry
Being pregnant in a heatwave is making me WANT
   TO DIE.

If Molly was honest, she felt completely fucking exhausted.

It was July.

It was hot and humid. And she felt terrible.

Tom had started in his new role at work, and despite her worries about him becoming too controlling, everything seemed to be working out. Cutting up her joint-account card, eating the packed lunches he made for her, and budgeting her life around the twenty quid he left her at the start of each week had been the least of her worries. If anything, it had taken the pressure off and made things simpler.

Her biggest problem was that this pregnancy was taking everything out of her. She'd been struggling and pretending that she wasn't. But she needed to admit defeat at some point. She was finding life hard.

Asking for help didn't come naturally to her. She'd always got by on her own. She'd travelled most of Asia with only a backpack, a ground-mat and a bamboo tooth-brush for company, you'd think she could handle being pregnant whilst living in a first-floor maisonette in High Wycombe. She was beginning to realise what the phrase 'it takes a village' really meant.

It was hard trying to do right by Marley and look after her pregnant self at the same time – the two things didn't really seem to be compatible with one another. How did other women do it? And why did it look like everyone else had their shit so much more together than she did? She couldn't remember feeling any of this when she was pregnant with Marley, but this time the self-doubt and constant sense of guilt seemed almost as stifling as the humidity.

It wasn't as if Marley was a difficult baby – if anything he'd been about as easy and chilled out as babies come. He was eleven months old and he'd only really just begun to show an interest in crawling and getting around on his own. She was grateful he'd waited until now, but it seemed as though just as she was beginning to feel quite enormously pregnant and immobile, he was beginning to discover the joys of the kitchen cupboards, the thrill of slamming doors and the unrivalled euphoria of trying to kill or injure yourself by licking, poking and impaling yourself on random household objects.

Molly knew she had nothing to complain about really. It had nothing to do with Marley, it was her. He slept, he ate well, he napped a lot, and was still reasonably happy being contained, so long as he had enough to entertain himself with. But Molly could see that keeping him cooped up in the flat was a fairly impossible task now. He wanted to be outside, he wanted to be stimulated and entertained, even if she was too hot and exhausted to do it.

She'd conceded that she needed to start going to a few more groups. Emily seemed to be like some kind of index of local baby- and toddler-groups, so she'd decided to tag along with her today. For £3.50 she'd get a seat, a cup of tea, and Marley would hopefully be entertained for a couple of hours by what she imagined to be a plethora of plastic toys and objects that wouldn't actually kill him. Some kind of light-up baby paradise. But probably a bit snottier and less hygienic than was ideal . . .

Whilst Molly hadn't been the biggest fan of baby-groups, Marley was, and she needed this, if she was going to remain sane for the rest of her second pregnancy. Plus she'd have Emily for company, and as much as she hated to admit it, she wasn't always enough for Marley when it came to play stuff. She was rapidly becoming less mobile and she wasn't one for brightly coloured plastic anyway.

She just knew that she tended to not fit in at these places. She loved the babies, it was more the mums that

379

were the problem. They'd take one look at her bump and then at Marley, and judge her. Or at least that's how it felt.

Molly began to have second thoughts again. She'd text Emily for moral support, hopefully that would be the motivation she needed.

Molly
Hey you. I'm feeling a bit freaked out about today.
Can you tell me to stop being a dick and pull my fat-ankled hormonal self together please . . .?

Emily
Oh hunny why?
You'll love it when you get there.
Plus they have cake and hot tea whilst this mental voodoo type lady called Lynsey with pink hair and magical baby-whispering powers entertains the children . . . it's fucking amazing.

Molly
Well that does sound good . . . I love a pink-haired voodoo baby whisperer. Obvs. I've just got this weird paranoia thing about being judged is all. I know I'm being a knob. I'm never normally

like that but this pregnancy is totally
fucking with my head.

Emily

You have nothing to worry about.
We all build stuff up in our heads.
You'll have a great time.
Everyone will be lovely and you'll
come home feeling silly for ever
worrying about it. Trust me.

Molly

Okay. I know you're right.

Emily

I am. It's one of my main skills.
And failing that there's a woman there
who doesn't put nappies on her baby
and it basically just walks around shitting everywhere while she frantically
tries to catch it in a little pot behind
him, so trust me, while that's
happening no one is gonna be giving
any shits about anyone else.

Molly

Wow – that sounds pretty special. I
might come just to see that tbh.

Emily

Knew you'd come around.

I'll pick you up in half an hour.
I'm wearing a big hat and haven't
washed in three days, plus I slept in
my T-shirt. Just so you're aware.

Molly
I wouldn't expect any less. Thank you
sweetie and thanks for making me do
this. Love you xx

Emily
Love you too see you in a bit! x

Chapter 64

THE FUCK-YOU MUMMIES

Sometimes you have to admit defeat.

Emily felt her heart sink and an overwhelming sense of territorial anger as she listened to the bitchy titters emitting from a group of mums huddled around the tea station. Emily hadn't ever seen them before but she could tell quite instantly they weren't here to make friends.

So many of the baby-groups she went to were packed with lovely mums, just looking for a bit of a natter, some chat about poo or greasy fringes, and it was a wonderful world to be part of, but sadly, every so often, you got the other type. The judgemental cows who moved in packs, preying on the innocent, with lip-glossed faces and toned thighs. They seemed to know nothing of wearing pants for forty-eight hours until they got to the crispy stage, and certainly weren't likely to be chomping on Toblerones in the dark whilst crying into Twitter at 4 a.m. . . . They looked down on other mums. They were fucking dicks.

And right now the dickishly dickish dick behaviour was thoroughly aimed at Molly. She knew it. And so did Molly.

It all seemed so ridiculous, the unspoken rules of the

baby-playgroup, how thou shalt not allow a child to snatch a toy off another child, hog the ball-pit area, or GOD FUCKING FORBID a toddler attempts to climb up the play slide the wrong way else he may be STRUCK DOWN AND HAVE HIS SKIN REMOVED AND MADE INTO A HAT OF SHAME WHICH HE SHALL BE FORCED TO WEAR AT ALL FUTURE BABY-GROUPS FOR EVER. Or something.

Marley was far from an aggressive child, he was a placid, happy, smiling baby – and not many eleven-month-olds know how to share anyway, do they? Well, clearly that wasn't good enough for these mums, because after a tussle over a Fisher-Price caterpillar, Marley came out on top, and someone's little darling ended up falling backwards and hitting their head. On the heavily padded baby-proof floor.

But Molly saw it too late, and when she did decide to rush over and see what the commotion was, the nursing clip on her maternity top caught on her bracelet and she spilt tea on herself, so she waded into the midst of the under-ones toy-zone with one boob waggling free in the air, and tea spilt down her harem trousers in a very unfortunate manner, just as precious little Amelie's mummy – perky-tits Penelope – began scolding Marley for his outrageous behaviour. Yes, a fully grown woman shouting and wagging her finger at an eleven-month-old baby on a play-mat, who had no interest or comprehension of what was going on and simply continued to chew on his plastic caterpillar.

Emily had made her way across the sea of toys and babies to try and help her friend, as Molly desperately tried and failed to reassemble herself, and perky-tits Penelope and her gang of well-plucked companions giggled and looked on bitchily. It was a bit like being at school. Molly clearly had no time for confrontation and once she'd finally got her boobs under control, she returned to her seat with Marley and the notorious caterpillar, looking flustered, upset and embarrassed by the whole thing. All in all, not the ideal end to Wednesday morning Starfish Stay-And-Play.

They'd left after that.

Molly pretended to be fine but it was clear she wasn't. She had a thick skin and generally didn't care about these things, but being heavily pregnant, tired and emotional had clearly made her more vulnerable than normal. Now that Emily had dropped Molly back at home and arrived back at her little house with William asleep in the back of the car, it was playing heavily on her mind.

She felt guilty for making her come. But then how was she to know something like that would happen? She felt a sense of responsibility either way. She looked back at William, sound asleep in the car seat and decided that she'd transfer him to his cot and get on her laptop. She needed to release some tension and she knew just how to do it . . .

The Fuck-You Mummies

We all know the Fuck-You Mummies,
The ones you try your hardest to ignore;
Porridge-free skin, getting through the day
    without gin,
Don't they know parenthood's what alcohol is for?

I can't stand those Fuck-You Mummies,
The ones who look at you down their nose.
'Coz you're hungover at soft-play and wear
    pyjamas most days,
And make breakfast, lunch and dinner out of
    toast . . .

I hate those Fuck-You Mummies,
Whose children eat salad through choice,
And don't speak until they're spoken to, or laugh
    when they've broken you,
And never make weapons out of their toys.

I loathe those Fuck-You Mummies,
Looking smug as their kids sit and play
Speaking three different languages, making their
    own cucumber sandwiches,
And actually doing what their parents say.

I've no time for the Fuck-You Mummies,
Who don't allow TV or eat anything with wheat.
The CBeebies bedtime hour, is my only chance
   for a bastard shower,
While my child eats sofa raisins and licks their
   own feet.

So fuck you, you Fuck-You Mummies,
I'm not perfect and that's okay.
My child's hilarious and quirky, unpredictable and
   always dirty,
And I wouldn't have it any other fucking way.

Chapter 65

YES TO THE DRESS

Liz
Girls. I found the dress.
I'm not going to show it to you so don't ask me! I want to keep it a surprise until the day.
But I just wanted you to know I found it.
And it's perfect.
Holly cried a bit so I'm taking that as either a really good or REALLY BAD sign lol
But it's everything I wanted and I can't wait to wear it. I had to let you know!
xx
I know this sounds a bit strange but I think this is the first time I've properly looked forward to my wedding! Is that weird?
I clearly just needed to go shopping!
There is a life lesson there I reckon ;)
#spendingmoneyistheanswer
Love you girls.

Can't believe I'm getting married in six weeks!
Eek!

Emily
That's wonderful sweetie!
There will definitely be an actual wedding now! Lol
I'm so jealous that Holly has seen it and I haven't. But okay – if you can't tell me about the dress, tell me you got fabulous shoes? Send me a picture of those? Give me something here! PLEASE!

Liz
I certainly did. I'm not sure they're particularly exciting. But I love them – they're simple, low heels but slightly embellished and beautiful.

Emily
Sounds gorgeous. I need photos now!
I can't wait to see it all!!
And I'm seriously hoping you didn't go for open-toed with your weird feet . . .

Molly
Emily! Lol
I'm so happy you found a dress Liz.

I'm sure it'll be stunning – you always look stunning. Can't wait to see it on the big day xx

Liz
Aww thanks Molly x
And hey Emily – there's nothing wrong with my feet thank you! You start on my feet, I'll start on your ear-lobes okay lady. THE BIG GUNS WILL COME OUT.

Emily
I mean yeah . . . your feet aren't weird at all . . . even if your big toes do look like they have their own knee joints.
(And leave my ears alone! They're individual. And that's the story I'm sticking to.)

Molly
Pahaha

Liz
That's what all the people without ear-lobes say . . . lol x Right, much as this chat is doing wonders for my self-confidence, enough about my toe-knees OK.

Emily

Okay. I am seriously happy for you
though Lizzy-Pants.
The dress is so important!
I just can't wait to see you get married
now!
It's all so exciting!

Molly

Me too. So close now!

Liz

And look, there's something else.
I've been thinking about everything
and I think I need to be straight with
you guys – I just don't want a Hen Do.
I know you'll be disappointed Emily
but honestly, I can't think of anything
worse than running around like a
drunken teenager with a comedy veil
on my head carrying a giant inflatable
penis . . . It's been giving me night-
mares!
It's just not my style.
Sorry. Please don't hate me.

Emily

Really?? Come on – it doesn't have
to be like that – we could do it
classily. Nice restaurant, some wine

. . . Only a few inflatable penises . . .
(that last bit was a joke).
It's just a fun night out with friends!
Molly's nearly eight months pregnant
– we weren't exactly going to go
crazy anyway! Lol x

Liz
I know.
But I really just don't want to.
That's the truth. I'm sorry.
But look – to make it up to you –
instead I thought what I'd love is for
you girls to come to the venue the
night before the wedding.
I've got a few rooms as part of the
package so we can all stay there.
Boys and babies included. And I
thought us girls could meet in my room
with a posh bottle of wine and have
room service. Just us, in our PJs, like
we did when we were teenagers, and
you can help me not get nervous and
we can chat girl-stuff for a few hours.
So I don't just sit there like a lemon
watching rubbish TV and fantasising
about tripping down the aisle over my
weird feet . . .
What do you say?

Molly

Oh that sounds brilliant. I'm in.

Emily

Actually yes, that does sound pretty
brilliant! I'm in too x
But only on one condition. I know
we're not getting drunk or anything
like that, and obviously it's not officially a hen do, but as I'd already
ordered them off Amazon and I don't
really think they'd be appropriate for
my son's joint first birthday party . . .
can I please bring my willy straws?
Liz . . .?
LIZ??!!

Chapter 66

BIRTHDAY BABES

How are you one? How can a whole year be done?
How can I be a mummy to a toddler?
This time last year, I was facing my worst fear;
Letting a human force its way out of my wobbler . . .

I've learnt so much, it's been bloody tough,
But so awesome even though I am knackered.
I've kept you alive, somehow we've both survived,
And I'm fairly sure you won't end up a crack-head.

How could they be one?

It did not seem possible that an entire twelve months had passed since Paul had tried to feed Emily some cheese in the delivery room while she fantasised about snapping him in two with her bare hands, as a perfect tiny bundle of William surfed his way into the world via her vagina. Slightly gunky but none the less incredibly beautiful for it.

It had been the day their lives had changed for ever – in some ways as expected, in some ways totally unexpected, and she hadn't really looked at Camembert the same way since . . . But brilliant bits, shitty bits, and 'just fine' bits included, the last year had been nothing short of wonderful. Emily could see that looking back now. That or she had been too exhausted through the really terrible parts to remember them properly and her mind was blocking them out. Either/or really . . .

It was also wonderful that Marley and William's birthdays were literally days apart. Ready-made best friends, who couldn't be more different, but then neither could their mums, and their friendship had stood the test of time. And also survived that phase in the nineties where you had to wear boob tubes with low-waist army combat trousers that had a lot of tassels. And if a friendship could make it through camo-print tassely-trousers and East 17 then they were clearly meant to be friends for life.

Today, Emily had invited Molly and Liz round with their other halves, and Marley of course, for a miniature-cake-based celebration in her garden. It was a celebration on three counts really – seeing as Molly and Marley actually shared the same birth date. Molly had said she didn't want to do anything for her birthday – she was fairly preoccupied being hot, sweaty and pregnant whilst looking after a just-turned-one-year-old – but Emily had ignored that and bought a personalised cake and had some bunting printed in her honour. It wasn't much – but she couldn't let her friend's birthday go completely unmarked. Everyone deserves bunting with their own face printed on it at some point in their lives, even if they have to enjoy it with significant pregnancy under-boob sweat.

It was a hot sticky August Sunday, and the sun was

beating down hard on Emily's small terraced garden. She'd put cushions and blankets on the lawn under a large parasol for the babies to crawl around on. Not that Marley seemed to have much interest in crawling around, he was quite content simply sitting on his mum's lap chewing on a breadstick at the moment, whereas William was up and into everything now and didn't have much regard for Emily's attempts at a cushion barricade. There was no stopping him, which was delightfully exhausting for them both, although it had meant he'd started to sleep a little better through the night – not every night, this wasn't Oz, but the occasional six-hour stint had left Emily feeling like a real human, and so drunk on sleep that she didn't know what to do with herself. Her twenty-year-old self would be horrified to know that a six-hour stint of sleep in yesterday's pants with little or no hope of showering in the morning was a luxury now . . .

Tom, Paul and Gerald stood happily chatting in the sunshine, drinking bottles of beer and trying not to sweat too much. Emily loved that the men all got on so well. It made her so happy that the three couples could happily spend time together.

She joined Liz and Molly under the parasol, after replenishing the breadsticks and rescuing a plant from William's clutches, sitting down with her legs to the side and enjoying the comparative coolness of the shade.

'Thanks so much for doing this, Em. The garden looks lovely!' Molly said, slurping on something icy, but still looking uncomfortably hot.

'Hey, it was nothing. I just sent Paul to Tesco this morning and then slung some stuff in bowls. Easy really!'

'Well, I really appreciate it. It's so nice to mark the fact that our little men are one. I'm not sure I would have had the energy to do this on my own. It's crazy that a whole year has gone, isn't it?'

'I know! I blinked and missed it. I can confirm I am slightly less knackered and wobbly than at this point last year though, so let's drink to that!' Emily said, laughing and lifting a plastic cup of Pimm's into the air.

'Well you look great, sweetie,' Liz said, tapping her Pimm's cup on to her friends' gently. 'You'd never know you were tired, honestly. And happy birthday to Marley and William. And congrats to you both for surviving!'

'Yes. Congrats to us all,' Molly said. Slurping away again.

'And happy birthday to Molly too, of course. Who gets more beautiful with every year, despite keeping us all on our toes with a series of outrageous and reckless decisions – we love her all the more for it!' Emily said, with another round of cup-tapping ensuing. 'And can I just say I think we've done pretty amazingly – all of us, I mean. Two happy almost-toddlers, two happy mummies, a new baby on the way, and a wedding to look forward to in four weeks!'

'Indeed. And yes. Thanks for reminding me it's only four weeks away . . .' Liz said a little weakly.

'Ah, you'll be fine. If I know you, you'll have it all under control even if you feel like you don't. And you've got flicky-haired Claire. She's been working her flicky-haired tits off to make it all as perfect as she can, I'm sure.'

'Yes. I know you're right. I'm excited really. Time just goes so fast these days . . . I just feel like I'm winging everything, and just sort of being carried along with it all, to be honest,' Liz said, thoughtfully.

'Tell me about it,' Molly said, slurping again.

'I know. I thought I'd be back into my size-ten jeans, novel written and back at work by now . . . turns out none of that was realistic in the first year!' Emily said, with an exaggerated tut at herself. 'But as I'm averaging more than about ten minutes' sleep a night now, I do want to try and look my best for your wedding. I've tried on everything I own and they all make me look like a potato in a dress. Even with a full-body Spanx suit my flab is still finding ways to escape.'

'I don't think *you* have anything to worry about,' Molly said, casting her eyes down to her spherical protruding tummy.

'Hey, you're pregnant – that's different! And you look great for it as well,' Emily said, smiling and frowning at the same time.

'And you look great too!' Liz said, interjecting. 'Stop being so ridiculous. Besides, it sounds like a nice excuse to buy a new dress anyway. Whatever you do, don't go on some stupid crash diet. You honestly look lovely the way you are.'

'Thank you,' Emily said, feeling a little like she was being told off. 'And don't worry, I'm not going on a stupid diet or anything, but William turning one has made me look at myself a bit. I'm not trying to lose loads of weight or anything, but I think now is a good time just to eat a bit more healthily and exercise a little more. I'm happy being a curvy size twelve, I just want to wobble a little less round the edges, and cutting down on chocolate, wine and takeaways should do that!'

'So you're saying your main diet goals are to go from six Toblerones a week to just the four?' Molly said, laughing a little.

'Basically yes,' Emily said, laughing back. 'I'm just going to sort my lifestyle out a bit. I've spent a year eating, drinking and doing what I want because I've had other priorities, you know. I'm actually quite proud of how few fucks I've given about how I look most of the time in the last twelve months – trust me. It's been quite liberating! But he's a not a tiny baby permanently stuck to one of my boobs any more, he's a toddling little person, so I think it's time to stop eating Wotsits in bed before I go to sleep every night . . .'

'Well, it sounds like you've got your head screwed on, sweetie. But if I see you only eating cabbage soup and snacking on dust, I am going to have stern words with you though. Okay?' Liz said, wagging a finger.

Emily held her hands up playfully. 'Absolutely. I'd expect nothing less. I've been saying on my blog Instagram feed that I'm going to eat a bit healthier and stuff, asking my mummy followers for recipe ideas, that kind of thing, and I've picked up this mental personal-trainer woman called

Brenda, who has a twelve-pack and lives in St Albans. The other day, I was complaining about wanting a chocolate bar and she took it upon herself to begin some kind of motivational intervention. It's getting weird. I think I'm going to have to block her.'

'Wow – that does sound a bit intense,' said Molly, looking a little bemused.

'I know. I was like, it's OKAY, BRENDA. I'm not saying I'm giving up on all healthy eating and exercise for the rest of my life. I'm just saying, there's only so much cottage cheese and sugar-free jelly one human can eat before they just fancy a fucking KitKat.'

'Ha!' Liz almost spat a mouthful of her drink out laughing. 'Well said. Why don't we drink to the babies becoming little boys, the birthday girl, brilliant times ahead, and saying fuck off to twelve-pack Brenda.'

The friends all laughed, clinked their plastic cups and couldn't resist an in-unison-toast . . .

'FUCK OFF, TWELVE-PACK BRENDA.'

Chapter 67

TOLLY NO SHOW

Liz
Have you had that bloody baby yet?

Molly
Oh that? Yeah.

Liz
What? Molly!

Molly
Yes. I've secretly had the baby but didn't think it was important so didn't bother to tell you.

Liz
Funny.

Molly
Well continually asking me if I've had it isn't going to change the fact I haven't, is it? Lol
I can promise I'm not going to NOT tell you when the baby comes okay!

Jeez – I expect this kind of pressure
from Emily, but not from you
Liz.
You've changed!

Liz
Sorry. I know!
I think this wedding might have
slightly altered me as a human. I'm
just panicking because I want you to
be there that's all!
There's only ten days to go!
I'm shitting it a bit.
How are you feeling?

Molly
Fat, uncomfortable and like my tits
have taken up permanent residency
resting on the top of my
bump.
And don't worry – I know. And I will
be. Uterus evacuated or not. I WILL
BE THERE.

Liz
Haha x I know you will.
I was just hoping because Marley
was early – this one would be too! I
feel like it's doing this just to taunt
me tbh!

Please have a word with your unborn
child and make sure their exit is within
the next week or so would you?
Thanks.

Emily
lol – I reckon you're right!
Don't worry. I'll sort this.
I'm coming round later with a pine-
apple curry, some of that raspberry
tea that tastes like actual arse, and
my birth ball.
WE WILL SQUAT THAT BABY OUT
TOGETHER WHILST DRINKING
ARSE TEA.

Molly
Ha! Look – I don't need curry, tea
made from arses (seriously wtf) and
birth balls. I'm fine. It's going to
happen, I can
feel it.
Have faith ladies.
And don't worry – you will be amongst
the first to know when he or she does
make an appearance.

Emily
Fingers crossed. Come on Molly's
fanny – you can do this!

Molly

Yes it can. And I appreciate the motivational vagina support. Obviously.
Now please excuse me while I get
back to wiping my under-boob sweat
away with baby wipes.
I will let you know if anything changes
xx

Liz

You promise?

Molly

YES!

Chapter 68

TOLLY TWO SAVES THE DAY

Molly felt intermittent rushes of euphoria, relief, happiness and exhilaration as she focussed on Tom's face right in front of her.

He looked calm, happy, excited . . . his eyes were full of love and admiration as he gripped her hand strongly whilst she sat in the warm waters of the birthing pool. She was trying hard to maintain eye contact with him throughout the contractions. They were coming thick and fast now – Molly knew it wouldn't be long. She was working hard to breathe through them and allow her body to do what it needed to. It seemed to be racing through the stages, but she felt confident and so much more prepared this time.

Her muscles were remembering; her body knew how to respond. The fear, the unknowing of the first time wasn't there. There was just the feeling of certainty that in a few moments this would pass, and they would meet their baby for the first time. She could barely wait for it. She could remember clearly what that felt like – the moment when all the pain and discomfort turned off like a tap, and you were left with nothing but joy as you held the child you'd been creating inside your body for the last nine months. It was a moment words could never do justice to.

As Molly blew away the end of the last contraction, she couldn't help but feel a sense of déjà vu. This moment compared so starkly with Marley's birth. She was sitting again in a birthing pool in the lounge of Tom's slightly cramped maisonette, trying hard to listen to the instructions from a midwife at her side, whose face and name she knew she wouldn't remember once this had happened, because of the all-consuming process of having a human being headbutting its way out of your womb.

Marley was there with them this time too, though. He seemed strangely unaware of how important the next few minutes would be. In fact, he was fairly disinterested, which wasn't a bad thing – but then at thirteen months old, why should he be? He'd spent most of the last hour trying to get in the birthing pool with his plastic red boat or sitting on the floor eating a sandwich. Tom was splitting his time between Marley and Molly, but she was so much more in control this time. She felt empowered. And oh-so-ready to meet her baby.

Molly felt the warm, soothing water lapping around her stomach. This birth felt quite different – she was able to relax more perhaps, knowing what was coming, trusting and confident in the midwife at her side, to whom she'd be so grateful for helping her to bring life into the world safely in the comfort of her own living room, with her family and all the things she loved and knew around her. This was exactly how she wanted it.

Molly suddenly felt the pain step up and the overwhelming urge to push consumed her. She was aware that Marley was in the room, so didn't want to sound like she was in pain, but she couldn't help but make some noise as her body began to get ready for the baby to come.

The next few moments seemed a blur, she breathed, listened, pushed, at the mercy of her body, unable to have much control over what was happening now. She was using her hypno-breathing techniques as best she could, and squeezing Tom's hand for dear life as she felt it. It was coming. It was happening. This was it.

At the midwife's instruction, she used every ounce of strength she had left and gave everything she had . . . it felt like for ever . . . but it could have only been a few minutes, maybe not even that . . . before she felt the familiar rushing sensation she remembered from before . . . and then . . . Relief. Tears. Stillness. The end of the pain before what she'd been waiting to hear – that amazing noise. Those tiny cries that let you know everything was okay. That you'd done it. You could stop. Your body didn't have to work now. All you had to do was feel love for the tiny little person that was being neatly placed on your chest. The screwed-up little bundle of human life. Life that you'd created. It was just as overwhelming as the first time.

Molly felt hot tears of emotion, exhaustion and sheer happiness fall down her face as she looked down at her baby for the very first time and listened to the cries it was making as she clutched it.

'It's a girl . . .' the midwife said, smiling, as Molly felt another wave of happiness and emotion wash over her.

Tom was right there with Marley. Who was still clutching his sandwich but looking at the baby too now. Tom's eyes had welled up, and he was unable to stop staring at their new baby girl.

She was so perfect.

So tiny.

Molly couldn't ever remember Marley being that small, even though she knew he was. She couldn't stop looking at her, and gently stroking the downy damp hair on her head as they lay there together in the water, sharing those first amazing moments together.

She was here.

Her little girl was here.

And she was even more beautiful and wonderful than she'd dreamed and hoped she would be.

And quite wonderfully she had arrived just in time for them to make Liz and Gerald's wedding.

Chapter 69

SHE'S HERE

Molly
Ladies.
She's here.
She's so perfect I can't stop crying!
I can't believe she's a girl.
It's so strange having a girl after a
boy . . .
It just looks really odd that she
doesn't have a willy. lol
But I'm very happy she doesn't ;)
I'd have been outnumbered otherwise
right!
I'm just so happy. We all are.
I still can't believe I made her. She's
amazing.
Anyway, I know it's late and you're
both probably asleep, but I couldn't
hold it in. I knew you'd want to know
straight away!
I'll send you some photos in the
morning.
We're both doing great.

She was six pounds ten, so nice and healthy and not too big (thank fuck! Lol)
Looks like we'll need an extra seat at the wedding now then Liz ;)
(Although obvs not an actual seat. She'll mostly be in a pram or on my boob I'd imagine.)
Right I'm waffling.
Oh and we've called her Luna-Rose. And she can't wait to meet you.
Okay I'm going x I'm off to try and sleep a bit and not think about how much my fanny hurts.
Love you xxx

Chapter 70

THE NIGHT BEFORE THE GEDDING – #GIZEVE

Nerves are normal
Doubts are fine
Just shut the fuck up
And drink some wine
This time tomorrow
The first day of your new life
You'll leave all the shit behind you
And call yourself someone's wife

Liz gently brushed her fringe into place with her fingertips. Then for a few moments she just stood there quietly, without any emotion registering on her face, and studied her reflection in the large bathroom mirror in the bridal suite at The Olde Bell.

Gerald was staying with his friend and best man, Peter, in a B&B down the road, so she had the room to herself for the night. Whilst she wasn't a particularly traditional girl, and neither were they a particularly traditional couple, she supposed, this was one thing she had wanted. They both had. For him to not see her the morning of their wedding, and for them to next

lay eyes on each other as she took her first steps down the aisle.

She wasn't sure if it was really 'tradition' that had prompted that arrangement at all, if she was honest; practically it just made sense. She wanted the space to spread out and get ready in the morning. She wanted her dress to hang neatly in the wardrobe unseen by him. And she wanted a night with her two best friends, so she could relax, laugh and unwind. Now that she thought about it, it seemed quite selfish that she'd sent him down the road to a tiny room above a crappy pub whilst she slept star-fished in the centre of a super-king-size four-poster bed . . . But hey. It's what he'd wanted too. Liz reassured herself of that.

She felt oddly unsettled being alone right now, though. A little nervous perhaps. She supposed that was normal the night before your wedding. She was glad she'd invited Emily and Molly to her room for the evening. She wasn't sure she could take an entire night of feeling like this on her own.

She knew they had both arrived at the venue, she'd had a stream of constant text updates from Emily throughout the day and Molly had let her know she'd got here a little while ago. They were due at her room shortly, and Liz was very much looking forward to escaping her thoughts.

She just needed to focus on spending the night with her friends, and NOT letting her mind run away with itself. She had a bad habit of doing that at the most inconvenient times, and she was fed up of beating herself

up just for being happy. Which she was. Even if she sometimes needed to remind herself of that. Soon Emily and
Molly would be here, and they'd relax, reminisce, tell silly
stories from their past, their friendships, their lives to
date, and guess at what the future held. She had a nice
bottle of wine in the fridge, although clearly she would
be taking it easy on the drink, and she'd ordered a couple
of cold platters to be delivered to the room for them to
pick at. She didn't feel hungry enough for a big hot plate
of food. That was probably the nerves again, but she
knew she needed to eat. Tomorrow was a big day.

She also couldn't wait to meet little Luna-Rose. It was
so brilliant that the timings had all worked out. She knew
Molly would be exhausted, but it had meant so much
that she had still come. She knew she would. It just
wouldn't have felt right getting married without her there.

Liz nodded firmly at herself, still staring into the bathroom mirror. She really needed them to turn up now.
She'd message them and see how they were getting on.

Liz
Hey. Are you coming? I am feeling all
weird and need you guys here!

Emily
No – we changed our minds and
decided to get shit-faced on posh gin
in the bar instead.
Of course we're coming!

> I'm just helping Molly get Luna-Rose
> ready.
> We'll be there in about 20 mins.
> Don't worry – get the wine open!

Liz
Okay. Hurry up!

Liz felt slightly reassured. It was just twenty minutes. Not even half an hour. She could do that. This was all in her mind. Liz moved from the bathroom to the bed. She was hoping she'd relax more there. She sat with her head resting on the headboard and her legs out in front of her.

She was still feeling odd. And could feel her mind wandering to places she really didn't want it to go. It was as if she couldn't be by herself any more. Which was frustrating, and actually quite strange for someone who'd spent so many years shutting everyone else out without much trouble at all. She'd lived alone, worked alone, and frankly had wanted to be alone for a lot of the time. But since Gerald had moved in, she was realising how used to being around someone all the time she'd become.

Liz was getting annoyed at herself now. She didn't want to spend any of the night before her wedding thinking about the mistakes of her past, but they were creeping into the back of her mind with an irritating air of inevitability. Maybe that was why she wanted her friends here, to stop her thinking about how life used to be. Stop her ever thinking about 'him' again.

Liz felt a sudden jolt of anger at the realisation that he had wormed his way into her thoughts. There he was. In her head again, at the most inappropriate time. She knew it was because deep down she still felt guilt over that night, but she needed to let go of that.

A thought tugged at the back of her mind – a strange daydream where he found out where she was getting married and showed up to confess his undying love for her. Liz shook her head at herself for even thinking it – at least that was as absurd as it was likely. Liz reminded herself that there was one reason that would never happen. Even though he was spiteful enough to want to fuck up her life – she had no doubt of that – he wouldn't do it, simply because he wouldn't want the attention. He wasn't one for bold or public statements. He needed deniability. That's how he worked. He was a snake that hid in the grass and only attacked from where he couldn't be seen.

Besides, she hadn't had any attempted contact from him in months, he'd clearly got bored and had no doubt moved on to some poor idiot who'd fallen for his bullshit. She pitied whoever that was. Liz huffed. It was ridiculous that she was even thinking about all this – tormenting herself with it.

Liz knew she needed to shake him away. Out of her head for good. She couldn't carry on beating herself up about the past for the rest of her life. She wasn't that person any more. She hadn't been that person when she met him all those months ago – she'd simply been in a vulnerable place. One stupid drunken night did not need

to define her. She needed to let it go. Tonight was the time to exorcise her demons. Because her new life started tomorrow. Her life with Gerald.

They were stronger than they'd ever been. And more in love. She only had to consider how desperately she missed him tonight to know that. And how much she couldn't wait to marry him.

Liz allowed herself a small smile as she thought about Gerald.

She felt the weight lift a little.

Tomorrow she was going to marry the man she loved in front of the people she held closest in the world. And that's all that mattered.

Liz blew out a long, slow breath.

There was a knock at the door. Her friends were early.

Liz let herself smile properly now. She was so ready for tonight.

To laugh and share a brilliant last night as an unmarried woman.

She jumped down from the bed and headed to the door.

As she opened it wide, ready to greet the smiling faces of her two best friends, she instead found herself instantly frozen to the spot unable to breathe or speak.

It was 'him'.

There he stood. As bold and real as she was stunned and horrified.

She hadn't believed for a second that he would ever show up here. Ever.

'Hi, Lizzie.' His voice was cool, calm, full of charm

and confidence like it always was. It sent a jolt of anger through her, which seemed to wake her from her temporarily frozen state.

She blinked a few times and closed her lips which she had only just realised were parted.

'What the fuck are you doing here?' Liz couldn't remember thinking before the words were spitting themselves out of her mouth.

'I've been asking myself the same thing the whole way here, Lizzie. I think I just needed to see you one last time. Believe for myself that you really were getting married, that it was truly over between us . . . I just didn't want the last time we saw each other, at the hotel, to be our final goodbye.'

His words made no sense. Liz knew that. This was just the same old routine – the words might be different, but it was the same old shit in different packaging. She wouldn't be sucked in. She forced herself to focus.

'How did you even know where I was . . . ?' Liz said, uncomfortably shifting her weight on her feet.

'Well. You have your friend with the blog to thank for that. Tagging herself outside the pub on Instagram, and captioning it something about her best friend the lawyer's wedding . . . it wasn't hard.'

Liz felt sick. The idea that he'd been following Emily's Instagram page was creeping her out. But she couldn't get distracted right now.

'I still don't understand why the hell you'd show up? Did you not get the message from the last ten months of

417

me ignoring you? How obvious do I need to make it!' Liz felt good. She felt strong. This was nothing like their meeting all those months ago when she'd been a fraction of her true self, weak and ravaged by everything that had happened to her. The real Liz was here now, and she would never let herself be so weak again.

'Like I said . . . I just felt like I should say goodbye properly . . .'

The smirk on his face made her stomach lurch. It was amazing that he was arrogant enough to show up here at all, let alone think that he might get lucky one last time. Liz had heard enough.

'Then goodbye,' Liz said, straightening herself up, her weight centred on both feet now as stared through him. She thought she'd feel hatred for him now, but she didn't. You have to care, to hate someone. All she felt was pity.

'One disappointing fuck almost a year ago doesn't give you the right to show up here, nothing does. Now piss off back to your poor wife and kid, and stop trying to fight your way back into my life with your pitiful bullshit and disgusting disregard for marriage. Both yours and quite imminently, mine. Tomorrow I'll be marrying a real man – someone who understands what it means to respect someone. Someone who knows what love is. And someone I can't wait to spend the rest of my life with, and I certainly don't need several vats of vodka simply to share a bed with. So there's your goodbye, you arrogant Instagram-stalking shitbag. Now kindly fuck off away from my hotel-room door and my life for ever.'

Liz slammed the door as the last words flew out. She hadn't shouted, she had calmly said her piece and it felt epic.

She waited just the other side of the door for a few moments and let the adrenaline that was surging through her body relent, before exhaling with relief as his footsteps headed away into silence.

He was gone.

Liz turned on her heel and headed to the minibar where the wine was chilling. She poured herself a large glass, sipped it triumphantly and perched herself on the bed, letting what had just happened wash over her. She felt so strong. She felt back in control. Which was handy really, considering her friends would be here any moment, and she had no plans to allow what had just happened to affect any more of her evening or her life from now on.

Within what felt like seconds there was a knock at the door. This one she was confident held no nasty surprises, and she heard the voices of Emily and Molly just the other side as she let it swing open.

The faces of her two best friends beamed at her from the lobby as she welcomed them in. It felt so good to see them.

Molly came forward first, clutching Luna-Rose to her chest like she was made of glass. Liz was so happy she got to meet her tonight. 'Hello, little one,' Liz said, as she stared down at her tiny face and rubbed her friend's arm gently. 'She's beautiful. And so small. Wow . . . Congratulations again, sweetie. Come in, come in!'

Molly nodded and smiled, then stepped into the room. She looked tired but happy. And surprisingly well, considering she'd given birth less than seventy-two hours ago . . .

'Happy #GizEve!!' Emily chimed, as she hugged her friend dramatically in the doorway, and made her way past her into the hotel room.

'Happy . . . er . . . what?' Liz said, smiling and frowning at the same time.

Emily flung herself on to the bed and laughed. 'Well, I'm not allowed to call it a hen do. But it's the night before Giz officially becomes a married couple . . . So Giz-Eve! No brainer really. Came up with it all by myself on the way here. Feel free to use it. Thank me later.'

'I'm actually okay,' Liz said sarcastically, rolling her eyes, before fetching the wine and some more glasses and looking over at her friends. She felt oddly emotional and really thankful for them suddenly.

Liz stood still for a moment, watching as Molly and Emily laughed and cooed over Luna-Rose on the bed.

'Are you okay?' Molly said, looking at her friend with slight concern on her face. 'You seem a bit distracted.'

'Just pre-wedding nerves,' Liz said as casually as she could manage – she'd never let her friends know what had happened only moments before they arrived. She was strong now. She never had to think about it, or anything to do with 'him' ever again. She knew that.

'Nothing a large glass of wine can't solve, I'm sure!' Liz added, confident Molly's concern had gone, as her face relaxed and she smiled back at her.

'Oh and just one small addition to those wine glasses . . .' Emily said, rummaging for something in a small bag she'd brought with her. 'I know this is not a hen do, and I've obviously done my very best to respect all your wishes, but I just thought I wasn't being true to myself if I didn't bring just the one novelty straw and an inflatable penis hat for the bride-to-be . . . so . . . ta-da!'

Liz laughed and rolled her eyes again. Although the hat was one step too far for her, she did concede on the willy-straw. It was #GizEve after all . . . and who was she to be a non-willy-straw-using party-pooper?

Chapter 71

THE GEDDING

It was the morning of Liz's wedding.

And Liz couldn't quite believe it. Maybe because she thought she'd never get married, maybe because she'd never thought she deserved to . . . but none of that mattered now.

It had been the best and worst year of her life. So much had happened. Some bits brilliant, some bits so terrible she wasn't able to let her mind go back there again.

But this day – her wedding day – celebrated all the brilliant and made up for all the terrible, and she couldn't wait to walk down that aisle in front of the few people that she and Gerald really valued in their lives.

There were only twenty-three people attending Liz and Gerald's wedding. His and her closest friends and immediate family, and that was it. It would be simple, and elegant, and totally bullshit free – just as she wanted it. As they both did.

She was never one for being the centre of attention. It wasn't a confidence thing, she had that in spades, she just had no desire for the limelight. Emily was far better at that – she loved all eyes on her, it suited her and she seemed to come into bloom once she had an audience;

she thrived. Liz was far happier to sit back and drop in the odd sarcastic comment from behind the crowd, with a well-groomed fringe. She felt no need to parade herself around in front of the masses today. She wanted it as intimate as possible.

Liz looked in the mirror, studying herself from head to toe as she gently swished her elegant navy-blue gown from side to side with her hips. The swooping fishtail cut of the dress created curves on her she never knew she had. A simple diagonal line at the neck left one shoulder exposed, and the other ruched into a small gathered embellishment, which then sent the material cascading down her back to the floor. It had a fifties feel to it and Liz had loved it from the moment she put it on. There was nothing traditional about it – it certainly wasn't something most people would want to wear on their wedding day – but that only served to make her love it even more. And right now, she couldn't have felt more beautiful.

A vintage hair-clip with deep blue stones, which her sister had given her, gently pinned her bob to one side, softening her usually sharp, angular style with the addition of some soft waves. It complemented her dress wonderfully. Liz couldn't help but smile at her reflection. She looked like her, but the best version of her. And of course, she'd insisted on keeping her trademark red lips for the occasion. They finished the look off perfectly.

Liz allowed her face to return to a neutral expression as she composed herself. There was a light tap at the door.

Followed by the unmistakable sobbing of her best friend Emily as she entered the room with Molly following behind, gently rolling her eyes.

'Wow. You look utterly stunning,' Emily managed between the snotty sobs. Liz knew she meant that.

'You really do,' Molly said, smiling broadly at her friend. 'I know you didn't really want visitors before the ceremony, but I couldn't keep soppy-bollocks here away. Sorry!'

'It's okay,' Liz said, realising how happy she was that her two best friends were here with her right now. 'I could do with someone to help me do up the last few buttons at the back anyway. I didn't realise I'd need to be a contortionist to get this on,' she continued, laughing a little.

Emily jumped into action at the sign of a task to complete.

Liz watched Emily in the mirror, soft happy tears running down her face still, as she attended to Liz's fastenings, with Molly looking on. None of them actually needed to say anything right now. The air was full of happiness and anticipation, and words weren't necessary. Perhaps that's how you knew someone really was your best friend – a few knowing glances and a hug in the right place were all you needed to know exactly what you were saying to each other.

No one was walking Liz down the aisle. Her parents were here, but her father was quite elderly and not very well or very mobile for that matter. And aside from that, they didn't really have that sort of relationship. If Liz was honest, she couldn't remember the last time she'd really spoken to them outside of inviting them to her wedding, but whilst she had never been particularly close to her parents, neither did she have any plans to substitute them for the occasion either.

She would walk herself down to meet her future husband. It seemed fitting. She had done everything else in her life on her own – she would do this too.

It was bizarre how overwhelming the sense of nervous excitement was that pulsed through her body right now, as she waited for the large oak doors to open into the ceremony room. She knew what was waiting for her quietly on the other side. She couldn't wait to see it full of people. With Gerald standing patiently at the other end of the aisle.

Her nerves suddenly seemed to step up a gear at the thought of everyone looking at her. The nerves weren't because she had any doubts; she'd established that last night. She knew this was right. This felt more right than anything she'd ever done.

They were simply an overload of emotions, bubbling away under the surface, sucking in the anticipation and importance of what was about to happen.

Flicky-haired Claire appeared and made a thumbs-up gesture as she moved in front of her. She placed her hand on the door handle and Liz nodded firmly to signal she was ready. Liz ignored how dry her mouth suddenly felt as she watched flicky-haired Claire slip inside, and the gentle scrapes of chairs and people getting to their feet could be heard through the crack.

Liz's stomach filled with butterflies as the strumming intro to her favourite Ella Fitzgerald song began to hum in the background. Those few seconds felt like a lifetime, but suddenly the doors opened and Liz took a sharp suck of the air in front of her as the room revealed itself and was as perfectly sun-dappled and magical as she had hoped and remembered.

She could barely take it all in – the sparkly eyes of all the people she loved fixed on her, the mix of birds and nature with the hum of people and children, with the open doors at the end revealing the orchard in all its splendour. And the man she loved. Smiling, his lips parted and his eyes unblinking as he waited for her, watching her every step. She ignored her pounding heart, and slowly moved one foot in front of the other. The aisle was short – only a few paces really – but she wanted to enjoy it. She wanted to remember and revel in the moment. As her eyes fully met Gerald's, her grin widened so far she thought she might burst out laughing, or possibly into tears, maybe both, but she didn't. She held it together and fixed her eyes on his. His wonderful, kind, beautiful eyes, that were looking at her like she was the most beautiful and dazzling thing he'd ever seen. She wouldn't forget this moment. Ever.

As Liz finally reached Gerald, she allowed herself a little laugh of relief and happiness. He took her hands, holding them tightly, and she felt her heart rate slow down a little. She could breathe again. He couldn't take his eyes off her and it was actually making her blush a little.

Liz took a moment to glance around the room as Ella entered the last chorus – there were moist eyes all around. Emily and Molly were near the front – babies on laps. Gerald's parents sat on the opposite side, along with a couple of his friends. She finally spotted her nieces, Clover and Isla. They were about three rows back, dressed in matching white satin dresses, and were currently using all their upper-body strength in a valiant attempt to escape Holly's clutches. Liz decided it was best not to make too much eye contact with Holly right now . . . She was in professional toddler-wrestling mode.

Liz looked back at Gerald – who didn't appear to have taken his eyes off her still, or even blinked. It was such a strange sensation to have everyone looking at you. It felt self-indulgent, yet weirdly addictive. She now felt silly for feeling so nervous about it.

As Ella was gently faded out at an appropriate point, the registrar appeared and the room fell silent as everyone took their seats again.

Liz barely remembered the next part – it's strange the parts of your wedding that become the most important, and those which fade into insignificance. Liz listened and said the right words in the right places, but really, the only part she remembered was looking at Gerald, and them both saying I do before a wonderful kiss. That part she had thought about – too quick and it could seem unromantic and cold; too long, or too much tongue, and

it would feel inappropriate. But the gentle lingering touch of lips that said 'we did it, we're husband and wife' felt like perfection.

Everyone cheered as they signed their names in the register and began their first steps as husband and wife back down the aisle. Liz allowed herself to glance around the room, taking in the happy noises and faces. She'd enjoyed hearing the odd gurgle from the babies near the back during the ceremony. If anything, it just made the occasion more personal and less stuffy. Now that she looked properly, she clocked a three-year-old Clover trying to swing from the drapes at the back of the room, with a slightly frantic Holly trying to coax her back to her seat with a lollipop. All whilst her younger sister attempted to steal people's shoes from their feet and chew them, with Dan politely replacing them and apologising behind her . . . What could be more personal than that?

Liz's cheeks were aching from smiling so much, as she gripped Gerald's arm tightly while Ella sang them out of the ceremony room. Liz was so happy. She felt like she had gained a real sense of perspective in the twenty-four hours approaching her wedding day, and seeing the people around her now, she knew what really mattered, what was important to her. And it wasn't the miniature cheese soufflés, or the pink-gin cocktails, or the cake that cost the same amount as a second-hand car. All that mattered was how amazing they both felt right now, and that she would never ever forget the way Gerald had been looking at her since that door opened.

Liz turned to him as they passed through the doorway, ready to be whisked off for a few photographs before they could relax, eat and drink with their friends. They didn't speak, but he kissed her again. Another lingering, gentle kiss that said so much more than any words could.

She felt so silly for ever resisting his advances, for ever not wanting to get married, for ever questioning anything, because right now, she couldn't wait to spend the rest of her life with him.

She couldn't wait to be #Giz for ever.

Chapter 72

PERFECTLY UN-PERFECT

Emily's head hurt quite a lot. And she was fairly sure that had nothing to do with the evening hog roast, and probably quite a lot to do with the pink-gin bar . . .

Liz and Gerald's wedding had been nothing short of amazing. Even if her memories of the evening section were a little hazy. But she had made it to her room, made it to bed and undressed herself somehow – a small victory against alcohol at least.

She was struggling to wake up properly and as she propped herself up in bed, she remembered Paul mumbling in her ear about taking William down to breakfast, sounding irritatingly fresh and not like his mouth tasted of arse. Undoubtedly, he'd skipped down there – smugly un-hungover, rolling his eyes as he mentioned to people that his boozy wife was currently in a gin-coma trying hard to recall the fuzzy events of the night before. Emily found it annoying that he never suffered hangovers . . . right now she was struggling to blink without it hurting.

Hangover anxiety was Emily's nemesis. It never served her well to even attempt to piece together the drunken fabric of the night before. Snippets of memories were poking at the periphery of her mind, images of questionable dance moves on table tops, terrible jokes and stumbling around in high heels, for far too long judging by the searing pain in the balls of her feet. It was best to leave them be. Nothing could be gained from dredging those up into the forefront of her mind right now.

She did remember that Paul had taken William up to bed around 10 p.m., and left her to party into the early hours alone. Probably sensible that one of them was able to parent effectively this morning, Emily thought, wincing at the pain in her temples. She rather wished right now that it had been she who had turned in early and not spent the night table-top dancing in expensive shoes she couldn't even walk in. She seriously hoped she hadn't made too much of a fool of herself. It had been the first time she'd drunk alcohol to excess like that since before she was pregnant. And right now she was vowing to never do it again.

Her hangover jitters were getting the better of her now, she'd text Liz and Molly and see how they were . . .

Emily
Hey. You guys awake? I'm dead.
Someone must have spiked my 74 gin
and tonics with extra gin . . . only
explanation.

Molly
Hey you. Yes – that makes sense
now.

Excellent dance moves by the way.
Just the right amount of fanny flashing
to be enticing but classy at the same
time.

Emily
Oh God. Really? That bad?

Molly
You are far too easy to wind up! Don't
worry you were fine. Pissed and funny
but fine. Dignity and fanny still intact
I'd say.
(Although I've never seen anyone do
the Macarena like that before . . . so
much gyrating . . . impressive hip
action.)

Emily
This is not helping! My brain might fall
out of my nose. I'm wondering if
bacon might help . . .

Molly
Please don't talk about bacon.

Liz
Morning ladies! How are you both?
I'm just heading down for breakfast –
you able to cope with solids yet
Emily?

Emily
Morning to our beautiful bride!
How does it feel to be waking up as
Mrs Gerald this morning?
Yesterday was absolutely stunning Liz.
Thank you so much for making us a
part of it xxx (and no – I'm thinking
coffee and Berocca first . . . safer all
round).

Molly
Yes it was amazing.
I honestly don't think I've been to a
better wedding! It was perfect.

Emily
Oi! What about my wedding!

Molly
Well obviously YOURS was perfect
too. lol
And sorry for turning in early xx

Liz
Haha x get that foot out of your mouth
Molly! And please don't apologise –
you had a baby only days ago! Thank
you so much for still coming x
I know it must have been hard work
yesterday.

433

Molly

Don't be silly. I wouldn't have missed
it for the world.

Emily

And neither would I. (Me and my
gyrating Macarena that is . . .)

Liz

Well I must have missed that – Gerald
and I headed up about midnight, so I
guess all the gyrating started once
we'd left! I never realised how tiring
getting married could be? I was dead!

Emily

Ah well you'd never have known. It
was seamless. Loved every bit of
yesterday.

Liz

Me too. It was everything I wanted.
But now all I want is a cooked breakfast so hurry up and get downstairs!

Emily

Okay. For you. I'm there.

Molly

Me too. We're on our way anyway. I'm
just tandem boob feeding. All the
glamour. Sneak me a couple of

sausages when Tom's not looking
would you? I need the meat.

Liz
Secret sausages it is. That's how
much I love you.

Emily
Me too. I really do love you ladies.

Molly
Me too. You steal me meat,
you keep me sane and you're the
best friends a girl could have.

Liz
Like an epic sausage-stealing, boob-
feeding, man-marrying girl band with
90s tendencies and a soft spot for
Spice Girls lyrics and Heather
Shimmer lipstick . . .

Emily
Absolutely.
HEATHER SHIMMER FOREVA!!!

Molly
Heather Shimmer for ever.

Liz
Now hurry up! xxx

Emily laughed as she placed her phone back on the night-stand and wearily pulled herself up to a slightly more upright sitting position. Her head was foggy but she was actually beginning to feel a little better. And perhaps able to face something edible and bacon-like with a strong coffee if she took it slow. Plus, she was beginning to feel guilty that she'd not properly said good morning to her son and husband yet. As much as she appreciated the lie-in, it was time to get back to being a responsible adult and parent again. There would be no twerk-based dance moves this morning, that was for sure.

Emily smiled as she sighed and contemplated the last year of her, Molly and Liz's lives. It had been so crazy, it had gone so fast, there'd been such riveting highs, and such sad moments, but they'd all remained the best of friends. She really couldn't imagine any part of her life without them.

And now her new journey was starting. The first year of parenting had been tough on her, even though she'd loved it. She'd cried so much more than she knew she would and struggled with parts of it way more than she expected, but mostly, she was proud of herself. Proud of her and Paul, and of William, for surviving the last year and beginning this new chapter. The baby days were over now, there was no more Angel PR, no more twatty Matilda and her stupid annoying face, just lots of exciting blogging in the pipeline and the opportunity to spend more time with William. She couldn't wait. It was the right decision, and for the first time in a long time she'd let go of the turmoil, let go of the constantly trying to be perfect and begun to accept her new life for what it was – perfectly unperfect.

Emily reached for her phone – she'd had an idea for a blog post that she didn't want to forget. The bacon could wait for a few moments while she quickly tapped it out in her notes page and transferred it later. She'd get it written, get dressed, and get downstairs very shortly.

Her little family, her best friends and all the breakfast meat she could ever dream of were waiting for her down there. And she couldn't think of a more perfect start to a Sunday morning, or a more brilliant end to an amazing year, than that.

Sometimes it's okay not to be okay,
To not be perfect after you've been up all night.
Sometimes you've just got to say FUCK. IT. ALL.
Because it's all right to not be all right.

Sometimes you *are* gonna lose it,
And call your baby a knob.
It doesn't mean you're not an awesome mummy,
It makes you a member of the 'We're-Not-Perfect-
    Mums-Club'.

Just because your house isn't spotless,
Doesn't mean you don't crave a raisin-free home.
But while your living room is a neon-plastic graveyard,
You're bloody entitled to a bit of a moan.

Some days you'll stay in pyjamas,
(And the next day, and shit, the next day after that)
Some days you'll just need a good weep on your own,
Because that twatting shop window made you look
    fat.

Not having your shit together every morning,
Or dropping the odd F-bomb and drinking wine.
Does not make you a totally crap mummy,
It makes you NORMAL and is totally FINE.

Somehow you'll make it to tomorrow,
Just brush the Weetabix and that sticky stuff into
    your hair.
Stick on ITV-Be, get the biscuits, make some tea . . .
And just don't shitting care.

So sometimes it's okay to see through it,
All the perfect-mummy-bollocks on your Facebook
    feed.
Because you know what, being not-so-bloody-perfect,
Makes you more than fucking perfect, actually.

xxx

Baby Boom!

No one said the journey to motherhood was easy . . .

Increased face-girth, back acne and gagging every time she's in the presence of vegetables isn't quite the beautiful start Emily had planned for her unborn baby . . .

Molly's unexpected pregnancy somehow turns her boyfriend into the poncy-vegan-nut-milk-enforcer, but she breezes it, as she breezes everything. (Including still being able to eat avocados much to Emily's annoyance.)

Liz quickly realises if she's to move her life on, she needs to get rid of the married man she's in love with – especially now she's realised he's been hiding more than his wedding ring . . .

The first novel from award winning blogger *Just A Normal Mummy* is available to buy now!

Read on for the first chapter.

Chapter 1

Pissy Wrist

'Shit.' said Emily.

As she sat on the loo, with her pants stretched awkwardly from one ankle to the other, feeling slightly undignified and more than a little exposed in the middle cubicle of Angel Public Relations unisex toilets.

Why the hell hadn't she waited until she'd got home? WHAT ON EARTH possessed her to use her lunch break to buy a couscous salad, a packet of diced coconut, and a double pack of Clear Blue pregnancy tests? Well – she'd only bought the coconut because she overheard one of the girls on reception say it made you thin and it sounded easier than actual real-life exercising – but she didn't even like couscous . . . And the pregnancy tests? Why was she doing this NOW? At work. Ten minutes before a whole agency brainstorming session about a luxury towel brand.

Yet here she was, with her Ted Baker pencil skirt hoisted up round her waist while her own lukewarm urine dribbled into her shirt sleeve.

Excellent, she thought to herself, pursing her lips and using her other (non-pissy) hand to hold back her mane of thick blonde curls.

The box said it took two minutes. Two minutes to show

a clear result. Well, frankly, two minutes felt like a bloody lifetime while you were sat with your vagina out listening to Brian from accounting trying to politely cough his way through a spot of IBS.

No. Not exactly ideal. But here she was: pantless, pissy wrist and all, watching in slight disbelief as two very distinct blue lines in the 'pregnant' window slowly appeared and stared back at her.

'Shit.'

'Hello?' Brian said tentatively from the sink area.

FUCK OFF, BRIAN.

'I'm fine. Thanks,' she called back at him.

Emily took a deep breath and tried to block Brian out as she fixed her gaze on the little white stick that was telling her her life was about to change quite a lot from this point. Probably. Right?

What did this mean?

OKAY, she knew what it 'meant'. Obviously. But what did it really MEAN . . . Did she need to call her doctor? Find a midwife? Stop eating cheese?

I mean – anyone could take or leave Cheddar, but Camembert? That was going to take some serious commitment. Just thinking about it now was making her crave a Brie-and-bacon sandwich and a large glass of Pinot Grigio.

THIS IS RIDICULOUS. IT'S NOT ABOUT CHEESE. PULL YOURSELF TOGETHER, EMILY. YOU'RE CURRENTLY SITTING WITH YOUR FANNY OUT AND PISS DOWN YOUR ARM WITH SIX MINUTES TO GO UNTIL A

MEETING ABOUT TOWELS AND YOU'RE THINKING ABOUT SOFT FRENCH CHEESES.

She took another deep breath.

A smile grew across her face. She couldn't help her teeth from showing. There were a lot of teeth.

But she was just so happy.

(And semi-naked . . .)

And her mind was racing.

However, in the interest of somehow pulling her shit back together so she could think creatively about towelling, Emily reassembled herself, quickly snapped a picture of the pregnancy-test result on her iPhone and then wrapped the test in loo roll, popped it back into the packet and into her handbag.

Pants and pencil skirt now firmly back in place, she fired a WhatsApp message off to her husband Paul with the photo and a caption simply saying:

> You're going to be a daddy . . .

Swiftly followed by:

> But can't talk now.
> Got to go brainstorm the shit out of
> some towels.
> I love you.
> I can't stop grinning.
> Everyone is going to think I REALLY
> like towels.

And with that, Emily checked her phone was on silent, took a final deep breath and, confident she was now alone, finally left the shelter of the middle cubicle.

As she washed and dried her hands, she imagined laughing in the future about finding out the happiest news of her life at the same time as Brian from accounting had the shits in the loo next door to her . . .

Emily shook her thoughts away, composed herself and left the toilets. She quickly made her way back through the open-plan office attempting not to make eye contact with anyone (especially not Irritable-Bowel-Brian). It felt like her news must be pasted all over her face and might burst out of her any moment. It was almost disappointing that no one so much as glanced at her as she returned to her desk.

Focus, Emily.

She sat in front of her Mac and pulled up the briefing document she'd prepared for the brainstorm.

She stared at the screen. It was impossible to concentrate. All she had to do was press print, but it was so hard to think about towels now that she knew she had a human growing inside of her.

MY UTERUS HAS AN ACTUAL TINY PERSON IN IT.

It was an utterly insane feeling.

Just then, her eyes met her colleague Matilda's. Matilda was a senior account manager who sat directly opposite her. She was a bit of a bitch, actually. Emily was fairly sure she was after her job, so she would literally be the *last* person on earth she'd let know it could be up for grabs, even temporarily, in about nine months' time.

'Everything okay?' Matilda suspiciously raised an eyebrow in Emily's direction. Which irritated Emily way more than it should do.

'Yes. Everything's great, thanks,' Emily snapped. Attempting to remove the persistent grin from her face.

'It's just you were gone quite a while.' Matilda responded with her eyebrow still suspiciously raised. 'And now you're grinning like some sort of lunatic. Had some good news?'

MEDDLING. BITCH.

'I just really like towels,' she retorted as she pressed print.

Matilda rolled her eyes and looked back at her screen.

Just then Natalie, the managing director, called everyone in to the large meeting room for the brainstorm.

'Right. Let's get going everyone. Got those briefing documents, Emily?'

Emily rose to her feet, grabbing the warm sheets from the printing bay on her way to the meeting room.

Right.

Don't think about what's in your uterus.

Think towels.

Towels.

Fucking towels.

445

When one book ends, another begins...

Bookends is a vibrant new reading community to help you ensure you're never without a good book.

You'll find exclusive previews of the brilliant new books from your favourite authors as well as exciting debuts and past classics. Read our blog, check out our recommendations for your reading group, enter great competitions and much more!

Visit our website to see which great books we're recommending this month.

Join the Bookends community:

www.welcometobookends.co.uk

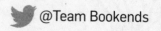 @Team Bookends 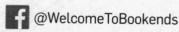 @WelcomeToBookends